The first lady was hiding some inner frustration

Bolan thought back to the aftermath of the battle with the Russian gunmen. While he never claimed to be psychic, the soldier was a good judge of a person's emotional state. The vibes he'd gotten off Anibella Brujillo in the wake of the skirmish had been of intense joy and pleasure.

She had swallowed that instantaneous reaction as soon as she'd realized she was being watched, but the blood was in the water. Bolan had tasted it, and even though he had nothing more than the word of a fugitive and a few rumors, he believed that there was something dark and ominous gliding under the calm, glassy surface of Anibella's exterior.

Something that would make even a crocodile quiver in fear.

D0188251

Don Pendleton's Mack Bolan®

Devil's Playground

A GOLD EAGLE BOOK FROM

W RLDWIDE®

TORONTO • NEW YORK • LONDON
AMSTERDAM • PARIS • SYDNEY • HAMBURG
STOCKHOLM • ATHENS • TOKYO • MILAN
MADRID • WARSAW • BUDAPEST • AUCKLAND

First edition November 2007

ISBN-13: 978-0-373-61520-9
ISBN-10:   0-373-61520-5

DEVIL'S PLAYGROUND

Special thanks and acknowledgment to
Douglas P. Wojtowicz for his contribution to this work.

Nothing more completely baffles one who is full of trick and duplicity than straightforward and simple integrity in another. A knave would rather quarrel with a brother knave than with a fool, but he would rather avoid a quarrel with one honest man than with both. He can combat a fool by management and address, and he can conquer a knave by temptations. But the honest man is neither to be bamboozled nor bribed.

> —C. C. Colton,
> 1780–1832

The liars of the world have cause to fear. I can play their game, but without their tactics of deception, confusion and coercion. My mind is clear and I cannot be tempted.

> —Mack Bolan

PROLOGUE

Even in the bright Acapulco sunlight, Rosa Asado felt invisible. Less than invisible, really. As part of Governor Brujillo's executive protection team, she was supposed to keep to the background, ever vigilant.

While Asado was an attractive woman, she was just second-rate compared to this crowd. A slender blond American singer with a vacuous smile laughed at Anibella Brujillo's latest witticism. The governor's wife was a stunning woman in her late thirties, with long, black silky hair. Brujillo's face was lean, with full lips that moved with facile ease as she spoke cultured English with a deep, husky breathlessness that sharply contrasted with the American songstress's cackles and nasal-braying speech. It was no surprise, Asado thought. While the young blonde was popular in the United States, Anibella Brujillo had been a national heroine in her younger days, achieving international fame from Argentina to Ontario with fans of latin music. She had even achieved crossover success with several Top 10 hits in the U.S. between the time she was eighteen and twenty-nine, when Anibella finally officially retired from pop superstardom and married a young, up-and-coming politician in Guerrero's state politics.

Brujillo's voice could be described in one word—spellbinding.

Asado's wide-brimmed hat, dark sunglasses and brunette curls were arranged to conceal the unobtrusive earpiece and throat microphone that kept her in touch with the rest of the executive protection team. If there was a battle, Asado wouldn't be alone.

"We've got movement at the gates of the resort. Military vehicles," a voice cut in on her concentration.

Asado's hand rested on her thigh, not far from a pocket containing one of her twin Detonics .45 CombatMaster pistols. "I thought we had a report of a base arranging transport through the area."

"They're off the given path," another one of the Mexican security team stated. "And I don't know about you, but I'm not keen on having jeeps with machine guns passing too close to the command trailer."

Asado's brow furrowed and her fingertips played around the snap of her pocket. While the mobile command center was armor-plated, against a .50-caliber machine gun that protection might as well be tissue paper. "Ricky…"

She was about to give a quiet admonishment to be careful when distant thunder rumbled through the air, the earpiece shrieking through her skull as Ricardo Bonases howled in agony, shrieking something about his arm being severed.

Other members of the protection team closed in around Anibella Brujillo and Asado tore the pistol from her right pocket, thumbing down the safety lever. At the sight of armed men and women around her, the governor's wife cut off her story in midword, green eyes scanning the area.

Asado caught Anibella's glance toward two men at one far corner of the pool area, reinforcing her suspicions about the two men who seemed to be stalking the first lady. Veteran members of the detail had dismissed Asado's warning about the pair, and others like them, pronounced as being harmless after background checks. Asado had been ordered to drop any inquiries about the mysterious shadows, and rumors among the rest of the security team had said those orders had come from Anibella Brujillo herself.

Right now, Asado didn't know who exactly the pair were, but at least she felt secure that they wouldn't make an effort to kill the governor's wife.

An explosion rocked Asado as she closed with the first lady, the shock wave knocking her to the marble-tiled deck and pushing her into the water. Caught off guard, Asado sucked in a lungful of water. She lost the first pistol in her grasp from the concussion or from striking the marble pool deck. Either way, her reflexes took over, powerful legs kicking off the pool bottom and driving her head above the water. With a vomitous exhalation, she voided water through her mouth. Her slender but tightly muscled arms reached for the terracotta lip of the pool to brace herself as she took a ragged gasp of life-giving oxygen into her chest. As she surfaced, she spotted green- and brown-mottled shapes with assault rifles rushing through a cloud of smoke and debris from the explosion.

Asado tucked down, holding her breath this time as bullets pierced the pool's surface, riding on spears of bubbles. She tore the other Detonics CombatMaster from her pocket, transferring it to her right hand and thumbing off the safety. With another kick, she broke the surface, spotting a Mexican soldier with a G3 assault rifle firing a short burst at the other end of the pool. Asado didn't waste any time identifying the target. Instead she punched out two fat 230-grain hollow-point rounds into the camouflage-wearing gunman's groin and lower belly. Wide-mouthed cavities scooped aside flesh and blood, hydrostatic pressure peeling back the bowl-like lips of the bullets and spreading them apart on impact, smashing out deep divots from the Mexican's pelvic bone.

Robbed of the skeletal structure he needed to stand, the rifleman tumbled headfirst into the pool, his rifle clattering to the tile.

Asado surged for the deck, firing another shot at a second armed gunman who raked a burst of automatic fire across the governor's wife and her party. Realizing that she heard nothing over her ear radio, Asado wondered if the water had shorted out the system when she was dunked. She would have to check on the radio, but not before she seized the enemy's rifle. The Detonics .45 was powerful, but nothing beat a rifle when it came to killing people engaged in homicide. With a hard shove, she flopped onto the deck and grabbed the grip of the Heckler & Koch G3.

Water suction and gravity dragged Asado back into the pool, just in time to avoid being cut in two by another assassin. As she sliced into the water, she kicked back from the edge, aimed the rifle and fired. Heavy recoil shook the weapon in her fist, but at a range of only ten feet, she was able to stitch the uniformed soldier from navel to throat with a 3-round burst of 7.62 mm bullets. The assassin jerked backward violently, as if propelled from a cannon, the rifle slugs coring through his torso as if it were made of soft cheese.

Asado spun and kicked for the far side of the pool.

When she did, she saw that the table where Anibella Brujillo had been sitting was surrounded with corpses, other tables overturned in a scene of carnage. Spearing the rifle ahead of her, Asado knifed through the water like a torpedo. Muzzle-flashes blazed around the side of one table, showing that some of her comrades were still alive and fighting. Asado clamped her hand on the lip of the pool and yanked herself up on deck. She stayed prone, rolling onto her belly so that she could take aim with the G3 rifle at any newcomers.

The two mystery men suddenly entered the fray, Uzi submachine guns blazing as they ambushed the marauding assassins. Raking fingers of 9 mm gunfire laced into the assassins with brutal efficiency as Asado discarded her empty G3 and reloaded her CombatMaster. Kneeling behind a stone planter, she fired three shots into a rifle-armed soldier, striking him in the upper chest and stopping him cold. Collarbone and ribs shattered by 230-grain bullets, his thoracic cavity was suddenly filled with rocketing shrapnel of deformed hollow-point rounds and bone splinters. Blood vomited from the dying man's lips as he collapsed limply to the ground.

Asado pivoted, looking for more targets when she saw Anibella Brujillo, armed with a gleaming, nickel-plated pistol, fire a shot into a dying assassin's face as she stood over him. Asado recognized the pistol as belonging to Montero, one of the protection team. Montero was sprawled on the pool deck, most of his face missing and his brains forming a fan around the cavern that used to be his skull. Physical pain speared through Asado's chest at the sight of her murdered comrade.

Anibella fired two more shots, taking a fleeing rifleman between the shoulder blades, and she spit a curse. *"Culo."*

Rosa Asado stood, glaring at Anibella Brujillo.

"You survived?" Brujillo asked.

"No thanks to the gangsters on your payroll," Asado answered, nodding toward the Uzi-armed gunmen who were escaping over the fence.

"My dear, I don't know what you're talking about," Anibella stated. "All I see are two killers you allowed to escape."

Asado clamped her teeth in her lower lip to restrain the urge to throttle the woman. She thumbed the safety up on her CombatMaster. "I don't know what this is all about, but I'm certain it has something to do with your links to those gangsters."

Anibella shook her head. "They were trying to murder me, because my husband is working hard to bring down the Juarez Cartel. This is proof that we are on the right track."

Asado took a deep breath and looked around. Except for Anibella, she was the only one standing. The blond American singer was facedown in a puddle of blood. However, looking at the wounds in the young woman's back, she could tell that they were too neat to have been made by a G3's rifle slug. They looked more like the bullets from a .38 Super, just like the one that Brujillo held.

Asado looked up to see the silvery muzzle of Montero's 1911 pistol leveled at her. A flower of fire appeared, and in that dying moment Rosa thought of her twin sister, Blanca, and how she'd never see her again.

A 125-grain slug smashed into her forehead and puffed out the wet tresses at the back of her skull.

The bodyguard collapsed in a jumble of limbs, eyes bulging in their sockets, staring vacantly at the clear skies of the Acapulco paradise.

"Oh, Saint Martha," Anibella Brujillo whispered, calling the goddess of death, Santa Muerte, by her nickname. "What a waste of a good scapegoat."

She flipped the nickel-plated 1911 back to Montero's side.

The two Uzi-packers were gangsters, but they were also Anibella's devotees. As the high priestess of the Santa Muerte cult in the state, she was never far from the protection of her flock members. She was a shepherdess not of sheep, but of Mexican wolves, predators who infested the drug gangs and lorded over neighborhoods.

It would take some time for the authorities to arrive, but she already had her followers acting on her plans to implicate Rosa Asado as the real perpetrator of this recent attack.

The Juarez Cartel was stepping up its aggression, and Asado had been correct. The drug lords were seeking to eliminate her not because her husband was a crusading politician, but because she was the heart and soul of the Santa Muerte cult conquering the heroin trade in Acapulco.

Anibella's brow furrowed. She would deflect attention for now, but the Juarez Cartel was still not going to give up so easily. A full paramilitary assault was only one sign of the extremes that Juarez was willing to go to, to eliminate her and the cult.

She needed an advantage over one of the most tenacious and lethal drug gangs in Mexico. The Mexican president had dropped a hint to her husband. A few years back, when the new president was under assault from multiple factions, an American operative had been assigned to assist him against drug gangs and military officers seeking to stage a coup.

This lone man was like an army unto himself. Anibella had heard rumors of a more recent savage conflict between Colombian cartels and the Hong Kong triads on Mexican soil, involving a similar one-man battalion. The president gave governor Emilio Brujillo a contact number to bring in this solitary crusader.

Anibella Brujillo knew that if anyone could level the playing field against the Juarez Cartel, even if they could arrange an army assault, it would be the mysterious lone warrior.

CHAPTER ONE

Jon Dever was tempted to pull a cigarette from the glove compartment of the U.S. Border Patrol Ford Bronco, but he was trying to quit. His partner, Daniel Hogan, saw Dever's gaze fall on the glove compartment door and smirked.

"Don't start, Dan," Dever muttered.

Hogan's smirk continued to grow. "You should try some nicotine gum, Jon."

"I did. Ate a whole pack at once and nearly puked my guts out," Dever grumbled. "Besides, if I light up, they'll smell the smoke a country mile away, even if they can't make it out through the windshield."

Hogan nodded sagely. That had been the younger man's intent, to push his older partner into rationalizing against taking another cigarette. Dever was twelve years older than Hogan, who was in his early thirties, and had about seventy pounds on the younger man. Most of it was muscle, but enough was the result of the thickening of age.

Hogan put his night-vision glasses to his eyes again. "Got a visual."

Dever picked up his glasses and looked. "Three trucks. They look military but—"

"Either the Mexican army's making extra cash selling surplus to heroin smugglers, or they went in for steady employment by doing the transportation themselves," Hogan surmised. "Either way, our orders are not to fire on anyone wearing a Mexican uniform."

"This is bullshit," Dever said. "My training officer would have had an aneurysm if he'd been told to let those bastards shoot at him without returning fire."

"Hey. Washington doesn't have a spine anymore. They'd rather beat their chests in a foreign country, but let the psychos next door do as they please," Hogan snarled.

Dever took a long, deep breath, then got out a digital camcorder with a low-light optical filter on the lens. At least they could document any efforts by the neighboring nation's military in breaking international law.

Dever's brow furrowed.

"What's wrong?" Hogan asked. He eyed the M-4 carbine locked in its clamp against the dashboard. It, and the Heckler & Koch .40-caliber pistol on his hip, would give any opponent a run for his money, if only his trigger finger hadn't been restrained by insipid rules of engagement. The official attitude was to not spark a border war, but apparently the men wearing army uniforms and carrying Mexican-issue rifles were under no such restriction.

Several Border Patrol agents had been injured in increasingly tense encounters across the past few years. It was only a matter of time before the bastards had collected the final breath of an American law-enforcement agent. Some had called for the end of the Border Patrol due to its failure to control or act against foreign invaders. Others had wanted the National Guard to step in. Still more took their own weapons and camped out at major thoroughfares for migrating illegal aliens, seeking to take the law into their own hands. The fact that the American Minutemen were looking only to turn back illegal aliens, and not gun down unarmed intruders who were coming merely to seek jobs had kept the situation from surging to a flashpoint of violence.

It had come close a couple of times. Military forces and federal agents had dealt with a crisis for the then-new Mexican president as powerful smuggling alliances actually engaged in brutal assault on American lawmen. Only the actions of people who existed in whispered rumor had prevented a second Mexican-American war from ripping the continent apart.

Hogan sighed. He hoped that the men who didn't exist would make their presence felt again to push back the encroaching and increasingly bold and deadly smugglers.

Dever looked at the feed on the screen. "Something is moving out in the desert behind the trucks, but I can't quite make it out. It might be a person. It's about the right mass, but it doesn't… No, it disappeared."

Hogan chuckled nervously. "Maybe you saw a Chupacabra."

"Not too many goats for a goat-sucker to feed on out there, Dan," Dever returned. "Nothing. I just see bupkis."

Hogan nodded. "We'll review the DVR later. Maybe image enhancement will—"

"Down!" Dever shouted, and Hogan's head slammed against the driver's window. The windshield cracked violently as something crashed into it. Plings and plunks of rifle fire sounded on the Bronco's metallic skin. Dever had his double-action-only USP .40 out, but instead of rising above the dashboard, he stayed hunched over the younger agent.

"Damn bureaucrats are going to murder us," Dever snarled.

"They will if we don't shoot back," Hogan said. He felt a knot rising on his battered skull, but he was in no more of a mood to rise and engage the enemy than Dever.

M-16s and the Heckler & Koch pistols were hot stuff against poorly trained "coyotes" armed with AK-47s. The human smugglers couldn't hit the broadside of a barn at one hundred yards, while both the Border Patrol's chosen pistol and rifle could score head shots at that same distance. Unfortunately, the enemy gunmen across the border were three hundred yards out. The short-barreled M-4s came up as inferior at that distance when compared to the older but vastly more powerful Heckler & Koch G3 battle rifles. The G3's 7.62 mm NATO bullet could kill at over eight hundred yards. Only the armor plating and the heavy engine of the USBP Ford Bronco had managed to stop the high-powered slugs from drilling into the two agents.

The windshield finally gave up the ghost and disintegrated into diamondlike cubes of broken glass that rained down upon the pair.

"Damn!" Dever shouted.

Suddenly, from across the border, another weapon discharged. It was deep and powerful, thundering across the plains. The Mexican rifles stopped firing.

Dever poked the camera up over the dashboard, the LED screen rotated so that he could use it as an electronic periscope. G3 rifles crackled again from the trucks, but the tongues of muzzle-flashes licked out into the desert behind them.

Someone else had entered the fray.

MACK BOLAN HAD INTENDED to make his incursion against the alleged Mexican military forces covertly, but the lives of two American lawmen were on the line. The Executioner rapidly pulled the suppressor off his Barrett M-98 rifle and mounted the muzzle brake. He was going to need to make noise to redirect the murderous gunmen's attention.

With his first pull of the trigger, the M-98 spit a .338 Lapua Magnum round into the head of one of the riflemen. The result was instant decapitation as the 300-grain slug detonated the Mexican's skull with hydrostatic overpressure.

Sprayed with gore, stringy brain mass and bone fragments, the other gunmen in the truck were struck momentarily numb. Bolan's first target slid over the rail of the truck, plopping to the desert sand below.

There was no doubt now that the enemy soldiers knew where the rifle shot came from. The Lapua Magnum round was designed to kill humans at over a mile and a half away, or punch through the engine of a lightly armored vehicle at closer range. That kind of power was accompanied by a throaty roar and a flash like lightning.

Just to make certain, the gunman right next to the first target caught a second Barrett round at the center of his clavicle. Windmilling backward as a fountain of blood vomited through the .338-inch hole in his upper chest, the Mexican was dumped next to the first target in the sand. G3s ripped to life, but the Executioner was in motion, leaving the area he'd fired from.

The semiautomatic Barrett punched out another slug as Bolan fired from the hip, catching a third smuggler through the center of his torso. The dying Mexican folded like a cheap shirt, collapsing as a grapefruit-size crater formed when the Magnum bullet excavated two vertibrae through the skin of his back.

Panic and screams had taken over the smuggling crew and one of the trucks fired up its engine. Bolan shouldered the Barrett and tapped off two .338 rounds which smashed through its grille. The engine seized up as the heavyweight slugs tore through gears and pistons. A commanding voice cut through the howls of fear.

"Track and fire! Split up! We're too easy a target in the trucks!"

Bolan slung the mighty Barrett and drew his Beretta 93-R machine pistol from its spot under his left armpit. Suppressed, its muzzle-flash would disappear in the desert battleground. Now that he had their attention, he needed stealth and the protective curtain of nighttime shadows. The foregrip lever folded down, and he flipped the selector to 3-round burst. A snarl of silenced Parabellum rounds coughed from the end of the Beretta's can, ripping into a man standing nearest to the leader shouting orders.

The leader of this group reacted not as a frightened smuggler but as a cold-blooded professional, pulling Bolan's quiet kill in front of him as a human shield. Whether the Mexican had been dead or alive, his commander had deemed his own existence more important. Bolan popped off another triburst that forced the enemy headman behind the cover of his vehicle, 9 mm rounds eliciting jerks from his human shield.

A grenade sailed high and wide of the Executioner's position, but he wasn't going to stay upright. The minibomb detonated, shrapnel singing through the air in a sheet of razor wire over his fallen form. Bolan sighted on the legs of another rifleman and chewed his kneecaps off with another burst. The gunman howled in agony, collapsing facefirst in the sand. Strangled sobs of pain resounded from the fallen soldier.

"Aqui!" a Mexican rifleman shouted. Bolan rolled quickly out of the path of a salvo of bullets, triggering a trio of 9 mm slugs into the shooter's chest.

Bolan took a momentary disadvantage and profited from it, grabbing the fallen rifleman's G3 and a bandolier of ammunition off him. He dumped the magazine and slapped a 20-round box into the battle rifle. A Mexican rushed toward Bolan, too close and too fast for the Executioner to shoot, but the heavy wooden stock was as lethal as any bullet. With a sickening crunch, the heavy rifle butt caved in the gunner's jaw on its way to splitting his palate and facial structure. Shards of jagged bone speared the unfortunate thug's brain, dropping him instantly into a pile of dying human meat in the border sand.

A second man burst into view and Bolan brought the stock down hard into the side of the newcomer's neck. The gunman's neck released a wet, stomach-churning snap as it failed to absorb the lethal impact. Spine crushed, the Mexican collapsed at the Executioner's feet.

Another truck engine turned over, and the Executioner whirled, burning off a half dozen slugs through the driver's door. The wheelman jerked violently as bullets exploded through sheet metal and soft flesh. A river of blood poured from his lips as he slid out the door.

"Fall back! Fall back!" the enemy commander shouted. He jumped from the bed of the driverless vehicle toward the third truck. He laid down a sheet of covering fire to keep the Executioner at bay, but Bolan didn't want to cut off the last vehicle.

Instead, he waited, letting the commander and the remnants of his group pack into the back of the remaining vehicle. A mad roostertail shot from under the wheels as the truck sought traction, driver in a panic and applying too much gas. Finally the treads bit into the sand and the vehicle lurched away from the death grounds.

Overloaded with men, it swayed as it made a wild turn back to its base, but the low center of gravity won out, keeping all the wheels on the ground. Bolan yanked the lifeless driver out of the cab. The Mexican riding shotgun with him was slumped, coughing up blood from lethal injuries. There was no way that Bolan could treat the horrific wounds inflicted by the powerful rifle. He unleathered the Desert Eagle and ended the gunman's suffering with a 240-grain skull smasher. He pushed the corpse out of the cab and started the truck.

The Border Patrol agents, hundreds of yards away, had gotten out of their vehicle, watching in consternation. They'd just seen nearly a dozen men who'd tried to kill them left dead or wounded on the desert sand, their black-clad savior commandeering the Mexican truck to take up pursuit.

Bolan hated to leave the patrolmen in the lurch, their vehicle destroyed. He opened his satellite phone, linking up to Stony Man Farm.

"Bear, send a recovery team. We have two Border Patrol agents who'll have a long walk unless they get a new ride," the Executioner said. He slipped on a pair of night-vision goggles so that he could watch the road without resorting to headlights, which would betray to the escaping enemy that they were being hunted.

"We're on it. Satellite imagery is following the remaining truck, if you should lose it," Aaron Kurtzman responded.

"Not likely," Bolan returned. "I put the fear of hell

itself into them. The enemy driver is plowing up countryside as if there were no tomorrow."

"ETA for the pickup on your agents is about five
minutes. Satellite imagery shows that they're unharmed.
Both are moving around normally."

"Great news," Bolan said. "I hated to blow the element of surprise, but I couldn't just stand by and let two
lawmen be murdered."

"Now we get to see where the rabbits hole up,"
Kurtzman told him. "You were right, though, Striker.
They couldn't be easier to track if they had a neon sign
on them."

The Mexicans' truck bounced and charged across the
terrain several hundred yards away from Bolan's vehicle. Finally, the two-and-a-half-ton truck swerved. It almost tipped again, two wheels rising a couple of feet into
the air, but the driver recovered the vehicle's balance.

"They're on a road now, Striker," Kurtzman informed him.

Bolan eased his "borrowed" ride onto the road with
far more grace than his quarry. Though the road was
paved, there were no lights along it, or even rails on either side, just soft, gravel-filled shoulders. The fewer
lights, the better. He didn't need his terrorized prey to
realize that he was still with them. As it was, he let off
the gas enough to increase the gap.

Judging by the speed and distance traveled, they'd already gone twenty miles past the Arizona-Mexico border. The G3 and the powerful Barret M-98 rested on the
bloody seat, in case he was being drawn into a trap. It
was hours from dawn. Hopefully, he'd arrive at his intended destination before sunrise so that he could make
a covert insertion.

If not, Bolan would do the best he could, even in

broad daylight, though he doubted that his quarry had much farther to go. Already, they had dropped from nearly eighty miles an hour to half that. Bolan matched their speed, and saw them turn onto another road. There was a sign at the intersection. The Executioner paused long enough to read that the road led to an Army base.

"What's the status on this base?" Bolan asked, reading off the name to Kurtzman.

"It's fully active, Striker. It's mostly a supply and transport depot, and according to reports, it's been on the bubble as far as closing. There isn't enough money to keep it going, with rising gasoline prices and the Mexican government just barely out of the red," Kurtzman explained.

"So they're taking odd jobs to keep the gates open?" Bolan asked.

Kurtzman sighed. "Sounds like it. A little dilemma."

"No dilemma at all," Bolan replied. "They tried to kill American lawmen. I've fought enough top-secret U.S. groups funded by drug money who murdered anyone in their way and shut them down. Slaughtering people and selling addictive poison isn't a valid option for any group to fund itself."

"Not everyone on the base is in on the cocaine cowboy rodeo," Kurtzman stated.

"I've got a face and a voice," Bolan returned. "When I cut off the head, the rest will die. I'm closing this connection now, Bear. Places to go. Things to break. Catch you later."

He turned off the sat phone and pulled the truck off the road as he saw the supply depot's lights in the distance.

The rest of this trip was going to be on foot.

BLANCA ASADO PUSHED HER auburn hair off of her forehead, kneading the skin below her hairline as she looked at the photograph of her twin sister lying on the morgue table. She squeezed her brow until it felt as if her skull was going to crack under the pressure, her eyes burning with tears. A swirl of sickness spun in her guts and air in the room felt unbreathable, despite the open window and the fact that Armando Diceverde wasn't smoking.

"Blanca…" Diceverde began. "Blanca, are you okay?"

"I don't know," Asado replied. Rosa's eyes had been closed, but she could tell by the way they had been shut that the force of a .38 Super slug to the brain had nearly disgorged the orbs from their sockets.

Diceverde wasn't a tall man, and he only came up to Blanca Asado's shoulder. The fact that Blanca was looking at the remains of her sister and best friend only made him feel spiritually smaller. A choked sob escaped Asado's lips and she shook her head.

"Rosa wasn't into making money with drugs. We've both seen what that shit does to good people," Asado explained.

"You're preaching to the choir, Blanca," Diceverde replied. "She'd been flagging things for me to look at. We've both noticed something new burrowing into Acapulco's drug scene. Someone has been giving the Juarez Cartel a real knocking."

"And this is why Rosa was killed? Brujillo and his wife have been working hard together to end the hold that the cartels have over Acapulco. Rosa told me that she was investigating all forms of threats detected against Madame Brujillo."

"And on the surface, they seemed to be antigovernment attacks, but Rosa was curious about the sheer ferocity levied against the first lady," Diceverde replied. "She sent me copies of her research into a new player on the drug scene, organized around a Santa Muerte cult."

Blanca wrinkled her nose at the mention of the death cult, a popular subreligion that had sprung up in the underworld. Loosely based on Santería, Santa Muerte was a more ethically flexible religion, its morality open enough to allow drug dealers and murderers with faith issues to make amends for their wrongdoing with prayer and sacrifice, without hindering their more bloodthirsty and highly profitable activities. Suddenly the sins of dealing poison or mowing down another human being could be washed away with a moment's contrition without renunciation of their previous crimes. Congregations sprung up in destitute slums and prison blocks across Mexico, and followers came from every walk of life, from the lowest gutter urchin to the most powerful drug baron.

"So if Rosa was picking up leads about Santa Muerte cultists taking over the state's drug scene and trying to kill the governor and his wife…" Blanca began.

"The cultists have never made an attempt against Señora Brujillo," Diceverde countered. "They have been hitting the Juarez Cartel and the smaller organizations hard, so much so that the Juarez group has been importing help from overseas."

"So why would they accuse my sister of being part of this Santa Muerte cult and its takeover bid?" Asado asked. "Or of trying to murder the first lady?"

"We might never know," Diceverde answered. "Maybe she saw something during the hit. There was a sighting of two men escaping the resort after the gunfight. An evidence technician I know also told me, off the record, that he was ordered to eliminate evidence of two 9 mm submachine guns from the battle scene."

"Two 9 mm SMGs?" Asado asked. She did some mental arithmetic, looking at the reports of the fight.

"The assassins were using Mexican-issue G3 rifles. The bodyguards had .45 and .38-caliber handguns and sub-machine guns. The first lady shot several assassins using a .38 owned by one of the protection detail…"

"And she shot your sister in the head," Diceverde punctuated.

Asado took a deep breath. "After my sister might have been responsible for at least four dead assassins."

"Too many shell casings to match with slugs," Diceverde countered. "But you know Rosa and her baby Detonics .45s."

"She was deadly with them," Blanca replied. Her brow furrowed and her eyes began to sting. "Rosa wouldn't have tried to shoot the first lady, even if she was responsible for a fake assassination attempt on herself. She wouldn't have pulled a gun on her!"

"Everything that First Lady Brujillo is saying contradicts the hints that Rosa and I had been gathering," Diceverde replied. His lips pulled into a tight line across his mouth. "Unfortunately, someone got to Rosa's copies of the records when she died."

"Someone on her protection detail who hadn't been killed at the resort, most likely," Asado said, her mind focusing on the problem.

"Not likely. The first lady liked to keep her personal staff close by. Anyone severed from her service usually ended up going somewhere far away," Diceverde explained.

Asado frowned. "So that's why the Feds want to talk to me."

"If they've been fooled into thinking that Rosa was dirty, they might want to know how much she told you," Diceverde added.

Asado took a deep breath. "I need to talk to someone about this. I know some people who know some people."

"How many trust you enough to give you that kind of wiggle room?" Diceverde asked.

Asado's shoulders fell.

The room was hot and cramped, bugs rattling against the rapidly disintegrating screen on the window. A small, naked bulb in a desk lamp glowed, throwing light on the reporter's copies of Rosa Asado's notes.

"The dent in the Juarez Cartel's activity came when Governor Brujillo was elected," Asado noted. "And it's only become larger the more the governor cracked down on the cartel."

"Circumstantial evidence. Nothing that would stand up in a court of law," Diceverde admitted, regret weighing his words.

Bugs fluttered en masse from the screen, buzzing away into the night, drawing Asado's attention. Something had frightened the tiny, sensitive creatures. Her hand slid under the loose tail of her blouse and she pulled out a hammerless .357 Magnum snub-nosed Ruger.

Diceverde's eyes widened at the sight of the revolver. "What—"

Asado put a finger to her lips and shook her head. The journalist fell silent, hazel eyes going to the window. She pushed him to the wall and guided him to sit, protected by brick and masonry.

"I didn't even see that," Diceverde whispered.

"Well, if you had, then it wouldn't be doing the job I wanted it to," Asado replied. "Shush."

A fist punched through the tattered windowscreen, an ugly, lime-shaped object locked in it. Asado clamped her hand over it, clenching it tight, and jammed the muzzle of the Ruger up into the wrist attached to it. Two thunderbolt blasts ripped through the confined room, the sheer power of the Magnum pistol enough to sever the appendage.

A howl of pain cut through the night and she hurled the disembodied hand back through the screen. A heartbeat later the brutal little round object exploded, rocking the walls and ceiling hard enough to rain dust in the room. Diceverde winced from the grenade blast, but realized that if the mysterious hand had let go of the bomb, the two of them would undoubtedly have been killed instantly.

Curses sounded outside and Asado swept the files off the table, stuffing them into Diceverde's briefcase. "Come on, Armi."

The journalist wasn't waiting for a second invitation. He was up and on the woman's heels in a flash. He paused long enough to retrieve a nickel-plated Colt 1911 from a drawer and thumbed the hammer back, short fingers wrapping easily around the slender autoloader's grip. He jammed two spare magazines loaded with .38 Super rounds into his offside pocket.

Though it was against the law for civilians to own guns in Mexico, that didn't stop people from breaking the law. As well, Diceverde had made enough enemies across his career as a reporter to know he needed a powerful and reliable handgun. They didn't get much more powerful and reliable than the Colt in .38 Super.

Asado grabbed a handful of Diceverde's shirt and shoved him through the door as an assault rifle poked through the window frame. She opened fire on the weapon in the portal, her pistol blazing like the sun. Bullets chopped just an inch over Diceverde's head, letting him know just how close he had come to dying. His stocky legs propelled him through the doorway and the front door to the building opened, a black shadow appearing in front of him.

The journalist saw the unmistakable profile of an AK-47 in the man's hands, and Diceverde triggered the Colt twice. The .38 Super roared in the darkness, creating bright strobes of light. The rifleman jerked, and Diceverde wasn't sure if he had scored hits or not.

A muzzle-flash flared from the mouth of the AK, but it was stretched and elongated. Having been present for enough gunfights, the little reporter knew that the shots had been discharged into the ceiling. Diceverde triggered the Colt twice more, cracking out 125-grain hollow-point rounds at well over 1300 feet per second, aiming just behind the origin of the muzzle-flash. He was glad he'd spent the money on having night-sights installed on the shiny pistol. By following the vibrant neon-green dot hovering in the distance between the more indistinct yellow rear dots, he knew exactly where he was aiming,

A strangled cry filled the air and the rifle clattered to the floor.

Thunderbolts launched from behind Diceverde and he jerked his attention to another figure in the door, which was writhing as Magnum projectiles speared through his body, soft, exposed lead peeling apart on contact with fluid biomass and tunnelling horrendous cavities through the chest of another gunman.

Diceverde ran to the door and pressed his broad back to the wall to the side. He took the momentary break to drop his half-empty magazine and pocket it, feeding a new stick of nine shots into the Colt.

He heard the clicking of metal as somewhere in the shadows, Blanca Asado reloaded the partially spent AK-47.

"We'll need the firepower," Asado stated.

"Blanca…" Diceverde began.

The words he intended to say were ripped from his memory as the wall suddenly exploded behind him, concussive forces hurling him to the floor, his vision blurring.

CHAPTER TWO

The Executioner snipped chain links in the fence with his multitool, a sharp, powerful vise for cutting wire set at the base of the folding pliers. The circle of fence fell away, and he crawled through the hole.

He'd left his Barrett and the confiscated G3 behind in the truck, knowing that going in, he needed stealth and their added bulk would make his large, powerful frame even more noticeable. Still, he had the wicked Beretta 93-R machine pistol with its 20-round capacity and blunt suppressor under his arm, and the .44 Magnum Desert Eagle riding on his hip. Both handguns had been chosen by Bolan for their power and range. The Desert Eagle had proved itself a killer at out to two hundred yards, and the Beretta 93-R was a match for any submachine gun in his skilled hands, out to one hundred yards.

Though it was the Executioner's plan to bring a fatal, final judgment to the commander of the smuggling forces who'd returned to the base, there was the possibility of uninvolved, honest Mexican soldiers staffing this facility. Opening fire without proper identification would put innocent blood on Bolan's hands.

Luckily, aside from his pistols, Bolan also had various knives, garrottes and impact tools, truly silent means of delivering death. He saw the last of the trucks pull toward the motor pool, overladen with soldiers. All it would take would be one grenade to eliminate the smuggling military men, but before Bolan took out the enemy commander, he needed to get answers out of the man. A grenade might not leave enough left of the traitorous military leader to question, and an open gunfight would result in a conflict with soldiers whose duty was the defense of the base, not pushing heroin across the border.

Stalking closer, a shadow among shadows, Bolan closed on the group as soldiers disgorged from the truck.

He got within ten yards of the milling soldiers, his comprehension of Spanish more than sufficient to understand what was being said.

"We lost a third of the heroin," one of the men reported.

"Juarez is going to be mad as hell," the commander replied. "What the hell are we going to do?"

"We? You're the one who ran away from one man," the subordinate countered.

"Is that so?" the commander asked.

"Wait. Munoz… Hold on…"

A muzzle-flash lit up the accuser's face an instant before it dissolved into a crater of spongy gore. Munoz lowered his .50-caliber Desert Eagle and looked around. "Any of the rest of you want to accuse me of running away?"

"No!" came the unanimous response.

"Good," Munoz replied. "I'll be in my office, contacting the cartel about the difficulties we've had tonight. In my version, we were struck by a significant force. It seemed as if they were Santa Muerte cultists."

The soldiers nodded.

"Get the heroin stored away for our next trip. We'll

see if the part of the shipment left behind was touched. I doubt it. The Border Patrol wouldn't cross two hundred yards into our territory to take out 150 kilos of Mexican Brown," Munoz concluded. "Remember— Santa Muerte cultists ambushed us."

It was one way for the commander to save face. The punctuation of his statement remained the dead man, his skull hollowed out by a thundering 350-grain bullet. Any deviation and the corpse would be joined by more. And apparently Munoz was in such a position of power that he could get away with burning his own men to the ground with impunity.

"I'm going to hit the bathroom," another man said. His authority among the others was sufficient that he was able to slack off menial tasks to take care of biological functions, and the minions below him didn't dare do more than grumble under their breath.

Bolan decided to shadow the loner instead of going right to Munoz. Kurtzman would contact him via his vibrating pager if anything of urgent interest were reported. The Farm undoubtedly had hacked into the phone system to spy on any communications coming in or going out, sifting for nuggets of gold in the streams of data running along fiber-optic wires.

The second in command had stepped into the latrine and begun to relieve himself when the Executioner snapped a powerful arm around his throat, pressure on his larynx strangling off a cry of dismay. Bolan rested the sharp edge of his commando knife across the Mexican's brow and cheek.

"If you make a sound other than to answer my questions, I'll carve out your left eye and saw off your nose in one slice. *Comprende?*" Bolan inquired.

"Yes," the Mexican soldier rasped softly in English.

Facial mutilation, especially the threat to his eye, had cowed the smuggler for now.

"How many on the base are in on the heroin pipeline?" Bolan asked.

"There used to be a dozen more," the man began.

A hard push and blood trickled from the officer's brow into his eye. A strangled whimper escaped.

"Minus them," Bolan advised.

"Me. Colonel Munoz. The gate guards on duty. And the dozen or so unloading the truck," the officer stated.

The answer sounded plausible, and the tremors in his captive's voice had added a sense of truth to the confession.

The Executioner tugged his forearm tighter against his captive's throat. "Let the survivors in your little bunch know that there's an American who disapproves of your moonlighting."

He jammed his thumb under the ear of the captive, pressing hard on the carotid artery long enough to render the smuggler unconscious without imparting any long-term harm.

Bolan turned the unconscious soldier around and deposited him on the seat of the toilet. He paused long enough to use a strip of plastic tape to take the man's thumbprint, preserving it by pressing it to a three-by-five card for later scanning.

He had business to attend to.

Fourteen men were unloading heroin from the truck, several pushing a rolling pallet toward the depths of a storage building. Others worked on cleaning the blood spatter off their vehicle and picking up Munoz's executed victim.

Bolan followed silently and stealthily after the quartet with the heroin. There were more than two hundred kilos on the pallet, meaning that Munoz's declaration of half was either an understatement or he was delivering for more than just the Juarez Cartel.

The Executioner made a mental note to get that information out of the colonel before he died.

One straggler in the group had hung back. His task had to have been rear security, and since he gripped a rifle in both hands, he was Bolan's first target. In two long strides, the wraith in black clamped a crushing hand around the throat of the soldier, cutting off any voiced protests just before spearing the seven-inch blade of his combat knife into the base of the gunman's skull. Speared right through his brain, the major trunk of his central nervous system destroyed by the razor-sharp edge, he instantly turned into dead, dangling weight in the Executioner's hand with only a whispered "squelch" of steel grating on bone betraying the swift kill.

The blade whipped out of the dead man's neck, and Bolan shoved the corpse against one of the two men pushing on the trolley, both bodies collapsing to the ground as the warrior closed in behind the second drug pusher. Slick blood was the only thing glinting on the nonreflective battle knife, and even the dully glistening fluid disappeared when the Executioner plunged the unyielding steel into the Mexican soldier's right kidney. A tortured sputter of pain was all that the smuggler had time to release before renal shock killed him. With a twist and a hard slice, the blade was free as the remaining pallet pusher grunted, shoving his lifeless friend off of him. There was a moment of complaint about the fool "playing around" before the Mexican realized he was complaining to a corpse.

He whipped his head around, but he only saw the waffle-tread of Bolan's combat boot filling his world.

The side kick smashed the Mexican smuggler's nose flat, driving bone fragments back into his brain even as his neck snapped under the thunderous force of the blow.

The sickening crack that signaled the pallet pusher's death alerted the man at the lead of the group and he whirled, reaching for a handgun in a flap holster.

Only the Executioner's battle-honed reflexes gave him the advantage in beating the trooper's quick draw. The black commando-style Bowie knife whistled through the air like a shard of night come alive. The gunman had snapped open his holster and stopped, fingers clawing up to the handle of the weapon jutting from his windpipe. Lips worked noiselessly as the last of the transport crew suffocated with an inch-and-a-half width of steel cutting off his air.

Bolan ripped a smaller, ring-handled knife from an inconspicuous sheath on his harness and charged in, two fingers through the loop base of the blade. A two-and-a-half-inch wedge of steel raked across both of the choking smuggler's eyes, the stocky knife swung with enough force to splinter bone and carve a furrow in his forebrain. Bolan took the handle of the commando knife as the Mexican soldier slid off the black-phosphate blade to flop to the floor.

In the space of a few moments, four men lay dead, blood spreading in puddles on the concrete.

Bolan had to deal with the two hundred kilograms of heroin on the pallet, without resorting to a fire that would alert the remaining smugglers or Munoz in his office.

It took only a short time to locate a janitor's closet, and bring back several cartons of cleaning supplies. He sliced open the necks of the bottled bleach, then punched air holes in their bottoms and upended them onto the packets of heroin. The air holes would allow the bleach to drain into the heroin more quickly to soak it into a useless morass of chemical paste. The perfectly squared blocks of black tar heroin deformed and swelled under the bleach's assault. It wouldn't take long for most of the remaining heroin to be ruined. And with the loss of the drugs near the border, the cartels that Munoz did business with would be enraged.

Though Munoz wouldn't live to see the morning, the thought of losing a million dollars in heroin to the incompetence of the Mexican army would slow the cartels in doing further business with them. It was a small pause, a tiny impediment. But in the long run, it would give the DEA and the Border Patrol time to shore up their defenses against this particular batch of smugglers.

In the meantime, Bolan had a visit to pay and information to get.

BLANCA ASADO HATED to admit it, gripping the handle of the AK-47, but she was back in her element. Dealing with the emotional crush of her sister's murder had kicked her around until she couldn't think straight. In a way, she wanted to thank the faceless marauders who were swarming Armando Diceverde's small motel room. She thrived on conflict, and because of that she was able to spend years struggling, alongside her sister, rising through the ranks of Mexican law enforcement before she quit and became a private security contractor.

Dread and sorrow were things she couldn't control, but gunmen coming after her was something she did know how to handle. It would put the agony of losing her sister on hold for a while.

The sight of another masked gunman focused her and she ripped off a short burst from the AK, a row of bullet wounds blossoming from his belt to his throat as she zipped him up the center with the assault rifle. With the stock welded to her shoulder, the recoil was controllable. No ammunition wasted, and through her peripheral vision over the top of the sights, she was able to see other targets popping into view.

Unfortunately, an explosion threw her off as a grenade detonated just outside the door. Diceverde toppled backward, taking the brunt of the concussion, and Asado had to take a couple of steps to regain her balance. Her ears rang, and she cursed herself for not equalizing the pressure in her skull with a loud shout.

Another pair of gunmen appeared in the doorway, expecting their stun grenade to have flattened all opposition within. They were cocky, and their weapons were held low, fingers off the trigger, staring at the flattened photojournalist as he struggled to recover his senses.

"Easy pickings," one man said.

"So you think," Asado growled, pulling the trigger on the AK-47 and letting the weapon buck and kick against her shoulder. She held on tight, though, fighting against the muzzle's rise just enough to keep from emptying rounds into the ceiling, slicing the cocky gunman up through his torso with a stream of 7.62 mm leaden scythes. The shooter slammed into his partner, giving Asado a moment to release the trigger, shift her aim and then tap it again. A trio of bullets spit into the face of the staggered second assassin, his hair and scalp flying back as though someone had thrown open a trapdoor.

Asado reached under Diceverde's arm. "Come on, Armando."

Diceverde got to his feet. He hadn't lost control of his Colt, but he wisely kept it pointed at the ground. His senses were scrambled by the concussion grenade, and if the bomb had gone off inside the apartment, instead of in the doorway, the compression wave would have left them both far more than merely stunned. Asado helped pull Diceverde onto the balcony, and by the time he reached for the railing, he no longer needed assistance.

There were no more signs of enemy activity, but that could have been a lull in the action, Asado thought.

"My car is down there. Follow me," Asado stated.

"Lead the way," Diceverde replied. He picked up speed as they reached the stairs.

Asado jumped when she was five steps from the bottom, landing on the sidewalk in a crouch, using her forward momentum to throw her against the fender of her sedan. Gunfire sparked, and Diceverde's Colt cracked into the darkness. The journalist ducked, having drawn the attention of the hit men, and Asado spotted the muzzle-flash, pinpointing the enemy gunners. She fired another burst, giving Diceverde a break to join her at the car.

Asado threw open the door and ripped off the last of the AK's load to cover for Diceverde as he crawled into the passenger seat. She let the empty rifle clatter to the ground and slid in behind the wheel. A twist of the key and the engine roared to life. Throwing the car into Reverse, she peeled straight toward the assassins as they rushed her. Diceverde lurched up after reloading his pistol, but Asado stomped on the gas and the Chevy Impala's rear bumper struck one of the gunmen. The Chevy shook, and Diceverde's shot missed the charging gunmen as the car rolled over one and quickly past the other.

The other gunman had thrown himself out of the way and Asado stood on the brake, momentum whipping the nose of the Impala around as she ground the gearshift into drive. With a tromp on the gas, she was off, shooting into the street as gunfire banged against the car.

Diceverde shouted in pain, his gun falling into the seatwell.

"Armando?"

"Took one in shoulder," he rasped.

"Just hang on," Asado told him. "I'll get you to some help."

"Feels like my arm is broken, but there's not much bleeding," Diceverde said, pained.

"I'm sorry I got you into this," Asado replied, swinging around a corner. She wanted to make certain no one followed her.

Once she was sure that they had no tail, she pulled off onto the side of the road and reached under her seat for the first-aid kit. She packed the gunshot wound with gauze and taped it in place to control the bleeding. Diceverde was right; there wasn't much blood. She taped his forearm against his stomach to hold it in place, then worked up an improvised sling from seat belt straps in the backseat, always keeping an eye out for enemies who would try to finish the job.

Blanca Asado couldn't believe she'd lost both her sister and her trust in her country in the same night.

COLONEL JAVIER MUNOZ put down the phone and massaged his brow. His mind reeled from the threats his Juarez connection had growled at him. He looked at the big chrome Desert Eagle on the desk next to him. If he didn't recover the lost heroin, they'd thread his tongue out his throat and staple his genitals to it, before giving him the sweet release of death.

He rested his hand on the pebbled rubber grips of the massive handgun. One pull of the trigger and he'd hammer out a .50-caliber slug. He'd never shot anyone with it before this day, and Sosa's death was illuminating. The man's head had been cored violently, brains squirting out the back in a fountain of human destruction. But even the power of the Desert Eagle might not be enough against the gunmen of the Juarez Cartel. Maybe if he put the muzzle between his lips and squeezed, he wouldn't feel it.

Something scraped behind him, a movement just outside the cone of yellowed light from his desk lamp. Munoz's fingers clawed the big handgun closer when another Desert Eagle chopped down like an ax, crushing his carpal bones between two slabs of heavy steel. A hand clamped over the colonel's mouth before he could let out a cry of pain over his shattered limb, bones floating freely in pulped meat. Munoz's eyes bulged in their sockets and he was stretched hard backward out of the chair, neck bones creaking against each other.

"Nice pistol," came a dry, grim voice. "Trouble is, I can lift mine."

Munoz's throat burned as his muffled howl of agony tried to force its way past his lips.

His attacker's Desert Eagle disappeared with the ruffle of steel sheathing itself in leather.

Bolan reached out and picked up the massive .50-caliber weapon, thumbing back the hammer, then sliding on the safety. "In your next lifetime, if Desert Eagles are still around, this is how you should carry it."

Munoz swallowed as the huge weapon's muzzle pressed to his cheek. He wanted to struggle, but with Bolan's knee shoved into the back of his chair, and hundreds of pounds of leverage hauling on his chin and stressing his spine, the colonel was left helpless and paralyzed with pain. His good hand clawed at the hand over his mouth as he struggled to speak past Bolan's restraining fingers.

"You've got something to tell me?" Bolan asked, loosening his grip. "Just remember, you call for help, I put one in your stomach, so it'll take you a long time to die."

"Yes, sir," Munoz whispered, making sure his voice didn't rise. His windpipe still felt choked off, but this time from fear not physical force. Tears burned down the colonel's cheeks.

"I listened to your phone call. Your bosses don't think very much of your performance tonight," Bolan taunted softly. "After all, losing nearly a dozen men to one enemy combatant?"

"You didn't fight fair…" Munoz protested, his voice a harsh, ragged exhalation.

"And you did, opening fire on two American lawmen forbidden to return fire against you?" Bolan asked. Munoz's neck twisted until he was looking at a pair of cold, merciless blue eyes. At first he was going to cry out in pain, but the icy gaze froze his soul.

"Skip the 'poor me' whining, Munoz," Bolan informed him. "All I want to know is who am I sparing the trouble of mutilating you by putting a bullet in your head?"

"Roderigo Montoya Juarez," Munoz replied.

"Right," Bolan returned. "As if Montoya-Juarez would get any of your foul fluids on his fingers. Tell me another joke."

"I swear. I swear!" Munoz replied, his voice rising.

Bolan ground the steel of the barrel hard against Munoz's cheek, the ridge of the bone crunching against the unyielding metal. His hand clamped tighter over the colonel's mouth. "If I didn't know any better, I'd swear that you were trying to make some noise in order to call for help."

"I'm not," Munoz whispered. "I'm not… I just don't want to die."

"You've done everything you can to convince me otherwise," the Executioner informed him. "You know how light the trigger is on these pistols, right?"

Munoz heard the metallic clink of the safety catch snapping off. His pants grew hot and wet as his bladder cut loose. "Please…"

"You're not giving me anything to make me want to spare your life," Bolan said. "But, considering I just emptied twelve gallons of bleach into what was left of your heroin, I could just spare myself some hearing damage and let Montoya-Juarez have you."

Munoz's dark eyes bulged, irises narrowing to pinpricks in sheer horror.

Bolan released the colonel and flicked on the Desert Eagle's safety.

"Wait…"

"For what?" Bolan asked.

"Juarez has competition," Munoz replied.

"I know the layout," Bolan told him. "There are six other cartels sweating Montoya-Juarez right now."

"A new player who only popped up recently," Munoz stated. "I gave Juarez a hookup to make a move the other day."

"With who?" Bolan pressed.

"Army officer by the name of Salvada," Munoz confessed. "Salvada called in some ex-soldiers to make the hit, but equipped them."

The Executioner regarded him coldly as Munoz ran the numbers in his head. Nearly one hundred pints of bleach would completely ruin one hundred pounds of heroin instantly. That was a quarter of the two hundred kilograms he had left. Together with the 150 lost at the border, and even more seepage, Munoz could kiss any chance of making it up to the cartel.

Bolan dropped the magazine and racked the slide, then lobbed the empty Desert Eagle onto the desk. "All yours, Colonel. I suggest you run like hell. You've got a few hours before Montoya-Juarez stops waiting for you."

Munoz nodded, looking at the gun.

"Who knows, maybe you can find mercy with the government and military you betrayed. Or you could trust that the Border Patrol won't kill you on sight," Bolan suggested. He lobbed one of the fat .50 caliber bullets to Munoz. "Or, you could find your own way out."

The Executioner turned and left the office. He'd gotten halfway down the hall when he heard the solitary roar of the Mexican's pistol, followed by the thud of a limp body striking the floor.

He was working his way up the Juarez Cartel, but now he heard about another player in this game.

One that might have been the reason why the governor of Guerrero State wanted the Executioner to join the conflict.

He'd cross that bridge when he got to it.

CHAPTER THREE

Anibella Brujillo looked over the railing of the patio at the tall American who was walking up the marble stone path. Over six feet tall, he had deeply tanned skin and a lean, powerful frame. His denim jacket was tight at the shoulders, but hung loosely enough at the waist to inform her that he had to have concealed at least one large handgun in its folds. Clear, ice-blue eyes looked her over and she smiled softly, her wide, lush lips curving as her eyes narrowed invitingly. Emilio Brujillo didn't even notice the man walking up the path until she gently cleared her throat.

"The American is here, darling," Anibella said, resting her hand on his thigh, delicate fingers giving his linen-sheathed leg a tender scratch.

Brujillo looked up from his newspaper, nodding absently. "Thank you, darling."

Brujillo was about twenty years older than Anibella, but even for being only in his midfifties, he was gray and wrinkled, a worn-down man. His run for the governorship of Guerrero had been long and hard, and his work since being in office had been relentless. It was as if the beautiful Mexican singer had married a withered old grandfather, instead of a vibrant, crusading politician. Physically, he looked a wreck, but he still managed to speak in a strong, forceful timbre. Some of her high-society friends seemed scandalized by her public displays of affection with the shrivelled politician, despite knowing about her dalliances on the side.

Emilio Brujillo walked toward the man his friend in the U.S. Justice Department had called Agent Matt Cooper. Anibella assumed it wasn't his real name, more likely a cover for someone who had a far more sinister history. She looked him over, seeing signs of faint scar tissue on the man's callused hands and the bit of fore-arm visible under the light, summer-weight denim jacket. He looked at her, and though his face carried an ageless quality, the glance carried the weight of a man who had been through more than one lifetime.

Brujillo shook Bolan's hand, and despite the wear and tear on the Mexican governor's features, his grip was strong, but not challenging. "Welcome to Acapulco, Señor Cooper."

"Thank you, sir," Bolan replied, nodding.

"This is my wife, Anibella," Brujillo introduced. "Anything you can say to me, you can say in front of her. She is a part of my government, and is one of my most trusted confidants."

Bolan looked at Anibella again, studying her. She reined in her charming, playful nature, instead presenting a curious and innocent facade. The Executioner tensed, watching the change wash over her, and Anibella realized that he was observant, noting the sudden shift in her outward nature. Anibella dropped the charade and simply smiled.

"A pleasure to meet you," Bolan said, burying his suspicion out of her sight. He was as facile in controlling his emotions as she had been, which set her on edge.

"A pleasure to meet such a man who has earned our president's trust as an ally," Anibella replied.

Bolan nodded, looking to Brujillo. "I generally operate off the grid, and alone. Perhaps if you had a trusted operative…"

"I was thinking of having you work with my wife," Brujillo began.

Bolan raised an eyebrow, glancing to her. "I'm sorry, sir, but…"

Anibella could sense his distrust, and her control over him slipping away.

That was when the Saint of Death tipped her hand, granting the high priestess her advantage back.

BLANCA ASADO RUBBED HER EYES and sighed. She hadn't gotten much sleep after making certain that Armando Diceverde was patched up and hidden in a safe place. She didn't want her friend to end up as a statistic or a victim of an overzealous assassin. Asado knew that the men who had struck the night before weren't *federales*. Even though she'd engaged in a few "black" SWAT-style operations with the police, they would have had the hotel more tightly sewn up, and wouldn't have even bothered with grenades through the window. They'd have simply opened up with some powerful rifles, not the relatively weak AK-47s, and just hosed through the walls for thirty seconds, then gone in and policed the corpses. The AKs would have penetrated the hotel walls, but these were gangsters, not working with the best knowledge of what a powerful weapon could do.

Asado's home was being watched by the police. She recognized the unmarked cars and the stakeout teams, not because she knew the men personally, but because she knew their style. That was all right. Blanca had fresh clothing and some tools in the trunk of her Impala. She'd showered and changed at a public beach. While she had a Remington 12-gauge shotgun and a Heckler & Koch MP-5 machine pistol in her trunk, taking the place of her spare tire, she'd left them alone.

Instead, she'd reloaded her stubby little Ruger and pocketed two speedloaders for it. The pocket-size .357 Magnum revolver was a good gun, but she needed something easier to reload and shoot quickly and accurately. For that, she went with Armando's Colt .38 Super. It was fast and powerful, but much more manageable in the recoil department. She would be able to conceal the flat pistol, as well. Considering that the .38 Super 1911 was one of the most popular handguns in Mexico, due to laws keeping citizens from owning military calibers like .45 auto or 9 mm, it would be easy to get spare ammunition and magazines.

Asado watched the gates of the governor's mansion, noting the arrival of a man in a rental car. As he waited for the gate to open, he scanned around. Taking a look through a pair of compact binoculars, she caught his face. The blue eyes betrayed him as a North American. He caught sight of her and made eye contact for several moments.

Her hand dropped to the chrome pistol on the seat next to her, lips drawn tightly.

Could Anibella Brujillo have hired an American assassin to clean up her affairs?

No. She saw the badge and Justice Department ID card that he'd flashed. He was here in an official capacity. Of course, that wouldn't exclude his presence as a CIA assassin sent to silence a potential threat to the first lady. But try as she might, she couldn't reconcile her paranoia with her instincts and experience.

The rental car went through the gates unhindered, and Asado relaxed. She had a knot of tension balled up between her shoulder blades that sent a spike of pain spearing out through her forehead. She wondered, idly, if it was anything approaching the pain her sister felt when she'd been shot. Blanca had been the skeptic of the pair, doubting Rosa's so-called psychic flashes. The phantom pain was still there, and Asado couldn't unkink her shoulders though she had already swallowed half a dozen painkillers.

After several minutes of discomfort, Asado tilted and stretched her neck and as she did so, the pain between her shoulders disappeared with a click. Out of her peripheral vision, she spotted movement and she instantly slouched in her seat.

It was a pair of black vans, quickly rolling up the street. Since this particular road led nowhere, there was no need for speeding. In a heartbeat, her hand flashed to the grips of the chrome Colt resting on the seat, the safety snapped off with a click that echoed the release of her tightened tendons in her neck. If it was a psychic message sent through her pain centers, she wished that she'd been able to tell Rosa about it. Maybe, though, it was her dead twin, warning her from beyond.

The lead van accelerated past her Impala, gunfire flashing out the passenger window. The guard at the gate jerked violently as he was torn crotch to throat by a line of automatic fire. He slammed back into the ground and the front grille of the van connected with wrought-iron bars. Peeled from their frame and their runners, the metal sliding gates hurled out of the path of the speeding vehicle. It jolted and rolled to a halt just beyond. The second van swerved around it as men disgorged from the rear of the stalled lead vehicle.

Asado fired up the ignition, but just before the engine turned over, she heard a shout in what sounded like Russian. Her stomach twisted as she realized that the Juarez Cartel had to have brought in outside muscle, namely the *mafiya*. The Russian organized crime Families were deadly men, culling the ranks of the Soviet military and intelligence to get their most ruthless soldiers and assassins.

As much as this seemed like an opportunity for the first lady to pay for framing her sister as a drug smuggler, Asado couldn't ignore the fact that innocent bystanders would be caught and killed in the cross fire.

And then there was that blue-eyed American. He was a mystery in this equation, as was Anibella Brujillo. Joining the conflict would give her a vantage point on the questions popping up in her mind.

She gunned the Impala and aimed for one of the men who had rushed to watch the gate. The man was pasty and blond, an obvious Russian, but the Uzi in his hands spoke its message understandable in any language. A volley of 9 mm bullets deflected off the streamlined hood and windshield of the Chevy before the gunner could compensate his angle of fire. Asado put the pedal to the metal and felt the jarring impact of her front fender against the *mafiya* thug, bones shattering on impact as he launched into her windshield and smeared torn flesh and gore across the cracked safety glass.

Asado regretted losing the Impala, but lives were at stake. She dived out of the driver's seat after popping the rear trunk. The MP-5 and a bag of magazines came immediately to hand, and she threw the satchel over her shoulder like a lethal purse.

Only one of the Russians had stayed behind to watch the gate, meaning that the killers had a plan to be in and out before a prolonged firefight could break out.

Thunder crashed in the distance, the deep and throaty bark of a .44 Magnum pistol cracking loudly as a counterpoint to the softer chatter of machine pistols.

The American had come, and he was prepared for a fight.

MACK BOLAN'S CURIOSITY about Anibella Brujillo was put on hold with the distinct rattle of an automatic weapon in the distance. In a heartbeat he had the .44 Magnum Desert Eagle out of its quick-draw leather, safety off, finger resting in register against the trigger guard. It took only a moment of hesitation to call out in Spanish to Governor Emilio Brujillo's bodyguards to get him to safety immediately.

Anibella pulled a Glock from underneath the breakfast table. She didn't rack the slide, and her finger was off the trigger, muzzle aimed at the ground.

"That means you, too, ma'am," Bolan snapped.

Her hazel eyes flashed brightly with indignity. "They are attacking my home, Mr. Cooper, and I have been trained by the best commandos Mexico has."

"They're also heavily armed," Bolan countered. He knew that the first lady hadn't run at the previous assassination attempt. Indeed, she'd picked up a handgun belonging to one of her fallen bodyguards and proceeded to fight back with savage proficiency. "If you want to help, protect your husband and fall back along with his security detail."

"But…" Anibella began, but the Executioner had no time to waste in debating with her. He took off in a long, loping run, keeping to the concealment of a row of planter-based hedges. The concrete would provide him with cover and he found a good position where he'd have protected fields of fire to control the rear entrance of the mansion.

A shape crouched beside him and from the smell of Anibella's perfume, he didn't even have to look to identify her.

"Not going to yell at me?" the woman asked, finding a notch in the concrete planter she kneeled against.

"It's too late now, and I'd give away my position," Bolan returned, containing the urge to growl at her. "It's your funeral."

Her wide lips curved upward in a smirk. "I don't think you'll allow that—"

"Incoming," Bolan cut her off. He took careful aim with the Desert Eagle, the front sight cutting across the forehead of a gunman. He was mildly surprised at the Slavic features of the hitter, as well as the Uzi submachine gun in his hands. However, that didn't slow his pull of the trigger, nor the screaming 240-grain jacketed hollow-point round he punched through the Russian's skull at more than 1300 feet per second. The dome of bone and scalp that had been the top of the assassin's head flipped back on strips of stretchy flesh.

Other *mafiya* goons dived wildly for cover as the Executioner tracked a second Uzi-armed killer and popped another .44 Magnum slug through his rib cage. Eight hundred foot-pounds of energy tore the Russian's heart in two, killing him instantly. Anibella's Glock .40 barked off to Bolan's right, taking down a third gunman with a double-tap to the upper chest.

Three down so far, but a half dozen SMGs ripped out a sheet of return fire that drove them both back behind the protection of concrete garden decorations.

"You wouldn't happen to have anything heavier…or maybe some grenades, would you?" First Lady Brujillo asked.

"Not right now," Bolan replied, shifting his position to the end of a long marble bench. Swinging around the side, he tapped off four quick shots that took two of the hit men off guard from their flank. Cut down by the Magnum heartstoppers, he drew the attention of the remaining four shooters. Bolan was letting the marble absorb the fire lancing in his direction, allowing the gunmen to burn up their reserves of ammunition on bulletproof stone. Suddenly, he noticed movement in his peripheral vision.

Anibella's Glock ripped off several quick shots toward a knot of Russians who were trying to slip up on Bolan's blind side. The Executioner's left hand ripped his Beretta from its shoulder holster as he emptied his Desert Eagle toward the mobsters, helping to keep them down. One of the shooters jerked violently, his neck geysering out a fountain of arterial blood as a .44 Magnum round ripped through it. Finally the 93-R machine pistol snapped out at full extension on his left arm. On semiauto, the six-and-a-half-inch barrel of the Beretta spun a 9 mm shot through the face of a second of the newcomers. The 93-R's extra barrel length gave him enough accuracy to make lethal shots at forty yards, while the 9 mm bullet still had enough velocity to cause major damage.

There was more gunfire in the distance, automatic weapons chattering on an exchange of fire that gave the Executioner pause. From his memorization of the mansion's layout, none of the other security on the scene would have been in a position to engage in combat with the invaders. Someone else had entered this conflict, and Bolan wasn't certain exactly who.

"Fall back to the house," Bolan ordered, capping off a pair of Parabellum rounds into the face of a Russian hitter. A gory splash churned up the assassin's features, whipping him to the ground like a sack of garbage.

"Why?" Anibella Brujillo asked. Her Glock roared twice more, fat bullets tearing through the shoulder of a second Uzi-packing killer. She bore down and finished off the wounded man with three more shots into his center of mass, 180-grain bullets churning internal organs into pureed slush.

"Do it!" the Executioner growled. He popped the empty magazine from his Desert Eagle, stuffed it into his waistband, slapped in a fresh stick and brought the weapon to bear with one hand, all while punching out two more accurate shots from his Beretta. "I'll cover you. Go!"

The first lady took off. Bolan rose, both handguns blazing. He was firing to draw the assassins' attention, but even as he sidestepped along the planters, Beretta and Desert Eagle barking almost in unison, he managed to tag two more of the *mafiya* gunmen, dropping their corpses to the lawn, leaking from multiple wounds.

The full-auto gunfight around the corner was growing closer, and Bolan didn't want to have to deal with a mysterious newcomer and the governor's decisively lethal wife at the same time.

Anibella Brujillo reached the back entrance to the mansion, security team members in the doorway with machine pistols barking. Uzis chattered angrily and one of the Mexican bodyguards let out a gargled cry of pain, collapsing to his knees. Brujillo whirled and hooked the injured Mexican under his arm and pulled him to cover as Bolan ripped out 9 mm and .44 Magnum retribution against the knot of gunmen opening fire on the first lady.

"Hurry up!" Anibella shouted.

"Get him to cover!" Bolan snapped. He stuffed the Desert Eagle into his waistband and dropped behind the concrete planter. His index finger stabbed the release on the Beretta, and the 20-round magazine slid freely to the ground. A spare stick snapped into place, and he released the slide to get the machine pistol into battery. The whole move took a second and a half, and he was up and shooting, 9 mm slugs punching into the heart of a bold Russian gunman rushing his position.

The Executioner swung from the dropped assassin and struck another *mafiya* thug in the throat. Vertebrae exploded from the back of the gunman's neck.

He turned and saw an auburn-haired woman step into view at the corner of the mansion. She had an Uzi in her hands, exchanging fire with one of the armed raiders. She stitched him from crotch to throat, dropping the Russian like a sack of laundry. She whirled and was feeding her partially spent machine pistol a fresh magazine, when she saw the Executioner. There was a moment of hesitation on her face.

Bolan recognized the woman instantly. He knew the face of the dead bodyguard from the resort assault, Rosa Asado. But, having read the dead woman's file, he also knew she was one of a pair of identical twins. This had to be Blanca Asado. He remembered, from his briefing with Hal Brognola, that Blanca was wanted for questioning about her sister's alleged activities as the mastermind behind the first kill-attempt against the governor's wife.

If the Asado family wanted the first lady dead, then why in hell was Asado here, shooting it out with Russian hired guns when they could have exacted revenge for the murdered twin?

Brognola had surmised, during the briefing, that the Russians and the murdered Asado had been at cross purposes, both seeking the death of Mrs. Brujillo.

All this flashed in a single moment of recognition, and Bolan left the questions to be asked later when he spotted another *mafiya* gunman sneaking up on Asado's blind side. Bolan pulled his Desert Eagle from his waistband and punched out a single 240-grain slug that took the Russian at the *V* of his collarbone. Windpipe, aorta and spine torn out by the heavyweight bulldozer of lead and copper, the gunman flopped to the ground in a bloody mess.

Asado exchanged a quick, wordless glance with the Executioner before her eyes scanned for other opposition.

"Gracias," she called.

Bolan scrambled, cutting the distance between the two of them, staying alert for any of the *mafiya* goons who might have retreated to regroup for another attack. He took advantage of the pause to feed the hungry Desert Eagle again, returning it to his hip holster before transferring the 93-R to his right hand. "Blanca?"

"You have the advantage over me, sir," Asado returned.

"You out for vengeance for your sister?" Bolan pressed.

"I'd like to know who I'm talking to," Asado answered, her eyes scanning the grounds.

"Agent Matt Cooper," Bolan introduced. "You here for blood?"

"I'm here for answers," Asado stated. She had the Uzi pointed between Bolan's feet, a gesture not lost on the warrior. She didn't trust him.

"So am I," Bolan replied. "The one answer I want is, are you looking for payback for your sister?"

Asado's eyes narrowed, lightning sparking behind

them at the accusation. "Someone framed my sister, and now she's dead, and the police want to 'question' me. And you know how they ask questions in a Mexican jail."

Bolan's lips drew into a tight line. "So do you want to stick around and find out the truth?"

Asado glanced toward the mansion. "You think you can pull the fangs on Anibella Brujillo?"

Bolan looked over his shoulder, then back to Asado. He fished a business card out of his pocket and flipped it to her. "Contact me if you can. Use the voice-mail line. It's secure."

"You sure about that?" Asado asked.

"It's ironclad," Bolan told her. "Get out of here."

Asado let the Uzi drop to the ground between them. "I'm trusting you for now."

She took off around the corner, heading for the front gate. Sirens wailed in the distance. Asado was going to have to hoof it to disappear before the law showed up, but with the strides she was taking, she'd have enough time to reach whatever wheels she had stashed away. He'd noticed a vehicle parked not far from the mansion's entrance, and with her appearance, he realized the occupant of the unknown car. Strewed corpses were testimony to the odds that she'd helped to cut down.

The Executioner was glad for the assistance, but Asado's presence was worrying. She was on the run, and she was convinced her sister had been set up. That she was willing to hang back and trust Bolan to keep her in the loop was an advantage he possessed now. He looked back to the mansion and saw Anibella Brujillo, packing an MP-5 from the injured bodyguard. Her eyes locked on him with smoldering suspicion, but Bolan knew how to play it cool and close to the vest.

The first lady wanted in on his hunt for the people out to kill her, at least on the surface, but she was getting a little too cozy for Bolan's tastes. Having someone out from under Anibella Brujillo's thumb would allow him some wiggle room.

It was going to be tricky, but when he'd been recruited by Brognola for this, he was expecting a maze of deception. For now, he had a string to lead him back out if he wandered in too deeply.

CHAPTER FOUR

Thirty-six hours earlier

"I'm glad you could take this meeting, Striker," Hal Brognola said as Bolan sat at the end of the polished oak conference table. Monitors displaying satellite- and computer-generated maps flickered, bathing the dimly lit room in a blue glow that conflicted with the low-powered amber bulbs built into the smooth railings around the sides of the conference room, the woodgrain and luster of the rail matching that of the finely made table that Bolan sat at. The two friends were in the operations center beneath Camp David.

"I had a little downtime after my last mission," the Executioner replied.

"You get damned little enough R and R," Brognola stated.

Bolan simply shrugged. "I'm no good at relaxing."

"That's because you need more practice," Brognola grumbled. "Unfortunately, this has the makings of a major crisis, and the Mexican president asked for help from 'Striker.'"

Bolan's brow furrowed at the memories of what had been dubbed by the press as the Border Fire crisis. It had flavored the more recent dissent against the illegal immigration problem that followed. Bolan had worked almost side by side with the Mexican president, fending off several factions attempting to overthrow him and bring Mexico into open conflict with the United States. Only the combined forces of Stony Man Farm had brought the crisis to an end, battling wildly disparate forces.

The lights built into the oaken rail flared brighter and lines built into the ceiling added to the illumination, dispersing shadow and heralding the approach of the President of the United States and his guest, the Mexican president.

"Striker," the Man greeted Bolan. "I believe you know my guest."

"Good to see you in good health, sir," Bolan greeted the Mexican president.

"I wish that we could have been reunited under more cordial circumstances, my friend," the Mexican leader replied. "But I am glad to see you are still healthy, as well."

"I know you're not one for small talk, so we'll get down to the basics, Striker," the President said. "There's a cartel war going on in the Acapulco area, Guerrero State."

"And it's struck uncomfortably close to home with your friend, Governor Brujillo?" Bolan asked.

"You must have your finger on the pulse of my nation," the Mexican president stated.

"It helps to know where trouble occurs," Bolan explained. "I put the Acapulco situation in the forefront of my mind."

"Because of the American singer who was murdered?" the Hispanic official asked.

"Because it appeared that an army unit was involved in trying to murder a government official in a blatant terrorist attack," Bolan corrected. "First Lady Brujillo is the governor's face on the war on drugs in the Acapulco area."

"With Americans going down there for vacations, it's one of the hotspots that cartels are competing for control of," the U.S. President noted. "And unfortunately, there's nothing constitutional that we can do to limit that sort of demand."

"I'm more interested in containing the violence that the cartels inflict upon people," Bolan stated. "Unfortunately, between street level control of neighborhood dealers to attempted assassinations of government leaders, that kind of violence can smother nations and continents. Believe me, for all the heads I've killed, the body still manages to live on and grow a new one."

"Sounds like you get discouraged," the Mexican leader commented.

"It takes more than me burning a cartel to the ground to end your problems," Bolan returned, no bitterness in his voice. "Treat the disease and forget about picking at the bandage I applied."

The man bristled noticeably, but he held his tongue at reprimanding the Executioner. Bolan had a point about what was really needed. The lone warrior had assailed the leaders of drug cartels for years, doing fantastic amounts of damage, and instead of seizing upon the momentary advantage he supplied, laboriously moving government agencies stumbled, hemmed and hawed, allowing new batches of thugs to swarm in to replace the severed head.

"Governor Brujillo is a good man, and he is trying to implement more than a slash-and-burn approach to fighting drugs in his state," the Mexican president replied. "He deserves all the help we can get."

"He'll get it, then," Bolan replied. He tapped the over-stuffed file folder in front of him. "I've got all the intel I need, and I have an appointment on the border tonight."

"The border?" the Mexican leader asked.

"I have word of a military unit making a heroin run tonight," Bolan explained. "They might not have been the ones behind Anibella Brujillo's assassination attempt, but maybe they'll give me a link to someone who would know."

"You'll be acting against my country's military, Striker."

"I'll be acting against traitors. Nowhere in their oath of duty does it say they have to assist in peddling poison to other nations," Bolan countered. "That doesn't contribute to protecting Mexico. It only breaks the laws of your nation and mine. And you know firsthand how I deal with those kinds of men. Their sentence has been dictated by their own actions."

The Executioner stood, took the file and left the two national leaders behind in the conference room to mull over his words. He had a flight to catch and drug smugglers to kill.

IT DIDN'T TAKE LONG for the fingerprints of the fallen Russian *mafiya* assassins to get back to Bolan. The Executioner had conducted an immediate inspection of the corpses, and using a digital camera, blood and a white sheet of paper, he was able to get the prints of a half dozen of the would-be killers before the *federales* arrived.

"Four of the six you nailed were former Spetznaz," Aaron Kurtzman informed Bolan. "The other two were combat swimmers. All of them have records with Russian Intelligence linking them to organized crime as muscle. They dropped off the radar two years ago."

"They moved to Acapulco to shore up *mafiya* ties with the Mexican cartels," the Executioner surmised.

"A reasonable assumption, considering their bloody fingerprints are all over a sheet of paper you photographed for us," Kurtzman replied.

"Any information on the Asado twins?" Bolan asked.

"Except for the sudden, recent accusations of Rosa being the head of a major drug gang while working out of Anibella Brujillo's security detail, they're clean, hardworking and exemplary lawmen, er, women," Kurtzman stated. "Frankly, if they had been in U.S. law enforcement, we'd have had both of them through the blacksuit program. It's just a shame that Mexico's lawenforcement community is an old-boy network. They'd have gone even further."

"One won't," Bolan mentioned. "And the other is on the run now."

"Nobody ever accused the *federales* of being white knights," Kurtzman mused. "There are plenty who are good and honest, but there's enough who will buy into any story to protect their careers with the heat on."

Bolan sighed. "It's amazing that Mexican law enforcement gets as much done as it can."

"The channels are tangled down there. I deal mostly in Internet, but this is Acapulco law enforcement. Word of mouth is still the most reliable means of these people getting in touch with each other, and if they're putting anything in writing, it's paper and ink, not digital," Kurtzman said.

"That's okay. I'll shake answers loose the old-fashioned way," Bolan replied. "Twist an arm, and listen to the music."

Kurtzman made a sound of disgust. "Damn it. I forgot."

"Something I said?" Bolan asked.

"Narcocorridos," Kurtzman stated. "What you said about listening to the music."

"Right. The tradition of putting the stories of crimes into song. Murderers and drug dealers keep their legends alive that way," Bolan said. "If there was anything, we'd hear it in music."

"I'll see about what's on the hit list," Kurtzman offered. "Some of the songs make it onto the Internet."

"Instead of pirated music, music about pirates," Bolan mused sardonically.

"Bingo. I can also see if we have anyone who has their ears open on that particular community," Kurtzman stated.

"It'll be a needle in a haystack," Bolan replied. "Murder is the flavor of choice for those songs. Drug dealers, while admittedly pretty sexy in that field, don't get noticed for their brand-new street corner deal, just for putting the hit on someone in their way."

"And anyone out to make Rosa Asado look bad will keep things mum about framing and murdering her," Kurtzman concluded.

"Keep working that angle," Bolan requested. "It's an alternate form of intelligence."

"What about the Santa Muerte angle that popped up?" Kurtzman asked.

"Digging into that is even further off the Internet grid," Bolan said. "And for now, I'm on my own."

"Wish we could get Rafael or Rosario to hit the streets for you down there," Kurtzman said, "but Able and Phoenix are busy."

"I have my own sources down here, Aaron," Bolan replied.

"The running Asado twin?" Kurtzman asked.

Bolan looked around the office that Anibella Brujillo

had provided for him in the governor's mansion. He'd performed a thorough sweep of the room, and had found three active bugs so far. A small white-noise generator next to the laptop he was talking into would mask any sound he made as he used a headphone and jawbone-contact microphone unit plugged into the computer to communicate directly with Stony Man Farm. The contact mike, taped to his jaw, wouldn't be affected by the white noise generator, since it picked up the vibrations of Bolan's voice directly through his body, not the air. The cyberlink between the laptop and Kurtzman's system was protected by powerful encryption software, so hacking the information flow would be difficult. Still, the Executioner wasn't willing to discuss his contact with Blanca Asado even over an encrypted line, protected by a cocoon of bug-disorienting noise.

"I have my means. And suspicions," Bolan returned. "Thanks for the background on the hitters. Any word on where they've been staying recently would help immensely."

"I'll track that, too," Kurtzman promised. "Good luck, Striker."

"Thanks," Bolan said, signing off.

He turned off the laptop and disconnected from his headphone and contact mike. Anibella Brujillo would want an update, and he didn't want to disappoint her.

BLANCA ASADO LOOKED at the business card that Agent Matt Cooper had flipped her in their brief encounter. Armando Diceverde took a sip of warm beer as he sat in the corner of the hotel room. The handsome little journalist had his laptop out and was hooked to the Internet via a satellite-capable modem.

"I've got nothing on Agent Matt Cooper of any

agency," Diceverde announced. "All results on his Justice files come up as access denied. Whatever he does is shoved into a deep hole that I can't pull up."

"There's no doubt of that," Asado returned. "But he has a voice mail and an e-mail contact."

"Probably a secure drop he can tap when he needs to," Diceverde mused. "Nothing we could actually use to check up on him."

"Your implication?" Asado asked.

Diceverde took a deep breath. "He's a spook."

"Oh," Asado answered, rolling her eyes. "That's news to me."

"Sarcasm will get you nowhere," Diceverde mumbled. He took another sip.

"Beer and painkillers don't go well together," Asado warned for the third time.

"Says you," Diceverde answered. "I'm feeling a nice buzz here."

Asado looked at the arm that hung in the sling around the reporter's neck. If the bullet had struck any closer to the joint, he'd have needed a serious hospital stay, and amputation would have been an option. The little journalist had been lucky, and she couldn't begrudge him his minor alcohol-and-painkiller-induced high.

"Want one?" Diceverde asked, motioning the base of his bottle toward the remnants of a six-pack she'd brought him.

"I'm good," Asado answered. "E-mail him."

"Cooper's people would be able to track us easily in that case," Diceverde warned.

"He could have put a bullet in my head instead of giving me his calling card," Asado countered. "I'll trust him. For now."

"You type, then," Diceverde said. "I'm good at using

a search engine typing one-handed, but doing anything more is testing my limits."

Asado patted him on his good shoulder. "Take a rest from typing. I'll send the e-mail."

Diceverde sucked down a long pull of his beer before getting up and plopping on the bed, letting the woman take his place at the desk.

"Establishing contact," she typed into the header and body of the e-mail. She sat back and waited for a response. Considering Cooper's mysterious air, he obviously had a large organization behind him. They'd be watching for any e-mails to his contact address.

She wasn't surprised when the phone rang after a minute. Plucking it off the cradle, she put it to her ear.

"Blanca Asado?" a woman asked on the other end.

"Speaking," she answered.

"You made an attempt to contact Agent Matt Cooper by e-mail."

"You're his secretary?" Blanca inquired dryly.

From the sound of Barbara Price clearing her throat, Asado knew that she'd struck a nerve. "I'm a liaison."

"I figured he's busy elsewhere," Asado continued. "Perhaps you can arrange a meeting for us, if you're not going to drop a team of *federales* into my lap."

"You're a Fed yourself, Blanca," Price countered. "And we're talking a Mexican Fed to boot. We've got, what, a fifty-fifty chance that you're crooked?"

"If that's the case, then why didn't I just take out the governor and his wife with the rest of those Commie soldiers?" Asado asked.

"A different faction," Price mused. "You're an unknown quantity to us."

"You've done a lot to earn my trust so far," Asado said, not bothering to keep the sneer out of her voice.

"If your sister was anything like you, no wonder she ended up dead," Price answered. "Don't trust authority, free-thinking, looking for what's right. It'd be a real wrench in the works of anyone trying to run something crooked."

"Flattery will get you nowhere," Asado retorted. "So how are we going to arrange contact with Cooper?"

"Do you have a cell phone?" Price asked. "Using the hotel's landline is secure, but it'll limit your mobility."

"I tossed mine last night," Asado explained. "Too easy to track."

"The airport's only a couple of miles away. Locker 171J will have something we can establish secure communications with."

"You have a key?" Asado asked.

"It's locked, but the key is in a secure area. Section D of the parking lot, space 44," Price answered. "We have the key lodged in a disguised box in the concrete pylon. The patch of concrete over it is marked with a rather large smear of bird crap."

"That's one way to keep someone from feeling around on it," Asado returned. "This would have been Cooper's 'backup'?"

"There is a cell phone and a few survival tools in a handbag," Price explained. "We have secure communications with you."

"And a GPS tracker presumably," Asado added.

"Actually, it's deactivated. The GPS signal could possibly give his position away on a stealth insertion," Price told her. "The tools are clean, as well. We'll contact you when you recover what you need."

"Very generous with someone else's equipment," Asado stated.

"This was a redundant supply drop," Price said. "He

has other means of reequipping. Call us on Autodial 1 when you retrieve the phone."

Price hung up and Blanca Asado set down the receiver.

"Well, they got the e-mail," Diceverde said. "You going to take them up on their offer?"

"What choice do I have?" Asado asked. "You're hurt, so if we get into trouble, you won't be able to effectively protect yourself."

"Rosa was my friend, too," Diceverde protested.

"Kicking ass isn't your specialty, though. Finding things out, that's where you're strongest. I need to follow this conspiracy smearing my sister, and you can cut through that mess far better than I could," Asado explained. "I need a source of information that isn't tied to Cooper."

"You don't trust him?" Diceverde asked.

"I don't trust the people on the other end of that phone," Asado told him. "But I met Cooper face-to-face, and he seems like a good man. I'm going to get the stuff."

She handed him her revolver. "It's stuffed with .38s, so you can control it with your dumb hand."

"Thanks," Diceverde replied.

"I just hope you don't have to use it," Asado added, heading out to the car.

"IF WE'RE GOING TO BE WORKING together," Anibella Brujillo began, putting two cigarettes between her luscious lips and lighting them both, "we're going to need to be open and honest with each other."

She took one cigarette out and turned it over to Bolan. He accepted it and could taste her. Bolan shrugged. "What makes you think I'm hiding anything?"

"Your birth name isn't Matt Cooper," Anibella cooed.

"It's the name I go by," Bolan returned, keeping irritation out of his voice.

Anibella took a deep breath, then sighed. "And who was outside helping us?"

"I exchanged fire with someone in the treeline. I couldn't get a good look, but whoever it was was interested in taking out the Russians, too."

"Ah…that's the thing. Russians," Anibella replied.

Bolan handed her a printout. "My people pulled the records on a few I got fingerprints on."

The first lady nodded in approval as she looked at the file. "Your people work quickly."

"Kind of a necessity in my line of work," Bolan said. "Quick intelligence can mean the difference between success and death."

"You seem to have both in droves, Agent Cooper. Quickness and intelligence."

Bolan nodded, keeping his mind off of the smoldering, seductive stare that the woman burned into him "I'd rather work independently. Being shackled to a bureaucracy will only limit my ability to hunt down those responsible for your assassination attempts."

"You think this was round two?" the woman asked.

"Round two of what we know so far. There might have been more attacks foiled by law enforcement that didn't filter up through your grapevine. These efforts seemed like acts of desperation," Bolan replied.

Anibella nodded, licking her upper lip. "I am the one who is the figurehead of the antidrug campaign here in Acapulco, Matt."

Bolan shrugged. "It's a possibility."

"I have a sizable dossier on local organizations, including drug processing and distribution centers, which we do not have enough evidence on to constitutionally take action," Anibella told him, her eyes glimmering. The glimmer sparked an even hotter fire as Bolan realized that his facial expression changed ever so slightly. She'd read him, the flicker of anticipation. She'd been trying, all conversation, to find a chink in his emotional armor to pull him in to her grasp.

A guide to good hunting, just outside of the law, had been the chink she was looking for. Her obvious sensuality hadn't been enough to bend him toward her, but now that she had the Executioner's measure, she thought she was in control.

He'd allow her to believe that. A less perceptive man would have been oblivious to her attempts at manipulation.

"I'll get to work on this. Maybe I'll shake something loose," Bolan answered.

Anibella Brujillo smiled, and despite her efforts to make it warm and friendly, Bolan felt a creeping cold sinking into his heart.

CHAPTER FIVE

Locating the locker wasn't a task of any great difficulty for Blanca Asado. The airport was crowded, and while it could have concealed any one of a dozen hunters, it also provided her with a shield of bodies that would hinder observation. Dressed simply, to avoid being noticed, she weaved through the crowd. She kept an eye out for any cues that would betray organized surveillance, but she saw no enforcement agents with earphones, nobody speaking into a collar.

The airport also had only sporadic video cameras located throughout the terminal. Security was in the form of uniformed manpower, and their attention was locked on nervous travelers who had visible concern on their faces about baggage searches. Police officers passed within a few feet of Asado, but large-framed glasses and a straw sun hat made her just another anonymous person in the crowd. Even if the *federales* were on the hunt for her, they weren't looking for her here.

She picked up the key taped to the bottom of one locker complex across the terminal from where she needed to pick up her "care package" as the American woman had called it. The care package was inside an oversize purse. She slid her own, smaller bag, complete with her snub-nosed revolver, into it. The "hobo bag" was stylish despite its plain appearance, meaning it fit in and was ubiquitous, not drawing a second glance. Inside the bottom of the voluminous purse was a hard-cased blue plastic container, probably holding a gun and some spare magazines, judging by the weight. She also noticed a small canvas money belt, and a brand-new cellular phone, with a plastic-bag-wrapped charging cradle.

The cash wasn't something she needed, but she couldn't leave it somewhere and trust that it wouldn't be used to hurt Cooper's allies back home. If she got to meet with him in person, she'd give him back the money belt.

Getting in her car, she popped open the plastic case. Inside, a stainless-steel Springfield Armory XD-9 stared back at her. A magazine was in the well, and three loaded 15-round magazines were nestled in the case. She took it out and did a quick press check, and partially dumped the mag. All told, she had 61 shots. There would be no fumbling with the slide-mounted catch to get it to fire. It was ready to go with a smooth, crisp 5-pound pull with a lightning-fast reset. Safe, and as sturdy as a bank vault, the stainless-steel XD-9 wasn't a concealment weapon, but it would pull her through gunfights in environments that would choke anything but an AK-47. Its polymer frame would allow it to weigh lightly in its waistband holster, as well. With the stainless-steel and plastic components of the weapon, the Croatian-designed, American-built pistol was rustproof and needed minimal maintenance.

She was well protected. The cell phone was innocuous, but on opening it, she noticed that it took a direct satellite signal. It had ports to hook to Diceverde's laptop using the Universal Serial Bus 2.0 hookup now en vogue in electronics. The USB cable would give her a connection at a whim, so if Cooper's information crew had computer data to send her, she'd get entire files at thousands of kilobytes per second, as fast as the satellite signal fed the phone, and the phone's processors pumped the data into the laptop, or any computer she needed access to.

She pressed the 1 key and hit Send. The woman who spoke to her before answered immediately.

"You've got our package?" she asked.

"Yup," Asado answered. "This phone's secure?"

"It would take an encryption program 1300 years to break the security on that thing," Price answered.

"Then we'd better keep these calls short."

There was a genuine chuckle on the other end. "I'll inform Cooper that you have a secure means of contact."

"He's hanging around with Anibella Brujillo, lady. She'll be all over him like flies on *caca,*" Asado replied. "Especially if she thinks that he might have been in contact with me."

"Not good news," Price responded. "We'll do what we can. I've already put your number on his sat-phone directory. If he gets a moment's freedom, he'll make direct contact. You can keep it active while it sits in the charger cradle."

"Thanks," Asado said. "Over and out."

"WE JUST GOT IN TOUCH with Blanca Asado," Barbara Price told Bolan over the phone. "We hooked her up with a secure line of communication with you."

Bolan replied with an "Uh-huh" over the phone, not providing Anibella Brujillo with any information as to the content of his conversation.

"You have an audience?" Price asked.

"I'm just in conference with the first lady. We're going over some locations where the cartels might be staging their assassination attempts," Bolan explained. "Can I get some satellite observation?"

"Absolutely, Striker," Price responded. "Asado doesn't think you should trust her, though."

"Good. I'll scan and send you the addresses First Lady Brujillo is giving me," Bolan stated.

"Please," the governor's wife said, resting her long, delicate fingers on Bolan's thigh. "Call me Anibella."

Bolan raised an eyebrow, pointed to the phone, then shook his head. Anibella winked, her fingernails trailing streaks of sensual fire down the Executioner's thigh. He couldn't deny the stirring of her contact, but his face remained a cold, emotionless mask. If anything, Bolan's emotional resolve only seemed to bring on more smoldering attention from the beautiful ex-singer. Her fingertips trailed off Bolan's knee and she leaned back, crossing her leg, the hem of her skirt crawling along its smooth, lean length.

"We'll download real-time satellite imagery to your laptop, Striker," Price said. "When will you need the data?"

"Give me a few hours to rest and recuperate," Bolan responded. "I'll make my move at sundown."

That elicited a few fractions of an inch more from the first lady. Her middle finger glided across the neckline of her blouse, exposing a half inch more of her tanned, soft breasts.

"Just be careful, Striker," Price responded. Though she didn't have a video feed through Bolan's cell phone, she could hear Anibella Brujillo's come-on over the sensitive microphone, and the cold professionalism in his voice. There was a battle of wills going on, the first lady and the Executioner feeling each other out in conversation, innuendo, and perhaps even physical contact. "We don't need the governor upset with you."

Bolan hung up on Price. He didn't need to dignify her last remark. It was less a catty jab at his ego than it was an admonition of concern for the deadly waters he was wading in.

"Rest and recuperation?" Anibella asked, her eyebrow rising over one hazel jewel of an iris.

"It's what I mean it to be. I've been up all night and have been involved in several combative actions since last night," Bolan replied. He pocketed the cell phone. "Do you have any quarters for me to wash up and take a short nap? All I need is a spigot and a comfortable chair."

Anibella's shoulders slumped almost imperceptibly, but she chuckled to hide her disappointment. "This is the governor's mansion, Señor Cooper."

She extended her hand to him and he took it tentatively. She guided him, launching into a practiced tour-guide speech, talking about the guest rooms and facilities that the grand home had for visitors and residents alike.

"I personally have gone to great lengths to ensure that guest accommodations are the equal of the highest-rated hotels on the beach," Anibella stated, her arm now crooked with his. She was tall, and her shoulder came up to the bottom peak of muscle that slid between Bolan's biceps and triceps muscles. She was only a fist's height shorter than the big American, wearing three-inch heels that she walked on with the grace and deliberation of a black widow. "Your quarters will not only have full high-speed satellite Internet connection to run a full office out of, but all the comforts of home."

She lowered her voice, thick-lashed lids drooping seductively over her eyes. "Wherever that may be."

Bolan shrugged, loosening her grip on his forearm. "I have a couple of places, but they're strictly utilitarian. I'm on the road too much to lay down roots."

Anibella grinned. "You're always welcome in Casa Brujillo."

Bolan stopped at the door. His laptop case and war bag hung from his left hand, and he disentangled his right arm from Anibella's to open the guest room. "Send me horchata and a burrito, carne asada."

"Legitimate or North American fast-food style?" Brujillo asked.

"Legitimate. I'll take a shower while I wait."

"Would you care for some company?" Anibella asked.

"I'm a man who usually stays away from married women."

Anibella Brujillo smiled widely. "I'll have to work on that 'usually.'"

"I'm certain you will," Bolan replied, closing the door behind him.

ANIBELLA BRUJILLO WATCHED the big American step into the shower and pull the curtain. She had a slender fiber-optic camera mounted just above the nozzle, enabling her to watch her quarry at all times. Some people felt that the shower was a secure location, with running water and loud echoes and the security of the shower curtain, but Anibella had made certain that she had technological means around those. She had microphones installed with digital filters that ignored white sound while picking up vibrations in the normal conversational range of the human voice.

Her husband knew that she had put in some extra

work to enhance security at the mansion. What he was ignorant of, however, was the tap that she had placed, so she could put anyone in the mansion under her magnifying glass without them being the wiser.

The American's body was lean, but rippling with curves of muscle. He had very little body fat, and his limbs moved with grace and agility as he washed off the stink of cordite and perspiration from the earlier battle. The Santa Muerte high priestess watched with rapt attention as Bolan turned and twisted, cleaning himself thoroughly, then stood, head hung, letting hot water splash onto his back to massage tired muscles.

Even when he was naked, Anibella couldn't tell the man's age. The tightness of his long, straight limbs showed the body of an almost fanatical athlete. The last thing she'd seen that resembled the man was carved from marble and meant to represent Ares or Herakles. Had the warrior on her screen been born two millennia sooner, he'd have been worshiped as a god-king. It was no wonder that Agent Matt Cooper had been considered a one-man solution to rampant organized crime and terrorism by the Mexican president.

Unfortunately, for the first lady, the tall, powerful warrior in the shower had made no phone calls that she could listen in on, accessed no computer data that her cameras in other rooms could glean off the laptop monitor.

"Ah, Martha," Anibella whispered. "He is a wily creature. He is aware that he is being watched. His senses are as sharp as his skill in battle."

"Did you say something, darling?" Emilio Brujillo's voice called from his office in the next room.

"I am just saying my prayers," she told her husband. "Giving thanks for Agent Cooper's protection this morning."

The governor stood in the door. Though his lined face showed weariness, he still was straight and tall, not leaning. His deeply lined smile shone with the light of a man of twenty. "And I give thanks for you, my dear. If you had not requested that I send for him, we surely would have been lost."

Anibella closed her laptop and walked over to her husband, embracing him, feeling the hidden strength in his frame. Strong arms wrapped around her and he kissed her passionately. For a moment, the first lady imagined the Greek god who had finished bathing on her screen, but the passion of the governor swept over her, and she remembered why she had married this man as he picked her up like a doll, carrying her to their bed.

As passionate a crusader for honest government, Emilio Brujillo was just as passionate a lover. Anibella pushed aside her thoughts of plotting, succumbing to a wave of sexual bliss.

THE EXECUTIONER WAS CERTAIN he was being watched by pinhole cameras, and didn't bother scanning the room for bugs. It was a matter of course that guest rooms in the homes of heads of state were under all forms of high-tech surveillance. However, since the only secrets Bolan would reveal were the contours of his naked body, he didn't pay mind to the omnipresent feeling of being watched. A quick, hot shower scoured him clean of the stickiness of exertion and the stench of gunpowder. He appraised himself in the mirror, looking for bruises or signs of lacerations that would need covering to prevent infection. As he made a visual check, he also stretched and tested his muscles and joints, looking to see if he'd overstressed anything, the effects of minor tendon or muscle tears hidden by the effects of adrenaline and seratonin in his bloodstream.

Satisfied that he was healthy and hearty, he slipped into a pair of cargo shorts and greeted the servant who had just knocked at the door. A cart was wheeled in. Bolan was impressed by the savory repast arranged on the plate, heaping side servings of delicious-smelling refried beans and spicy rice accompanying them. The burritos were thick and bulging, in soft wraps. They were delicious and filling to the point where he was nearly groggy. He washed them and the side dishes down with two soft drinks, drunk straight from chilled glass bottles. He saved the horchata for after his nap.

Bolan looked around the room, then crawled onto the bed. Silk sheets enveloped his freshly scrubbed flesh, and the ceiling fan pushed down a cool breeze over the soldier's bare skin. Though he tried not to concern himself with the hidden cameras and microphones, he couldn't help but know where they were situated, if only from his familiarity with covert surveillance. There were eyes and ears in likely places, his sharp combat senses picking them out with little difficulty. The Executioner pushed his Desert Eagle under an extra pillow, not far from his fingertips. Nestling atop the sheets, his cheek resting against a decadently soft and comfortable pillow with a satin case, he was fast asleep within a few moments, taking a quick combat nap.

A RUSTLE OUTSIDE THE DOOR snapped Bolan awake what felt like mere moments later. The noise tripped his mental alarms and he was fully seated, the cocked and locked .44 Magnum pistol aimed at the door.

From the deepening blue of the sky out his window, it was close to sunset, and the rap of delicate knuckles on the door preceded the voice of Anibella Brujillo. "Are you awake, Agent Cooper?"

"Come in," Bolan said. He set the mighty Israeli pistol back under the pillow.

Anibella opened the door. Gone was the linen white blouse and black, short skirt she'd worn before. She wore no rings or earrings, and her black hair was pulled back into a bun. She wore a long-sleeved, navy-blue shirt, fitted to match her contours. Her long, lean legs were tucked into black jeans, which were just loose enough not to constrict her movements. High-top black gym shoes clad her feet, comfortable and sensible in opposition to the pumps she'd worn earlier. She was also wearing a belt with a flap holster and spare magazine pouches on the opposite hip.

"You said you would make your move at sundown," Anibella told him.

"You look like you're dressed to kill," Bolan replied. He turned and dropped his cargo shorts, pulling on his form-fitting blacksuit. He didn't doubt that Anibella was appraising his body as he wrapped it in the high-tech battle uniform he'd made his second skin. A pair of blue jeans went on over the bottoms of the blacksuit and he pulled on combat boots over socked feet. "I know you feel like you deserve a shot at these—"

"I'm just going to be your driver, Agent Cooper," Anibella cut him off, her voice hard, all wisps of seduction drained. "I know the places you wish to go."

"They also want you dead," Bolan replied. He strapped quick-draw leather around his waist, and retrieved the Desert Eagle for it. The Beretta 93-R and its harness slid around his broad shoulders. A black, untucked linen shirt concealed the warrior's battle gear, and he rolled the long sleeves of his blacksuit up to the elbow where they would disappear under their linen covering. Heavier ordnance was in his war bag, which he hefted.

"I'm not stupid enough to stand and fight," Anibella said. "Not alone. If they come after me, I'll take off. I've got a backup rendezvous in case we end up separated."

Bolan regarded the woman in front of him. In the hours that he had slept, a change had washed over her. Instead of seeming as if she were trying to crawl under his blacksuit, she was all business now. "What kind of wheels do you have?"

"A 1992 Toyota 4WD," the first lady replied. "It looks rusty, but we have a few armor plates under the hull to take care of the important components and cargo. V-8 engine, run-flat tires and a full communications suite."

"You usually have a stealth vehicle assigned to you in your job?" Bolan asked.

"It was something I'd bought from the DEA when they were cleaning house a few years back," Anibella explained. "I told you, I'm the one in charge of my husband's efforts to clean these jackals out of our state. I needed an inconspicuous vehicle."

"For what?" Bolan inquired.

"Meetings with sources outside of the system," she responded. "And some observation."

"I can't say I approve," Bolan told her.

"Why? Because I'm not six foot three and two hundred pounds?"

"Because a face like yours is hard to miss," Bolan countered.

She slid on horn-rimmed glasses. Combined with the tautly pulled bun of hair, and a lack of makeup or jewelry, any resemblance between the creature in front of the Executioner and the finely attired beauty he'd met that morning was tenuous. Bolan knew the maneuver well. Role camouflage. He had been able to pass himself off as a harmless reporter to a hardened, desperate thug looking for brute work in the past, blending into underworlds across the globe. Accepted as an Irish terrorist by the Islamic jihad or an Italian businessman in Greece, Bolan had slid through enemy expectations by playing on their perceptions. Disguise was more than makeup and prosthetics, it was body posture, tone of voice, and even gestures.

Bolan didn't want Anibella along for the ride, though. She would cramp his style, especially if he picked up a lead. And there was the problem of contacting Blanca Asado, and sorting out the stories of the two women. His gut trusted Asado, but he wasn't infallible. Anibella's facility at changing her colors like a chameleon was worrying and concerning, especially how she seemed to try to manipulate him, but until Bolan had solid evidence, he couldn't really act against her, especially if he wanted to make use of her resources in his crusade to bring cleansing flame to Acapulco.

"I'll be behind bullet-resistant glass and armor plate, and can go zero to sixty in 5.6 seconds with the 4WD," the first lady told him. "They might not miss me, but they won't be able to punch through."

"Why you and not an agent?" Bolan pressed.

"Because this is the second time that these animals have come close enough to me to shoot me. I've been working too hard to clean up this state, and now it's personal. I want this place to ditch its seedy reputation, and I want to put anyone between me and the perfect paradise in the ground," the woman stated. "You've been shot at. There's no doubt of that."

"It's my job," Bolan explained.

"Job? Or duty?" Anibella asked.

"So you're driven?" Bolan asked. "What about earlier? Sharing a shower doesn't sound like someone on a crusade."

Anibella's hazel eyes narrowed to razor slits. Rage radiated from her in palpable waves.

"I was just checking to see if you thought with your dick," she growled. "You blunted some of my best efforts, so you passed my trustworthiness test."

"I see. If I'd been weak enough to get naked with you, then I'd be too incompetent to take on the cartel," Bolan mused.

"Not incompetent," Anibella said, softening slightly. "But too easily distracted."

"You *are* distracting," Bolan returned. "I just know how to put it in a pocket and zip it shut. Fine. You want to drive, drive. I'm not the one dragging you into the field to get killed. You volunteered. I wasn't hired to be a babysitter."

"I don't want a babysitter," Anibella replied, her voice taking on a hard edge once more. "I want someone I can trust to gut the cartels so we can sweep in and clean up the state."

"Then you've got your man," Bolan told her.

"Good!" Anibella exclaimed. The corners of her wide sensual mouth turned up in a relieved smile. "Let's go."

CHAPTER SIX

"So what is the deal with Cooper?" Blanca Asado asked. "He hasn't gotten in touch with me."

"He's still at the governor's mansion, and he's under heavy surveillance," Barbara Price replied. "He tried to get out from under Mrs. Brujillo's thumb, but she's insisted on accompanying him."

Asado's shoulders tightened into a knot and she took a deep breath.

"Yeah, we feel the same way," Price responded.

"You're awfully cavalier with his position," Asado told her. "What about operational security?"

"We're not giving away exact locations or privileged information," Price replied. "I'm certain you'd have figured it all out on your own."

Asado's lips tightened into a straight line. The woman was right. She'd had her suspicions about Cooper's detention by Anibella Brujillo. She had no solid proof, only copies of her sister's notes shared with Armando Diceverde, and those notes weren't conclusive proof, only observations of seeming coincidences. Circumstantial evidence, not enough to convict the governor's wife, let alone launch a war or retribution, but Blanca felt in her gut that Rosa's instincts were sharp, right up until the moment that conniving witch put a bullet in her brain.

"I'll leave a message. I presume Cooper has access to voice mail, right?" Asado asked.

"It's safer than having his phone ring while he's on a stealth penetration," Price explained.

Asado grinned. "Do you have anything for me to do, or need something?"

"We could use a look at your sister's notes," Price replied.

"I'll have Armando e-mail scans," Asado told her.

"That'll be perfect," Price said. She paused and heard the rustle of paper. "I was just handed… Get on the phone to Diceverde, now! The Feds have located him!"

Asado pulled her personal phone and hit the speed dial. Diceverde answered on the first ring.

"No time to talk. Move now!" Asado ordered.

"Halfway packed," Diceverde replied. "I got a buzz from one of my friends on the force."

"Get going. And don't forget the notes. Cooper's people need them," Asado reminded him.

"I know that," Diceverde said, sounding out of breath. Moving quickly, hauling his briefcase and laptop, using only one arm, and perhaps having the shoulder strap cut into his injury, was taking its toll on him. "We'll meet at the clubhouse."

Asado took a moment to think. She remembered her time with Armando and Rosa as part of a tutor's group. It's where they'd grown to be friends, the twins seeing Diceverde as a sweet brother they never had, and the young writer being not only torn between deciding which sister to ask out, but developing a deeper affection. He was their brother, and they helped him find good girlfriends, and to guide him in keeping in their good graces. She remembered their secret little "clubhouse," something no one else would ever know.

"I'll be there. Just get out safely," Asado admonished.

"I'm out the door already," Diceverde responded.

Her stomach flopped and twisted as the phone disconnected, but she dared not try to contact him. With two healthy arms, a quick escape was difficult enough without being distracted by a cell phone. Having only one hand to devote to all his tasks, Asado knew she might as well be smacking Diceverde in the back of the head with a tennis racket as ringing him again.

"You don't have an eye in the sky watching him, do you?" Asado asked over the secure phone to Stony Man Farm.

"No," Price answered. "Just good ears. The *federales* were just tipped off about Diceverde's location. But from what we heard from your call to him, he's safe."

It didn't surprise Asado that the woman could hear her conversation. It also wouldn't have surprised Diceverde. "Cloned" cell phones and hacked signals were all too common, even in the alleged "third world" back streets of Mexico. Phone hacking was a cottage industry in Mexico, especially among tourists in Acapulco. Cloning registrations enabled drug dealers to communicate unhindered, under the electronic disguise of being American tourists using their own cell phones. Diceverde had done stories on "phone phreaks" in Mexico, and had gotten more than a few of the "cellular" criminals irate at him.

As such, Diceverde was very terse and spoke close to the vest when on any telephone. His e-mail programs were protected by powerful encryption, allowing him to be more verbose. Diceverde's vague statement about the "clubhouse" was a layer of paranoid armor for the journalist.

"Nothing about you, Blanca," Price added. "You've dropped off their grid."

"Maybe of those who wear token badges," Asado answered. "But there are other hired guns who don't need badges."

"We've been trying to tap their network, but it's like trying to catch an airplane by building a brick wall on the ground under their flight path," Price replied.

"Welcome to Mexican law enforcement," Asado said. "Unless you have someone down here beating answers out of the small fish to get to *los tiburones*, you've got nothing."

"Luckily for you, we do," Price reminded her.

"Well, you told me he's busy now," Asado countered.

"Luckily for us, we've got a backup," Price stated.

"Another operator?" Asado asked.

"No. You," Price said.

"Oh, great," Asado groaned.

"Welcome to our world, Blanca. Hope you survive the trip," Price said, signing off.

Asado slipped the phone back into her pocket. She had a man she loved like a brother to take care of before she could take another step into this twisted maze.

ARMANDO DICEVERDE WOKE from feverish dreams, his wounded shoulder throbbing and his ears ringing when he realized that the clanging warble wasn't in his gunfight-blasted eardrums, but coming from his cell phone. He reached out with his left hand, fumbling for the folded device and snapping it open.

"Hello?" he asked, mouth feeling dry and gummy.

Blood loss and pain had taken its toll on him, but fortunately, Blanca Asado had enough antibiotics on hand to keep infection at bay. He'd resisted the painkillers, if only because the amount he'd need to control the pain in his shoulder would leave him a drooling lump of meat, ripe for the killing if Blanca's enemies closed in on him.

"Armi, it's Delgado," a familiar voice rumbled on the other end. "You at the Motel Azul?"

Diceverde blinked the blurriness from his eyes. "Yeah."

"We've got a team rolling out. I saw the description of one of the suspects, and it matches you to a tee," Delgado answered. "You're in deep shit, amigo."

Diceverde rolled out of bed. He was fully dressed, except for having to slide his feet into boat shoes. "It's a warrantless operation?"

"They don't intend to bring anyone in, Armi," Delgado warned. "They pulled AKs out of the evidence room, and they're dressed for a ski trip."

Diceverde sneered at the implication. Delgado was a *federale* who he'd worked with quite often, getting stories on bloodthirsty criminals in the Acapulco underworld. As such, the two men had developed a level of trust and friendship that was unshakable. They'd gone after the savages enough times, and Diceverde had kept his mouth shut and looked the other way when Delgado and his allies went outside the law to take down particularly stubborn opponents.

His hand went to the grip of his chrome Colt on the nightstand and he tucked it into his waistband in a cross-draw position, hidden under his sling-wrapped arm. He snapped the laptop shut and looked around the room. Nothing irreplaceable had been left behind in drawers, simply toiletries bought at a corner store, and a few bottles of water.

The cell phone rang. It was Asado, and she sounded nervous. It took him a few moments to calm her, all the while putting his laptop into its carrying bag and sliding it over his neck. The strap pushed against his wounded arm, causing grunts to mix with his speech as he hauled ass to the door. He thought for a few moments about the fact that their current hideout had been compromised, and immediately came to a decision.

"The clubhouse," he told her. There was a moment of silence while Asado processed the memory. Then there was a nonverbal acknowledgment that she understood. He hated to hang up on her, but considering that Delgado didn't waste time, he wasn't going to handicap himself by keeping his only functional hand occupied with a cell phone.

As soon as he stepped outside the door, the hairs on the back of his neck stood up. There was a hush in the air, and he wondered how much of it was simply his paranoia. Either way, he wouldn't stop to overanalyze. His car was parked right in front. He tossed his laptop clumsily into the backseat. The computer was designed to withstand shocks, and the shoulder case was well padded to provide extra protection. If worse came to worst, he could rip out the hard drive and install it in another computer to preserve the vital information inside.

Diceverde slid behind the wheel, performing a few tricky twists and turns, inserting the key into the ignition with his left hand, then pulling the gearshift into Reverse. It was tricky, and he was glad he wasn't driving a stick shift, since he couldn't reach the gearshift and keep his foot on a clutch at the same time, using only his left. He backed out and did a J-hook turn, twisting again to throw the car into drive.

A black van glided into the parking lot as he stepped on the gas. The man riding shotgun glanced at him through the windshield, but Diceverde kept his cool. Eyes on the road, he turned out and drove down the road. He gave himself a hundred yards before he accelerated past the posted speed limit, weaving through traffic.

If the van was packed with a handpicked death squad, then they would immediately start looking for any vehicles that recently left the lot. The motel owner had the description of his car, as well as Asado's, and the gunman riding shotgun would instantly recognize how closely they had missed catching their prey. Melting into the nighttime traffic, his car became another pair of anonymous taillights down the road from the Motel Azul.

Diceverde kept one eye on the rearview mirror at all times, looking for signs of the deadly black van in the distance. So far, so good, but just as quickly as he had evaded a mortal fate, he could end up in another trap. His knuckles tightened on the wheel, and the weight of the chrome-plated Colt .38 in his waistband was a heavy reminder of the dangerous world he'd stumbled into.

He hoped that Asado was having a better run this evening.

ANIBELLA BRUJILLO WAS A DEFT helmsman amid the stormy streams of late-night traffic in Acapulco. Bolan kept watch from the shotgun seat, his senses sharp for any shadows that might have attached themselves to their tail. While the early-90s SUV was innocuous, it wasn't invisible, and it would have drawn attention leaving the governor's mansion. Tucked into the leg well of the passenger seat, resting against Bolan's calf, was a 9 mm mini-Uzi submachine pistol. Only a foot long, but capable of tearing out Parabellum devastation at an astounding 900 rpm, it was good for close-quarters combat. If anyone was going to get a shot at Brujillo in the old SUV, they'd have to swing up bumper-to-bumper or door-to-door to get it, given the choking traffic surrounding them.

In those conditions, the SMG was ideal. It wouldn't tear through both sides of an enemy car and spray other vehicles with lead, and with Bolan's trained finger on the trigger, he could milk out quick, lethal bursts before recoil threw his aim off and toward an innocent bystander. If he'd had to use a compact assault rifle, the danger of overpenetration would have been too much for the warrior and his code of conduct.

There was someone following them. Anibella had noticed, and she immediately tagged them as part of her undercover task force against the cartels.

"I'd introduce you to them, but it would compromise them," Anibella stated.

"No offense taken," Bolan returned. The men obviously weren't in any form of unmarked police vehicle, but that could be easily explained. A luxury sedan, seized by lawmen for use against the drug dealers who'd formerly owned it, perhaps.

Logically, he had no reason to doubt the identity of the men in the luxury car as being on the side of angels. Instinctually, though, the Executioner's mind was in a storm sorting relevant data. If Anibella Brujillo was somehow involved, would she try to eliminate him on his first night on the job? Or were these men meant to serve as a backup, in case Bolan got in over his head?

Their exact identity was irrelevant. His primary concern was who they would shoot at if they had to draw their weapons. And if they were cops…

Bolan had never knowingly shot an officer of the law, not even one who had sold out his badge. To kill a policeman, honest or otherwise, for whatever reason, was an inviolate rule. Some would have called him foolish for hindering himself in such a manner, especially in a world where crooked lawmen were common as grains of sand, but it was a line he'd drawn. To step over it would begin a slippery slope. He'd begun his crusade for justice as an outlaw, and his focus was an act of almost fanatic willpower. A dishonest policeman here, and the next thing Bolan knew, he'd be considering a few civilians as acceptable losses.

The only thing that kept any semblance of guilt for the thousands of murderers and crazies that Bolan had put down over his career was the fact that he knew that no one he'd taken down in combat was anything less than completely guilty, and untouchable except by his methods. Crooked cops could be brought to justice by more legitimate means than a lone man skirting the edges of society, and the Executioner's tactical acumen made it unnecessary to risk a single noncombatant's life.

"We're almost there," Anibella stated.

Bolan took the nut off the barrel of the mini-Uzi, exposing the threads to which he would attach the sound suppressor. The machine pistol slid into a tanker-style holster that Bolan hid by closing his windbreaker over it. "Ready."

"I'll slow down enough for you to get out," the first lady reminded him. "Don't get run over."

"And here I was hoping to try Mexican hospital food," Bolan replied.

Anibella fought a smile as she tapped the brake. Bolan opened the door and disembarked, weaving amid traffic. He was glad his reflexes had been honed by countless battles with enemies holding automatic weapons. Trying to dodge the streams of cars filling the roads was like dancing between the hosing slugs of an AK-47, except instead of being 123 grains of steel-cored lead, he was avoiding 3500-pound vehicles.

He made it to the sidewalk, whole and untouched by bumpers. Anibella and her SUV were out of sight, down the road, and Bolan pulled out his cell phone.

"I've got a window," he said after speed dialing the Farm.

"We just got off the line with Asado. The *federales* were sent after her reporter friend, Diceverde," Price answered. "We're trying to track down the origin of the tip and the warrant on them."

"How's Aaron doing on the *narcocorridos?*" Bolan asked.

"We're running some of the latest through our translators and trying to correlate the information," Price said. "So far, all we've got is the solutions to about thirty murders in Los Angeles."

Bolan grunted. "L.A.P.D. should be happy about that."

"Except the murderers won't be deported," Price groaned. "It's a 'free city.'"

"Put it on my to-do list, Barb," Bolan returned. "Anything else?"

"Satellite imagery of your location. You've got a lot of heat masking the defense there. They're cooking up heroin, looks like, so the numbers are fuzzy," Price replied. "Somewhere between eight and fifteen, I'm told."

"Narrows it down," Bolan stated. He walked closer

to the abandoned apartment building. He could smell the heroin-refining operation in full effect. "Thanks. I'll get in touch with Asado."

"Good luck," Price said just before he cut the connection.

"Cooper?" Asado's voice called as he connected to her.

"It's me," Bolan said. He ducked into a darkened corner of a hallway. Sentries moved on the balconies above, but the main courtyard was empty.

"Finally broke free?" Asado asked.

"For a moment. She's playing chauffeur and she dropped me off at a drug lab in an abandoned apartment building," Bolan stated.

"So you have company," Asado said.

"Not quite yet, but they're close," Bolan returned. "What's the news on Armando?"

"He called me from his car. He got out safely," Asado explained.

"Good news," Bolan admitted. "How are you holding up?"

"Luckily, I've been keeping myself busy. Thanks for the phone and the guns," Asado said. "I missed the little one on first examination of the kit you provided."

"That's the point of it," Bolan answered. "Keep in touch."

"I've got your voice mail, Matt," Asado replied. "Be careful."

"You, too." Bolan signed off.

He unzipped his windbreaker and wrapped his fingers around the handle of the mini-Uzi. With the stock extended, he shouldered the compact subgun. Asado had made a good point. Dealing with the minefield of Anibella Brujillo's intrusion into his investigation had at least a temporary solution in the form of straightforward action.

A stealth approach for a kill on an unknown number of enemies wasn't exactly straightforward, but it was a scenario he was familiar and comfortable with.

The silenced mini-Uzi scanned the shadows in front of Bolan as he listened for movement above. He heard low conversations and footsteps on the balconies. The minute he reached the mouth of the alcove, he'd be spotted and bullets would fly with merciless efficiency. The courtyard ahead of him was a death trap, upper walkways providing the defenders of the lab with clear fields of fire, while the floors and railings, planked off with two-by-fours, gave them positions of cover.

Putting intrigue behind him, he focused on taking down the enemy. Anibella had given him a general layout of the abandoned apartment complex, but as far as she knew, none of the apartments was directly connected to another. Since he was after intelligence as well as crippling this particular facility, even if he could gain direct access to the boiler room and arrange a catastrophic destruction of the empty buildings, he'd be left without a living prisoner to question.

Bolan came up with his plan. He unhooked a flash-bang grenade from his harness, thumbed out the cotter pin and hurled the bomb. As it flew, he left the corridor, going outside of the complex, swinging around toward a small parking enclosure. The crack of an explosion was answered by sudden ripping hails of automatic fire, informing the Executioner that his diversion was effective.

Letting the Uzi hang on its sling, Bolan spotted a pair of guards just inside the shadows of the parking alcove. He pulled out his .44 Magnum Desert Eagle and cut loose, the big handgun bellowing out its thunderous death messages, 240-grain slugs screeching violently into one of the gunmen. A dying cry roused further alarm as the surviving guard opened fire, burning off his entire magazine, howls of warning ripping from his lips in Spanish. He let the gunman reload and fire a few more shots at him before burning off the rest of the Desert Eagle's magazine.

The death shriek, followed almost instantly by a second distraction device brought the defenders of the laboratory running. Bolan raced back to his original entrance, unscrewing the mini's suppressor on the run.

Already, some of the cartel gunmen had ventured into the courtyard, moving cautiously and making themselves low targets for the attacking force. The green tritium dot sights informed the Executioner that his Uzi was aimed right at the pair of hardmen, and he raked off long and sloppy bursts, sweeping the gunners with 9 mm slugs that bowled over two of them.

Dropping prone, Bolan avoided being cored by a sheet of enemy gunfire that came in retribution to the initial attack. Firing from the ground, he blasted out the knees and thighs of another rifleman. The shooter collapsed in a messy heap, thrashing as he tried to control the blood spurting from his ruined limbs. As the agonized gunman put on his show, Bolan retreated and returned his focus to the parking garage. He reloaded the Desert Eagle on the move, and from behind cover he sniped at a newcomer to the enclosure. As the .44 Magnum round punctured the defender's skull, he dropped the rifle in his hands and tumbled nervelessly to the ground.

Autofire blasted crazily, aiming at the muzzle-flashes of Bolan's Desert Eagle while he emptied the rest of the autoloader's payload at the drug soldiers. Exposing only a tiny sliver of himself to cut loose with the mighty pistol, he frustrated the protectors as they wasted their ammunition in trying to wing him. He unhooked a third concussion grenade, armed the bomb and whipped it toward the alcove where he'd begun his engagement. The minibomb bounced off one side of the short corridor, ricocheting into the hall before detonation. Smoke vomited from the opening and a stunned gunman staggered out, ears and mouth pouring blood.

Bolan whipped around and stitched the gunman from crotch to throat with the mini-Uzi, then charged to the hallway. Other victims of the flash-bang were strewed across the floor like broken toys. One man, his face covered in a mask of blood, struggled to lift a long-barreled handgun, but the Executioner pumped a thunderous slug from his Desert Eagle into the enemy's face. Jagged segments of skull burst apart at the back of the Mexican's head as his face imploded under the .44 Magnum hammer blow.

Another cartel defender struggled to his hands and knees, but Bolan swept the back of his head with the muzzle of the powerful .44. As the Mexican's hand clawed the ground for a fallen Uzi, Bolan tripped the trigger; 240 grains of lead pinned the corpse's shattered face to the tiled floor of the corridor, a growing puddle spreading from the gunman's ruined skull.

It hadn't taken too much of an effort to convince the defenders that they'd come under a double-tiered assault and waste their ammunition and reaction time accordingly. When they finally realized that it wasn't a two-pronged assault force, and more likely only one man, they went for him through the courtyard. Bolan tipped his hand and continued his assault on the parking enclosure. It had been a gamble on the Executioner's part that they would get the clue so soon, but it paid off. Counting on the gunmen to try to blindside him, Bolan took his time in a prolonged firefight with the guards in the parking enclosure to lull the other protectors into committing to a counterattack. When that happened, all it took was a good concussion grenade to buy him the vital seconds required to punch a clear route through the enemy defenses.

The shielded walkways still presented a challenge, but with the Uzi and the Desert Eagle fully loaded, and another stun grenade in reserve, the Executioner felt sufficiently equipped to make the nearest stairwell. No gunfire sought him as he clung to the shadows. He noticed a head pop up, a guard returning from the garage. Bolan fanned the sentry with a sputtering blast from the Uzi, a wet, sticky cloud informing him that he connected just before he turned to run up the stairs.

All he had to do now was to follow his nose into the heroin processing lab itself, and break loose a few answers.

CHAPTER SEVEN

It sounded like a war going on outside to Francisco Casas, automatic weapons roaring and grenades thundering, shaking him out of the process of mixing the ether and hydrochloric acid for the final step of transforming morphine into heroin.

"What the…"

"We're under attack! We have to go now!" Oswaldo Duarte, the head of security, shouted.

"But the batch, the chemicals!" Casas complained.

Duarte looked at the liquefied ether. Both men, and the others in the lab, wore protective filter masks to keep the fumes from rendering them unconscious. There was a danger that a spark could ignite the airborne, gaseous ether, something Casas had been proud of avoiding for the past five years as a heroin processor. Others had their careers end in a fireball when the mixture of acid and ether went up in their face at flesh-melting temperatures.

"It's a write-off," Duarte announced.

Casas frowned. He'd never given up on a batch yet, but Duarte, at six and a half feet in height, arms sleeved in prison tattoos, wasn't a man to be trifled with. In his midforties, Duarte had been through the U.S. prison system, steeling himself in the forge of hard jail time, learning to kill to gain respect. Upon getting out, Duarte had proven himself to El Eme, the Mexican Mafia. They wanted him to protect their assets across the border. Not willing to ride the revolving door out of and back behind bars again, Duarte went south, and hadn't regretted it, carving a new legend for himself in broken bones, splintered teeth and pulped flesh.

When Duarte said to jump, Casas hopped to it. He glanced back to see Duarte hooking a grenade up to the door. Anyone opening it would pull the trip wire and spark the grenade, which in turn would ignite super-flammable fumes, turning the abandoned apartment into a pile of rubble and a tomb for any invaders. Meanwhile, they'd rush out the back to escape the blast radius.

Duarte was a cold-blooded killer, but he didn't intend to die for his masters in the Juarez Cartel.

Casas rushed to the back door and threw it open in a mad dash to escape. Something smashed hard into his face, and he felt his right cheek collapse as if struck by a hammer. His brains swam around inside the tumbling caldron of fevered bone before his back hit the floor. Dazed, he looked up at a shadow who was only a shade shorter and one hundred pounds leaner than the hulking Duarte. A gas mask made him seem like an armored, inhuman wraith, the only sign that this was a mortal man being a pair of cold blue eyes blazing through the lenses.

"Bastard!" Duarte bellowed in Spanish through his gas mask, and he pulled his gun before realizing that the action would be automatic immolation for himself.

The Executioner, as he stood in the doorway, let the silenced mini-Uzi hang on its sling. The suppressor would contain enough of the muzzle-flash to prevent a lethal spark from igniting the airborne ether, but if he opened fire, Duarte would shoot in self-defense, seeking to take the road to hell with Bolan.

"You can leave this death trap the easy way, or the hard way," Bolan told him in Spanish. "Your choice."

Duarte's chuckle was muffled by his mask. "Easy for me, I think."

Bolan tilted his head to one side, tendons loosening with a sharp crack. "Your funeral."

Casas curled up into a fetal ball, rolling out from between the two masked men. The evasion wasn't a moment too soon as Duarte lunged, his gas mask's filters exuding a snarling cry of inarticulate rage that distorted into something unholy. Casas tucked his head down, tears streaming through clamped eyes, his mind floating lazily, from shock and ether seeping through the cracked right eye of his gas mask. He missed the result of the hulking Mexican's charge.

For all the sound and fury, it signified nothing as the Executioner spun out of the human bull's path with a grace that would put a panther to shame. Bolan snapped out his forearm to catch Duarte across the back of his head as he passed. The impact jarred the feeling temporarily out of his left hand, but the Juarez strongman tumbled out of control, hitting the railing of the rear balcony with enough force to shake the entire fire escape.

Duarte's lungs emptied on impact, and his legs buckled, but even as Bolan turned to grab the big Mexican thug, he recovered enough strength to spike his elbow back into the warrior's chest. Kevlar and trauma plates saved the Executioner from shattered ribs. Bolan had once been shot in the chest with an enemy's Desert Eagle while wearing his body armor, and it had been a bone-jarring experience, especially from a .50-caliber Magnum round. Duarte's thunderous elbow made a Magnum impact feel like a love tap, and Bolan flopped to the floor of the apartment-turned-lab.

Casas looked up as he heard the wraith strike the carpet next to him. Pain and ether mixed in his consciousness to turn the Executioner into a fallen armored knight, clad all in grim black plate steel. Duarte staggered into the doorway, hallucination giving the drug soldier the appearance of a fanged dragon, thick drool pouring from an elongated, armored snout.

In reality, Duarte had vomited from the force of Bolan's dodge and strike. Bile dripped from the filter knobs, and the acidic smell burned through his sinuses, turning his eyes red with rage. The cartel thug was ready to move in for the kill.

Bolan dodged as Duarte stomped hard, the Mexican's combat boot missing the warrior's head by inches. Had Duarte connected, Bolan's skull would have burst apart like a rotted melon under a sledgehammer. The Executioner couldn't take chances on a fair combat with the looming hulk above him, but the only firearm he had in quick-draw was the Desert Eagle. Pulling it and flicking off the safety would be too slow, and the muzzle-flash would turn the flammable atmosphere of the lab into a roiling inferno that would lick the flesh from charred black bones in instants. The only other option available to the racing combat computer in the Executioner's mind was the nine-inch bladed Bowie knife in his harness.

A swish of steel singing from its sheath betrayed to Casas that the black knight had drawn his blade, a gleaming mirror ribbon burning in the reflected light of luminescent lamps. Duarte kicked out again, hoping to crush Bolan with a second foot stomp, but instead of feeling bone collapse under the sole of his boot, the burning agony of the razor-sharp knife speared through his arch. Duarte's own immense strength had impaled himself so that the point of the massive Bowie cut through the top of his foot and sliced into his calf. Casas heard the rattling shriek of agony escape Duarte, and he reared back through the doorway, pulling his attacker with him.

With a savage twist, Bolan tried to get the Bowie free, but Duarte kicked wildly in pain. The combined strength of the two men, augmented by survival-spurred adrenaline rushes, was too much even for the powerfully built Bowie knife. The full-steel tang, strong enough to survive being pounded into a car door, snapped like a brittle icicle.

The dragon was hobbled, spewing out spine-ripping roars of anger and pain as it glared at the rising armored knight. Even hallucination provided no logic to Casas as he clawed the stub to his chest, clinging to it as if it were a holy relic that could protect him.

Bolan stepped in quickly, a clawing hand tearing Duarte's mask from his face. He hoped that the ether fumes would slow down the giant even further, but two sinewy arms lashed around Bolan's lower back and squeezed him tight. Madness burning in the unmasked drug soldier's face and the unbearable pressure fueled by a maniac's strength were proof that the cloud of ether wasn't going to drop Duarte fast enough to save Bolan's life.

With two powerful chops, he hammered the sides of Duarte's neck, but knotted muscle blunted the lethal, spine-snapping force of the Executioner's axlike hands. Rippling arms increased their force and lightning jolts of pain flashed up to Bolan's brain, warning him that his own back was on the verge of splintering.

Sparing no time for squeamishness, the Executioner plunged his thumbs through Duarte's eye sockets, popping the orbs from their resting places as his fingertips sank into the flesh at the Mexican's temples. Squeezing with everything he could put into his grip, he levered his forearms to the side. Bone crunched sickeningly as Bolan closed his hands into fists. Even through agony-induced madness, there was no way that Duarte could shrug off the shattering of his orbital bones and the tearing of his face. Eyes flopped, drained of their aqueous fillings at the end of limp, overstretched optic nerves.

The maddened Duarte let go of the Executioner, hands clawing at his shattered, ruined face. He tried to stand, but his Bowie-destroyed foot gave out from under him and the Mexican collapsed. Wet, ragged cries for mercy bubbled from frothing lips. Bolan brought about the suppressed mini-Uzi and jammed the muzzle through bile-caked lips to lessen the odds of igniting the flammable atmosphere.

Casas, hanging on to consciousness by a thread, watched as Duarte was speared through the head, brains jetting out the back of his punctured skull. The wounded man shuddered for a moment, then lay still.

"Drop the weapon," Bolan ordered.

The chemist looked at the broken knife handle in his grasp and Bolan slapped it away. Losing the wood-sandwiched steel tang, Casas spun into a void of unconsciousness.

The Executioner hauled the man across his shoulders in a fireman's carry and rushed down the fire escape.

He had a prisoner, despite the ferocious battle with Duarte.

It might just give him a chance.

Blanca Asado rolled to a halt in front of what they'd affectionately called "the clubhouse." The old bookstore had belonged to Armando Diceverde's cousin, where they had hung out in the back room. All three friends, and the cousin, had been avid readers, voraciously devouring books, forming a small book club where they bounced ideas off one another.

The bookstore was quiet and dark, but that didn't mean anything. She had the full-size Springfield tucked away, hidden against her hip, but she gripped the small Ruger pocket cannon as it hid inside her jacket pocket. She pulled the car around the corner and slid it onto a patch of gravel that was an abandoned lot. Since the car was a dilapidated Volkswagen Beetle, it wouldn't be noticeable. Even if the car did get stolen, the thief wouldn't get much more than a half tank of gas and an engine wheezing after 120,000 miles.

She checked over her shoulder, trying to balance between paranoia and caution. No one was out at that time of night in the small affluent neighborhood. Small stores dotted the way up and down the street, but for the most part, everything had been closed down for the day. It was too far inland and too far off the tourist trail for many outsiders to provide after-hours business.

Just as well. A couple of storefronts, far down the road, had lights burning through their windows and half a mile away, a gas station, illuminated by a solitary yellowed lamp, was kept busy by an eighteen-wheeler, either going to or coming from a delivery of supplies to one of the resort towns up and down the coast. It made strangers easier for Asado to spot.

So far, halfway between the gravel lot and the bookstore's front door, it was clear. It was late, though, and Asado was nervous to see how Diceverde was doing. He sounded like hell on the cell phone, and she hadn't been able to get back in touch with him, but that could have been explained by damage to the tiny device while he was moving, or a dead battery.

Keep your mind on business, Asado scolded herself, walking slowly, carefully, eyes sweeping both sides of the street, and back the way she came. The front door was closed, and she wasn't certain if it was locked. Every instinct and concern for one of her oldest friends ordered her to pick up the pace, to check on the wounded journalist, but such activity would attract undue attention.

Not only was the law on her trail, but she had also earned the enmity of the cartels. And both had a shallow, unmarked grave with her name on it, so to speak.

A phone call to the police about a woman rushing to a closed bookstore in the middle of the night would be all that the conspirators within the *federales* needed to steer their death squad to this tiny little storefront. She rested her hand on the knob and gave it a tentative twist. The latch clicked and it came free, opening for her.

Her heart skipped a beat. Would Diceverde have left the door open to any stranger wandering in? Or had he collapsed just on the other side, succumbing to blood loss from torn stitches?

She let go of the revolver in her pocket and thumbed the switch on a pocket flashlight.

No trail of blood on the floor, but her mind didn't relax. Perhaps someone had taken Armando hostage, waiting to get the both of them in the same room and finish off their line of inquiry into Anibella Brujillo's conspiracy.

"Armi?" she called gently, trying to keep the worry out of her voice.

"Here," came a faint croak. She swiveled the light to

see Diceverde's face, pale and wan, smiling at her. He squinted, then feebly raised one hand to shield his vision. "Hi, Blanca."

Asado slipped over to him, killing the flashlight.

"What did I tell you about staying up late?" she mock-scolded him.

Diceverde sighed. "You're the one who's making me nervous, staying out all hours."

Asado gently slid an arm under his good shoulder and they walked to the back room that they had claimed as their clubhouse. A shadow moved in the darkness, and Asado froze for a second.

"It's okay, Gloria," Diceverde whispered. "It's Blanca."

A woman in her thirties, standing not much over five feet, stepped into the open, the muzzle of a double-barreled shotgun aiming at the floor. "Blanca…"

Asado nodded in reply. "Sorry for the scare."

"Since he claims that he's the one responsible for drawing you into this mess, I won't blame you," Gloria Ramirez stated. "Yet."

Ramirez opened up the back room for them and flicked on a light. The woman's father used to own the little bookstore, and in the years since they'd finished school, she'd inherited it. Over the course of a decade, she and Diceverde had grown very close. Blanca and Rosa had worked hard to get the couple together, despite Ramirez's distrust of the twins.

Asado helped Diceverde gently onto a comfortable old sofa. "You're soaked with sweat."

Diceverde nodded, his lips drawn thin around his mouth. He looked as if he were reaching for a clever quip, but exhaustion and strain had taken their toll on him. "Yeah," he answered defeatedly.

Ramirez had gotten some water for her wounded

boyfriend, then looked to Asado. "Help yourself. The fridge is full."

"Thanks," Asado replied. She stepped back, feeling lost as Gloria fawned over the wounded journalist. The woman dabbed Diceverde's face with a damp cloth, cooling his feverish skin.

"Maybe it'd be a good time to take a trip. Go see your aunt," Diceverde whispered.

Ramirez shook her head. "And leave you alone?"

"I'm serious. This is a dangerous place to be," Diceverde countered.

The woman looked over to Asado, her dark eyes burning with spite. "And you're any more suited for danger, especially in your condition?"

Diceverde looked to Asado for help, but Blanca wasn't going to get between them. She needed someone to look after Armando, and Ramirez was well suited to the task. No one had tracked either of them here so far, so it wasn't likely that the bookshop owner would need to use her shotgun. Still, it would have been even better if Diceverde went with the woman to see her aunt.

"You should go with her, if that's the case," Asado suggested, knowing the answer.

"No way," Diceverde growled weakly. "You need help."

"I've got it," Asado said.

"Can you trust Cooper's people?" Diceverde asked.

"I'm getting there," Asado replied. "And you can help me over long distance, just like they do."

Diceverde's eyes narrowed. "As if they'd find me here?"

Ramirez looked back to Asado, mouthing a silent, "Thanks for trying."

Asado took a deep breath. "Concentrate on getting over your fever for now. I can't have you collapse on me."

Diceverde smirked, patting his stomach. "Not exactly your safest fate."

Ramirez gave Diceverde a kiss on the cheek. "You're perfectly fine the way you are. Blanca, you should get some sleep. I'll make sure Armi's okay. I've been giving him antibiotics I borrowed from a nurse friend of mine."

"Does the nurse know who it's for?" Asado asked.

"My other stubborn goat," Ramirez answered with a chuckle, nodding to the animal her family had kept in the yard for years.

"Baa, baa," Diceverde mumbled. "Get some rest. You look worse than I do."

Blanca Asado was asleep a minute after her head hit the pillow, the grip of her gun still clutched in her hand.

CORSARIO GARZA ENJOYED the feel of the bucking hips of the young blonde, her giggles bouncing in the air like champagne bubbles. The floozy, a college-aged tourist, had discarded her bikini fifteen minutes ago after the third line of coke. In the middle of her deeply tanned face, her eyes stood out, red-rimmed and unfocused puddles of murky blue.

Garza felt the presence of another person in the room.

"Sir?"

"What is it, Jorge?" Garza asked.

"Duarte called a few minutes ago. Someone is attacking his laboratory," Jorge Pueblo told him. "We haven't heard anything since."

Garza felt his erection fade. He pushed the woman away, crawled out of the bed and glared at Pueblo. "You've tried calling back?"

"No response," Pueblo returned.

"Anything from the police?"

"It sounds like a war, according to what our source is saying. Explosions and automatic weapons. It's quiet now," Pueblo stated.

Garza grimaced and pulled on a pair of jeans.

The blonde reached out for him, tugging on the cuff.

Garza yanked his foot from her grasp and as an afterthought, kicked her in the side of the head. She let loose a squeal and rolled up into a fetal ball. The cartel governor grimaced, turning away from the trembling blonde heap at his feet. "Damn it! Tonight was the night that they were doubling production to replace the stuff lost by Munoz!"

Pueblo nodded. "Roderigo's not going to be happy."

"Corrie," the woman murmured. She reached one hand up to the mirror where two lines of cocaine still remained. There was a bruise on her temple where Garza's naked toes struck her. The only reason she still had any coordination was that the Mexican was barefoot. "Corrie…please…I just want…"

Garza slapped the mirror off the bed. White powder flew everywhere in a cloud that snowed onto the carpet. "Stop calling me Corrie, you bitch!"

The blonde looked up, bloodshot eyes wet and hurt. "But…"

She glanced back at the scattered cocaine. She nosed into the deep shag and tried to sniff some up, but it was useless. Garza shook his head in disgust at the little bimbo trying to get one more free hit. She was just like all the other leeches he'd picked up. There were only two females in this world he truly loved.

"That reminds me, have Zilla and Moda eaten yet?" Garza asked.

"Not until a little later tonight," Pueblo replied.

Garza looked at his lieutenant, not needing to ask the question.

"The ones who let Asado and her reporter friend escape," Pueblo answered.

Garza nodded, then looked to the mewling creature on the floor, trying to sniff residue off the upturned hand mirror. Snot and slobber dripped from her face, forming a slimy bridge to the reflective square. Pueblo nodded, as he understood what Garza wanted.

"How many men did you send to check on things?" Garza asked as Pueblo spun a sound suppressor onto the end of his stainless-steel Beretta.

"Just one. A reconnaissance. Duarte has twenty soldiers with him, so sending a dozen more probably would just be throwing more bodies into the fire," Pueblo stated. He thumbed the hammer back as he continued to discuss business.

"Good point," Garza grumbled. He glanced back to the naked blonde. He'd already forgotten her name. Showing up in a bar, flashing American dollars and promising easy blow, he managed to score a line of quick and easy women. Many were good at paying him back for what he gave them, but some simply ended up as pains in the ass. Not needing a pathetic sack of meat like that hanging around, he disposed of the trash in the most expedient manner. Pueblo's Beretta coughed and a quiet bullet smashed into the girl's forehead. Her blond hair was stained dark red as bloodshot eyes stared glassily at the ceiling.

Pueblo grabbed the dead woman by the ankle and dragged her away to Garza's private zoo. The Juarez Cartel governor let the warmth he felt for his very large Komodo dragons wash over him, the gentle love he felt for the cold-blooded meat-eaters cutting through his dread of informing Roderigo Montoya-Juarez that they'd lost one of their labs.

CHAPTER EIGHT

A little duct tape, cable ties binding his wrists and ankles, and a seat belt securing his waist and the chemist, Casas, was wrapped up in the back of Anibella's SUV. He'd passed out, delirious from inhaling ether fumes. When he awoke, Bolan would grill him for information on the Juarez Cartel. In the meantime, the prisoner slept as the first lady steered him toward a new location.

"Two hits in one night?" Anibella asked, steering through the thinning traffic.

"Striking while the iron is still hot," Bolan answered.

"You just finished with a brawl. I can see how winded you are."

"Don't worry," Bolan said. Already, thanks to the comfort of the passenger seat, and a few sips from a canteen, his reserves of strength were returning. He poured a little water into his hand and wiped his face. "I'll be fine."

The first lady looked at him, uncertain. "We don't have to finish this all in one night, Agent Cooper."

"We're not heading for the finish line. We're giving the enemy a few shakes," Bolan countered. He'd set the war bag in the seatwell at his feet. The mini-Uzi was stripped down and replaced in its compartment. For the next mission he'd take an assault rifle, the compact M-4 carbine. He hadn't used the more powerful weapon simply because the suppressor on the submachine gun could trap the gases from the muzzle more readily. If the situation had gone down where he'd had to shoot inside the drug lab with hydrochloric acid and ether fumes in the air, he'd have been immolated within moments, even with a suppressor on the rifle. The muzzle-blast would have still produced enough heat to cause combustion out of the short-barreled rifle.

His next stop, he would need power. An ACOG rode on top of the stubby rifle, and a vertical grip hung under the barrel furniture on a Picatinny rail. A 30-round magazine of 5.56 mm NATO ammunition rested in the well, a live round in the chamber. One flick of the safety and the Executioner would be in business. He snapped pouches of spare magazines onto his modular vest and replaced his supply of grenades.

He'd be prepared, regardless of however many men would be guarding the yacht and its attendant speed-boats at a private mooring on the coast twenty miles west of La Marina Acapulco. Along with the Acapulco Yacht Club, and Marina Ixtapa and Puerto Mio a hundred miles west, the four major marinas were public and tourist attractions, each capable of housing hundreds of boats for tourists traveling the world. Such a setup would leave a Juarez Cartel boat operation too open to prying eyes to be of any use. A private marina, however, between the cities of Acapulco and Ixtapa, would allow the Juarez group to move, blending in with other sea-going craft, while still maintaining the privacy of their personal mooring.

Anibella had explained to Bolan that any attempts to

serve a warrant on Marco Careyes's operation inevitably met with failure as the canny cartel lieutenant cleaned up at the first whisper of law-enforcement intervention.

Careyes, however, had never dealt with the Executioner. Without sanction or warrant, the lone crusader struck like lightning and with just as much warning. By the time the drug smugglers could react to his presence, it was already too late.

Bolan wasn't going to seize and arrest. He intended to grab a prisoner or available intelligence and then to destroy the capabilities of the Juarez Cartel to smuggle into and out of Acapulco. He glanced over and saw a dour, angry look on Anibella Brujillo's face.

"What's wrong?" he asked.

"That bitch Asado," she hissed, a queen cobra releasing a death sentence.

"She's dead. You shot her," Bolan stated.

Anibella looked at him, her eyes unfocused for a moment before her anger resumed. "It's because of her, operating out of the governor's mansion, that the Juarez Cartel thinks my husband is involved with the heroin trade. Because of her, my family and home are in danger!"

Bolan nodded, letting the conversation drop. Anibella continued to keep watch on him out of the corner of her eye as he double-checked his gear as they closed on Careyes's private marina. The first lady was hiding some other frustration; he could tell that by the sudden panic, the gears spinning in her brain as she drew up a preset response. If he only knew what it was…

He thought back to the aftermath of the gun battle with the Russian gunmen. While he never claimed to be psychic, he was a good judge of emotional states. The vibes he'd gotten off Anibella Brujillo in the wake of the skirmish had been intense joy and pleasure. She swallowed that instantaneous reaction as soon as she realized she was being watched, but the blood was in the water. Bolan had tasted it, and even though he had nothing more than the word of a fugitive and a few rumors, he believed that there was something dark and ominous gliding under the calm glassy surface of Anibella Brujillo's exterior.

Something that would make even a crocodile quiver in fear.

JORGE PUEBLO SIGHED as the guards looked up.

"Garza had another letdown?" one of them asked, looking at the corpse Pueblo deposited on the tile floor.

"Jorge, you're making a hell of a mess," the other said. "At least wrap her head up."

"Shut the hell up and open the cage," Pueblo snarled.

"What about the other guys? If the sisters eat…" one began.

Pueblo locked him with a stare. "They don't care if the meat is fresh or if it's rotten. There's still chunks of meat on the bones of the judge we tossed in there last month."

"Moda does love to nibble on the gooey stuff," the second guard commented.

The first shuddered and unlocked the overwatch. The pungent reek of carrion flesh and thick humidity struck Pueblo's nostrils. He picked up the blonde and hurled her over the railing to the dirt ten feet below the platform.

Zilla was the first one out. She was so named because of an unusual maple-leaf-shaped floral pattern along her spine. Most Komodo dragons were shale gray, with only a few yellow spots mixed in along their head and sides. Zilla, however, had a familiar pattern on her back, earning the nine-foot lizard her name. She and her "sister," Moda, were bought at the same time, though the illegal wildlife salesman didn't know if they were from the same egg clutch. But, according to Garza, they were lovely sisters. Moda was the larger of the pair, ten feet, three inches and three hundred sixty-five pounds, one of the largest verified Komodo dragons.

Moda lifted her head with regal disinterest as the lump of flesh struck the dirt. Her tongue flicked in the air, tasting the newness of the kill, but it would be several hours before the recently slain mammal would attract her interest.

Zilla, on the other hand, tore an arm from the corpse and scurried to the corner.

Pueblo chuckled. "Bring in the failures. Let them see what's going to happen to them after we shoot them."

"Damn shame such a hot woman needed to be turned to lizard food." The second guard sighed.

A wooden slat was opened on the far side of the lizards' habitat. Two bruised and battered men on the other side of a chicken-wire fence were stirred to consciousness by the first guard's prodding with a nightstick. They looked and saw that Zilla had curled just outside of their cage, ripping stretchy, stringy tendrils of meat from an arm.

Pueblo could hear their sudden wails of horror and surprise. Zilla lifted her head, still chewing and sprayed out a punitive hiss, blood and stringy slobber hosing all over the chicken wire. That always made the cartel lieutenant laugh when Zilla "commanded" humans to stop reacting in horror to her meal.

This prompted Moda to rise to her feet and to walk behind Zilla, black eyes staring menacingly at the failed hit men. The queen of the habitat licked the air, her tongue picking up the scent of horror on the naked, half-starved, stinking prisoners. She let out a sigh that was halfway between a lawn mower and distant thunder, disappointed that the terrified humans were neither intruders for which to prove her mastery of this domain nor rotted animals. Moda sensed that they would belong to her soon enough, though. She stomped over to the still too fresh corpse dumped at the bottom of the observation deck and clamped her jaws onto an ankle. With a violent thrash of her neck, she popped the hip joint apart. Razor-sharp fangs shredded the sheath of muscle and flesh still connecting the dislocated limb to the lifeless torso, and then Moda dragged the leg back to her nest, pausing every few feet to level black, soulless eyes at the doomed humans.

"Moda sure knows how to put on a show," the first guard said, returning from the enclosure where the prisoners were kept.

"That," Pueblo said, pointing for emphasis, "is why Moda is the queen, and Zilla's only a mere princess."

The guards laughed, a tinge of nervousness in their tone. Pueblo smiled, enjoying their fear. Anyone who failed under Garza's command would be dumped into the dragon pit and left to be mutilated, torn to shreds, and to rot all for the appeasement of two carrion-devouring monsters. Gangsters who didn't fear being shot at or stabbed turned to quivering pudding at the thought of being left as an open-air buffet for the mighty reptiles below.

Only one person had ever angered Garza enough that he was thrown in with the sisters while alive. Stupid with panic, the mewling cop thought that he could fight his way past the sisters of doom. Instead, Zilla's whiplike tail smashed out his kneecap as he took the first offensive.

Collapsing into the dirt, the poor bastard looked up to see Moda's jaws part, strings of saliva forming a hideous web between her razor-sharp fangs. Moda took only a tentative nip, opening a six-inch gash in the cop's shoulder. He howled and flopped away from the lizards.

Then the poisonous bacteria that had grown between the rotten-meat-clogged fangs, breeding in the reptile's saliva, took hold. Respiratory shock set in within fifteen minutes, but the fever and dementia hit within only five. It took an hour and a half for the undercover cop to finally die, rasping and wheezing, gibbering madly as hallucinations rushed through his mind.

The prisoners wouldn't dare try to escape, even through the chicken-wire. The Komodo dragons, satisfied with the 120 pounds of carrion just dropped off for them, wouldn't be interested in chewing through the metal webbing to reach the living prey, and trapped as the humans were, the reptiles didn't feel the need to fight to defend themselves. Surrounded by heavy steel bars on the other three sides, the two failures were trapped, watching their future playing itself out in front of them.

Pueblo smiled. The cameras that Garza had put up in the habitat would have digitally recorded all the latest fun and games. Provided that the cartel governor wasn't placed under a death sentence by Montoya-Juarez, Garza would be cheered up by this latest show.

And if not? Pueblo smirked. Garza's ass would be chewed out for Pueblo's entertainment.

"Santa Muerte," Anibella Brujillo whispered in soft prayer as Mack Bolan went to the water's edge. He'd stripped down to the skintight, waterproof blacksuit he wore under his street clothes. It looked as if he'd been carved from the solid blackness of a starless night sky, and already her body yearned to taste the pleasures of the walking god of death.

That was all she could think to call him now, Pluto, lord of the underworld, striding the world, harvesting the lives of the damned. The battles she'd witnessed, the obliteration of Montoya-Juarez's Russian allies and then the destruction of the drug lab, were not the acts of a mere mortal. He moved with a grace that defied human measure and struck with an efficiency that left her staggered.

The man she knew as Matt Cooper most assuredly was the handpicked executioner of the goddess of death.

No, Anibella thought, looking at Casas, their prisoner, in the backseat. Had Cooper been a tool of wrath, he would have slain the chemist immediately. And yet, nearly two dozen gunmen had been cut down like wheat before the threshing bullets from Cooper's weapons. She knew, though, he was no mere engine of destruction. He was at once subtle and explosive, hiding his thoughts from her canny senses while proving capable of turning an entire fortified apartment complex into an inferno.

You want this man's power more than his body, a voice cut through Anibella's thoughts. She looked around and realized it was the same voice that called to her when she'd first joined Santa Muerte. It was the voice of Martha herself, soft and seductive, promising power and the ability to do what she would. In a way, the "do what thou will" tenet of Santa Muerte paralleled the beliefs of American Satanism as proposed by Alastair Crowley and Anton LeVey. But where so-called Satanists did their best to exist as innocents in the eyes of the law, Santa Muerte's children held no such restraint. The law of man was a thing to be scorned. Only a token of appeasement to Death herself, and sins were washed clean.

The dark saint's voice continued to speak, cooing to her. *He is a man who has fought me across the world, across decades. My minions, in their wars against him, have fallen a thousandfold, and with each defeat, he has sapped my might in your world. The reason why we hide in the shadows, and not rule like queens, now cuts through the waters to destroy our opponents. Cooper is my ultimate adversary, bleeding me dry. Kill him, and the world will be ours. We shall reign over a golden age as surely as Zeus and Odin ruled previous eras.*

Anibella's mind spun at the thoughts that broke free in her consciousness.

To destroy such a man would grant her unlimited power. He was the avatar of death, as surely as she was the voice of death. Killing him would unleash a flood of spiritual energy, bathing her until she would become immortal and omnipotent.

"I would be a goddess," the woman told herself.

But first, this lone warrior would have to clear the field, making Acapulco the seat of her godly throne. Anibella could almost taste the heady wine of ultimate power.

IT WAS THREE HOURS before dawn, but the Executioner was under a deadline. He had to verify that Careyes didn't have noncombatants confined to the boats, either women brought in to entertain the sailors, or hostages to ensure lawmen didn't poke their noses too closely into Careyes's operation. For now, Bolan slid from boat to boat, winding detonation cord around the driveshafts of the speedboats, inserting a small waterproof detonator in the puttylike explosive snakes he left behind.

The det cord would destroy the propulsion of the craft, and the detonators had a range of two miles. If the speedboats were taken out of commission, they wouldn't explode with destructive power, but be left crippled beyond immediate repair. The explosives could easily be deactivated on one of the craft, should he need to appropriate one to get noncombatants out of the battle zone.

He had already intended to board Careyes's yacht to deliver a fatal judgment to the smuggler after sweating some answers out of him. Scouring the boat for prisoners or female entertainment added little into his factored timetable. Still, the opportunity for the doomsday numbers to run out and turn his soft probe hard was always there. If there was one thing about the Executioner, he was flexible, within the confines of his morality.

Rushing in, guns blazing, could result in innocent lives lost, and while some could debate that a prostitute was hardly an innocent, there were few women of the evening that Bolan could call a cold-hearted murderer, like the heavily armed thugs in Careyes's employ. A rundown of the smuggler's acquaintances read like the reunion of a cell block with murderers and rapists who had been disgorged from some of the worst prisons in Mexico, Cuba and Guatemala. They were hardened men who were released thanks to a bribe and overcrowding, sentences shortened to a mere vacation away from their usual litany of death and destruction.

Putting the heat on Careyes's bodyguards wouldn't put Bolan in a moral quandary. He swam up to the personal watercraft launch for the yacht and hauled himself aboard. His blacksuit's waterproof high-tech fabrics kept him from dripping and sloshing as much as he could have.

The smell of a cigarette reached Bolan's nostrils and he lowered himself between the bulky frames of two Jet

Skis. Footsteps clanked down the walkway and Bolan spotted the outline of a sentry. Over the glow of the cigarette, he made out the rough features of one of Careyes's army of ex-con soldiers. The smoker paused, looking out over the water, then sighed.

When he turned, Bolan rose silently, gliding forward. He'd need some answers, and the guard would provide them.

The Executioner lunged and ensnared his prey in an unbreakable grip, a crushing hand clamping the guard's mouth shut. Bolan spared a few seconds, confiscating the guard's radio and weapons before he pressed a cold length of steel against his prisoner's eyebrow.

"You can live, or you can die," Bolan whispered to the sentry in Spanish. "You can also decide how easily you can die. Disappoint me, and your end will be very slow. Understand?"

The guard grunted in agreement. Blood from where the razor-sharp edge slit his eyebrow poured, stinging into the guard's eye. The threat of six inches of steel carving out his eye had cowed the thug easily.

"Does Careyes have any guests on board?" Bolan asked.

There was a nod.

"Business or pleasure?" Bolan pressed.

"Both," the guard croaked softly, not daring to cry out when the combat knife rested on his face.

"Entertainment?" Bolan asked.

"A couple of girls," the guard whispered.

"The business?" Bolan growled.

"Russians," the sentry explained.

"How many?"

The guard held up four fingers.

"And how many guards and crew?" Bolan inquired.

"Nine, without me," the sentry replied.

"And where would you be?" Bolan quizzed.

"Swimming like a bat out of hell for the shore," the man replied.

"Get to it," Bolan ordered, loosening his death grip. The knife slipped into a sheath while he drew the silenced Beretta 93-R. The guard looked at the blunt can on the end of the handgun and knew full well that any action he'd take would be futile. With the noises of a floating boat, the sound of the suppressed handgun would be easily lost.

"Don't make me waste a bullet," Bolan reminded the guard.

The sentry turned and knifed into the water, stroking powerfully for the shore.

There was no guarantee the guard wouldn't try to alert Careyes when he got to land, but the time it would take for the man to locate a phone would give Bolan vital minutes to get the women to safety.

He took a moment and plugged an earphone from his harness into the guard's radio. The earpiece came alive as he heard the brief chatter of guards communicating with each other in Spanish. Bolan would be aware if Careyes's hardforce became alerted of an intruder in their midst. The guard's weapons, a 9 mm Taurus pistol and a small MAC-11 machine pistol, were excess clutter, considering his already impressive arsenal. After stripping ammunition out of the guns, he hid them under the seat of one of the Jet Skis.

A figure appeared at the top of the gangplank.

"Ed, hurry up. I'm thirsty," a guard called down.

Bolan lined up the Beretta, targeting the silhouette of the sentry's head. He stroked the trigger and the pistol chugged once, no louder than a polite cough. A spray of blood spread in a halo around the bodyguard's skull before he toppled down the steps.

Two down, thirteen to go.

And unlucky number thirteen, Marcos Careyes, was going to go down the hardest of them all.

CHAPTER NINE

A rap sounded on the door. "Marcos needs to see you," a voice called through the door in Russian. "There's something going on."

Vassily Roykov pushed aside the prostitute who'd been servicing him. Something bothered the *mafiya* lieutenant about the interruption.

"Kopolev?" Roykov asked. "Is that you?" He went to the door and turned the knob. As soon as the latch was released, the door swung violently, the corner cracking him in the middle of his face. The Russian mobster toppled backward, another figure crashing into him. It was Kopolev, at least what was left of his partner, half of his face removed by a burst of bullets.

Framed by the doorway, Roykov saw a grim shadow. The gangster struggled to get out from under his mutilated friend, pushing on Kopolev's corpse and reaching for his gun. One hand snaked toward his holster, but a machine pistol in the tall wraith's hand burped, fire burning through the Russian's hand and forearm. Pain strangled the cry in his throat as he saw his middle and index fingers skitter on the hardwood floor, landing just short of the handgun he'd desperately sought. Roykov folded his arm back under the protective shield of the dead Kopolev, eyes staring in horror at the grim gunman in the doorway.

"You and I have to talk, Vassily," Bolan told him.

Roykov's mouth worked for a moment before he recognized the shadowy figure. For years, the man in front of him was considered a myth, but he remembered fellow gangsters, former KGB agents, explaining about the lone American agent who had dared to wage a one-man war against the Soviet Union. "It's impossible...."

"Ask Kopolev," Bolan whispered. "Though he doesn't seem talkative, he should be able to tell you everything you need to know."

Roykov felt the blood draining out of the corpse's torn face onto his shoulder. His stomach turned and twisted. "T-t-talk?"

The Executioner stepped into the room and looked at Roykov's "entertainment."

"Get dressed," he told her in Spanish. "Your friend is at the Jet Ski launch. Get to shore."

The woman glared at the Russian, then looked to Bolan.

"He'll pay," Bolan reassured her, answering the unspoken question.

It had taken the Mexican prostitute only twenty seconds to wriggle into her shorts and toss her blouse over her head and shoulders. She didn't bother with shoes. As soon as she was gone, those chilling eyes turned back to Roykov.

"What's your kind doing in my backyard?" the Executioner challenged.

"B-business," Roykov sputtered. Bile crawled up the back of his throat, tears burning down his cheeks from the pain of his shattered hand.

"No kidding?" Bolan asked. He rolled Kopolev's

corpse to the side, allowing Roykov to crawl to a seated position. "Specifics."

Roykov cradled his ruined limb. "Montoya-Juarez wanted us to supply some muscle in exchange for control of European distribution."

"Against who?" Bolan pressed.

"Someone in the governor's mansion was making a push against his control here," Roykov stated. "But she apparently died. At least, that's the story."

"You don't believe it, and you sent a death squad against the governor and his wife," Bolan prompted.

"Brujillo is hard on us, and there are still elements of the newcomers working against him, behind the scenes," Roykov explained. "So maybe there's someone yet at work in the mansion."

Bolan nodded. "Any idea who?"

"You don't know?" Roykov asked.

There was only a cold, piercing silence from the implacable wraith. The Russian swallowed hard. "They say it's a woman. That's all we know, except for the mutilations."

"Mutilations?"

"The cartel lost some men. They were found later carved up," Roykov described.

"Like the Colombians?" Bolan inquired.

"No. Ritualistic, a human sacrifice. Heart removed and the bones shattered," Roykov told him.

"Sounds Aztec," Bolan said. "But it might be a borrowed ritual."

"Yeah," Roykov replied, shock numbing the pain in his hand. "Cults do that."

"Your kind's spent enough time around backwater countries manipulating those kinds of groups. What's your guess?" Bolan asked.

"Santa Muerte," Roykov said.

Bolan's brow furrowed. "That's not really an organized cult. So that would explain the lack of information about what's going on."

"All I've heard is that the *narcocorridos* have been abuzz with Martha's priestess," Roykov replied. "She's the one in charge."

"Saint Martha. Santa Muerte," Bolan mused. He remembered hearing Anibella Brujillo whisper the name before.

Roykov glanced toward the gun. With his left hand, he'd never be able to reach it, not with the black sound suppressor pointed right at his heart. Naked and helpless, the mobster had no options open to him.

"How long are you going to make me sweat before you pull the trigger?" Roykov asked.

Bolan thumbed down the hammer on the Beretta and stuffed the weapon back in its holster. "Kopolev told me that you're just the ranking *mafiya* thug on this boat, not the one running the show."

Roykov's cheeks went white as he realized what the Executioner implied.

"If your boss gets a hint that you sold him out, he'll take it out of your skin slowly," Bolan informed him. "If you cross me, you're just nine millimeters away from your judgment. I own you, and you know that I expect results. Don't disappoint me, Vassily."

Roykov nodded. The Executioner stepped over to the holstered handgun and drew it. He pressed it into the gangster's good hand, but only after dipping the grip in the puddle of blood that seeped from his forearm injuries.

"Fire out the magazine before you get to shore," Bolan ordered. "Otherwise, they'll wonder how you got off this ship without firing a shot."

Roykov swallowed hard, nausea rolling through him like a tidal wave. Bolan helped him to his feet.

"Nine millimeters, Vassily," Bolan reminded him.

Roykov looked at Kopolev's cored face and the 9 mm holes in his own forearm. Nine millimeters wasn't far enough away for the gangster's taste, but at least he was free to live another day.

PAYING PERIPHERAL ATTENTION to the earphone connected to Ed's walkie-talkie, and secured from sight in Roykov's cabin, Mack Bolan dialed up Stony Man Farm on his satellite phone.

"We've been watching Careyes's yacht," Kurtzman announced as soon as the phone link connected. "The women are safely ashore."

"I let a guest go. He's going to be my ears inside the Russian Mafia," Bolan informed him.

"I picked him up on deck," Kurtzman stated. "You get anything good out of him?"

"Vassily Roykov," Bolan rattled off. "Check the *narcocorridos* for Saint Martha or Saint Martha's priestess."

"Martha?" the Bear asked. "We're dealing with Santa Muerte?"

"That's what Juarez and the Russians think," Bolan answered. "If it pans out, we might be another step closer to figuring out what's really going down here."

"And you want me to check out Mrs. Brujillo's possible links to the cult?" Kurtzman inquired.

"You'll have to be subtle. The *federales* might not notice, but Anibella's sharp. She undoubtedly has access to resources beyond mere law enforcement. Especially if she was able to plant a frame on Rosa Asado so easily," Bolan explained.

"I'll be careful," Kurtzman replied. "You, too. We've still got eight heat sources on board. And they're agitated."

Bolan heard the curses in Spanish. "Yeah. They found the body I stuffed under some steps. Where's Roykov?"

"Halfway to shore," Kurtzman said. "They won't see him. It's too dark."

"Good," Bolan answered. "Can't let them know my rat abandoned the ship before I sank it."

The alarm raised, Bolan heard the order for the yacht security force to check out the Russians' cabins. Careyes's men were organized and sharp. Even though the Executioner's stealth and skill had enabled him to get the drop on many of them so far, it hadn't been easy. The 125-foot yacht had plenty of places to hide for a canny, experienced warrior, but Bolan's familiarity with the ship and its crew would allow Marcos Careyes no such haven.

"They're heading toward your cabin, Striker," Kurtzman warned.

"Numbers?" Bolan asked.

"Three. They look heavily armed."

"I've got it," the Executioner answered. He unslung the M-4 carbine. Its 5.56 mm rounds would pierce the flimsy doors on the yacht as if they were made of rice paper. And without the potential to harm a noncombatant, he was in a free-fire zone.

There was a rap at the door.

"Roykov? Come on out," a voice ordered in Spanish.

Bolan held his fire. The command was filled with too much authority to be just a member of Careyes's guard. Instead, the soldier rattled off a string of angry curses in Russian.

"Damn you, leave my mother out of this," Marcos Careyes snapped. "We've got a situation!"

Bolan smirked. Naturally the smuggling yacht owner would understand Russian. That's why the Juarez Cartel had insisted that he host members of the organization while they were in Acapulco.

"Come in," Bolan said, mimicking the Russian's voice.

The door opened and Bolan recognized Careyes immediately from his file photo. He was behind two of his men and the Executioner snapped off two rapid shots, taking each of the guards in the center of his face. Blinded by a spray of blood and brains from cored skulls, Careyes flinched and spun, trying to escape.

Bolan surged into the hallway, grabbing a handful of Careyes's shirt. With a violent yank, he pulled the Mexican gangster off his feet and powered a hard punch into the nerve juncture at the back of Careyes's jaw. An explosion of nerve impulses washed over Careyes's brain and the Mexican shook like gelatin as his CNS misfired. Overloaded with pain, the smuggler flopped limply to the floor.

The roar of the assault rifle was unmistakable, as were the two single shots in a space no longer than a second. Bolan jammed his unconscious prisoner under the bed, securing his wrists and ankles with cable ties, and prepared for an enemy assault.

Having set up a killing box and drawing the attention of the remaining mobsters gave the Executioner full control of the coming battle. Gunshots were like blood in the water, chum to attract sharks.

"What's the disposition of the enemy force now?" Bolan asked.

"Tearing ass right toward you," Kurtzman stated. "These guys must have never heard of an ambush."

Bolan smiled, but there was no mirth or joy in it. Just an acknowledgment that everything was going according to plan. The smile disappeared and he lay in wait to spring his trap.

MARCOS CAREYES'S EYES fluttered open, his head pounding. He'd been jammed under a bed, and his hands and feet had fallen asleep, pricking with cold needles that informed him that the blood had been strangled off them. He tried to move his mouth, but his jaw hurt like hell, and his tongue felt as swollen and limp as his fingers. He spotted movement from under the bunk, black combat boots with skintight black leggings tucked into them.

"What…" he muttered when the figure dropped to the floor.

Careyes's struggling consciousness exploded. Thunder ripped through the room and his pounding head took on a whole new level of discomfort. It felt as if a herd of cattle were stampeding across his skull, their thick hooves trampling his brain.

Splintered wood flew in a cloud, choking off visibility in the gap between the bunk and the floor. The man in black, having fallen to his side, stroked the trigger on his rifle and stitched the wall with long ragged bursts. As soon as the storm subsided behind a wail of clattering bells roiling in his ears, Careyes realized that his security men had opened up with their AK-47s, the powerful slugs snapping through the fragile walls of the cabin.

Hammerlike 7.62 mm slugs tore through the paneling, reducing it to airborne splinters and sawdust.

"Stop firing, you idiots!" Careyes roared at the top of his lungs.

Bolan glanced back to his prisoner, then nodded in grim satisfaction, mouthing the word "good." The Mexican smuggler's bowels tightened as he realized that he'd placed his bodyguards at a sudden disadvantage by ordering them to hold their fire. They had no way of knowing that he was tucked safely under cover. The instantaneous knee-jerk reaction to call for the cease-fire had been why he'd been left ungagged. He had been only half conscious, his thoughts not up to speed.

"No! Shoot! Shoot this bastard!" Careyes bellowed.

Bolan rolled over and huddled against the bulkhead under the porthole. He whispered something into a throat microphone, then nodded as he received an answer to the unheard question. Careyes struggled, trying to push out from under the bunk, but his bound wrists and ankles left him with no leverage to maneuver. AKs ripped out short bursts, firing high to avoid perforating the bound smuggler. The Mexican knew that he'd thrown his men into a deep enough confusion that they were actively missing.

They gave the Executioner an opportunity in which to rise and throw open the porthole. Careyes froze, not knowing whether to shout another warning or to hold his tongue. Another mistake could give this one-man army everything he needed to get the drop on the smuggler's protectors again.

Bracing his thighs against the other side of the porthole opening, Bolan hung only a few feet over the water, M-4 carbine drawn tightly to his shoulder. He aimed at a section of wall that would give him an angle on the men firing from down the corridor. He counted down the milliseconds before the head smuggler would give another warning.

"He's outside the porthole!" Careyes shouted.

One bodyguard poked his head out of the window and Bolan milked the M-4's trigger, obliterating the guard's face with a salvo of 5.56 mm skullbusters. The stump of a neck hung, ragged strips of face and scalp dangling off the decapitated corpse. Bolan loosened his grasp on the porthole and slithered to the deck outside of the cabin, tucking his legs behind him barely in time to avoid having them severed by a vicious eruption of return fire. AK slugs punched through the cabin's walls, scything into the water after smashing through fiberglass and wood paneling.

"He left me alone!" Careyes announced. "Get me out of here now, damn it!"

The Executioner trained his rifle on the cabin wall, just under the metal frame of the porthole, waiting for the sound of gunmen entering the cabin to rescue their commander. So far, every gut-instinct command that Careyes had given had played right into Bolan's battle plan, allowing him to steer in response to the dazed smuggler's own strategy. The gunmen had trusted their boss implicitly; after all, he'd gotten them past several instances of Coast Guard interception and to victory against pirates looking to make a fast profit by ripping off heroin runners.

What they hadn't counted on was the lethal cunning of Bolan's years of experience and ability to maneuver around an enemy's strategy.

Footsteps could be heard in the cabin; Careyes sputtered the first word of an order to get him to safety.

Bolan held down the trigger and swept the cabin at waist height, screeches of agony erupting from the mouths of gunmen. Careyes howled in terror and rage, throwing out curses with too much coherence and forcefulness to indicate that he'd taken a hit. Bolan dumped the M-4's magazine for a new one and then kicked a hole in the perforated fiberglass, making a window through which he could see his captive, drenched in the blood of his slain bodyguards. Two more Mexicans lay sprawled in the cabin, their bellies opened up by a saw of 68-grain penetrators that whirled through their torsos. Rubbery loops of bowel and intestine gorged from the hideous slashes of abdominal muscle, dark eyes staring lifelessly toward the ceiling.

"You…you son of a bitch," Careyes hissed.

Bolan contacted Kurtzman. "Any other heat traces?"

"One still moving, aside from you and Careyes. Looks wounded," the Stony Man computer genius replied.

"I've got him," Bolan said.

Reaching the end of the gangway, Bolan glanced around the corner. A lone gunman sat, his ruined arm painting his white linen shirt a deep red. His good hand held a Colt .45, but it was pointed at the deck. The wounded man looked pleadingly at the tall wraith in black.

"Drop the gun, and I'll stop the bleeding," Bolan ordered.

The injured bodyguard loosened his fingers and the pistol clattered to the wooden deck. Bolan moved in quickly, kicking the .45 under the railing and into the water. He tore off the wounded man's shirt and used strips of sleeves as a pressure dressing. Utilizing a roll of duct tape from a pouch on his web belt, he secured the pressure dressings to the gunman's wrecked right arm. Four rounds had destroyed it, smashing bone and slicing blood vessels, but fortunately avoiding the major brachial artery running through the arm. As it was, Bolan ended up choking off the upper arm with a cable tie, pulling it taut. The plastic cable indented the wounded Mexican's arm a good inch in circumference, cutting off blood to the shattered limb. Blood loss through severed veins would render most of the flesh necrotic, and they'd have to amputate such a completely destroyed limb. But he would live.

The Executioner would take no pleasure in allowing a wounded enemy to die, especially after taking the offer to surrender.

"You'll live," Bolan promised him. "Stay put."

The gunman nodded, and he returned to Careyes. In his state, and unarmed, he was no threat.

The smuggler was still where Bolan had left him, but fueled by rage and panic, Careyes had dislocated his thumb and despite tearing half the flesh from his left hand, he'd pulled out of the cable ties. A dead gunman's weapon was in his hand and Bolan barely had time to duck out of the path of a spray of bullets.

"You are a devil!" Careyes cursed. "I will send you back to hell!"

"Not before I collect my due," Bolan returned, staying behind a support strut in the bulkhead. Careyes fired off a few more shots, but they couldn't penetrate the heavy steel of the girder. "Heaven isn't getting you."

The smuggler cleared his throat, covering up the noise of a reload. Bolan had a grenade on his harness, but he had come for answers, not just to eliminate an evil man.

Careyes snarled in defiance. "Who really sent you?"

The Executioner decided to play a gamble. He remembered what Roykov had said about the Aztec-style sacrifices. "Huitzilopochtli."

"Bullshit!" Careyes snapped. Autofire blasted from his rifle. A 7.62 mm bullet bounced wild and nicked across the back of Bolan's arm, stinging him and drawing a trickle of blood from the shallow graze.

"The devil has nothing on me," Bolan continued. "When my lady sent me, she wanted more than a heart. She wanted skins."

"Wh-what do you want?" the smuggler asked, his nerve breaking.

"To know who to flay in your stead," Bolan explained.

Careyes looked down. The Executioner was banking on the smuggler's knowledge of his nation's mythology and history. Traditional sacrifices to Huitzilopochtli were made while the victim still lived, his skin removed in one continuous action. The gangster might have been a tough guy, but when it came to the slow, relentless agony of being flayed, he wasn't so tough anymore.

"You're still not going to let me go," Careyes replied coldly.

"You'll get the mercy of a bullet. And a chance to shoot back," Bolan said.

"Garza," Careyes betrayed.

"And where will he be dying?" Bolan asked.

"There's a ledger in my cabin, taped under my desk. It has a map, and it has the layout of everything we currently have running in Acapulco and the neighboring states," Careyes stated.

Bolan nodded.

"It was an insurance policy," the smuggler confessed. "In case they ever thought I wasn't useful anymore. I have enough in there to turn the Juarez Cartel into a third-rate corner bakery."

"Paying the devil your due," Bolan concluded.

"Maybe it'll ease my sentence in the afterlife," Careyes admitted.

"Maybe," Bolan replied. He tossed his M-4 to the floor. "Get your pistol."

Careyes dumped his AK into the hall. His shadow spilled from the doorway. "Like a Wild West duel."

"Fill your hand?" Bolan asked.

Careyes stepped into the open. He had a Glock stuffed into his waistband. "Count of three?"

"All yours," Bolan conceded, his hand inches from the grip of his Desert Eagle.

The smuggler smirked. His hand shot for the handle of the Glock. "Three!"

Careyes had hoped to trick his adversary, beginning his draw and skipping the countdown. He hadn't counted on the lightning reflexes of the man in black, however. The Glock's muzzle hadn't even cleared his belt when the mighty .44 Magnum pistol was up and leveled at his face.

The Executioner fired through the bridge of the smuggler's nose, the jacketed hollow-point round splintering bone and detonating in the seat of the Mexican's brain. There was no time for pain to register for him, just the instant release of death.

Bolan turned and went to the smuggler's cabin.

Marcos Careyes had been as good as his word. Pressing the thumb stud on his radio detonator, Bolan watched as the smuggler's fleet of speedboats shook, their propeller shafts and hulls torn apart by the explosives he'd planted. The Juarez Cartel had lost its shipping division in the space of a few hours, and with the information in Careyes's ledger, the Executioner would sever the hydra head nestled in Acapulco.

Anything else would go to Mexican law enforcement and the DEA to bring the cartel to greater ruin. Unfortunately, there was still the problem of the cult, and the Russian Mafia operating in Mexico.

One hydra head lopped off, with two more remaining.

But the Executioner knew he had more than enough steel to take care of them.

CHAPTER TEN

Casas felt miserable when he came out of his stupor. One side of his face was swollen, the broken cheekbone grating every time he winced in pain. His feverish hallucinations of knights and dragons and a flaming hell around him had vanished.

He just couldn't move. Logic kicked in and he knew he'd been taken prisoner by the big man in black who had broken his gas mask and cheek. Duarte was undoubtedly dead, the scene tormenting his unconscious mind even as he struggled to awaken and escape the hellish dreams.

All told, it was still better than being fed to the deadly reptilian sisters that Corsario Garza kept at his mansion. Even if all that happened was that he received a bullet in his head, he still wouldn't be torn apart by savage carrion eaters. The fact that he had awakened to see another morning was icing on the cake. He just wasn't in a hurry to find out what was under that icing.

Gummy eyes scanned the room and he saw her. Even with a thunderous headache and his body bound by flexible plastic restraints, arousal struck him like a freight train.

Anibella Brujillo had transformed from the plain, darkly clad professional into a more familiar role. Her red satin dress stopped midthigh, and the neckline was cut down to her navel, tied off with a crimson sash that hugged the glimmering red skirt to her curvaceous hips. She smelled of jasmine, and her lips were full and livid, hazel eyes smoldering as they bore into him. Her tongue glided across her upper lip as she stepped closer, long delicate fingers tickling across Casas's bare chest.

"I must be hallucinating again!" the chemist exclaimed.

Anibella simply smirked and her red fingernail scratched across Casas's right nipple, a jolt of pain followed by a hardening of the nub. Casas felt an uncomfortable tightness in his pants and he couldn't wriggle his hips around enough to relieve the sudden pressure.

"You poor thing," she murmured, her voice deep and husky. "It must feel like you're being strangled. Let me loosen that up."

Despite what his nerve endings were telling him, the chemist still believed that he was in the throes of hallucination. A gurgle bubbled in his throat as she undid his pants, fingers massaging his engorged member with a skill he had never known existed. Garza had some quality call girls available for his favorite employees, and as the cartel's chief chemist in the region, he'd been entertained by some of the most beautiful women in Acapulco.

None of them had driven him so wild with the touch of their hands. His skin glistened with sweat and his lips quivered.

"Now, I'm going to ask you a few questions, Francisco," Anibella announced.

"What do you want to know?" Casas asked.

"Everything you know about the cartel. Answer me truthfully, and I'll make your dreams come true."

"But, if Montoya-Juarez finds out…" Casas began.

Anibella's seductive gaze grew cold and hard. She cupped his injured cheekbone, then squeezed. Agony like nothing he'd ever experienced speared through his brain. Tears rolled down the chemist's cheeks as his throat constricted in agony.

"I can make your nightmares come true, as well," Anibella snapped.

The pressure on his broken cheek eased, and while his stomach turned, he no longer felt the urgent need to vomit. Those hazel eyes returned to being warm and inviting. "Heaven or hell, Francisco? Trust me, I'll have fun either way."

Francisco Casas decided to take the ride to heaven. Even if Montoya-Juarez found out, the taste of torture that she'd given him had been enough to shatter his loyalty and fear of the deadly cartel.

WHILE ANIBELLA BRUJILLO WAS PLAYING seductress, Mack Bolan got in touch with Stony Man Farm. They tracked Vassily Roykov easily. As soon as the Russian mobster had reached the shore, he contacted his bosses and spun a tale of an armed assault on the yachts, and how he had barely escaped with his life. In the face of overwhelming odds, the gangster had struggled to freedom and warned his masters of the looming threat.

It was a performance that would have gotten the Russian an acting award if it had been caught on film. The fact that he was in mortal terror of the Executioner had painted his words with a genuine fear that simply couldn't be faked.

Roykov remained on the line long enough for Aaron Kurtzman to triangulate the location of the Russian Mafia's headquarters in Mexico.

After that, it was simply a matter of setting up wire-taps and pointing geosynchronous spy satellites right down the throat of the compound. Infrared, radar and high-resolution satellite imagery were all downloaded to Bolan's laptop. While it was so easy that it amounted to cheating, there was no guilt on the soldier's part. He hadn't survived countless campaigns against American organized crime, international terrorism and international espionage by playing fair.

While there were lines he wouldn't cross in terms of harming noncombatants, using every ounce of information from illegal wiretaps and unauthorized satellite surveillance came nowhere close to tickling his ethics. Anibella Brujillo's sexual charms were another weapon Bolan felt no qualms about employing. Some men could be broken more easily by a taste of sugar than a stinging lash. The woman wielded her beauty and the desire it fired like a surgeon employed a scalpel, and if anything, the governor's wife could cut even more deeply Bolan felt his own figurative scars from dealing with her machinations.

Unfortunately, he couldn't completely ditch the first lady.

She could become a deadly opponent, but she was also a powerful asset.

For now, the Executioner would have to sleep with the devil he knew to bring down those he was less familiar with.

"Gold mine, Striker," Barbara Price said on the other end of the e-conference. "I thought you intended to go scorched earth."

"You know how flexible I can be," Bolan answered. He caught a glimpse of her grin at his innuendo. "I decided I'd be better served with Roykov as my patsy. And the first guard…there was no need to kill him. He was interested in survival."

"It was a chance," Price admitted.

Bolan nodded for the camera mounted on top of his laptop. "A small chance. I know how to read people."

"All this time and you still haven't lost faith in people," Price said, shaking her head.

"Well, there was some cynicism involved. I had the guard dead to rights. The same for Roykov. And Roykov knew about me. Or at least the boogeyman that the KGB veterans lived in fear of before they quit and joined the Russian mob."

"Missing the old days of leaving a calling card and spreading nightmares across entire countries?"

Bolan's smile was noncommittal. "Nope. Just glad that those I have to hunt are three-quarters dead from living in fear of something."

Price nodded. "Would you need any help with the Russians?"

Bolan studied the layout of the mob's compound. It was a spacious estate atop a hill, surrounded by a ten-foot wall. Several outbuildings housed three dozen men, and a fleet of vehicles. The main house was wired half as well as the Farm, making it a formidable electronic fortress for gathering information, and covered by high-tech security.

"Ideally, I could use Jack in an F-14 to just drop a few JDAM cluster bombs on-site," Bolan mused. "But as they say, that's not how I roll. I can handle this. I know the setup."

"What about Garza?" Price asked, looking over the intel that Bolan had supplied to the Farm.

"Still narrowing down his habits and his location. One fire to douse at a time," Bolan told her. "The Rus-

sians are in the neighborhood to launch a major operation. They want a slice of Central America and working with the Juarez Cartel would give it to them. I need
to make Acapulco seem like a complete disaster to the
thugs in the old country, otherwise they'll slip in the
back door as soon as I'm done here."

"So, it's going to be standard blood and thunder and
cleansing fire?" Price asked.

"Go with what works," Bolan replied with a wry grin.
He heard the door open. "Over and out, Barb.
Anibella's going to brief me."

Price's gaze narrowed as she caught view of the first
lady as she stepped into camera range. "Over and out."

The video conference ended, Price's frown fading on
the screen.

"Get anything?" he asked.

The corner of Anibella's mouth turned up and she
nodded. "All recorded for your perusal." She handed
him a DVD.

"A combat nap is in my immediate future."

He shut down the laptop and gathered it, the DVD
and the printer into his portable case. "Will the *federales*
keep Casas under wraps so Garza doesn't know we
nabbed him?"

Anibella smiled. "Oh, he'll be kept out of sight for a
while."

There was a hidden smugness in that statement that
put Bolan's spine on edge. The chemist was to have
been promised jail time and safety in return for betraying the Juarez Cartel. Every instinct in the Executioner
was screaming that the poor bastard wasn't going to live
to see the inside of a jail cell.

If he gave voice to that doubt, however, he'd lose his
handle on Anibella Brujillo's scheme to control the heroin

trade running through Acapulco. He reminded himself of Casas's lifestyle, riches built on a foundation of drug abuse, victimization and violence that crossed continents.

"Good news," Bolan stated. He left the first lady and went to his room for a fitful sleep.

IT WOULD LOOK AS IF Francisco Casas had been spirited away from the governor's mansion by an unmarked car full of *federales*. Indeed, one of the men in the SUV was an official member of Mexican federal law enforcement, but his life on the edge of the underworld had made him one of Anibella's flock. Having lived a double life, he surrendered to the spiritual simplicity of Santa Muerte. Guilt was appeased by offerings.

Being part of a group that was on the verge of conquering the heroin trade of the Pacific coast of Mexico also provided its own form of soothing to a troubled soul.

As drained as Anibella Brujillo felt, she revived in the company of her fellow believers. Their reverence for her was an energizing tonic that brought her around.

The hood protected Casas's identity, and hid the swelling of his shattered cheekbone. There was nothing really that could be done with it outside of a hospital, and in a few hours, there wouldn't be any need to preserve his features, anyway.

Though most of their sacrifices were in the realm of small animals, such as chickens, Saint Martha demanded lives in exchange for her largess. For truly important endeavors, more was required.

The war with the Juarez Cartel had provided some in that regard. Men would satisfy the embodiment of death far more than a small bird that would end up as food for humans. The goddess wanted more preferential treatment. Captives of the enemy were what she had been used to in the olden days, back when victims were dragged to the peaks of ziggurats, flayed and their hearts removed. Anibella had made many sacrifices to Santa Muerte over the years, skeletons crowding her closet with each new success and rise in prominence.

There had been times when Anibella wondered if it wasn't just coincidence, or cold-blooded machination that had vaulted her from a teenage nightclub singer to international stardom and being the wife of one of the most powerful politicians in Mexico. Murdering her rivals and enemies certainly made slipping up the ladder of success easier, but murders could easily be uncovered, and all of her progress could collapse once the foundation of rotting corpses was laid bare for the world to see. But now, Anibella knew it was more than luck and providence. Something divine and powerful watched over her, giving her breaks, covering up her underhanded dealings as she strode between the sun-drenched Acapulco spotlight and the shadows of its back alleys with impunity.

Only a death goddess's subtle hand could have granted Anibella such boons that she was only steps away from the peak of greatness.

"Thank you for the gifts of this night, Martha," Anibella prayed. Her men also bowed their heads in reverent thanksgiving. Only the frightened whimper of Casas under his hood interrupted the solemn proceedings. The chemist had gathered enough clues to realize that he had been dropped into the lap of the enemy who had assailed his cartel with relentless abandon.

The drive took a half hour, but when they finally reached the coastal cave systems, Anibella was glad. The caves had been modified by Spanish settlers as fortifications against pirates, more than merely a back door, but an entire underground complex that provided the groundwork for even further exploitation.

Anibella had discovered the cave system a decade ago, while she and her then boyfriend, a director, were looking for places to shoot videos. The director had been a part of her coven of Santa Muerte adherents, and over the past few years had arranged with other cultists to develop the hidden caverns as the base for their unholy temple.

A few well-placed cave-ins had separated the underground caverns from the escape tunnels of the coastal fortress, leaving the winding maze and heavily built-up complex of great halls and fortifications as nothing more than a half-remembered rumor. Technology was brought down, electric lighting, modern communication and other amenities. The hidden underground base gave the cult a place to hold their meetings and their grand sacrifices with all the pomp and circumstance befitting their goddess. The place also provided vast storage for riches, drugs and weapons that Anibella had accumulated.

But Anibella knew this base was but a mere stepping stone. Acapulco was only one step toward a higher peak. The presidency of Mexico wasn't out of her husband's reach. And with control of what the cartel had commanded in one state, expansion to rule the whole of Mexico's underworld would be another step.

All of this can be yours. I ask only one more token of your loyalty. The life of the man you know as Cooper. The whispers of her goddess echoed through her mind.

"Soon," Anibella promised. "But for now, I have only a small morsel for you."

She could feel the satisfied smile of the goddess of death even as they parked the SUV for a moment in an underpass, transferring Casas to an eighteen-wheeler semitrailer. The vehicles remained idle during the transfer, which took place quickly, and roughly for the captive chemist. The eighteen-wheeler picked up speed to make up for its loss of time, and Anibella's SUV came out of the underpass, steering toward the location she'd given to Cooper as the safe house where the prisoner would be kept. Her paranoia had been stepped up a notch. She knew that she had the mansion tight under her command, electronic eyes and ears everywhere. When she saw how deftly the big American had charged through the cartel's defenses for their drug lab and smuggling fleet, she knew that he had eyes in the sky. That was why she'd taken the precaution of handing her instructions on a slip of paper to her renegade, Santa Muerte-worshiping *federale* follower. All the electronic intelligence in the world couldn't spy on a folded piece of paper handed off, no matter what the resolution capacity of the orbital cameras on a spy satellite.

The information age had proved one truth. A courier, with a sealed envelope and a sharp mind, was one of the most secure methods of transferring information. Unless the courier was a planted spy, the odds of intercepting him without betraying the interception were very thin. Encryption codes could be broken, phone calls listened to, meetings photographed. She set her orders in motion through a whisper stream of lips to ears, slipped notes and blind phone calls for last-minute meetings in person. The extent of her cult was such that she had been able to come up with doppelgangers for Casas and herself. At the network of caverns that served as her home base and temple, alternate transportation was set up that would rendezvous with her stand-in, which would be equally obscured against eyes watching from the edge of space.

It was a tiring game of charade and deception that would allow her to outthink Agent Matt Cooper and his allies back in the United States, but Saint Martha wouldn't give her a free road to complete, unchallenged power without making her earn it. Even if the Americans somehow managed to detect her ruse of the transfers, she had layered the deception well enough to make finding the cult's home base impossible. Not expecting Anibella to make such a switch, they should concentrate on paving Cooper's path of war against the Juarez Cartel and their Russian Mafia followers, she mused, but with two hours of preparation time, she'd managed to set up a suitably twisted trail.

Finally she felt the trailer come to a halt. She glanced at her watch and nodded. Her doppelganger, a beautiful actress who could have been her twin sister with the proper accessories, was tasked with handling a few minor-level functions, burning through a slow, inconsequential morning of public appearances. As high priestess, Anibella required a stand-in so that she might engage in far more important activities, such as waging war in the shadows with the cartel, or committing to her religious duties. It would be out of character for Anibella Brujillo to attend a late-afternoon luncheon with the blood of a sacrifice staining her fingertips. As long as Cooper was resting or preparing for his evening of knock-out assaults, her personal presence wasn't required. Emilio Brujillo was busy with his own responsibilities, freeing her up for the morning, so that she could send Francisco Casas to the goddess of death with proper pomp and circumstance, leaving Cooper and his allies none the wiser.

Her minions took Casas firmly in their rough hands, pulling him from the SUV and to the loading-dock door installed in the cliffside. Hidden by copses and rocks, it was protected from prying eyes.

"Feel glad this day, Francisco," Anibella cooed to the hooded prisoner. "Today, you meet a goddess."

Despair escaped Casas's lips in a low, miserable groan.

BLANCA ASADO HADN'T GOTTEN much sleep, despite being in a supposedly safe place. She'd left Diceverde and Gloria alone for the morning, seeking to make herself useful. She imagined the kind of life she'd have had if she'd subsumed her need for action and hunger for justice, then had to fight a wave of jealousy and bitterness that swelled within her chest.

Armando would have given himself completely to her, or Rosa, if they had only weakened in their resolve. Manuel Asado had wanted the twin girls to emulate the sons he never had, and thus discouraged their interest in boys. He had been a respected lawman, but there was something missing in him. He could have taken pride in their beauty, and found happiness with them if they'd developed affection for strapping men who exuded machismo. Instead, the rough-and-tumble tomgirls found themselves attracted to boys like Armando, who had intellect and creativity, but were lacking in physical ability.

It was no wonder that Gloria existed in a world of unspoken tension whenever Blanca or Rosa had been around Armando. She had seen through the twins' sisterly affection for him, and could feel the jealousy that stirred beneath Blanca's emotional armor. Asado took a deep breath and fought her feelings, pushing every negative back into her subconscious. Only the fact that she didn't want to hurt Armando, or the woman he loved, gave her the resolve to shove her envy aside, caging it in the armor of her hardened heart.

"Thank you, Papa," she whispered, grateful for the emotional buffers he'd instilled in his girls when they'd lost their mother. She just had to focus on bringing down Anibella Brujillo, and so she was off to watch the governor's wife as she attended the opening of a new clinic. Diceverde had managed to obtain a copy of the woman's itinerary for the day, and Asado decided that if she had to be the prey, she was going to evade her hunters by stalking the mistress of the hunt.

It was a foolish gamble, she admitted to herself, but only by pushing her luck was she able to submerge the pain of the loss of her sister. When she'd been at the mansion and stumbled across the Russians' attack, it was like a salve to a badly charred soul, shedding her impotence and uselessness in an explosion of violence. Being part of Cooper's investigation granted her a greater purpose, and more importantly, a greater distraction.

By concentrating on whether she was being followed by lawmen or assassins, she didn't have time or energy to waste on bittersweet memories of her childhood. Focusing on how Anibella Brujillo framed Rosa Asado, she blunted and directed the aimless need for revenge, turning it into an intellectual tool instead of something that pulled at the leash of her self-control. Now she could smother the urge to pull her handgun and put a bullet into the first lady's forehead just as the conniving witch had done with her sister.

Despite her survival instincts operating in a constant buzz of activity, she'd developed a soothing calm.

Entering the crowd to watch Anibella's dedication of the new clinic, Blanca scanned for signs of the shadows that Rosa had mentioned in her notes to Diceverde. None was in evidence, and the security detail was at full strength, eyes like hawks as they perused the crowd.

Asado willed herself to not exist, blending in with the crowd. When the bodyguards swept their gaze across her, they saw nothing that would alert them, no nervousness, no agitation, nothing that would betray her true identity.

Dispassionately, she observed the first lady when something nibbled at the edge of her instincts. Something was wrong about the woman standing at the podium, giving her speech. The voice was unmistakable, and her carriage was nearly perfect. It was enough to fool a crowd, and unfortunately, Asado had never personally met the woman.

If Rosa had been present, maybe she could have put Blanca's suspicions to rest when she suffered the same kind of headache that had warned her back at the mansion.

This wasn't the governor's wife. Deep down, without need for any evidence, warning flags raised.

"You keep this up, Rosa, and I'll start believing in an afterlife," Blanca whispered. She raised her digital camera and called out to the first lady, snapping off several rapid pictures.

She'd need evidence if she wanted to convince Cooper's allies that Anibella Brujillo had given them the slip.

A man in the crowd locked her with a predatory, penetrating gaze. Asado knew in a heartbeat that she'd given herself away. Under his linen jacket was a concealed handgun, and he was bearing down on her.

CHAPTER ELEVEN

With the crowd surrounding Asado, there was no way she could justify pulling her weapon and opening fire on the tall man cutting through the crowd toward her. He hadn't pulled his weapon yet, but even as a fugitive, she couldn't allow anyone to get hurt if the stranger returned fire. She had to avoid a gunfight. The memory stick loaded with photographs had to get to Cooper's people so that he could be alerted to the fact that Brujillo wasn't on the up-and-up.

Ducking behind a news camera crew and slipping through the throng of reporters and well-wishers, she had a plan: get to a side alley and ditch the bystanders, and possibly the armed man in the linen jacket. There was no guarantee of the latter, but at least she'd be able to minimize collateral damage if the gunman opened fire. Besides, considering her luck so far, the gunner was in communication with other allies throughout the crowd and they would hem her in.

If it came down to that, what would she do?

These killers were also on the trail of Diceverde, and the wounded journalist and his girlfriend, despite

Gloria's double-barreled shotgun, weren't up to the task of holding off a team of professional murderers. They would pull the information out of her through torture and tie up their loose ends.

The gun in her waistband would be the only barrier between the hit men and Armando Diceverde and his girlfriend. One bullet, through her brain, would deny them any knowledge of the two isolated lovers. Anibella Brujillo would get away with her ruse, but Asado was determined. The lives of Armi and Gloria were more important than her own.

But that's only if they penned her in with no way out.

The crowd was thick, and Asado threw elbows hard into sides to carve her way through the knotted mass of humanity. All the while she kept her eyes open for pursuit. A quick glance toward the stage showed one of Anibella's bodyguards talking into his communicator, his gaze locked on her.

Her sudden escape path had drawn attention to her, blowing the cover of harmlessness that she'd put on only moments ago. Exposed by her flight, she now had two enemy forces to deal with, one that she didn't want to open fire on in case they were only honest lawmen doing their jobs. She was desperate, but she didn't want to murder an innocent cop. She had one bit of advantage, though. The *federales* would announce themselves as authorities before opening fire on her.

There was always the possibility that the murderers would use that ruse to get her to hold her fire, her paranoia reminded her.

Just run, she ordered herself, and she burst through the edge of the crowd, disappearing into an alley. It was a narrow squeeze, and she couldn't get a good head of steam running, but glancing back, she saw another well-dressed gunman fill the mouth of the alley. The man ripped a pistol from under his jacket and snap-aimed at her just as she reached a large garbage bin that blocked the way. She surged ahead, grabbing one end of the bin and lunging up. The gunman's bullet sliced the air between her rising legs, copper-jacketed lead deforming against steel. The shooter adjusted his aim as Asado tumbled in a shoulder roll across the corrugated hatch door. The next shot flew high, stabbing into brick and raining splinters on her. Before the gunner could get off a third shot, two things happened. Asado rolled into the open hatch, landing atop padded garbage bags, pulling her out of the path of fire, and a riot of terror exploded in the crowd behind her.

The third shot missed her and any subsequent gunfire was smothered as security personnel and crowd members lunged, pulling down the pursuing gunman. Agents shouted orders and warnings over bullhorns in the courtyard, and Asado lunged over the edge of the garbage bin, landing on the other side. With the big metal container acting as a shield behind her, she had a free run. She kept her head low and broke into a run toward daylight shining down on the other end.

Commands to halt resounded from the mouth of the alley as she raced away from the orders. She couldn't risk getting into a fight, not now, and capture would only end in one possible outcome—her eating a bullet. Bursting out onto the side street, she looked around for signs of pursuit. Nothing yet, but she wasn't taking chances. Her car was two blocks farther on, and she would have to lose any tails she picked up if she didn't want to bring a strike force of murderers down on Armi and Gloria.

She circled around, taking the long route to her car, walking with purpose, as if she were out on an errand, not fleeing from the law. It had taken only a few brushes of her fingers through her hair to unkink it from her tumble into the garbage bin, and observing herself in the windows of storefronts, she was glad she'd worn dark clothing. Any stains she'd have picked up from the garbage bags were invisible, not that she'd felt any dampness on them.

So far, so good. No one was the wiser to her identity after she'd escaped from the first lady's photo opportunity.

She paused for a moment after ducking into a bakery. Her heart was hammering and she needed to calm down. She ordered a *churro* and some hot chocolate. The sugar-rolled pastry and the similarly loaded drink wouldn't do much to calm her nerves with a rush of glucose through her system, but it was spiritually calming, and she wanted to replenish her reserves of endurance. Sitting in the back of the bakery at a small table, she kept her eye on the entrance as she munched and drank. After she'd downed half of her first refill of the chocolate, she waved off the waitress and left the woman a tip. If no one had come in to check to see if she was in the bakery by now, they wouldn't. No one matching the man who had shot at her appeared in the windows, and she'd have recognized a plainclothes federal agent even through tinted glass. She was safe.

For now.

Steeling herself, she left the bakery and wound a spiral path toward her car.

Cooper's people were going to need the pictures on her camera.

ANIBELLA BRUJILLO SET down the phone, taking a deep breath.

Something had happened at the clinic opening. Her

mole inside the security force hadn't provided any information, but her body double was unharmed, and the event continued without interruption. Anibella's reputation as a brave and dynamic woman wouldn't dissuade her from her duties to the public.

It was a small setback, but not an insurmountable one. Her double would keep up the ruse. The Santa Muerte high priestess picked up her knife and looked to Francisco Casas, pinioned through his forearms and shins with steel spikes, secured to a stone altar. The surface was carved in a prayer to the embodiment of death, and would catch every drop of the victim's blood. Anibella caressed the wounded chemist's cheek and smiled at him.

The razor-sharp blade sliced along one side of his throat, then the other, shallow, capillary-draining cuts that poured blood, but weren't instantly lethal. Smaller vessels bled readily, without leaving the sacrifice with an oxygen-starved brain. A little deeper and she'd have severed the carotid artery, resulting in a swift demise.

The blood was for show, and she sliced almost completely through the skin holding the cartilage shells of Casas's ears to his head, more of the red fluid pouring and filling up the inscribed letters hewn into the surface of the altar. Casas would have babbled, but she'd had one of her minions administer a stupefying drug. As if stroking a lover, she swept the point of the sacred blade down each side of the sacrifice's chest, bisecting his navel and ending at his pubic bone. The cuts met at his sternum.

Casas's brown eyes darted wildly around the room as the cultists surrounding him began to pray. The chant was a variant on an ancient Aztec prayer to Huitzilopochtli, the flayed one, god of war. Anibella had taken to co-opting the ancient Aztec ceremony, sacrificing enemies captured from the Juarez Cartel in a manner befitting the life taker. It was a simple logic, really. In her infinite existence, the goddess of death had taken Huitzilopochtli as her aspect in war as much as her guise as Saint Martha was emblematic of her role as a benign guardian and epitome of forgiveness.

Anibella licked the flat of the knife, tasting the chemist's life on the bloody steel.

"Martha forgives and guides, Huitzilopochtli strengthens and destroys," she said out loud. "Death rules all humankind, and on the day we are born, we move every second toward our inevitable fate. To embrace Martha is to live to the fullest, for there is only one toll to be paid, and all other sins are sublimated by fealty."

The chant in Aztec reached its crescendo, and Anibella proceeded with her cuts. Instead of having to crack the heart's skeletal armor, she severed the sheet of muscle that allowed the captive to breathe. She reached in and clutched the still beating organ and pulled. A sudden seizure struck the sacrifice as she squeezed and wrenched the heart from its place, tearing blood vessels.

The chemist died moments later, a small mercy as his blood completed the writing of the sacrificial prayer to a god's avatar of war.

The spikes were wrenched from the speared limbs, and with a brutal shove, Casas's corpse bounced down a flight of stairs that led deep into the lower bowels of their cavern. By the time he reached the bottom, his skeleton had been fractured in dozens of places.

Anibella set the heart in a metal basin, surrounded by kindling and oil. With the touch of a tongue of flame, Casas's heart was incinerated.

The cult cheered the successful sacrifice.

Anibella's cold, hard gaze silenced them.

"Clean off and get dressed. We have business to attend to," she ordered. "We have been blessed. But we still must earn our place. That means we must destroy the American we know as Matt Cooper."

Their mood not dampened, the cultists walked under a powerful spout, its spray scouring blood from their fingers and faces. Massaged by fingers of water, Anibella Brujillo lost herself to the dream of tearing Matt Cooper's heart, still beating, from his chest.

AARON KURTZMAN INTERRUPTED Barbara Price's examinations of the files.

"We've got some data coming in from Blanca Asado," Kurtzman replied. "Looks like images. No virus."

"Open them. She wouldn't be sending photos without a good reason," Price stated. She followed the wheelchair-bound computer genius back to his station. He pulled up the e-mail that had eventually made its way to his computer and several high-quality digital photos were revealed. Most of them were blurry "hail Mary" shots, but a couple were distinct enough to identify a woman who resembled Anibella Brujillo.

"Blanca says that she doesn't think that's the real deal. She might be a body double," Kurtzman explained.

"Luckily a few of them were in focus," Price said. "But judging by the crowd, it's easy to see why quality suffered."

"The blurrier ones look sharp in thumbnail mode," Kurtzman added. "I'll run these past file photos we have of the first lady."

"Even then, that might be iffy," Price replied. "Some

of them might match up, but then those pictures might be of the double herself."

"I'll work on multiple checks, but the image match programming will take an hour or two."

"I'll see if Striker's awake. He's met the woman and might have a better gauge of who's who," Price suggested.

"Good idea," Kurtzman replied. "I've got a few transcripts of *narcocorridos* that I've been compiling that might shed some light. Nothing about who is in charge of the Santa Muerte cult in Acapulco, but it is a confirmation that the cult is active and it is waging a war against the Juarez Cartel."

"That lead worked out?" Price asked.

"The lyrics match the ritual sacrifices of several members of the cartel over the past couple of years. The cartel itself has 'warning songs,' but a lack of victory ballads and descriptions of fallen foes shows that the cults are still untouched by retribution," Kurtzman explained.

Price looked over the description as she transmitted the photo over Bolan's satellite phone. The laptop would have proved a better medium, but Kurtzman noted that the governor's mansion, and the Executioner's quarters in particular, were under heavy electronic surveillance. The liquid crystal display on Bolan's sat phone would give him a preview, and he could take measures to obscure the image should he be forced to upload it to his laptop.

The descriptions of the murders were gruesome, but one cryptic line disturbed her the most. She read the lyric out loud.

"'And the blood of the enemy will write out our prayers to Huitzilopochtli.'"

"Aztec god of war. He wore the skin of a defeated foe as his cloak," Kurtzman said.

Price frowned. "I figured that's who Huitzilopochtli was. One of the things the Aztecs did was to slay the survivors of enemy armies, to take their strength and add it to their own."

Kurtzman looked at Price, an unspoken question hanging in the air.

"If Anibella is the high priestess of this cult," Price continued, "well, we know she's been watching Striker in action."

"It's superstition, Barb," Kurtzman interjected.

"Like the superstitions that spurred the Simbas or the leopard cults that Phoenix Force fought?" Price countered. "It might be a myth, but that doesn't make the believers any less dangerous."

Price got a reply on her system. Bolan had answered, and the Stony Man mission coordinator frowned deeply. "Things are just getting more and more twisted."

BOLAN AWOKE after four hours of sleep and ate enough to fill the void in his gut. He had allowed himself the luxury of a large meal before getting some sleep the day before, but now he was on war time. Despite the battering he'd taken, he didn't want to become sluggish with overindulgence. He cleaned up and pulled on a black T-shirt and jeans.

He felt the dull pain where Duarte had elbowed him in the chest. The bruise was just over his sternum, and it felt as if some phantom talon was dug into his ribs, trying to pry at his heart. He swallowed a couple of aspirin and focused on what he knew, running off his mental notes, coordinating everything in his mind's eye.

So far, Roykov had provided the Executioner with a trace on the Russian Mafia's presence in Acapulco. With the organization working with the Juarez Cartel, it was only a matter of time before the Mexicans recovered their steadily slipping control over that part of the country's drug trade.

Corsario Garza was the figurehead on top of the cartel's holdings in the state. The man had a fearsome reputation, and was said to have Komodo dragons at his beck and call, foul beasts who could shred a man to the bone in minutes. The creatures were capable of running as fast as a man over short distances, and their jaws could generate thousands of pounds of force to shatter bone and cleave flesh. Being merely bitten would be dangerous, as the meat-eating reptiles weren't the most fastidious of creatures, rotted flesh in their teeth breeding colonies of highly poisonous bacteria that the giant lizards were immune to, but that could kill a man-size mammal.

Having quantified the nature of that threat, the Executioner turned his attention to the far more pedestrian opponents in Garza's employ, dozens of former Mexican army soldiers and cast-off troopers from other military organizations. The Juarez Cartel's connections with Colonel Munoz were no fluke. Allegiances between the Mexican army and the cartels were strong, enabling access to vehicles, uniforms and weaponry with relative ease, and actual army manpower in a pinch.

Dolan had carved a rift between the cartel and their minions in the military with Munoz's destruction. The officer corps were out for easy money, and with several of their own visited by an implacable Executioner, that quick cash was going to have to come from a safer venue. It wouldn't dent the numbers of the dregs kicked out of active service, however. Mexico wasn't a land of opportunity, and jobs for people skilled with rifles and grenades were in even shorter supply. The cartels could take their pick of gunmen from Central and South America.

First the *mafiya* had to be brought down. The Juarez Cartel's reliance on foreign muscle had to be shown as a weakness. If Russian gangsters turned up dead, the cartel's leadership would lose faith in Garza. Losing not only Munoz but the mobsters in the space of a few days would paint Garza as a failure. Whatever manpower that the cartel could muster would be held in reserve as the failed leader of the Acapulco chapter was burned to the ground.

It was a classic strategy that Bolan had used to collapse organizations expanding into new territories. Such ventures were gambles, and although Garza's organization had been in place for a long time, it was still only a branch of the cartel. The heart of Roderigo Montoya-Juarez's concerns was elsewhere. If Acapulco fell, it would hurt, but not enough to engage in a potentially suicidal conflict with a superior force. Bolan simply had to emulate a superior force, and that meant using every trick and weapon in his repertoire. He would need only a few more days of intervention, plowing through Garza's allies to cement the idea that Acapulco was too expensive as a territory. Others might move in, but the jockeying for control would take time and effort, and local law enforcement would be able to minimize the spread.

Bolan felt the phone vibrate in his pocket as he was in the midst of organizing his thoughts. He checked the screen and saw that it was a call from Stony Man Farm. Instead of a voice mail, he looked at the tiny screen, taking in information from a text message.

"Need identity confirmation."

Bolan received an image over the satellite phone's

screen. The resolution of the photograph was good on the liquid crystal display. He studied the photo closely. At first glance, it was Anibella Brujillo, but something was off. He took a USB cable and connected the phone to his laptop and blew up the likeness of Brujillo to examine it in finer detail, his broad shoulders and the angle of the computer notebook's screen making surveillance of the image impossible.

What he saw tensed his jaw in grim recognition. Using the satellite phone, he texted the message back two words.

"Not subject."

When he was out in the field later, on his own and away from the electronic eyes and ears of Anibella Brujillo, he'd be able to ask directly. Until then, he suspected what was going on. Instead of dropping off their prisoner, Casas, and then going about her more public appearances, she'd arranged for a double to put on her face and attend to other matters.

He remembered Roykov's description of the murdered cartel soldiers, their mutilation resembling that of a ritualistic sacrifice.

It didn't take much of an effort to guess who had acquired the photographs of the false first lady. Blanca Asado had promised to make herself useful, gathering information for the Executioner, evidence that would exonerate her murdered sister Rosa. The surest route to that knowledge lead straight through Anibella, and shadowing her at public appearances would be a sure way for the Mexican ex-cop to pick up a lead.

The lead she found was that the first lady had strayed from the schedule she'd given Bolan when she left that morning.

It was likely that the captured chemist was dead. A

loss, but not a tragedy. Casas would be avenged, though. It was a simple matter of course, but he was another mark in Anibella's debit column. Bolan shut off the phone and laptop after clearing their memories. He checked the news and there was a report of a disturbance at a clinic dedication.

He mentally filed the new information. By now, Kurtzman should have gotten a lead on the *narcocorridos* about the Acapulco war. However, the official check-in wasn't for another hour.

He spent the intervening time breaking down his weapons, cleaning them and testing their function. He paid close attention to the gas systems of the M-4 carbine, and that of the Desert Eagle. He'd never had either weapon fail on him, but that was due to diligence and careful ammunition selection on the part of the Desert Eagle. The mighty Magnum cannon was finicky about what it worked with, but years of working with its predecessor, the AMT Automag, had inured Bolan to the needs of a fastidious handgun. The advantages of a fast-loading .44 Magnum pistol that he could carry in a belt holster outweighed the gun's disadvantages. Range, power and penetration, as well as intimidation and its fit to his large hands factored into his choice for it as his signature weapon, so Bolan simply worked with the pistol until he knew it would never fail him. His knowledge and experience were all that he'd needed to render the Eagle a reliable combat handgun.

He had enough ammunition for the assault on the Russians' compound, but he would need to get more for when he went after Garza. He'd have to arrange to have his war bag restocked. If he couldn't arrange that, then he'd simply have to improvise. There was also the potential conflict with Anibella and her followers, but until the Juarez Cartel and its allies had been expunged from Acapulco, she wouldn't force her hand, and Bolan couldn't eliminate her without positive proof that she was a murderer. He needed more than rumor.

It was a delicate balance. So far, everything that pointed to the first lady was merely circumstantial. While Bolan had struck with less evidence to go on, he had acted in the middle of a conflict, when it was shoot or die. His instincts hadn't failed him yet, but so far, she had presented herself as a soldier on the same side.

Her vigilance against the drug trade might only have been a ploy to eliminate competition, but even if it was just a ruse, her information was giving him a straight line into the Juarez Cartel's Acapulco holdings. Still, there was something that tripped Bolan's danger sense toward her. If she came at him, he wouldn't be caught flat-footed, and he'd respond as he always had to attempts on his life.

He'd fight fire with fire.

CHAPTER TWELVE

Vassily Roykov thumbed down a curled corner of medical tape that kept his bandaged, nearly destroyed hand and forearm in one piece. He was doing it to avoid the hard, burning glare of Anatoly Kuriev, but even without seeing those furious eyes, he felt the searing hatred radiating off the crime boss. When the man in black told him that he'd pay, Roykov knew that this was only a small down payment, but the discomfort of being in Kuriev's presence was overwhelming. The silence hung in the air like a choking cloud, thick with surly rage.

"You got away from him?" Kuriev finally snarled.

"I was shot," Roykov replied. "You saw… I'll never use this hand again."

Kuriev stomped over, looming like a wall of obsidian grimness. "He let you run away."

Roykov looked up, blind fear of being found out flashing across his features like lightning. "No, no, he didn't!"

Kuriev growled. "As if you would know what the man in black would have in mind for us?"

Roykov realized that the hulking mob boss's statement

referred to the wraith using him as an unknowing dupe, not a willing accomplice. One hand, wide with fingers like sausages, rose, tensed for a jarring backhand swipe that Roykov had seen snap necks. He tensed, flinching for the blow he knew could rip his head from its socket on top of his spine. When no hammerblow washed over his cheek, he peeked through one slitted eyelid. Kuriev had lowered the massive paw and walked away.

"The…man in black?" Roykov asked. "What is his real name?"

"He has a litany of identities, and each one is false. The only reality we can count on is that he exists, and he is one of the deadliest men on Earth," Kuriev replied. "He is skilled in all forms of combat, and he is as cunning as a nest of serpents. It's no surprise that you got off that yacht. He wanted you to escape so he could follow you to us."

Roykov felt a cold hard lump congealing in the pit of his gut. So far, the mob boss was giving him enough alibis so that if this man did come to rain hell upon the Russian mobsters, he would survive. But what if Kuriev was playing on his sudden guilt over betrayal? The wounded gangster cupped his ruined limb and lowered his head again, trying to swallow his racing thoughts lest they be picked up by the furious mob boss.

"As soon as you called and mentioned him," Kuriev began, "I mobilized the men and acquired some extra backup."

Roykov swallowed. "But he's just one—"

Kuriev's deep-set eyes swiveled toward Roykov, cutting him off like a noose snapping taut at the end of a short drop. When confronted by the man in black, Roykov was engulfed in a state of fear, enough to make him forget his intimidation by Kuriev. Now, back in the mob boss's spotlight, he wished that he'd never taken the wraith's free pass. Every second was like basking in the runoff heat of a blast furnace, his skin baking and cracking. It wouldn't be long before he was a charred, blackened skeleton, and unlike true immolation, he felt every single moment. There was no nervous system to shut down, and every molecule of his being was sensitive to the roasting rage that lashed over him. Roykov never wanted Kuriev to look at him like that again. He'd rather put his remaining good hand over the muzzle of a shotgun and have everything up to the elbow blasted to a pulp of stringy sinew and splintered bone.

"Careyes, his crew, and three of your partners are dead," Kuriev said softly. The calmness of his tone didn't blunt the weight of his words. "Fifteen men. Eliminated in the space of a half hour. That's not counting the boats that the cartel used as their transportation fleet. What manner of ignorance are you suffering that you can't imagine someone as skilled as that one man could come into this compound and leave every one of us a corpse?"

Roykov shook his head. "I'm sorry…"

Kuriev sneered. He looked out the window of his office, watching. Roykov staggered to his feet and looked around the mob boss at the truckloads of men entering the compound. From his new vantage point in the office, he could also see Kuriev's AK-47 propped against the desk. Mounted under the barrel was a 30 mm grenade launcher, and the AK's 30-round magazine had been replaced by a 70-round RPK machine-gun drum. Roykov blinked and looked out the window as the gunmen unloaded from the trucks. Assault rifles with grenade launchers, as well as rocket launchers and medium machine guns, were brought out.

The last time Roykov had seen such a show of firepower was when he had been a teenager fighting on the front lines of Afghanistan. Kuriev was hardening the compound like a forward fire base against a mujahideen assault.

"Too bad we can't get artillery support," Roykov whispered.

"We have it," Kuriev responded. "There are 81 mm mortars hidden outside the compound. I'm willing to bring down high explosives on any part of this place to take out the man you described."

For a moment the blistering anger of the *mafiya* commander had been cooled by a frigid blast of fear. He swallowed again, trying to dispel the hardening knot of fear tightening in his bowels.

Armed with machine guns and grenade launchers, the local mercenaries would bolster Kuriev's forces to turn the compound into a killing box, but even then, there was a shade of doubt in the mob boss's words.

Roykov took a deep breath. If Kuriev was victorious, then his betrayal would disappear like smoke. If the man in black was victorious, then Kuriev wouldn't be able to hurt him from beyond the grave.

It was a precipitous balance, though. One man against a hardened, coordinated, heavily armed army of thugs and murderers. And either side could turn on him at any time.

Roykov was glad when Kuriev pressed the Glock into his hand.

"You're going to fight for your life, too," the mob boss said, his voice a low rumble. "No one sits this out."

Feeling the grip of the polymer frame in his hand, the Russian knew he had to make a choice. Would he fire on his·own compatriots, or would he burn down the man in black? If Kuriev noticed the dilemma he was thrown into, Roykov was oblivious. He went to his quarters, mind racing.

ANIBELLA BRUJILLO RETURNED on schedule, and Bolan was waiting for her.

"Heard there was some excitement this morning," he said.

"Someone opened fire in the crowd," the woman replied. "My bodyguards got me out of there. I guess they were tired of me doing all the shooting for them."

She smiled, but Bolan wasn't laughing.

"Maybe you should keep a lower profile over the next couple of days," Bolan suggested. "I'm not even certain if I want to bring you into the field with me."

"Last night wasn't an inconvenience, was it?" the first lady inquired. "If it was—"

"No. You stayed out of the way, but there are people at work trying to eliminate you. It might even be more than one enemy," Bolan said. He dangled some bait for her. "Don't forget, not only do you have to deal with the Juarez Cartel and their Russian Mafia allies, but there's also the remnants of Rosa Asado's organization. I've heard rumors about what it could be."

Anibella tilted her head as Bolan handed over the transcripts of the *narcocorridos* that Kurtzman had gotten a hold of. Like all such songs, they were vague enough to apply multiple interpretations, but to anyone on the inside of an underworld culture, they would be deadly accurate.

The first lady's eyes narrowed as she read the lyrics. "What the…"

"We've been doing some deeper digging. I have a feeling that we're dealing with a cult that's trying to rise through the ranks and become a power unto itself," Bolan said. "Santa Muerte. Ever heard of it?"

Anibella looked at Bolan and shook her head, still looking at the lyrics, as if the atrocities described within the songs had stunned her into silence.

"It's a pretty crazy cult, not much better than some of the more violent strains of Satanists, except these people are in the service of the embodiment of death," Bolan explained. As soon as he gave that obviously biased and distorted opinion, he could feel waves of tension flowing off her. She glanced up from the file description, fist clenching and crushing the papers between her fingers.

"That's…" she began before she regained control. Anibella's ego had taken a hint when Bolan had slandered her religious beliefs. It nearly had made her lose her cool and correct him, despite only recently "confirming" that she'd never heard of the cult or its religion. "That's pretty intense. I mean, live human sacrifice?"

The governor's wife made a motion of shaking off the information. "Sorry for crumpling these."

"Don't worry. I have them saved on my laptop," Bolan told her. "This isn't the first time I've dealt with psychopathic cults before."

Anibella turned toward him. In her mind, she remembered the whispered encouragement of Saint Martha. *This man you call Cooper has thwarted me before. He has constantly been a thorn in my side.* Her head started to swim and she turned to Bolan's desk. "Can I have a sip of some of your water?"

"Be my guest."

She put the bottle to her lips and tilted her head. Bolan watched as her throat undulated with each swallow, her beautiful hazel eyes hidden behind heavily lashed lids, her black hair spilling over her slender shoulders. Again, Bolan was reminded of a phrase he'd used many times before. One hell of a lady, he pegged her in his mind. His subtle gambit had paid off in labeling her cult as irrational, psychotic and evil. Shaken, she had to recoup her composure and build a strategy as she drank.

"Sorry. Being the first lady by day and a crime fighter by night is thirsty work," she apologized. She put on a dazzling smile that would have disarmed any other man. Only the blood-chilling knowledge that she had most likely murdered Francisco Casas earlier, and the means of his gruesome demise, hardened the Executioner's nerves against her more seductive qualities.

"Need to get some sleep?" Bolan asked. "A nap would do you some good."

Anibella took a deep breath. "I managed to catch a few minutes here and there while in the car."

It was the truth. After cutting out Casas's heart, she'd dozed off on the drive back, awakening only for the transfer from one vehicle to her old SUV. It was a deep, restful nap, the same soothing slumber she'd had after a night of passionate lovemaking with her husband, Emilio. She tried not to think too much about it, but the act of sacrificing an enemy to Santa Muerte had left her with a feeling that could only be described as postcoital.

"Still, it's another two hours until sunset, and we won't be going after Kuriev and his men until then," Bolan told her. "It was a long, tough night, and the day wasn't so easy, either. You sacrifice too much."

Anibella blinked at the reference. Bolan had picked the wording to sound innocent, but cold calculation was the order of the day. If Anibella was involved, then she would be put on the defensive, but it would be the unmistakable proof that the Executioner needed to take her down. So far, the only men he'd seen her slay were mercenaries and thugs taking shots at her, men Bolan himself had engaged in mortal combat. However, by shaking her tree, he'd get a feeling for just exactly what he needed to do.

"I do what I have to do," Anibella said softly. "I have my duty as you do."

Bolan favored her with a smile. She returned it, confused and off balance.

"Get some rest, Señora Brujillo," Bolan replied. "I have some final equipment checks to make, and advance intelligence to go over."

"Thank you, Matt." She stood on her toes and gave him a kiss on the cheek.

She turned and left Bolan's quarters.

He took Kurtzman's scheduled call. "Anything new on the home front?"

"Bad news. Kuriev tripled the manpower at his compound."

"Tripled. Sounds like he knows about me," Bolan said.

"Well, you've developed a reputation that no amount of computer trickery can erase," Kurtzman reminded Bolan. "Kuriev was around when you were paying attention to the more…nefarious schemes of the Soviet Union. He remembers your shoot-on-sight order."

Bolan looked at the footage downloaded to his laptop. He spotted the unmistakable setup of heavy and medium machine guns, and mortar positions dotting the countryside around the compound. It had truly become a hardsite, and his mind went to work. The mortar positions were able to be covered by two machine-gun nests, and two other mortar positions. Redundancy and provisions for loss of control of weaponry cut into his strategy of infiltration and elimination.

"Times like this, I miss the launcher on top of the old War Wagon," Bolan said with a sigh.

"They've got RPGs, too. Not too many of the Families had access to bazookas when you were driving that rolling target," Kurtzman replied.

"Ah, but it had a remote-control launcher and a camouflage system," Bolan returned. He took a deep breath and studied the map. Kuriev had to have had access to a defensive protocol, or worse, had been through one of his blitzes against the KGB high command. "I can handle this. I've had enemies ready for me before."

Kurtzman sighed. "They're not just ready for you. They're ready for an assault by an armored division."

Bolan printed out the aerial photographs. Kurtzman had given him several exposures for him to work out patrol patterns. Kuriev had built up a fortress, and the Executioner knew he was going to be in for the fight of his life. Even if the *federales* could be called in with the thin, minimalist evidence against the Russian and his army, they would be chopped to ribbons. Utilizing the army would give Garza a heads-up that trouble was coming to his doorstep, and even then, soldiers would be lost in throwing themselves against such a defensive position.

Bolan would find a way. He'd attacked more heavily defended installations before. While he would have liked to have had the firepower of Able Team and Phoenix Force on his side, there was no use wishing for things he didn't have. He double-checked the countryside around the compound, searching for advantages. The Executioner might not have more firepower than his opponents, but he had more experience and far more tactical flexibility. A direct attack would be suicide, and considering the firing arcs of the mortar emplacements, even sneaking into the midst of the enemy only meant that Kuriev would fire upon his own forces.

"Bear, any meetings going on tonight?" Bolan asked.

"Kuriev has been asked to come out to see Garza," Kurtzman answered, "but he's not moving after hearing about your presence in the area. He's buttoned up and waiting for the blitz to hit."

Bolan rubbed his jaw. "Is Garza sending representatives in tonight?"

"Nope. The Acapulco boss is too smart to send his people right to the spot where the hammer meets the anvil," Kurtzman announced. "Short of an airstrike or burrowing from the center of the earth, you're not going to have an easy time getting in."

The burrowing line sparked something in the Executioner's mind. "Sewer pipes?"

"I spotted a runoff a few miles away," Kurtzman replied, "but it's surrounded by a guard team, and there's consistent radio traffic to and from."

"So they'd be waiting for me on the other end and be able to send in a kill team, or just fire down the pipe," Bolan concluded.

"Pipes, as in multiple," Kurtzman said. "Let me check something. It'll take a minute."

"I've got the time," Bolan replied.

True to his word, the Stony Man computer genius was done, with ten seconds to spare. "I've got some laid-out pipes connecting farther inland to other resort-style compounds. Kuriev and his crew took over an abandoned resort and reconstituted it over the past year, since the Juarez Cartel began taking some heavy losses against the cult."

"How'd the place end up abandoned?" Bolan asked.

"Garza had it bought out. It wasn't doing well business-wise, so he bought the property and then put it in perpetual development," Kurtzman explained.

"That explains the construction equipment on-site," Bolan noted.

"It'd have been nice to use one of those as a tank," Kurtzman mused.

"Too static. It's easy for a determined man to take out one of those," Bolan countered.

That elicited a chuckle from Kurtzman. "Just because you've done it five or six times…"

"I'm not the only one, Bear," Bolan admonished. "Besides, they still have artillery. An 81 mm might not take out an M-1 Abrams, but a bulldozer would be torn apart."

"Point taken."

"So where would I enter the sewer network without attracting the attention of Kuriev's army?" Bolan asked.

"There's a property two miles up the road. It's in the process of demolition." An aerial photo appeared on the laptop. Bolan printed it out, examining the screen.

"I see the trunk lines for utilities," the Executioner noted. "And it looks like the area's day shift is clearing out."

"And we're checking the highways. No one is coming in for evening work," Kurtzman added. "You'll only have a skeleton crew to deal with at most. At least one security guard, and he'll be bored."

"How are the pipes laid out underground?" Bolan asked.

"We've got a map. There might be a few changes," Kurtzman replied. "There you go."

Bolan laid out the new pipe map out against the satellite photo of Kuriev's defensive emplacements. A plan formed, as did a small smile.

It wouldn't be an easy task, but it would be easier than he'd imagined. Kuriev had kept his eyes open for every avenue of approach except for one. It was a small fracture in an otherwise perfect set of armor, but the Executioner was prepared to mercilessly exploit it. However, it all came down to one man against an army.

If there was one thing Bolan knew how to do, it was how to take advantage of a weakness.

He formulated his plan, noting exactly what he would have to borrow from the demolition site's supplies to augment his own arsenal.

BLANCA ASADO WAS AWAKENED by the warble of the cell phone supplied by Cooper's people. Her hand flopped to it and it flipped open.

"Hello?" she muttered.

"Sorry to disrupt your sleep, Reservist White," Barbara Price's voice said. "We are in conference with Agent Matt Cooper and First Lady Anibella Brujillo."

The mention of Cooper's and Brujillo's names was like a splash of cold water in her face. She jerked to full wakefulness and sat up in the bed, fingers running through her hair. "Not at all, ma'am."

Asado wasn't quite certain why Cooper was talking to her, but the sound of the name "Reservist White" meant that he was trying to arrange a buffer of anonymity to get her closer to him in the investigation.

"Nice hearing from you again, White," Bolan greeted. "It's been too long."

Asado knew that Bolan was establishing a prior level of contact. She wasn't sure exactly how much she "knew" him for the current charade. She opted for a noncommittal, one-word answer. "Sir."

"Agent Cooper informs me that you had been present at the attack on my home the other morning," Anibella said.

Asado raised an eyebrow. "Permission to disclose the nature of that operation, sir?"

"How many times do I tell you guys just to call me Matt," Bolan said. "I explained that you were there as advance overwatch for the meeting. In case people from Asado's infiltration of the governor's mansion and administration might try something."

The cover story had an element of sting in it for Asado, showing distrust for her long-dead sister, but in an earlier conversation, Price had informed her that Bolan would do everything in his power to exonerate Rosa. Asado swallowed. "So that was need to know."

"I also informed her that you were there this morning," Bolan added. "In case anyone tried anything against her while she was making public appearances. Good save."

"No problem, sir…er, Matt."

"I'd like to meet you, Ms. White," Anibella said. "When all of this is over, of course."

"Likewise, ma'am," Asado returned.

"You'll meet me at the original supply drop-off, White," Bolan interjected. "I'm making the first lady sit out this thing tonight. My force options have changed, and I'm going to need an operator with me on this."

"Yes, sir! I mean, Matt."

"We'll convene in an hour," Bolan concluded. "Headquarters will fill you in on updated intelligence."

"All right. See you then," Asado said. Bolan hung up on his end of the conference call.

"Still on the line?" Price asked.

"What's the deal?" Asado inquired.

"He's trying to get some breathing room from Anibella. He confirmed with us that the woman you saw this morning wasn't the first lady. He's also suspicious that the prisoner he and the first lady had taken was murdered earlier today. By her."

"So he's using the excuse of an assault to split from under her watchful eye," Asado concluded.

"Yeah. He'll bring you into the fold, and you'll have time to brainstorm while prepping for the attack," Price said.

Asado looked at the laptop. Blood drained from her cheeks. "We're attacking that? *¡Dios mio!*"

"Cooper has a plan," Price explained. "It's not going to be easy, but you'll have a chance."

Asado didn't notice she'd let loose a low rumble of concern from her throat at first. "Right now, it doesn't look like he's taking it too hard to Anibella to clear Rosa's name."

"He's doing his best," Price replied. "But right now, we have an opportunity to make major inroads against two other criminal organizations while convincing a third that we're aware of their presence and proximity. We're continuing to do what the enemy wants, to get deeper into her good graces."

"And if she's aware that we're on to her?" Asado asked.

"That's why you're still being played close to the vest," Price replied. "You're the ace tucked in the cuff."

"Every Western I've ever seen that used in, ended with the cardsharp holding a belly full of lead," Asado countered.

"That's a risk that Cooper is willing to take," Price told her. "Remember, no one ever shoots the ace in reserve."

Asado took a deep breath. "Dangerous game."

"Tell me about it." Price sighed. "You've got Matt's battle plan now. Study it. He'll go over it in detail with you."

Price hung up and Asado hit the Print function and the portable printer spit out maps and notes while she got dressed, slipping handguns into various hideouts under waistbands or in pockets. By the time she was ready to roll, the printing was done. She looked over the battle plan and was surprised at the audacity of the maneuver.

She just hoped it worked.

CHAPTER THIRTEEN

Mack Bolan was an unmistakable presence to Blanca Asado. She'd only seen him once before, but she couldn't mistake him for anyone else. Tall and powerful, with cool eyes of blue ice, he stuck out in the crowd like an obelisk. He spotted her and a smile crossed his craggy, handsome features.

She paused, standing a few feet in front of him. "So, how do we greet?"

"Like dear friends," Bolan answered. He spread his long, sinewy arms and she stepped into the embrace. As she held his waist and lower back, it was like feeling living, pliable marble. His grip was soft and gentle, but firm.

"It is nice seeing you again," Asado admitted.

Bolan nodded and broke the embrace. He offered her an elbow, and she hooked her hand through it. "We're going to head over to a storage locker not far from here. My people have supplied us with a few extras to make this action work out."

"Does it happen to include the United States Marine Corps?" Asado asked. "Because we're going to need it."

"My group can arrange some weaponry, but unfortunately we can't get everything we want," Bolan replied. "Don't worry. I'll be in the middle of it. You'll be providing my cover and diversionary firepower."

"I'd read that," Asado answered. "You want me on hand, but not in the thick of it?"

"Fire support is never an easy task," Bolan commented. "And given that the enemy has long-range weaponry, it'll be dangerous. I'll work on setting up firing positions for you, but you've got your work cut out."

Bolan turned and started walking for the parking lot. Asado fell into step beside him, jogging a short stretch to get parallel with him.

He tossed her a side glance. "How's your friend Diceverde?"

Asado looked up at him. "He's on the mend. He doesn't want to leave my side. It's frustrating."

"I know how that goes," Bolan replied. "I've had a few friends who didn't want to back out on me."

"They made it out all right, though, didn't they?" Asado asked.

The Executioner took a deep breath, his pace slowing by a half step. "Not often enough to like it when that question's asked."

Asado turned her attention back to where she walked. "But it's not an automatic death sentence?"

"Far from it," Bolan returned. "But it's the losses that stick to you. The thoughts of what might have been."

"You're not trying to keep me out of this, are you?" Asado asked.

"No. I've lost family, too," Bolan told her. "I know what uselessness and loneliness feel like."

"So what did you do about it?" Asado pressed.

"I ended up with my government wanting to arrest me, and with a large criminal organization wanting me dead," Bolan replied. "That's why I want to clear Rosa and you both."

Asado paused and locked eyes with him. "So you gave up your life to keep the rest of us from feeling like you?"

"Too late for Rosa," Bolan lamented.

Asado nodded. "I've got a gut feeling that she'd appreciate what you're doing for us. Thank you, Matt."

Bolan rested a hand on her shoulder. "Small steps. Now come on. Activity is the best tonic for a tortured soul."

Asado continued on to the Executioner's van.

HAL BROGNOLA KEPT UP a network of contacts that steadily grew in size and reach around the globe. Most of them weren't even aware of exactly whom they were working for, while others stayed silent about their work out of loyalty or gratitude to the big Fed. The end result was the ability to arrange supplies for the operatives of Stony Man Farm out in the field. While a great majority were within the United States, Canada and Mexico, he was able to call in favors from overseas, as well. While most would never hear a call to duty, simply because Bolan, Able Team and Phoenix Force helped so many around the world, when they were called, they acted.

In this instance, Brognola had brought together the talents of two of his contacts. One owned and operated the dry storage dock, and arranged windows of inactivity where the Executioner's requested items could be delivered and picked up. The other was a sergeant in the Mexican army. Not all of Brognola's contacts were voluntary, and the sergeant was one of them. He'd been involved in an Able Team operation, on the losing side. Carl Lyons had let the man live, letting him know that he'd be called upon for assistance from time to time.

Now, Brognola called in a favor. The sergeant hadn't

liked what he was asked to obtain from his base's armory, but the thought of the blond *norteamericano* with the chilling eyes and the deranged intensity of a berserker had been all the enticement Brognola needed.

"Do what I say, and you won't see him again," Brognola promised. "Let me down, you can count your days on the fingers of your right hand."

Brognola and the man both knew that the sergeant had had three of his fingers severed by a shotgun blast fired by Lyons. Wanting to live more than two days, the sergeant did as he'd been told.

When the Executioner and Asado arrived, the garage-size storage locker was stocked with Bolan's requested armament. An M-2 Browning machine gun with a tripod, spare barrels and 5000 rounds of ammunition sat alongside an 81 mm mortar and its crates of ammunition.

"Wow," Asado whispered. "You weren't kidding when you said 'fire support.'"

"I've checked your dossier," Bolan said. "Your father behaved more as if he wanted sons than daughters."

Asado nodded quietly in agreement.

"And part of that meant that he arranged for training, so you could be good little *soldadas*," Bolan continued.

"I know how to work the M-2," Asado said. "And how did you know about my training on the mortars?"

"My people have been digging into your father's old contacts," Bolan told her. "It took a while, but my team was able to confirm you could handle this part of my plan. However, it wasn't one of your father's friends who taught you how to use a mortar."

Asado raised an eyebrow, then smiled in appreciation. "Who was it?"

"We picked up hints of a black operation to take down a group of smugglers. Official reports showed that the survivors saw only men, and mortars were used to soften up the group," Bolan said. "You were in the area, but unaccounted for."

"So you know I'm not exactly an angel," Asado replied.

"Anyone who takes the battle right down an enemy's throat never is," Bolan told her. "But checking the dark operations you have been involved with, no civilians were ever harmed."

"Not counting the civilians who just happened to be criminals," Asado amended.

Bolan nodded. "Pardon my imprecise wording. I never consider criminals 'civilians,' no matter how they dress. They're targets. They can either surrender or die fighting."

Asado sighed. "Where have you been all my life?"

Bolan tilted his head. There was no denying an attraction to this brave young woman in front of him, a greater attraction than just the raw animal lust stirred by Anibella Brujillo. It wasn't a purely physical attraction, though. Blanca was an ordinary-looking woman, dressed plainly, with her face clean of makeup and her hair pulled back into a tight, unflattering bun. However, Asado's courage and her ability to survive hardship resonated with Bolan on a deeper level than mere hormonal reaction. This was a woman who not only had felt the same things he had, but had done her job and restrained her bloodlust, killing only to defend herself or others. Anibella worked at seducing Bolan, but Asado's appeal blossomed just by her existence. There were a number of tempting answers that fought for the right to be blurted out, but the Executioner maintained his discipline.

"I've been doing my job. The same as you."

"Not the same," Asado replied, shifting gears from

her momentary lapse into schoolgirl-like admiration. "You've got the license to kill."

"I haven't always had it. But the government decided that if it couldn't stop me, it might as well give me its help," Bolan told her. "And even then, it doesn't always agree with me on who the bad guy is, at least until said villain is finally placed in the ground."

"Which is why you're taking so long to take down Brujillo," Asado said.

"Partly," Bolan answered. "I want to make sure I can get the goods on her. I also want to take advantage of her inside information and her position, too."

"Sounds like playing with a rattlesnake," Asado returned. "You're close enough that she can bite you anytime she wants."

"If she does, then I'll get to take off her head, no compunctions," Bolan replied.

"I want to be here for that," Asado said.

"I know," Bolan answered.

Asado looked at the big man's arctic-blue eyes. She realized that he knew that sometimes, revenge was a catharsis. It enabled someone to dispose of his or her pain. Of course, it could also be a heady, addictive drink that slowly rotted the spirit. It was a finely balanced edge that Cooper walked. Every step he took had to be directed by a greater duty, not just killing for the sake of feeling better.

"He's expecting one," Asado stated, "but you're giving him two."

Bolan nodded. "He's going to look for me to come at him with everything I have, but that's only going to be an attack from one front. Add in a second, and his defensive strategy falls to pieces."

"Let's hope," Asado whispered.

Bolan began loading the arsenal into the van, Asado assisting him with the heavy lifting.

The most important part of the current arsenal was twenty kilograms of plastic explosives. Each brick had the power to shatter an armored vehicle's chassis, and Bolan intended to sow the battlefield with them, utilizing the underground tunnels at the compound. When the blasts shook Kuriev's stronghold, Asado was going to start hammering the Russian's defenses, throwing them off balance while the Executioner did his thing in the heart of the viper's lair.

It was a brutal plan, but against men such as Kuriev, there was no other option, especially considering that the *mafiya* headman was armed to the teeth. Bolan intended to shut him down.

ARMANDO DICEVERDE HEARD the noise and his hand immediately wrapped around the grip of his pistol. He thumbed back the hammer. Gloria stirred in the bedside chair and at the sight of the mirror-polished slide of the pistol, she reached down for the double-barreled shotgun leaning on her armrest.

"You heard that, too?" she asked softly.

Diceverde nodded. He kept his finger off the trigger of the cocked pistol in his hand. It had taken a full day of rest, but he was already feeling stronger. He sat up and didn't feel dizzy. His shoulder still hurt like hell, but the journalist wasn't going to allow that to slow him down.

He got to his feet and stalked closer to the window, keeping close to the wall, letting it shield him. Behind him, he heard Gloria thumb back the hammers on the double-barrel shotgun, two clicks representing an ounce of lead ready to fly with devastating force, capable of shredding a torso to hamburger. He glanced out the window, looking for movement in the shadows beyond, the Colt waiting for four pounds of pressure on its trigger to speak its lethal message.

Meanwhile, his mind raced, analyzing the sound that set him off. It was the roll of a van's panel door that had stirred him to wakefulness. Adrenaline kicked in to bring his thoughts to clarity, the dull throb of his aching shoulder fading away. He made certain that his index finger rested on the trigger guard, because the others clenched around the grip, the checkering on the scales grating like the teeth of a file on his fingertips.

A shadow shifted in the distance, and Diceverde tucked farther back into the darkness of the room. His eyes locked on the movement. Natural epinephrine, released by his body's fight-or-flight reflex, burned through his bloodstream, enabling him to see farther and more sharply. He could make out the silhouette of a head and shoulders. Something flickered in the shadow's form, and Diceverde let out a warning shout, diving to the floor. The window exploded, bullets tearing through the wall.

Gloria's shotgun thundered, the fireballs of the muzzle-flashes strobing violently.

"Gloria! Get down!" Diceverde spit.

There was a thump on the floor. Diceverde's gut tightened and he popped to his knees, Colt blazing out shots toward the gunman. "Gloria!"

"Get down! I'm fine!" she growled. "I hit the floor like you told me to…on the other side of the bed!"

Diceverde took a deep breath. The gunner outside was joined by another. He could see the man's shadow shining through the window, placing him nearly parallel to the stocky little journalist's position. With a twist, he spun and fired the last of the Colt's magazine through the wall. The high-velocity .38 Super bullets tore through drywall and wood, and a strangled cry sounded on the other side. The shooter lurched into view in the window, clutching bloody gut wounds. The crack of Gloria's .22-caliber revolver punctuated the lull in gunfire. The attacker jerked violently as lightweight bullets punched into his riddled body. He collapsed.

"One down," Diceverde whispered, slipping a new magazine into his empty pistol. "Reload and watch the door. They might try to come through the front."

"I'm on it," Gloria replied. "Just watch the damn window, and find some cover yourself!"

Diceverde looked around. There was nothing solid to hide behind, except the other side of the bed. The mattresses and box spring would provide concealment and impede the penetration of the assassins' bullets, maybe even enough to save his life, but if he did so, he'd be bunched up with Gloria. He couldn't allow her to be hurt. He heard the click-clack of shells being fed into the breech of the shotgun. The noise was followed by the tinkle of empty brass as she dumped the shells from her revolver, feeding it fresh rounds.

"I'm fine here," Diceverde lied.

The bell on the front door jangled. Their attackers were in the bookstore. Meanwhile, assault rifle fire chopped through the window and wall, glass remnants of the panes splintering and raining to the floor, gouts of drywall bursting into dust. Getting out the shattered window would be impossible with the enemy penning them in the bedroom.

"Gloria…"

"I know," she whispered in reply. "I'm ready."

Diceverde felt a twinge of uneasiness in his gut, as if he were hearing her final words. He wasn't going to let that happen. Blanca might have been off, meeting with her mysterious ally, but as much as he adored the girl who'd been like a sister, she wasn't here to fight his battles.

He wanted to be there to help her. He kicked himself for being shot in the first place, a wounded albatross hung around Blanca's neck. In a way, he was glad that she'd hooked up with Cooper. At least she could act now, not be left as a bystander while her sister needed justice done, to be avenged and have her name cleared. Diceverde knew that there was very little that he could do to help her anymore. His contacts were nowhere nearly as extensive as Cooper's people.

That just left Gloria as his responsibility. His eyes narrowed and he took a deep breath.

"Gloria," he whispered. "Get on this side of the bed. Slide under if you have to."

"What? Why?" Gloria asked.

"Get over here now, damn it!" Diceverde gritted. He turned and fired his Colt through the door to the bedroom, aiming at chest height. As soon as the bullet holes appeared on the door, thunder ripped the upper panels to splinters. "Move!"

Gloria slithered under the bed as AK-47 fire slashed through the air. Diceverde had guessed correctly. They didn't want to kill the pair outright; they wanted prisoners. Firing high, despite the obvious fact that their targets would be hugging the floor, the rifles were merely distractions. Something else was up. Diceverde lowered his aim and fired out the rest of his magazine. The assault rifle fire abated for a moment, a cry of pain ringing out followed by angry curses. The 130-grain bullets in Diceverde's Colt were from his second magazine, round-nosed copper-jacketed slugs designed to slice through wood and flesh easily. He wasn't certain how effective they'd be against body armor, but it definitely sounded like it had some bite.

"What now?" Gloria muttered, pulling the shotgun behind her.

Diceverde wrapped his hand around the barrels of the scattergun. "I'm going to open the back door for you. You just have to run like hell."

"Leave?"

"They want me alive. Otherwise they'd have just fired through the walls. You've seen what those rifles can do," Diceverde told her, nodding toward the ragged holes torn by enemy slugs.

Gloria sighed. "No. I'm not going."

"Chances are they want only one prisoner. They don't know that much about you," Diceverde said. "They came to take someone back, but they're not going to want excess baggage."

Gloria's dark brown eyes watered at the thought.

"You have to run, baby," Diceverde said. "I'll be okay."

"Damn it…"

"Run," the journalist said. He shouldered the shotgun and pulled both triggers, blowing any remaining glass out of the windowpanes, spitting a cloud of lead pellets into the night toward the sniper that was pinning them in.

Gloria moved like a snake, darting through the cleared window and slithering bonelessly to the ground outside. Her revolver was clamped in her fist, and she scurried on her hands and knees through the low foliage around the wall. Diceverde reloaded his Colt and opened fire, blazing away to keep his lover covered.

The gunners outside returned fire, sweeping high so as not to harm the journalist. That gave Gloria a chance to escape. The Colt ran empty, slide locking back at the bottom of his third and last magazine. After that, all he had were four shells for the shotgun. He dropped back down, listening for enemy gunfire. The rifles continued to hammer, sawing through the wall and blowing out plaster from above his head. Powder clogged the journalist's eyes as he fumbled one shell into the breech, the other tumbling and rolling on the hardwood floor. He didn't want to waste time hunting down the shell and maybe lose another trying to load a replacement. He snapped the shotgun shut and lifted the gun up, blasting away with his payload. The rifles outside stopped.

He broke the shotgun open again, thumbing in shells. He didn't lose any this time and the shotgun closed, locking with a snap. The tattered bedroom door slammed inward with a kick and he swiveled, opening fire. Both barrels blazed at once, a grunt rewarding Diceverde. Something clattered on the wooden floor.

"God da—" was all he could get out before the world turned into a white-hot sun of pain.

Blind and deaf, there was nothing he could do. Someone tore the shotgun out of his hands. Something crashed across his cheek and jaw, and he heard a muffled utterance on the other side of the curtain of numbness that had suffocated his ears. Another impact bounced off his desensitized head. Someone had to have been taking out his frustration on Diceverde. His only saving grace was that the stun grenade had obliterated his senses. When he came around, he knew that his face would be a wrecked mass of bruises.

Hands hooked under his arms and dragged him half to his feet, pulling him along. He tried to allow himself to go limp, his toes skittering along the wooden floor. It felt as if he'd been staring into a spotlight, his ears filled with cotton, but eventually he could make out movement and shapes. He crashed into the back of a van, sprawling on the floor. A kick in the ribs pushed him deeper into the vehicle. Already, his face was regaining feeling, minor sparks fanning into roaring fires. He could feel the blood congealing on his lips, chin throbbing.

"Bastard!" one of the gunmen growled. "You killed Chewie!"

"She wants him in one piece," another snapped. "He'll get it. Don't worry!"

Diceverde tried to spit, but his lips were so busted apart, all he could do was drool. "Who wants me?"

"You'll meet her soon enough, prick," the angered thug growled. "It'll be the interview of your life."

The pissed-off goon chuckled malevolently, giving Diceverde a slap on the cheek before he added, "The last interview of your shit life."

CHAPTER FOURTEEN

Bolan held the choke hold for another two seconds after the night watchman stopped struggling. He didn't want to strangle an innocent man to death, and he lowered him to the ground, checking his pulse. The guard's pulse was strong, and his chest rose and fell, sucking in air. With Bolan's fist jammed under his carotid artery, it had taken only a few seconds for the hapless Mexican to slump into a dreamless slumber.

"He'll be okay," Bolan said to Asado, who watched with concern.

"Good," she finally replied after a few moments of staring at the unconscious watchman. Until this moment, she'd been glad that she hadn't needed to engage in a gunfight with otherwise honest lawmen sent after her by Anibella Brujillo. She didn't think that she could take down an armed cop with the stealth, speed and certainty of Cooper, and she knew she couldn't have done it without killing him.

Bolan looked at her for a moment before binding the guard's wrists and ankles with cable ties. He scanned the construction site looking for a safe spot for him.

Given the firepower at Kuriev's base, he knew the site was going to take a massive pounding.

"Blanca, I'll set up our equalizers. You have to take him out of the bombardment area. A mile down the road will do it," Bolan ordered.

Asado looked quizzical. "I'm not afraid—"

"But I am afraid that this guy will get chewed up in the cross fire," Bolan admonished. "I'm not going to leave you behind. I do need you to cover me."

"All right," Asado said, helping Bolan load the unconscious guard into the backseat of the car.

Asado was gone for ten minutes. In that time Bolan was able to mount the .50-caliber machine gun on its tripod, and was in the middle of placing the 81 mm mortar when she'd returned.

"How'd it go?" Bolan asked as Asado helped him adjust the aim of the mortar tube.

"I put him in a roadside ditch. When he wakes up, he'll be able to crawl to the road, but the ditch should provide some shielding in case a mortar shell flies a little too far," Asado replied.

"How does the setup work for you?" Bolan asked her.

Asado studied the scene and frowned. She scanned Kuriev's distant compound with her binoculars and checked her companion's wind charts. A stiff breeze could mean the difference between taking him out or the enemy. The launch tube, and the breeze taken into account, Asado nodded. "Better than I could have done it. I wish you'd been on hand for that op."

"You didn't harm any civilians, and you didn't hit any of your own people," Bolan replied. "That's all I need to know."

"And you'll give the signal when you're ready to

go?" Asado asked. "I don't think I will be able to communicate with you in the tunnels."

"When you see the earth shake and the enemy compound start to collapse, that's when I want the party to start," Bolan replied. "We still have another twenty shells to bring from the van."

"I found a dolly," Asado replied. "Who'd have thought that they'd have things to cart heavy materials around a construction site?"

Bolan grinned. "I take it you want me to go?"

Asado nodded. "I'll be able to get them over here by myself. I just want you to be able to make your hit and get out. There's a hell of a lot of rot in Acapulco, and you've only been taking baby swipes at it."

"The nest had to be stirred up so I'd know where all the drones would go to fight," Bolan replied. "Now that they've set up their defenses, they've focused me right on them."

Asado nodded. "Be careful, Matt."

Bolan gave her a warm smile and a squeeze of her hand. "You, too, Blanca."

THE TUNNEL WAS WIDE enough for Bolan to move through with ease. Though only four feet tall, its width allowed the tall soldier to stoop as he pulled along an improvised sled laden with explosives from the construction site. Normally he would have wanted to carry such an arsenal on his person, but given the firepower he'd already been loaded with and the fact that he wanted to spectacularly upset the foundations of Kuriev's compound, literally, there would have been no way for the Executioner to move with nearly a hundred pounds of C-4 plastique.

Fortunately, thanks to Bolan's great strength and endurance, the smoothness of the sled bed's bottom, and the foot of water in the sewer tunnel, hauling the war load was easy. The width of the tunnel also helped him to accommodate his M-4 with its grenade launcher. While he had an earpiece communicator, he wouldn't be able to make contact with Asado until he broke above ground. Not that she would have the power to do anything while Bolan was under ten feet of dirt and half a foot of concrete.

Still, if the underground tunnels were a weakness that Kuriev was aware of, an encounter in the dark would prove disastrous. To alleviate the potential for an ambush, Bolan wore night-vision goggles and had an infrared illuminator "lighting" the tunnel for the NVGs. A defense force would see Bolan's flashlight coming from a mile away if resorting to conventional observation abilities. There was the possibility that they, too, had goggles that would pick up the infrared light coming off his illuminator, but it was a risk Bolan was willing to take to get the element of surprise.

Despite the relative smoothness of pulling the parcel of high explosives, Bolan took his time to spare his back extra strain. He took rest breaks periodically, as well, turning off the IR light to check for distant lamps with the amplification goggles. Seeing none, he continued along, counting off the paces until he knew he'd reached the edge of the compound. There was a crimp in the tunnel as it met the outer wall, branching off into smaller pipes off the main. The narrower passages were barely large enough for Bolan to put his arm into.

The Executioner had assembled half a dozen pipe bombs back at the construction site. These he took, implanted a radio detonator and set in the mouths of six of the branching pipes. The radio detonator was set to fire the pipe bomb like a bottle rocket, sending it down the tubes to blow up after traveling a certain distance. Even if Kurtzman's records of the plumbing plans were off, the detonation of five pounds of C-4 in the pipes would cause considerable damage.

And then there was the hundred pounds of C-4 that perched where the compound wall parted to allow the underground pipe to enter. The radio detonators stuck into the massive bricks were on a separate frequency. It took a few moments for the Executioner to set up the huge mound to go off. He shouldered three improvised satchel charges and turned, going deeper into the main pipe as it ran under the compound.

Checking a pedometer, which measured his movements against a printed map on waterproof paper and ink, Bolan managed to place the demarcation line between the pipe outside the compound and inside within five feet according to the scale. It wasn't perfect, and with the main blaster seated right at the wall junction, he hoped to at least raise a major distraction. The pipe bombs would increase the amount of confusion, and even if the scale of the pipe layout had been off, the explosions would still sow chaos. Bolan's three remaining satchel charges and the M-203 attachment under his rifle would provide the rest of his punch against Kuriev's assembled army of killers. He had plans for the placement of the satchel charges, but if the actual layout strayed from the original, at least he was able to improvise on-site.

Bolan paused, killing the power to his infrared illuminator. Movement scraped on the sides of the tunnels ahead of him. There was no sign of light, either visible or detectable only by night-vision goggles, so it could have been tunnel-bound creatures, rats or snakes.

The skittering movements continued. Again, he thought of rats, but there was no attendant squeaks and chirps associated with a large number of rodents. Bolan turned on the infrared illuminator and scanned the darkness ahead. The walls seemed to be covered in some form of shifting surface. At first, he assumed it was simply moss, but one "branch" danced away from the edge, a low flat form, no longer than three inches, with a curved tail that curled up over a flat, broad back.

Scorpions. The walls of the tunnel ahead were blanketed in scorpions. Bolan usually was prepared for any local wildlife and he had antivenin for species of Mexican serpents, but he hadn't anticipated scorpions, since the only native species with significant venom to threaten an adult human was the Arizona Bark scorpion, a species that usually was no threat to a healthy man, barring anaphylactic shock. As such, the only antivenin for the Arizona Bark scorpion was merely experimental, and the point was moot because the species only occurred in the wild in Northwestern Mexico, not down in Acapulco.

Not naturally, at least. Bolan knew that scorpions only utilized small amounts of their venom for taking prey, saving the heavily concentrated reserves their body kept for protection against large predators, which was the only reason the creatures stung human beings. One scorpion sting would prove to be painful and debilitating, and in an extreme circumstance, put a person into shock. Multiple stings by frightened scorpions would result in a flood tide of poison coursing through his system and would definitely set off a body-wide allergic reaction, causing his respiratory tissues to release histamine, suffocating him. The venom of one scorpion would make him more sensitive to the next sting, and so on.

One stab with the barbed tail would be painful, but if he overreacted and disturbed others, it would be fatal.

The Executioner took a deep breath, cinched the satchel charges a little more tightly, and continued past the shifting mass of poisonous arachnids. He only needed to maintain his cool. Most people would end up in a panic, and their thrashing would only incite the barb-tailed desert predators to lash out in self-defense. The creatures shifted, plopping into the knee-deep water around him, which meant that Bolan would pick up several stowaways as he moved through the tunnels. As he reached the beginning of the mass of scorpions, he felt their tiny bodies bounce off his shoulders.

The blacksuit would provide some protection against the stingers, but his head and neck were exposed, as well as his hands. Fortunately, Bolan's skintight suit had snug cuffs at the wrists, neck and ankles. Years of fighting in jungle environments with all forms of biting insects had clued him in on the ideal form of clothing. The high-tech fabrics he wore were breathable and retained their shape, never stretching and distorting. Initially, the design was to avoid snagging on barbed wire or branches, but an added benefit was to keep parasites and pests from crawling into Bolan's clothes with him. But that snug protection had its limits, unfortunately.

Only having progressed ten feet into the now-living tunnel, Bolan felt scorpions land in his hair. The spiny claws at the end of their spindly legs pricked his neck as they crawled from his hairline. He gripped the handle and handguard of his M-4 more tightly, fighting off the desire to brush the crawling creatures from his skin. The last thing he wanted to do was to antagonize them.

One of the scorpions walked down onto his forehead, crawling over the housing of his night-vision goggles. Its claws suddenly flashed into Bolan's view and he tensed, slowing. The hooked feet of another scorpion pricked at his right ear, tickling.

"Move," he whispered to himself. One foot in front of the other, smooth and stealthy strides so he didn't splash, breaking the surface of the accumulated dirty water and making noise, he continued to advance. Knots formed in his neck and shoulders where tension seized him. The only sound he made was the plops as scorpions fell off him into the stagnant sewage.

The excessive moisture wasn't the ideal environment for the scorpions. They were designed with the ability to retain fluids from the insects they captured and ate, but landing on the thick, polluted water hadn't harmed many of them. Some, embedded in sludge, kicked and struggled, breaking surface tension and choked in slime covering their airholes. The rest struggled, cleaving to islands of muck or paddling furiously to reach the wall. The ones that had landed on thick flotillas were better off, scurrying to the wall and pushing to join their brethren. This wasn't a natural situation for the horde of miniature desert predators. They'd been imported as a line of defense. No wonder Kuriev hadn't wasted time with other guardians in the sewer tunnel.

The scorpions at the edge of the water didn't like being jostled, however, and they started fighting against one another to keep from being knocked back down into the sewage. Tails lanced violently, bulbous claws snapping in the air as the displaced scorpions struggled to regain their place on the wall. Bolan slowed as he spotted a cone of light burning down into the tunnel. A small mound of staggered and dazed scorpions sat on a mountain of sand that had been dropped into the sewer. Bolan could see spindly claws still breaking the surface of the sand as the scorpions struggled free.

The sand created a land bridge where the scorpions could get to the walls over the top of the water. The cone of light emanated from an open sewer hatch. A lit cigarette tumbled through the opening and sizzled out as it hit the sand pile.

"No! You want to blow us up?" someone snarled in Russian.

"If you're worried about methane in the sewer, the hole has been open for hours. It's well ventilated," came the bored, irritated reply.

Bolan slowed his pace, crouching. The two Russians weren't looking into the sewer entrance as they hadn't cast shadows in the spilled light. He slowly lifted one leg and stepped across the sand pile. He pressed the satchel charge into the mound, digging it down. Scorpions lanced their tails at the canvas-covered explosives, then scurried away harmlessly. With gentle ease, he scooped up handfuls of sand and poured it over the top of the charge, granules pouring on top of the bomb to disguise it. By gingerly handling the sand beneath their feet, Bolan avoided attracting the defensive reactions of the scorpions as he let it cake the soaking satchel charge. The radio detonator inside had been primed before he'd set it down, and now, half buried and wrapped in dirt-colored canvas, it was invisible. All the while, Bolan kept his attention on the cone of light falling down on him.

If he'd been seen in the sewer, he'd have milliseconds of life left.

As it was, he also had to make certain he didn't disturb the scorpions. While the venom of one sting wouldn't be fatal, it would make the tissues of his hand swell to the point of temporary uselessness. He didn't want to start the battle already handicapped. With a shift of his weight, he crossed the sand bridge and continued deeper into the tunnels, pausing as he heard a sudden curse in Russian. Bolan tensed as he lifted the M-4, ready to begin shooting.

"Goddamn it! The fucking bugs are crawling out of the sewer!" the guard snapped.

"So keep an eye on the entrances, Nikolai!" a voice shouted back. "What would you rather have? A scorpion coming out of the sewer or assassins?"

The sullen silence that followed was an answer.

ANATOLY KURIEV SNEERED at the sentries scurrying away from the sand-colored scorpions crawling around the sewer entrance. The scorpions had been a last-minute idea. The crates dumped into the open manholes in the compound were a stopgap, especially since he didn't want to waste any more men guarding tunnels. He had a small team out on the shore, where the runoff dumped out of the pipe, and they were connected to him by a solid landline. Jamming would prove too easy to simulate, and if the line were cut, his defenders would be aware instantly.

On his desk was a .44 Magnum Smith & Wesson revolver, a weapon in the same caliber the deadly man in black carried when he struck Moscow's high command all those years ago. Kuriev had been on the scene as part of the guard force. He'd watched in numbed terror as one of his compatriots fell dead from nerve gas after rushing into the room full of murdered KGB leaders. His right cheek twitched, spurring the memory of how his face became partially paralyzed by the passing whiff that would have killed him if he hadn't jammed the atropine injector into his chest. As it was, the right side of his face had remained numb, without sensation for years. He could see and hear, but the motor controls of his face had been damaged. His right eye drooped from the gas' sting.

"Get bitten by those little bugs, you bastard," Kuriev growled. "If you're coming through the sewers, get bitten and die screaming and paralyzed like my friend—"

"Sir, scorpions don't bite, and their venom doesn't cause para—"

Kuriev's hard gaze fell upon the lieutenant who had spoken up. The younger Russian swallowed, realizing that he had committed a grave error, correcting his commander.

"I'm sorry," the young man replied.

"Be glad I need you as cannon fodder far more than I need to take out my anxiety on your misbegotten head," Kuriev growled. "But go on, stupid one. I'm bored waiting for death to come. Let me educate you."

The subservient mobster nodded. "Yes, sir."

Kuriev took a puff from his cigarette, letting the smoke burn in his lungs. "I'll leave it to the man in black to punish you for me."

"You really think he exists?" the lieutenant asked.

"I was there at the Moscow massacre, fool. Why do you think I speak so stiffly?" Kuriev asked. He slapped his right cheek. "Why do you think that my face is not so animated?"

"I thought it was your Afghan assignment," the lieutenant replied.

Kuriev studied the younger man for a moment. "You fool. He won, you know. He destroyed the KGB, turning it into just another pathetic police agency, instead of the brilliant conglomerate that had the whole world caught in its clutches. We were gods ruling the Earth, until he came and destroyed our power."

"I thought it was the cold war overspending," the lieutenant said. "I can't believe that one man was responsible for crippling the entire KGB. And even—"

A thundering detonation threw Kuriev to the floor as the western wall of the compound suddenly disintegrated, hurled skyward in a cone of choking dust and debris. The young lieutenant, cut off in midproclamation by the blast, was now screaming in horror, his shoulder crushed by a rock the size of his skull, blood jetting from severed arteries, the limb dangling from a spot six inches lower than it should have.

"No," Kuriev snarled, "the man in black does not exist? And he's not going to attack us?"

The lieutenant fell silent, perhaps due to blood loss and shock, but Kuriev felt it was the realization that he was wrong.

The monster was real, and he had announced his existence with a peal of thunder and the screams of the wounded and the dying.

CHAPTER FIFTEEN

The first blast went off like a charm, shaking up the entire compound. Secondary blasts followed, as the pipe rockets finished their hurtling paths through plumbing into various buildings in the hardsite and impacted with jarring force. Bolan hit the third detonator's button and the sewer accesses hurled up thunderous volcanoes of fire, smoke and debris, throwing more shock waves among the defending Russian mobsters.

The Executioner had come up through the basement of the main house. He hadn't placed any charges under the building, but he wasn't going to spare Kuriev's temporary palace. Screams split the air from the wounded and dying outside, finally audible after the rumbling of multiple blasts died down. A rush of air, dust and flying scorpions flew up through the basement's sewer access, pushed along by the backblast pressure of the multiple explosions. Most of the arachnids were dead, but a few of the creatures skittered crazily away from the Executioner.

"There's your signal, Blanca," Bolan whispered as he kicked open the door to the basement.

Four of Kuriev's bodyguards whirled at the sound of splintering wood from behind them. Bolan's sudden appearance froze them in surprise, giving the Executioner three seconds of unimpeded freedom to whip up his suppressed M-4 and sweep the quartet with a salvo of high-velocity tumblers. Open-tipped bullets struck soft, yielding mass and upended, spinning like a rotary saw through pulping flesh, carving apart internal organs with savage power. The Russians dropped their AK-47s unfired, bodies collapsing moments later into mounds of jumbled limbs.

Bolan reloaded the partially spent rifle and let it hang on its sling. So far, with the distraction of his wake-up call, no one had noticed the ripping slash of the silenced assault weapon. He moved over to the dead men as the first warble of Asado's mortar shells sounded outside. He scooped up an AK in each hand and poked them through the window as an 81 mm shell detonated in the middle of the yard in front of the house. A powerful wind caused by overpressure blew through the broken windows, the remaining splinters of glass flying everywhere, forcing the Executioner to shield his face with his arm.

Roars of anger resounded on the second floor, dissolving into shouted orders. Kuriev was recovering his command of the situation, bellowing out the window. Rifle fire erupted upstairs, and through the shattered windows, Bolan could see the flare of Kuriev's muzzle lighting the compound.

"Open fire! Open fire!" Kuriev roared.

Bolan rested the handguards of his confiscated AKs on the sill, leveling their front sights at a squad of Mexican hardmen added to Kuriev's forces as they rushed to take up defensive positions at the compound wall. Leaning into the rifles, he held down their triggers, burning off sixty rounds in a long, sweeping burst that raked the mercenaries.

Kuriev's rallying orders suddenly turned to a litany of curses. "He's downstairs! He's inside! Open fire! All perimeter units! Fire on the main house!"

The Executioner saw Kuriev hurtle from the second-floor window, land in the dirt and roll with the impact. He was about to lunge out after him when the wall next to the window shattered with a torrent of .50-caliber bullets. Bolan hit the carpet and crawled as heavy machine guns and assault rifles opened up on the house. The upper floors shook violently as mortar shells slammed into the roof, smashing out massive craters of destruction with each hit. The ceiling spewed cracking plaster dust with the shattering blasts as the walls were shredded under the sweeping arcs of autofire.

Bolan let out a roar to equalize the pressure inside and outside his head to protect his hearing from the ear-splitting torrent of fury that Kuriev unleashed in response to the Executioner's infiltration. Meanwhile, more of Asado's fire arced in, spears of lightning that shattered men and buildings. Sooner or later, the defenders were going to realize that Asado wasn't one of their own displaying a lousy aim. Fortunately, Bolan's plan had been fine-tuned not to expose her for that long. The shells were for softening up the main force of Kuriev's mobsters, and the perimeter fire bases were to be targeted by a different heavy weapon after a set amount of time.

Meanwhile, Bolan aimed his M-203 grenade launcher through the shattered wall of the house and triggered a 40 mm charge into the courtyard. The fragmentation grenade detonated with body-ripping power, hurtling more Russian and Mexican gunmen in lumps of mangled flesh and shattered bone. He opened the breech and fed a new round into the chamber. A second blooper stabbed toward the spot where a mobster was coordinating others, visible partially through the wrecked wall. The round fell short, only splashing the crowd with shrapnel and shock waves, instead of engulfing them in the full fatal force of detonation.

Bolan rolled to the side, crawling for cover as rifles ripped into his old position. Streams of steel-jacketed lead tore the floor up, spraying splinters everywhere. He crawled on all fours, zipping through a hallway and gaining the cover of a broken wall just in time to avoid the concussion of a hand grenade. Stingers of razor wire plucked at Bolan's shoulder.

The Executioner kept low to the floor as enemy weapons chewed at doors and windows, rifle rounds stopped by the wall. The heavy machine guns no longer tore mercilessly through the main house. He heard a beep in his earphone.

"Matt?" Asado asked.

"You've got the other positions busy?" Bolan asked.

"Knocked out two before the third one started on me," Asado returned. "But it's occupied with me, not you, and I'm behind enough dirt and concrete."

"Good. What about the fourth position?" Bolan inquired.

"You mentioned before we might not get a clear shot. I tried with the mortars, but it didn't reach, and the machine gun didn't hit. The good news is that they can't shoot me, either," Asado replied.

"I'll do what I can. Pull back," Bolan ordered.

"What about the Barrett?" Asado asked. "It has the range and it is lighter."

Bolan's lips tightened into a hard line. "Be careful."

"From the sound of things on your end, you're not one to talk," Asado retorted.

"Business as usual for me," Bolan answered, firing off another 40 mm grenade through a shattered wall. The shell spiraled into a group of ex-Soviet army commandos who were closing on the wrecked mansion to confirm Bolan's end. Six ounces of high explosive launched razor wire at blinding speeds, perforating the mobsters. Shredded, their corpses collapsed into the dirt.

Bolan scrambled away from his vantage point, avoiding hammering salvos of assault-rifle fire that sought him out. Switching back to his M-4, he raked a pair of gunmen with 5.56 mm flesh rippers, knocking them to the ground like rag dolls. With a shoulder roll, he tumbled under even more return fire, hearing the shouted orders of Kuriev outside.

"I missed him," Bolan murmured. "Have to fix that."

"Yes," a voice croaked to one side. The Executioner whirled and saw Roykov, pinned under a collapsed section of ceiling. His face was splattered with blood, but where it hadn't been painted with crimson gore, it was pale and clammy. The crushed gangster was in his final moments of life. "The bastard killed everyone in this house just to get rid of you."

The Executioner crawled over to Roykov. "Almost everyone."

Roykov shook his head. "A man knows when he's dying. Just kill that arrogant fuck before he gets away."

Bolan reached down for his Desert Eagle to give the Russian a mercy shot, but Roykov's head drooped to his shoulder, his eyes glassy and unfocused.

The Executioner dug battered AKs out of the rubble and checked their loads, his own assault rifle slung across his back. By the time he was finished, he had a half dozen rifles ready to go, six chunks of disposable firepower at hand. He looped five over one shoulder and poked the first AK up, emptying thirty rounds in a hammer storm that chopped into an unwary thug, hurling him backward into two of his friends. Pinned by a corpse, they were easy targets for the final shots in the magazine. He dumped the empty weapon and whipped a fresh one off his shoulder. Pressed against a doorway, Bolan fired from the hip and ripped a 3-round burst into the belly of a fourth of Kuriev's defenders, folding him over.

"Damn you!" Kuriev shouted. His rifle blazed angrily in the distance, but his shots bounced off the chunk of wall that Bolan had braced himself behind. The Executioner popped around the other side and triggered a burst, trying to seek the mob boss, but the Russian threw himself to the ground to escape his judgment. Bolan pulled back and ran into the depths of the house as the survivors tried to penetrate his cover. Finding another position was easy, and he burned off the last of the second AK's magazine, taking out a sharpshooter who had scaled the perimeter wall in an effort to get a better angle against him. The rifleman tumbled eight feet off broken adobe with a sickening crunch that punctuated his death cry.

It was a nickel-and-dime defense. With the wreckage of the house to work from, Bolan was in a position of strength, with considerable firepower to fight back.

The ceiling above him creaked and groaned, drawing his attention from the mobsters trying to root him out. Bolan threw himself away from the wall, charging for a more stable section, but snapping floorboards and support struts signaled that he would be too late. The roof collapsed, and the Executioner was slammed into the floor by the crumbling ceiling.

BLANCA ASADO GRABBED Bolan's Barrett M-98 in its case and, as an afterthought, a mini-Uzi submachine gun with a pouch of magazines. The surviving enemy fire bases had yet to find her range, and were peppering the countryside up to and including the construction site with mortar shells and .50-caliber bullets. Thanks to use of a PVC pipe wrapped around the muzzle of her own M-2 Browning, she was able to utilize both the 81 mm mortar and the heavy machine gun with relative impunity. Only the sound of explosive shells arcing through the air gave the Russian defenders a direction to target her.

It was a large area for two mortar tubes and two heavy machine guns to cover, and Asado raced across the sands, despite the twenty-pound weight of the long Barrett rifle bouncing on her shoulders. It wasn't going to be easy, but she darted between clumps of cover. More than once she felt the shock waves of an 81 mm shell landing nearby, close enough to rattle her, but still far enough away to avoid shrapnel. When a stray .50-caliber bullet cut the air near her, she could feel the rush of wind in its mighty wake. She remembered the cartridges that fed into the Browning back at her own position, and the fat, long rounds were massive and intimidating. Pushed to nearly three times the speed of sound, she knew that if she were in the path of one, her suffering wouldn't last long. She remembered the devastation the slugs could produce when they struck a human being, bones turned to splinters and muscle and organs hammered into soft pulp by a ton of kinetic energy.

Asado hit the dirt as a line of machine-gun fire tore up a row of explosions along the ground. The gunners had to have spotted her through binoculars, and only the uneven ground gave her a moment of respite as

750-grain mankillers punched into the berm she'd dived behind. Sand vomited skyward, raining down on her as the machine-gun team cut loose with savage abandon. She unslung the Barrett and crawled on her elbows back the way she had come, sidetracking into a gully behind the berm to lose them temporarily. She pushed the long barrel out over the lip of the gully.

Through the high-powered Bushnell scope, she saw the tongue of flame erupting from the enemy machine gun. It was still firing at the small mound she'd initially taken cover behind, and the optics made it seem as if she could reach out and touch the gunners. She could make out their faces, and she pressed the stock against her shoulder.

Asado pulled the trigger on the suppressed Barrett M-98, and the recoil of the .50-caliber round spiked violently against her collarbone. The image in the crosshairs blurred as the rifle jumped and she struggled to hold the weapon down, looking for her initial point of aim. The two men manning the machine gun were still firing at the mound. She'd missed with the first shot, and she had no idea if she'd gone long, or the bullet had landed short. She cursed herself for not having made accommodations for the extreme range. She could only assume that she'd fired short and, not wanting to spend several minutes fiddling with the scope, she lifted the crosshairs until one of the ranging hatches beneath the center bisected the face of the man at the spade triggers of the enemy machine gun.

"Come on, Blanca," she grated. She held on to the Barrett tight and this time when the trigger broke, she rode through the recoil, the scope only jumping a little before settling back down on her targets. The machine gunner jerked violently, spinning away from his weapon. She'd gotten her range, but she was uncertain if she'd scored a kill or if she'd only injured the enemy.

The loader lunged toward the big D-handles of the machine gun and Asado fired again, feeling the bruise on her shoulder grow with the subsequent abuse. The second member of the gun team ducked and sprayed wildly with his weapon, .50-caliber bullets tearing the air over Asado's head. Three shots and two misses weren't doing anything to help her gain a sense of confidence with the heavy rifle, but she had nothing else with the range. She held high again and fired.

The Russian at the controls of the machine gun disappeared in a blossom of crimson. The big rifle round had torn through the man's skull in an explosion of gore, and his headless corpse flopped over the frame of the heavy weapon. Asado rested her forehead against the gully's lip in relief. One fire team down, she thought. She lifted her head and looked through the scope again. What she saw made her stomach drop as the wounded gunner fought to pull the dead man off the machine gun. His left arm was a shorn stump, but his right arm was in good condition as he wrestled with the corpse.

Asado grimaced in disgust. "Damn it, stop it!"

The gunner had the body almost dislodged. The surviving Russian was dead set on getting revenge. Her teeth grit tightly, grinding, and her finger caressed the trigger again. The Barrett kicked, and this time she didn't feel the pain of recoil anymore. Only soul-numbing emptiness as the one-armed Russian jerked under the horrendous impact of a 300-grain bullet turning his torso into a bloody cavern of excavated meat.

Asado sagged against the rifle stock, gnawing at her lower lip to contain her anger. She punched the sand in frustration that the Russians didn't want to give up. "You didn't have to fight to the death, idiot."

Silence reigned on the battlefield, and it took a couple of seconds for the lack of gunfire to sink in.

The Russians' compound had gone quiet. She keyed her communicator.

"Matt? Matt?" she asked.

There was no answer.

Asado scooped up the Barrett and lurched toward the compound. The man in black was in trouble.

BOLAN GRIPPED the AK-47 tightly, his forearms bulging with the effort of keeping the rifle straight over his head. The barrel had bent under the weight of the slab of ceiling that had fallen on top of him. Three feet of steel and wood were all that gave the Executioner breathing room. Unfortunately, it was one of the rifles that had been looped over his shoulder, its sling snared tightly around his upper arm. He removed one hand from the rifle's forearm and reached for the combat dagger in its chest sheath.

The thinner wood of the forearm cracked almost as loud as a rifle shot. Bolan wasted no time, lashing the razor-sharp edge across the leather sling. Unfortunately the sling was so twisted it snarled the Executioner's blade. He'd avoided being crushed under a wide section of ceiling, but his ankle was pinned under a heavy piece of masonry. Thanks to the rifle's length, despite its folded barrel, he had a few inches of room to squirm around in.

He clutched the blade even more firmly and twisted the knife free, splitting the leather sling a little more. The splintering forearm forced Bolan to grab it, holding it so that he could add his strength to the rifle's support. He could feel the barrel bend and warp under the massive weight over him.

Flexing the biceps and forearm trapped by the sling, he stressed the leather strap. The initial cuts whitened, splitting. He didn't dare let go of the rifle to cut at it again. The roof pushed hard on the length of the weapon. Fortunately, the stock was of thicker construction than the forearm. Though enormous pressure was being applied by the roof, it was holding. Bolan couldn't count on it to last much longer, and sooner or later, Kuriev would realize that his nemesis was in trouble and send in a swarm of angry Russians to finish what the collapsing building had begun.

He flexed his arm again, the leather stretching and tearing under the force of his muscles. One more pull and he'd be free. Bolan felt something tickle against his neck and he thrashed his head to remove the annoyance. Suddenly fire exploded under his skin, burning deep to the core of his being. With a shrug of his shoulder he popped the leather strap, but he already felt the tugging of the scorpion's tail, its barb still hooked in his flesh and pumping poison into his tissues.

The barrel bent further as he relaxed his grip, the wooden forearm furniture splintering in his grasp. It didn't matter as he couldn't restrain the primal urge to reach over and spear his fingertips into the stinging arachnid, tearing it from his neck and crushing it, feeling its hard chitin armor pop in his grasp. That didn't stop the coursing poison from surging through his system. He'd been stung by scorpions in the past, so he knew that he wasn't vulnerable to venom allergies, at least to the degree that he'd suffer anaphylactic shock. However, he felt the poisoned tissues under and inside his ear beginning to swell in response to the burning venom. His right ear felt congested, closing off as a hammer thumped at the base of his brain.

Get out from under the ceiling and get ready for Kuriev's men, he ordered himself. With a hard snap of his left heel, he cracked the masonry trapping his right foot. A second and a third kick pounded into the chunk holding him, crumbling the pinning weight. With a fourth kick, his right foot popped free from the broken masonry. The barrel groaned as it deformed further, wood crackling as steel bent in its grasp.

He dug in and pushed out from under the slab. The ceiling lurched and ground against the floor, plaster snapping like eggshells just as he got his legs out from beneath the crushing weight. The AK and its counterparts, including the M-4, were left behind. Underneath that enormous weight, they might as well have been locked in a concrete tomb.

It didn't matter. He had the Beretta and the Desert Eagle and various other small, unobtrusive weapons hidden in his harness.

A flashlight burned through one of the gaps in the wall and Bolan ducked behind a pile of rubble. The beam hadn't crossed him, but he wasn't certain if his rush of movement had betrayed him. No gunfire tracked him, which was a good sign so far. He drew the suppressed Beretta and he followed the progress of the mobsters in the reflections of their flashlights through the shadows. He counted three distinct beams, but those could have been only the point men, or support troops. Hushed, indistinct voices were hard to pinpoint, special forces training benefiting the gangsters as they began to flank through the wreckage.

A shadow lurched into view to his left, and Bolan snapped a single 9 mm pill into the silhouette's head, bowling him over. The quiet round elicited cries of dismay as the mobster crumpled with 115 grains of copper-jacketed lead drilling into his brain.

Assault rifles ripped to life, lances of flame and lead spearing into the darkness. Bolan took the opportunity of their initial panic fire to pluck a standard fragmentation grenade from his harness and lob it over his protective section of wall. The minibomb went off, shrapnel shrieking through the blazing flowers of muzzle gases from the automatic weapons, slicing deep into their owners and slashing arteries, leaving organs perforated lumps of useless tissue.

Bolan's head was fuzzy, feeling as if it were jammed full of cotton, but he was still able to walk and fight. With the gap blown by the fragger, he had the room to pop up and rake two more of the gunmen with 3-round bursts. The Russians crumpled under the assault.

Kuriev lurched into view, his face scoured by shrapnel.

"So, you took one side of my face with your nerve gas," he growled. "And you took the other side with your grenade."

"Nerve gas?" Bolan asked. "Moscow. I don't remember you."

"That's because I lived to fight another day," the ex-KGB thug snarled. He opened fire with the AK, but Bolan ducked back behind the wall, bullets stopped cold. "There he is! Kill him!"

One of Kuriev's soldiers rose up, rifle shouldered, but he snapped to one side violently, a fist-size divot blown out of his upper chest. Kuriev dived into the wreckage of the house as a second crack filled the air, another of his surviving gunmen dropping lifeless to the ground.

Bolan knew what was going on. Asado had heard the lull in the combat and knew he needed some assistance.

With a burst spraying from the Beretta, he took out a third of the Russians, leaving Kuriev alone, in the shadows with him.

A sudden cry cut through the darkness. "Damn it!"

The Russian thrashed out of his hiding place, clawing at a scorpion stabbing its tail into his forearm. Others crawled on his face, stinging his cheek. Kuriev's rifle dropped to the floor as he twisted, slapping at the arachnids climbing him.

"Hoisted by your own petard," Bolan said.

The venom-racked gangster looked up, his face ruined by two clashes with the wraith in black in front of him. Already his lungs were overproducing histamine, his breaths coming in thick, heavy wheezes. In a few moments he'd collapse and ultimately die a slow, agonizing death. Kuriev dropped heavily to his knees as his strength gave out. "I had an army…"

Bolan stepped closer, but not too close. His head hurt like hell from just one sting, and he didn't want to feel any more poison coursing through his system. "Nothing I haven't beaten before."

Kuriev coughed, a twisted smile crossing his lips. "No…"

Bolan triggered the Beretta, ending his suffering,

CHAPTER SIXTEEN

With the death of Anatoly Kuriev, and the silencing of three of the fire bases, whatever remained of the Russian *mafiya* forces and their Mexican mercenaries was in no condition to fight for a blasted wasteland crawling with scorpions and living nightmares. The legend of the man in black among the ex-Soviet hardmen was still strong, and this battle was merely one more skirmish that had proved the incomparable might of the grim American. Bolan could see them racing away across the countryside, guns discarded, terror gripping them and commanding them to flee.

Asado applied disinfectant to the scorpion sting on his neck. She'd scored a tiny cut to open the skin to let the disinfectant soak to the swollen tissues underneath. Bleeding would also wash away the excess venom, one of the human body's simple yet elegant defense mechanisms. Bolan could feel the trickle of blood seeping down his neck and into his blacksuit.

"You know how to make an impression," Asado stated.

"I don't go for half measures, Blanca," Bolan replied.

He winced as she squeezed the puckered lips of the tiny cut, a crimson flood carrying out poison. She squirted more disinfectant into the injury, which burned his tenderized flesh even more. Still, the bleeding gave him a phantom sensation of the pressure in his head disappearing.

"That goes for showing off how tough you are, too," Asado added. "Bad enough you let them drop a house on you, but then you shrug off a scorpion sting without a life-threatening allergic reaction."

"I'm a lucky man," Bolan returned.

"Luck? I'd hate to see when fate turns against you," Asado told him.

Bolan frowned, memories stinging him more painfully than the most poisonous of creatures. "You'd be safer if you weren't around when that happened."

She looked at him for a long, uncomfortable silence. "Feel up to getting back to the van?"

"Yeah. We'll have to police the construction site first," Bolan answered.

"It's a lot of work," Asado said.

Bolan picked up the large Barrett rifle as if it were a squirt gun. "I can handle it. We unloaded most of the ammunition so far."

Asado nodded numbly. "Where next?"

"We drop the van off at the airport. There'll be facilities for us to clean up, and I can check my scorpion sting again," Bolan replied. "Then I thought I'd check out your safe house."

Asado smiled. "That sounds good."

"We'll still have to prepare for going against Garza," Bolan added.

"We can't just sail mortar shells into his estate?" Asado asked.

Bolan shook his head. "According to my people,

there are noncombatants on-site. Kuriev had his entire force here, and every one was armed to fight. Garza has prisoners and regular civilian staff. I don't want any of them caught in the cross fire. This will have to be a more subtle approach."

"The charge up San Juan Hill was more subtle than this plan," Asado commented.

"Worked, didn't it?" Bolan inquired.

Asado nodded, looking at the carnage surrounding them. "Yes. It did."

Bolan grimaced at the distaste in the woman's voice. In the Executioner's world, a successful battle wasn't a pretty thing. "Welcome to the world of absolute last resorts, Blanca. It's not a pretty place, and I hope you return home from it."

Asado frowned. "Me, too."

ARMANDO DICEVERDE'S SENSES returned to normal as he was dragged out of the van. He could see that the ground ahead of him was smeared with a long streak of fresh blood. He blinked away the cobwebs and tried to lift his head, but the punishment he'd endured had taken its toll on him, neck muscles felt unable to bear the weight of his skull. All he knew was that he was dragged into a freight elevator, where a pool of blood congealed on the floor. When the door rattled open, he saw the streak of gore painted down the hall.

He didn't dare ask any questions, lest he antagonize his captors, and he assumed that if he remained quiet, he'd find out who else was here. Deep in his gut, however, he suspected who the other prisoner was, and the thought nauseated him.

"Gloria," he whispered as the two kidnappers hurled him into his dark, damp cell. He collapsed in a huddle on the unyielding stone floor, wild thoughts torturing his soul alone in the inky blackness of the dungeon.

BLANCA ASADO STIRRED AWAKE. It had taken hours to clean up, and on the drive back from the airport, she'd fallen asleep in the passenger seat. Cooper was driving, and he allowed her to rest after the shattering carnage of the night's battle. She'd awakened when she felt the car come to a gliding halt, hearing Bolan's grim rumble at the sight that greeted her gummy eyes.

Police cars surrounded the burned-out wreckage of Gloria's bookstore, and Asado sucked down a nervous breath.

"I see two ambulances," Bolan said. "There are multiple bodies, but I can't make out anything from here."

He flipped open his cell phone, getting in touch with Barbara Price, obviously hoping the Farm's electronic ears could hear news.

"Gloria's car is still there," Asado offered silently, spying the burned shell of the powder-blue Volkswagen Beetle. "But that wouldn't mean anything if they had to run."

"Around the time we made our hit, there was gunfire reported here," Bolan explained. "It sounded like a war."

"No wonder no one rolled by Kuriev's place," Asado muttered. "They were busy here."

Bolan nodded. "The bodies of three adult males were found in and around the bookstore. All of them were burned badly, but none of them was Armando's height."

Asado managed a weak smile. "That means he's alive, at least."

She snaked her hand down into Bolan's war bag and pulled out a pair of binoculars. She scanned the scene and spotted a pair of *federales* with a clear evidence bag. Asado couldn't quite make out what was in the bag while they were conferring with each other, so she swept the scene. Bullet holes had been torn in the walls, still visible where the fire had not licked them to ashen black.

The Feds with the evidence bag moved, and Asado whipped back to them. It was a large bag, a quart size, and in the bag was a human foot. Asado winced at the sight, not because it was a gruesome souvenir of an attack, but because the limb was so dainty. She doubted it belonged to one of the attackers, especially when she caught the glint of nail polish on one of the curled toes.

"They blew off Gloria's foot," Asado hissed.

Bolan nodded, his face an impassive mask, but the intensity in his eyes betrayed the anger boiling behind the calm exterior. "She could still be alive, too. Her body wasn't found."

"They blew her goddamned foot off," Asado swore. "How well off could she be?"

Bolan remained silent, and Asado knew that was because he didn't want to lie to her. This was an ugly scenario that was all too familiar to the big soldier. "No sign of either Diceverde or Gloria. But this was done to attract our attention."

"So what do we do?" Asado asked.

"We head back to my fallback safe house. Anibella Brujillo hasn't learned about it yet."

"Would have been nice to put Armando and Gloria there," Asado snapped.

"I know," Bolan answered, disarmingly sympathetic. She couldn't maintain her anger when he sounded as if he were suffering the same crushing guilt that had gripped her. "We'll rescue them."

Asado nodded. "How could they have known? And who the hell took them?"

"I doubt it was the cartel," Bolan mentioned. "Right

now, they have more important things to do than to send a strike force against a small house. The only ones with the freedom of action would have to be Anibella's cult."

Asado swallowed. "You're certain it's her?"

"She's been steering me right down the throats of her competition. Thanks to her, over a few days I've crippled any coherent threat to her ability to dominate the state of Acapulco's heroin trade. That kind of inside information might have come from a woman who is on a crusade to protect her home from the ravages of drugs," Bolan began.

"But…?" Asado asked.

"A chemist named Casas has left the safe house where Anibella and I had put him, or at least the heat signature we had assumed was Casas," Bolan answered. "I believe the real chemist is dead, sacrificed in an ancient Aztec war-god ritual. The same kind of sacrifice that had been responsible for several members of the Juarez Cartel turning up mutilated."

"Then let's head to the mansion," Asado growled. "We'll get the truth out of that bitch."

Bolan shook his head.

"We leave Armando and Gloria in their hands another day while we tackle Garza?" Asado asked.

"Not we. I will take on Garza, with Anibella's help," Bolan told her. "That will occupy her so she won't be around to subject Diceverde to the same fate as Casas and the other Juarez Cartel thugs."

Asado frowned. "And then I'll do what I can to find out where Brujillo is holding them?"

"It's not going to be easy," Bolan said. "But it's the only chance your friends have of rescue. I'll report that you were killed in action."

"She won't believe you," Asado replied.

"No, but it will provide a good excuse for me to operate out of the mansion again," Bolan answered. "She'll definitely suspect me of being up to something, but she won't act on it."

"Why not?" Asado asked.

"She's too busy moving her forces into position to fill the void left by the Juarez Cartel in Acapulco," Bolan answered. "That's why she has me doing all of the hammer work. I'm her weapon, and she can keep her people in reserve to take over when the surviving cartel soldiers head back to Juarez, limping and bloody."

"And when she does take over, no matter how much she can cover it up with a body double appearing in public, you'll be smart enough to put things together about how she set you up," Asado replied.

"That's the other hard part of this plan," Bolan added. "According to the legends I've read about Santa Muerte and Huitzilopochtli, it's believed that the sacrifice of an enemy warrior increases the power of those who make the sacrifice."

Asado's eyes widened.

"I'd be a big catch for a god of death and war," Bolan concluded.

"And you're just going to let her take you?" Asado asked.

Bolan's lips tightened. "I have a feeling that I know how she's going to take me, and she'll want me alive. Which means she'll take me to her sacrificial altar."

"Which is part of the reason why you want me to look for Armando and Gloria on my own," Asado said. "So I'd be in place to lend you a hand in case you get in over your head."

"In case?"

"You'd have to be naked and pumped full of scorpion

venom for a bunch of cultists to overwhelm you, Cooper," Asado quipped. "Though, knowing that bitch Brujillo, and what you've told me about her 'assistance,' I don't doubt that you will end up naked."

Bolan nodded. "The things I do for justice."

Asado fought back a chuckle, the sobering reality that Bolan was going to use himself as bait to spring the Santa Muerte high priestess's trap stifling the grasp at humor in the soldier's comment.

"Please, be careful on this. She knows that you're bad news for her. She might just decide that a bullet in the head is all the ritual she needs to 'absorb your death powers.'"

"Like I said, the things I do for justice," Bolan returned. "I don't expect to grow old and die in my sleep. If she makes a move to shoot me in the head, I'll stop her. I've handled worse with less."

The pair pulled away from the perimeter of the crime scene. Bolan plucked his cell phone out and got on the horn to Stony Man Farm to inform them of his plan, and his need to communicate with Anibella Brujillo.

ARMANDO DICEVERDE struggled to get up, but only got a few inches before the chains around his wrist stopped his movement cold. He could only see the woman in silhouette, her shoulders and the outline of her hair highlighted by light spilling through the door of the cell. When Diceverde realized he was chained in place, he tugged against his bonds, trying to pull free, knotted cords of muscle in his forearms bulging against new, rust-free steel manacles encircling him.

"Where's Gloria?" Diceverde asked.

"First you tell me where Blanca is," came the smooth-as-butter reply.

"Burn in hell, slut!" Diceverde cursed.

Anibella Brujillo leaned in closer, her soft, smooth lips brushing his cheek before coming close to his ear. "Oh, I love it when men talk dirty to me. Being a high priestess of a death cult and the first lady of the state intimidates people. It's so hard to find someone with the nerve to actually call me a slut."

Anibella rolled back on her haunches. In the half light, he could see her cheek swell with a smirk moments before she raked her nails across his face. Diceverde winced as flesh parted, blood pouring into his left eye an instant before he felt fire lance across his cornea. His lower lid tugged down under the clawing fingernails, splitting and tearing, hot fluid flushing down his bruised cheek.

"Why do you insist on being such a tough guy, Armi?" Anibella asked.

"Goddamned whore," Diceverde snarled. "I'm not tough, but even I have some ethics."

"Oh? Hiding a suspected drug dealer and murderer?" Anibella asked. "Or how about professing love to that dim little bookstore owner, while all the time you want to be with the aforementioned fugitive?"

Diceverde was off balance from the unrelenting pain burning in his left eye. He didn't know if she'd punctured the orb, but the agony speared deep into his brain, and it didn't fade like the throbbing in his balls. He struggled against the chains to cup his wounded eye, his opposite arm hauled back by the pulley system he was hooked to as he gingerly felt through the intact upper lid. The eye was a round, firm dome beneath, but blood poured from torn flesh.

"Quit avoiding the question, Armi," Anibella whispered. "Right now, I own you, body and soul."

"What question?" Diceverde asked. "In case you hadn't noticed, you fucked up my eye."

Anibella chuckled. "So do you really care about Gloria?"

Diceverde took a deep breath. "Yes."

"Oh, good. Then it wasn't a waste of time dragging her in here." She snapped her fingers and the light clicked on.

Gloria was strapped to a table. Diceverde struggled to get up and to her side, but the chains and his beatings over the past few days had taken their toll. He couldn't get up as he listened to the woman choke out a sob. She was bound and naked, a tray of stainless-steel surgical instruments by her side.

"See, that's the problem. If I torture you to find out where Blanca is, you'll just clam up and keep pushing your luck until you die of the strain and damage I inflict," Anibella explained. She walked over to Gloria. "However, if I torture this little plain Juanita here..."

Anibella picked up a scalpel and with a flick of her wrist, laid open Gloria's cheek. Diceverde let loose a bellow of rage as Gloria screamed in pain.

"See?" the first lady asked her female captive. "He does really love you. You can't fake concern like that. I doubt he'd ever betray you for Asado."

"Don't say anything," Gloria snapped.

Anibella flicked her wrist again, and Gloria jerked violently, part of an ear plopping onto the concrete floor.

"Stop it!" Diceverde begged.

"You know how to stop it," the woman taunted, slowly drawing the tip of the scalpel along Gloria's chest.

Gloria looked at him, her dark eyes wide in horror.

"Blanca went to the Russians' compound with

Cooper," Diceverde confessed. "She and Cooper have been in contact."

Anibella smiled broadly. "See? Was that so difficult?"

The cell phone on the surgical tray warbled and the torturess picked it up. "Anibella Brujillo."

"This is Cooper's support team," Barbara Price said on the other end.

Anibella rested the scalpel blade against Gloria's throat, to ensure Diceverde's silence. "Yes? What happened? I haven't heard from Matt in so long."

"There was difficulty at the Russian compound," Price replied. "Unfortunately, he won't be able to rely on any more field support from our end."

"Operative White had come to an unfortunate end?" Anibella asked. She threw Diceverde a wink.

"Yes. We have no other agents in the area that we can tap," Price replied. "Cooper will be returning to the mansion. He had to take care of—"

"Yes, yes," Anibella responded. "I'm a little busy at the moment. I sincerely hope that Matt is all right."

"He's taken a few knocks and was stung by a scorpion," Price explained, trying to keep the cell-phone conversation going, giving the Stony Man team time to home in on her cellular signal.

"Oh, that's horrible. But I have some pressing matters right now. When I return to the mansion, I'll expect a full briefing from Matt. Goodbye."

BARBARA PRICE HEARD the phone click dead. "Tell me that you managed a trace on that, Aaron."

"I narrowed it down to a barren stretch of road on the southern coast," Kurtzman replied. "Take a look at the satellite photos we have."

"It's a cell-phone tower," Price said. "No buildings for miles."

"It allows coverage of the beach, which is part of a resort," Kurtzman said. "It's a pretty well-known surf spot, but there's nothing built up in the area, except for an old Spanish fort about five miles away."

"Any chance that the fort could be somehow routing their calls through the tower?" Price asked.

"It's a possibility, but I've got Akira and Carmen going over the plans," Kurtzman told her.

Price grimaced. "Let me guess… The old fort is a busy tourist attraction. There's no way that Anibella could get away with using it as her secret death-cult-slash-heroin-empire headquarters."

"Not according to the architectural records," Kurtzman replied. "Archaeologists who have been over the place have mentioned a few hidden passages discovered over the years, and a few more that have been hinted at, but the historical documents on the fort show that the Spanish simply didn't put in any more tunnels than they had to, mentioning cave-ins and problems with pirates and privateers."

Price rubbed her hand down her face. "It's the only thing in the area receiving any traffic whatsoever, except for surfers looking to catch some barrels."

"Akira is going to try to get a hold of a geophysical satellite to see if there is anything under the fort," Kurtzman offered.

"Tell Asado about the fort," Price replied. "It'll take at least a couple of hours to divert a satellite into position to make the necessary scans. A pair of eyes on the ground in thirty minutes beats a seismological scan from low orbit in two hours any day of the week."

"Striker just dropped her off at the safe house,"

Kurtzman said. "It's been a hard night and finding out that Diceverde is missing—"

"I know, but this might just clue us in on where Diceverde is," Price answered. "And since Asado didn't let her twin sister's murder and frame-up slow her down, I really don't think she's going to take a nap while her childhood friend is in enemy hands. She might sound tired…"

"But she'll do just like Striker does," Kurtzman answered. "Dig in deep and find the energy to finish the job."

"And who knows, maybe we'll get lucky," Price replied. "She can bring down the death cult while Mack knocks Garza out of the picture."

"Without risking being Anibella's next sacrifice?" Kurtzman asked.

Price nodded. She swallowed her burning concerns for Bolan as if they were red-hot coals.

SHE CLOSED THE CELL PHONE and tossed it onto the surgical tray. "It seems that Cooper is suspicious of me. Luckily, these caverns have receptors built throughout, and route through hard lines to a cell tower about five miles from here."

Diceverde's brow furrowed. "They're trying to track you down, Anibella. Give up."

Anibella smiled and caressed Gloria's cheek. Her wrist flicked again, never having left the woman's throat. The bookstore owner gurgled and sputtered, arterial blood spraying like a pressure hose.

"Alas, poor Armi, you and I are very much unalike," Anibella responded as Gloria spasmed, her throat carved wide open, curtains of gore pouring down her chest as each beat of her heart squirted a stream of blood out of the severed artery. "You are the one who gives up easily."

The first lady paused long enough to lick the blood from her fingertips.

"Gloria!" Diceverde roared.

"Me, I hang in there until I get exactly what I want," Anibella added. Gloria stopped struggling, and blood no longer pumped out of the sliced artery. "Cooper intends to come into my lair, feigning the role of the fly, when really he is the tarantula hawk, hunting the web spinner. Do you know anything about tarantula hawks?"

Diceverde wasn't answering, choking back sobs of rage as he stared at Gloria's limp corpse bound to the table.

"A quick science lesson. A tarantula hawk is a wasp that hunts spiders by pretending to be prey. Unfortunately, the tactic is highly dangerous. As often as the wasp succeeds in killing a tarantula, it ends up as the prey of a smart, tough and well-prepared spider. I am ready for Cooper and his tactics. Unlike you, I know my enemy is capable of great ruthlessness. That is why I have a large underground base and an army at my command, and you have a dead girlfriend."

Diceverde turned his head slowly, glaring at the witch who'd murdered Gloria. "I'll see you dead."

Anibella smiled, "Don't hold your breath, little man."

CHAPTER SEVENTEEN

Bolan waited for Anibella Brujillo in the foyer of the mansion. The servants had poured him a vegetable drink that he sipped, savoring the cinnamony flavor as if it were the last sweetness he'd taste for the rest of his life. It wasn't overdramatization. He still had to attack Garza's mansion, and the first lady no doubt was aware that he was on to her. Almost a day had passed, and the only visible sign of the scorpion sting was the small incision that Asado had cut to let the poison be washed out by bleeding, and a red inflammation that encircled the scalp around his ear and extended partially down his back. His right ear still felt a little fuzzy, as if he had water trapped in the auditory canal. Closing his eyes, he focused on his ability to place movement by sound.

The stuffiness in his ear didn't affect his balance, and he could locate sounds on his right utilizing his hearing. He wasn't impaired, just left with some discomfort. Pain was an old friend, and Bolan had long ago learned that he could take whatever lumps he was thrown without a complaint.

He heard footsteps at the entrance and looked up.

Anibella Brujillo had arrived, with her personal body-guards and the rest of her entourage. She walked toward him, her flowered skirt fluttering like wings around her shapely legs.

"Matt, are you all right?" she asked. "I was so worried when I heard about White."

"This is a dangerous business."

"Oh, Matt." Anibella cupped his cheek with her delicate hand, her hazel eyes probing his with genuine-seeming concern. "I wish I could make this up to you."

"You have Garza's address," Bolan stated. "That'll go a long way to making the hurt disappear."

Anibella's worry lines disappeared as her eyes narrowed. "Can I join you this time?"

Bolan shook his head. "I lost a trained soldier in my last battle. Sure, you can shoot…"

The woman sneered in frustration. "You're certain?"

"Positive," Bolan told her. "We could use your SUV to get me in close."

"Instead of utilizing artillery and heavy machine guns like last night?" Anibella inquired.

"That was an armed camp, and there were no non-combatants," Bolan explained. "Garza's mansion might be different."

The first lady nodded. "I understand, Matt. There's too much of a chance of a bystander being caught in the cross fire."

"Precisely," Bolan replied. "Which is why I suggest using your SUV. We might encounter some prisoners in Garza's hands, and need to get them to safety."

"So you'll need me at the wheel to arrange a fast pickup," she stated.

"It's not as glamorous as being in the middle of a

commando assault, machine guns blazing, but it'll be a great help."

Anibella smiled. "All right, Matt."

Her fingers brushed down over his chest. The tender familiarity was coldly calculated to make Bolan feel more amicable to an intimate encounter after all the blood and thunder was done. But he was fully aware that the duplicitous manipulator fawning over him was going to be part of the blood and thunder he needed to finish.

The first lady smiled reassuringly. "Let me go get changed. Have you had a chance to rest?"

"Yeah."

"Then we can be on the move by sunset."

Bolan nodded. He took another sip of his drink and retired to his quarters.

ANIBELLA BRUJILLO SNEERED as she entered her bedroom, tossing her purse aside. Her staff remained in the hall. When Cooper's controller had called earlier, she was primed and ready to carve Armando Diceverde into tiny slivers of human flesh once she learned Blanca Asado's whereabouts. Unfortunately, she wanted to relish the end of the interfering journalist, so she left him alive. The fact that he was chained to a wall, unable to cradle the body of his butchered lover only a few feet away, gave her satisfaction that his torture wasn't put off.

"It's so much better to slice up their soul instead of their body, anyway," she softly mused as she shimmied out of her dress. The servants had laundered her commando outfit and it lay, dark and crisp, on her cream-colored satin sheets. She opened her closet and took out her pistol rug to examine her personal Glock Model 22. She then placed it and its shoulder holster with four spare magazines next to the commando outfit.

"Ana, darling?" Emilio Brujillo called. He looked out from their large bathroom. "Did you say something?"

Anibella froze at the sight of her husband. He was only wearing pants, and his silver hair was damp, traces of shaving cream at his sideburns and decorating his neck. "I didn't know you were there."

"I got back early from my budget meeting," the governor said. His gaze tore from Anibella's nude, bronzed form to the weapons and dark clothing on their bed. "I thought Cooper didn't want to put you at risk anymore."

"He has no choice," Anibella answered. "His partner was killed last night."

Brujillo nodded, a frown deepening the lines on his weathered face. "It's truly sad. Will they release his real name to us, so we can arrange an appropriate honor for him?"

"It was a woman," Anibella said.

"Even more tragic," Brujillo replied. He stepped forward and cupped his wife's face. "Oh, Ana, I wish that you hadn't taken this crusade onto yourself. It is dangerous business. These drug dealers are tricky as well as lethal."

Anibella nodded, then rose on her toes to kiss him. He returned the kiss with a fierce passion. "I will be just fine, Emilio. They've tried their worst against me, and they've failed at every turn."

"They only have to get lucky once," Brujillo warned her. "Couldn't you send someone else to do your dirty work?"

While Anibella's face remained locked in a gaze of adulation on her husband, her mind sparked with the suggestion. Suddenly, the mystery of why Bolan had claimed that Asado had died faded away. He was using her to look for Anibella's base of operations under the immunity of being reported dead. "Sorry, Emilio."

She gave her husband a kiss on the cheek. "Thank you."

Brujillo quirked an eyebrow. "For what?"

"For being my inspiration," she told him. She kissed him again, then turned to get dressed. Brujillo chuckled and went back to cleaning up for his public appearance that evening. Anibella didn't dare phone the temple until he was dressed and out of the bedroom, so she changed quickly, weapons ready and exited the bedroom into the hall.

She flipped open her cell phone, keeping an eye out for Bolan.

"Castillo," she said as soon as she heard the pickup.

"Mistress?" Castillo, her head of security at the temple, asked.

"Send some men up, incognito, to the Spanish fortress. We may receive some company," Anibella said. "Blanca Asado."

"But they told you she was dead," Castillo began.

"What better way to keep us from looking for her?" Anibella asked. "Five men, in plain clothes, with sidearms. If she doesn't show up, then we've got no problem. If she does, then take her down."

"But, if she is alive, and in contact with Cooper's people," Castillo interjected, "the Americans will know where we are."

"They'll suspect, but what are they going to do? Launch a commando assault on a tourist attraction? Even if they did come, we're in hidden tunnels that they can't find and we'll be moving into our new headquarters after tonight."

"Garza?" Castillo asked.

"Well, someone might as well make use of his facilities," Anibella replied. "And when we're done, I'll bring Cooper in. A going-away party, so to speak."

"We will be ready, mistress," Castillo offered.

"Good. And make certain that Diceverde remains healthy. I want him to see the other great love of his life dragged before him as a corpse," Anibella said. "I figure if I'm going to kill any man with complete satisfaction, I'll want to destroy every shred of hope and love in him first."

Anibella hung up and slipped the phone into her pocket, setting it to vibrate, not ring. Tonight, she was certain she was destined to see the sun rise on her new empire, freshly christened by the blood of not only the Executioner, but Diceverde and Asado.

Life was good.

"STRIKER, YOU'RE MAKING the Farm look bad," Brognola complained over the satellite phone connection.

"How so?" Bolan asked. "Because I'm actually doing the right thing?"

"You were asked to help the governor's wife deal with the drug trade in her state," Brognola said.

"I am," Bolan answered.

"So why are you having Farm resources diverted to spying on the first lady?" Brognola asked.

"Because she framed Rosa Asado as the mastermind operating the drug trade in the governor's mansion," Bolan explained. He was standing on the balcony, and he'd clipped a white noise generator to his pocket to keep his privacy. Powerful encryption keys made the call itself impossible to break into. "Anibella Brujillo isn't going to be oblivious to anything in this house, especially since she's installed more electronic surveillance capacity than there is on an AWACS plane."

"Just because Mrs. Brujillo has her ear to the ground," Brognola began.

"Hal, how many times have I been wrong about someone?" Bolan asked.

"All right." Brognola sighed. "So you think Mrs. Brujillo is involved in subverting the government investigation into the Juarez Cartel's operations in Acapulco. For what reason?"

"She's getting rid of the competition," Bolan explained. "And since the legal method isn't working as fast as she'd like, she called in an ace in the hole."

"You," Brognola surmised.

"Right. The Juarez Cartel has caught on to her, and they've started applying more pressure. She needs something to break them up, and given my track record, who better to call in?" Bolan asked.

"And only because the Mexican president confided in the governor and his wife do they even know about you," Brognola grumbled.

"Anibella is expecting to stage the final knockout of the Juarez command structure in Acapulco tonight."

"So you're still going to help her?" Brognola asked.

"You know me, Hal. I can't pass up a chance to take a bite out of a major cartel if it's handed to me. I've already taken down the local representatives of the Russian *mafiya*," Bolan told him. "The Juarez Cartel is a big, powerful organization that would take a year to bring down. But hacking off a tentacle in Acapulco will do for now."

"So how are you going to keep Brujillo from moving her organization in to take over?" Brognola asked.

"I won't be able to stop everyone from entering the void in power. But I'll take down Brujillo and her closest allies," Bolan stated.

"I don't like the sound of this. You're talking about assassinating a governor's wife."

"It will be self-defense, Hal," Bolan countered. "She'll try to take me prisoner, and hell, she might even succeed."

"Prisoner. This just gets worse," Brognola groaned. "Why take that risk?"

"She wants me to be the sacrifice. My blood will be the icing on her cake," Bolan stated. "She's a believer in Santa Muerte."

"That's like Santería, right? A Mexicanized version of voodoo," Brognola began.

"Not quite. Santería is a blend of African and Catholic imagery with Mexican culture. Santa Muerte is more of an outlaw religion, adhered to among the lower class. It's the same twisting of religion to grant criminals and the disenfranchised a feeling of empowerment that fundamentalist Islam and extremist Christian Identity give to terrorists and militias in other parts of the world," Bolan explained. "It's a spontaneously created religion that provides a basis to engage in cathartic violence and lawbreaking. Brujillo has built up a powerful cult. I suppose you've read the *narcocorridos* that the Bear sent you."

"It's not proof that Brujillo is involved," Brognola said.

"No, but the records the Farm has uncovered on Rosa Asado's real bank accounts put her in the clear of running a heroin ring out of the governor's mansion," Bolan returned.

Brognola grunted in disgust. "It will never hold up in a court of law."

"I deal in justice, Hal. Not law," Bolan told him.

"So she's going to carve you open. Why?" Brognola asked.

"In the *narcocorridos*, mentions are made to Huitzilopochtli, the flayed god. He was an Aztec god, and the Aztecs believed that by sacrificing a brave enemy warrior, you made his strength your own," Bolan said. "I don't know if Anibella believes that personally, or if she's stirring up her troops with that lie, but it also adds a bit of cushion between the U.S. government and her activities. If I die and disappear, then she'll be free and clear to become the godmother of Acapulco's heroin trade. And since she has a body double, she can even fake her own death to blind the Farm to her new whereabouts until she's too entrenched to root out."

"Damn it, Striker. Pull out. We can wait twenty-four hours and bring in Phoenix Force and Able Team on this," Brognola said.

"No can do, Hal," Bolan replied. "Garza isn't going to sit on the top floors of his hotel forever. And because he's in a major hotel, I can't just go in like I did against Kuriev, heavy machine guns and rockets blazing. We wait long enough to bring up Able and Phoenix, Garza will be long gone to another secure location, and Juarez won't be hurt badly enough. They'll rebuild. And if I pull out, Armando Diceverde and Gloria Gonzales are as good as dead."

Brognola sighed. "You'll never let a civilian down if you can. You want to get captured so that you'll be in a position to rescue Diceverde and his girlfriend."

"That's how I roll, Hal," Bolan said.

"And if they're dead already?" Brognola asked.

Bolan looked at the door to his quarters. There was a soft rap. It was time for Anibella Brujillo to join him in the raid on Garza and the Juarez Cartel's last centralized stronghold in Acapulco.

"If Diceverde and Gonzales have been murdered already, then their murderer has already been judged. I'll just deliver the judgment."

He hung up and went to meet with the woman who was on a collision course with her judgment.

IT WAS SUNSET when Blanca Asado finally reached the old Spanish fortress. The parking lot was still full as outdoor cafés on the walls enjoyed the evening breeze off the ocean, providing a romantic location for dinner and drinks. As the sky darkened to night, the tables were dotted with candle bowls, adding to the intimacy of the outdoor dining. Meanwhile, on the beaches below the walls and the cliffs, less affluent tourists rode the last waves of the day on their surfboards, or gathered around driftwood fires for parties.

Asado could smell the beginnings of those fires, with a hint of mesquite and hickory added to several grills where the partyers could cook their dinners. Standing at the base of the fort's wall, she looked down on the beach, bathed in the orange glow of the setting sun, people of all ages gathered in knots, enjoying themselves. Over the rustle of distant voices and the breaking of the waves, she heard the strumming as guitars were pulled out, or the electronic tinniness of battery-powered boom boxes blasting out music. It was a glimpse of a friendlier, happier life, a moment of tranquillity that washed over the young woman, stinging her heart as she realized that it was something that Rosa would never get a chance to experience now.

All their adult lives, Blanca and her sister had been living the hard life of a woman in Mexican law enforcement, not only dealing with the day-to-day threats of lawless thugs, but also with the ingrained prejudices of their coworkers. Through perseverance and sheer guts, the two of them had managed to make themselves into what their father wanted, good cops who could carry on his legacy. Rosa Asado had risen high enough to be trusted with the protection of the governor and his family, and in the end, that honor had been the end of her life.

Asado thought about the past couple of days, and she realized that her career was now on the fast track to the toilet because of Anibella Brujillo's demonization of Rosa. With Armando Diceverde missing, and maybe already dead, Asado didn't know how much more strength she had left. The only thing keeping her on her feet was a grim, burning ember of hatred and revenge against the conniving witch who had taken everyone she'd loved.

In her pocket was the little 5-shot .357 Magnum Ruger. Hidden under her untucked blouse was the high-capacity 9 mm pistol and spare magazines. Cooper had given her no admonishment to maintain a low profile, and his controller had gone so far as to warn her that the enemy might be expecting visitors. Asado didn't need to skulk, and if she ran into Brujillo's Santa Muerte cultists in force, it would only be proof positive that Cooper was right about the duplicitous first lady.

Brujillo wouldn't go to jail for circumstantial evidence, however, and Rosa Asado would still be framed as nothing more than a traitor who used her position to spread heroin throughout Acapulco.

"We'll be all right." The whisper came to Asado's ear and she turned suddenly to look for the speaker, but there was no one who could have dropped such an intimate phrase. However, twenty yards away, on the cliff, there was a man standing in a windbreaker that flapped open in the breeze, exposing the handgun jammed in his waistband.

"Damn it," Asado snarled. She turned and started up the walkway at the base of the fortress wall. She didn't want to get into a gunfight out in the open where a bullet would ricochet and plow into the people below. A small wave of confusion bubbled over her, and she didn't know if it was her sister's spirit actually speaking to her, or her subconscious mind pinning memories of her twin to sensory input that sparked her survival instincts. Right now, Asado didn't care which. She'd seen an enemy packing heat, looking right at her, and she had to move.

Asado walked quickly toward one of the gates when she saw another windbreaker-wearing goon appear in the doorway. He looked at her with recognition in his eyes and Asado slowed. When the man spoke into his collar, she knew that the jig was up and she had stumbled right into the enemy's backyard. "Rosa, subconscious, instinct, insanity, I don't care who you are. You've been looking out for me for the past few days. Get me the hell out of here."

The goon at the gate stepped out and began his trek toward Asado along the narrow walkway. A breeze plucked at her hair, waving out over the railing that separated the walk from a plummeting cliff drop. Asado looked down and saw that she'd stopped cold right at a spot where the incline of the cliff wasn't a steep drop off, but an angled, slender slope of straight rock. Asado climbed over the rail and dropped onto the slope, the soles of her shoes providing just enough traction to slow her descent as she plopped onto her haunches. Gravity overcame the rubber grip of her shoe treads and she disappeared down the slope, the seat of her jeans protecting her backside from abrasions as she slid down to the sand below. Wind whipped past her face as she straightened her legs to provide more of a steering surface, keeping her course from deviating. The slope decreased in angle halfway down, slowing her somewhat, but she still plummeted quickly.

Gunshots cracked against outcroppings of the cliff face around her, and Asado curled into a tight ball, rolling off the slope and landing hard in a rut off to the right of the narrow strip she'd been sliding down. The cultists seemed reluctant to join her on the wild ride down the stone slide, and Asado was in no hurry to pull her pistols to return fire. She glanced at the beach below her. The gunfire had incited a panic among the people at the base of the cliff. Underneath a finger of stone, she was safe from above. In the sand below, however, two more men wearing dark blue windbreakers and jeans were running to the cliff, pistols in hand.

Asado pulled the XD-9 and fired down at one of them. A 9 mm bullet burned into one of the shooters, and he collapsed onto the sand as his partner took cover behind an outcropping.

More gunfire rang out up above, but no bullets pinged or cracked against her rocky shield. Asado took a moment to glance upward and saw that the two men in the windbreakers were dueling with a security guard in a white uniform shirt. The guard's clean uniform suddenly smeared with red as the duo shot him mercilessly. Asado gave in to a rush of anger, pulled the .357 Ruger and in one smooth, lightning-fast movement launched a sizzling Magnum round through the head of one of the murderers. The jacketed hollow-point slug punched through the cultist's neck just under his ear, exploding in a spray of brains and skull fragments as it exited. The killer flopped over the railing, bouncing like a rag doll from outcropping to outcropping.

The other gunman spun to the railing and leaned out to get a good shot. Asado leveled both of her handguns at him and pulled the triggers as fast as she could. The 5-shot Ruger ran empty quickly, and she held her fire as the second murderer simply folded atop the railing, hanging like a grisly flag saluting the woman's anger.

A spray of stone splinters exploded just over Asado's left shoulder and she whipped around, firing her Springfield at the base of the cliff. Pure instinct locked her aim on target as she punched three rounds into the head and neck of the last of the cultists.

Asado put her guns away, climbed back onto the sloping slide and ran down the flat ridge of stone to the sand below.

She'd attracted too much attention and needed to get away from the fortress before she also had the law to contend with.

CHAPTER EIGHTEEN

Corsario Garza, the regional commander of operations for the Juarez Cartel in Acapulco and the surrounding area, had set up his headquarters on the top two floors of the Hotel Rey del Oro, the Golden King Hotel. Because of that, Mack Bolan's options were severely limited when it came to his plan. The M-203 grenade launcher, fragmentation grenades and satchel charges that he'd used on Kuriev's compound would not only prove to be overkill, they would be a menace to civilians and noncombatants in the resort. A 40 mm shell that went out the window would land on a subroof, or in a crowd, killing dozens. Structural damage to the top two floors would also menace noncombatants in their rooms below Garza's bi-level headquarters.

The M-4 carbine, loaded with lightweight hollow-point rounds and affixed with an integral suppressor, wouldn't punch through drywall and endanger unarmed staff who were tending to Garza and his people. Bolan hoped to minimize potential hostage situations, but he'd done battle with enough gangsters to realize that the cowards would hide behind a screaming maid while jamming a .45 in her car, barking orders to whoever threatened them.

The top two floors were a maze of corridors according to Kurtzman's blueprint research, and the roof had been plated so satellite infrared imaging was worthless. There was no advance data for the Executioner to utilize against the Mexican gangster's guard force. Bolan had gone into situations with less inside information before. He would simply have to rely on his expertise and well-honed reflexes to get him through the battle until he'd gotten the lay of the land.

The M-4 carbine was placed into a three-foot-long toolbox, along with a silenced Uzi for Anibella Brujillo. Spare magazines, knives and handguns were concealed by coveralls worn over their commando clothing.

"I'm sorry I don't have more for you, Matt," Anibella said softly as they walked through a service corridor at the back of the hotel. An oversize ball cap shadowed the first lady's face, and her load-bearing vest underneath the thin coverall masked her feminine figure. Smears of dark greasepaint along her jaw provided the illusion of five o'clock shadow, lines under her cheekbones making her appear even more masculine, furthering her disguise. Bolan's dark tan helped him blend in as a Mexican, and he covered his eyes with tinted safety glasses, their green plastic rendering his blue eyes an indecipherable darker shade. The coveralls were generously cut for both of them, and Bolan was able to conceal both the massive Desert Eagle and the Beretta 93-R, as well as pouches containing spare magazines for his rifle.

"Hey! Where's Tony?" someone shouted. Bolan turned at the question. The man was looking at the expertly forged work order on top of the three-foot-long toolbox he carried. "Tony's usually the one who does the contractor work on the upper floors."

"I don't know," Bolan answered in Spanish. "I'm pulling overtime and they asked me to come in here. I guess something came up."

"Maybe his wife finally had that kid?" the man asked. Bolan mentally translated the hotel worker's badge. He was in plant services, so he would be familiar with outsiders who came in to work on the ducts.

Bolan shrugged, tinting his response with irritation. "Like I said, I don't know. I don't know Tony. It's late, and I've been on my feet all day. I just need to take care of this work order, and I can grab a cold beer."

"All right, all right. No need to bite my head off," the plant manager said. "You need to be shown the way?"

Bolan took a deep breath and sighed heavily, glaring behind the green-tinted safety glasses. "Oh...so I don't know Tony, and suddenly I need to be lead by the hand by some pencil pusher? Give me a break, and quit treating me like an idiot. It's on the work order, and I do know how to read the map drawn on it."

"Sorry," the plant manager replied.

He glanced at Brujillo. "This kid doesn't talk?"

The woman sneered, then tilted her chin up, showing a strip of fused flesh across her throat. The plant manager paled.

"He talked once. Then he got too nosy," Bolan growled. He turned and walked toward the service elevator.

The plant manager shrugged and Anibella pointed from her eyes to the man, then joined the Executioner. Once in the service elevator, doors closed, they peeled out of their coveralls. Anibella tore the rubber prosthetic off her throat. "You always keep scar tissue on hand?"

"If you have a rather graphic injury, people pay more

attention to that than any other detail," Bolan explained. "It's not quite a subtle touch, but he didn't even notice your face."

The woman tapped the ridge of the false Adam's apple that the "cut" went through. "Pretty impressive."

Bolan opened the toolbox and withdrew the M-4 carbine. He handed Anibella her Uzi. "Repeat the plan one last time."

"Secure the elevator access panel on the roof. Guard it, and do not let anyone up and behind you."

Bolan nodded.

"I have a good turret position as pointed out on the satellite photo of the roof," Anibella added. "Meanwhile, you'll enter through the greenhouse and move in directly on Garza."

The elevator reached the top floor and Bolan opened the car's access hatch, climbing up the rungs in the wall of the car. He slipped through the trapdoor, and Anibella followed suit after handing him the toolbox.

Bolan waited until the first lady took the toolbox to the scouted position. He could tell that she had a good field of fire on the access hatch. The toolbox, with its lid lifted and locked in place with a crossbar, was resistant to bullets up to hunting-rifle power. She also had a climbing harness and extra rope inside, in case she needed to rappel down the side of the hotel to make her escape. The Executioner wouldn't need that much rope, and decided against the climbing harness. The waxy yellow windows of the greenhouse were lit from within, and the support struts of the structure proved strong. The only weaknesses were the vents in the roof, and its link to the bi-level structure.

Bolan knew what was rumored to be nestled in the greenhouse—Garza's flesh-eating dragons. He also knew he had to watch his back. Anibella could possibly try to make her move now. She didn't have access to high explosives, but there was always the chance that she had people inside the hotel. Standing on the edge of the roof, he looked down at the top of the greenhouse. To either side, he knew of the presence of two penthouse balconies, but those would be under heavy guard, especially on the night after Kuriev was scoured from the Earth. As well, the balconies were heavily defensible, with only bottleneck openings that could be sewn up by two gunmen with automatic weapons, holding Bolan at bay, or even dropping him off the seventeenth floor to the ground below.

Garza's little jungle den was a safer approach. While he was certain that the legendary dragons were real creatures, ten-foot carnivores that could have been anything from an alligator to a Komodo dragon, he also believed that such creatures would only attack in self-defense or to capture live prey smaller than they were, and were loath to expend more energy than necessary. If it came down to conflict, he had his firearms, but years of experience informed him that reptiles weren't exceedingly dangerous.

He scratched at the healing skin under his ear, remembering the scorpion bite the night before, and realized that he might just be tempting fate. It didn't matter. He didn't expect a ten-foot reptile to be a match for an assault rifle or a Desert Eagle.

The Executioner hooked his grapnel to the lip of the roof and lowered himself to the greenhouse so he could begin his climb to the vents.

MODA LIFTED HER HEAD, her tongue lapping out to taste the tension of the humans in the air. Their emotions converted into something she could scent utilizing the sensitive cells in her reptilian tongue. When she sensed fear her interest was always piqued and kicked her metabolism into gear. She lifted herself to all four legs and headed toward the wall, watching two of Garza's security guards at the railing.

She let out a long, rolling hiss that made the pair of humans whirl in surprise. One of them made a sound, and Moda licked the air, letting them know she was not to be ignored. Her sister, Zilla, was pacing.

Something made a sound above her loud enough to register, and Moda craned her head up and back, black beady eyes locking on a vent cover in the ceiling. To her primitive brain, it was as if someone were opening a door in the sky, but since the creature responsible for making the hole was all too human, it only spurred her to circle underneath the newcomer hanging forty feet above.

Moda fell silent as she stalked in a small orbit. Zilla picked up on her sister's movements, detecting the presence of fresh prey. Together, the great reptiles swirled in small spirals, the antithesis of soaring vultures waiting for their crawling prey to die, instead they were crawling beasts waiting for their next meal to descend from the above.

THE EXECUTIONER HAD EXPECTED there to be deadly, large creatures hanging out in the greenhouse. However, the sight of two ten-foot lizards perking up as they noticed him, gave even the experienced warrior a moment of pause. Surrounded by skeletons partially stripped of flesh, the great beasts were an imposing sight. Gently lowering himself through the hatch, he spotted two of Garza's security guards, packing submachine guns, standing on a walkway ten feet above the two monsters.

Hungry, anxious reptiles were only a reminder not to slip and fall the forty feet to the dirt. The two men with guns were his primary concern. Bolan didn't target them just yet. He scanned the greenhouse and looked for surveillance cameras. If Garza fed failures and foes to the flesh-eating monitors, then he'd want a camera on hand to enjoy the show of ripping meat and cracking bones. His four-power scope homed in on a camera overlooking the two lizards. He stroked the trigger and a suppressed hollow-point round tore into the device's housing. He adjusted his aim and took out a second camera with another hushed shot, the clatter of breaking plastic and electronics catching the attention of one of the gunmen.

Bolan flicked the selector switch on his M-4 and ripped a burst across the turning mobster's back. The impact of a trio of rifle rounds threw the hapless Mexican to the deck in a jumble of tangled limbs. His partner whirled at the sound of the dead man's collapse. He opened his mouth to raise a cry of alarm, but the Executioner guillotined the warning shout with a pair of high-velocity bullets tearing through fragile flesh and bone.

The corpse toppled over the railing and gave off a sickening crunch as it hit the dirt.

Moda and Zilla didn't even acknowledge the fresh carrion littering their dwelling. Their black, soulless eyes burned holes in Bolan, hissing reptilian invitations to him to become the main course. Bolan declined the invitation, and lowered himself on the rope until he was almost level with the railing.

With a kick, he began a pendulum swing that took him in an arc over the excited reptiles. He had to get on the walkway soon, otherwise the security force would notice that the cameras in the greenhouse had been knocked out. Reaching the apex of his swing, he released the rope, and momentum hurled him toward the scaffolding. Bolan tucked his legs up so he wouldn't jam himself against the guardrail and twisted in midair, bouncing off the far rail and coming down on the metal grating with a clang.

The door at the other end of the walkway opened and a security guard walked in, holding his Uzi lazily, calling out to the pair that Bolan had taken down. "Dave, Tommy, did you guys know that the cameras are… Oh fuck!"

Bolan whirled, bringing up the M-4 and firing from the hip. Garza's sentry jerked under multiple high-velocity impacts and he stumbled backward into the doorway he'd entered through. Screams on the other side of the door told the Executioner that he'd lost the stealth approach, but now that he was on solid ground, and inside the heart of Garza's lair, he was in blitz mode. He charged the open doorway, ripping off short bursts at figures on the other side, his rifle chopping into the gangsters as they sought to close the sudden breech in their defenses.

He reached up to his harness and pulled a flash-bang grenade, lobbing it with deadly precision through the doorway. The blast gave him the opportunity to feed a fresh magazine into his hungry rifle when he heard a feeble shout from below. A battered and abused figure in a chicken-wire cage wrapped spindly fingers through the mesh, big brown eyes looking up despondently toward the warrior.

"Help," the prisoner croaked. "Help!"

"Stay put," Bolan said, charging the bolt on his rifle. "I'll get you out."

Moda looked between the prey that had avoided her and the thing in the cage. In a moment of almost human inspiration, she lashed her tail violently against the chicken wire, feeling it sting against her armored scales. The human trapped within released a wail of terror as the massive reptile began attacking him.

On the catwalk, Bolan paused, watching the agitated monster attack the captive. He opened fire, raking the dragon with a trio of soft hollow-point rounds. The beast thrashed in pain, scurrying away from the chicken-wire cage, but the 40-grain bullets didn't have the structural integrity to do more than carve shallow gashes in her armored hide. Moda hissed angrily, glaring at the Executioner as he was distracted by a group of other gunmen coming through an alternate entrance.

Bolan didn't see the drama below, as his attention was held firmly by a pair of gunmen who fired across the U-shaped walkway. The wood-topped handrail splintered under Uzi fire, 9 mm bullets shattering against the wrought-iron mesh underneath the paneled railing. Shooting from the shoulder, the Executioner tapped off half a dozen rounds that hammered through the skulls of the sloppy gunmen. Bone fragments and gray matter exploded from the gangsters' heads, and that was all Bolan knew of their fate as he entered Garza's two-level suite.

The Bolan blitz had arrived for the last of the Juarez Cartel's leadership in Acapulco.

CASTILLO PICKED UP the phone on the first ring. It was Ypez, one of the men he'd sent out to hunt for Blanca Asado. He could tell by monitoring the police band that the law had been alerted to a gunfight at the cliffs, but the details were sketchy as panicked tourists yammered discordant stories to the lawmen who had arrived.

"What's wrong?" Castillo asked.

"We found Asado," Ypez answered. "She killed the others, though."

"Did you get her?" he asked, already knowing the answer. The moment of uncomfortable silence confirmed his suspicions before Ypez cleared his throat.

"I'm tailing her. I figured that if she'd taken out the other four, joining them would be counterproductive. She's moved onto the trail from the beach," Ypez explained.

"The one leading to our hidden loading dock?" Castillo asked.

"That's the one," Ypez replied.

"I'll increase the guard there. Keep on her," Castillo ordered. "I need to relay this information."

"Right." Ypez signed off.

Castillo's stomach flopped. Anibella had ordered five men sent out to intercept Asado, and apparently it had proved to be a good strategy. In exchange for four dead men, he received intelligence about the woman's escape and approach to their back door. It wasn't as if the secret loading dock entrance was recognizable as such, the doors covered with plaster replica rock colored to match the natural face of the cliff. The road was shaped like a cul-de-sac and composed of gravel, kept raked to disguise the tire tracks of trucks and cars entering through the dock's entrance. He hit the speed dial for Anibella's phone.

She picked up almost immediately.

ANIBELLA BRUJILLO HEARD the sounds of automatic weapons and the stun grenade only a minute after the Executioner entered the greenhouse. She gripped the Uzi tightly to her side when she felt the cell phone on her belt rumble. She plucked it from her waist, keeping a sharp eye on the elevator hatch.

"Mistress? You were right. Asado is at the fortress, and she eluded the force you had me send out. Only one is alive," Castillo reported.

Anibella frowned, wrinkling her brow with concern. "We don't want to draw too much attention to our headquarters. Not when we're only a few hours from moving out of there."

"I've beefed up security at the cliff entrance. She's heading up the trail from the beach," Castillo added. "One of our men is on her trail."

"Why doesn't he shoot her?"

"Because she killed the other four who had tried the same tactic," Castillo answered. "But it's better we know where Asado is than lose five men."

"You've got a point. But reinforce him as soon as you can. What about the fort?" Anibella asked.

"We've got police on the scene. A security guard was also killed, and the gunfight panicked several tourists. No one is quite sure what's going on, which is to our advantage," Castillo responded.

"But if Cooper's people are monitoring the site, they'll know that we have people on the premises," Anibella countered. "Keep your ears open. Watch the radar, and have more men watching the water. I don't want to get so close to my prize and have it ruined by a Navy SEAL team dropping into our laps."

"You still think it wise to bring Cooper back here?" Castillo asked.

The first lady bit her lower lip. "Santa Muerte demands it. I cannot refuse her. Just be ready to move out."

"Yes, mistress," Castillo returned. He broke the connection.

Anibella closed her eyes. "Martha, you'd better make this worth my while. This is getting too close for comfort."

BLANCA ASADO ALMOST DIDN'T notice Rosario Ypez trailing her as she padded up the sandy road leading from the beach. Trees clinging to the base of the cliff made it hard to watch the path behind her, and provided plenty of opportunity to hide. That was why she'd chosen the narrow trail, all the better to elude the law-enforcement personnel who had shown up at the fort above, their sirens' wails reaching her ears. She kept her hand on the revolver stuffed in her hip pocket, ready to pull and fire, only the knowledge that she might encounter a *federale* giving her pause. She didn't want to open fire indiscriminately and burn down a brother in uniform.

She took her hand off the grip of the revolver and slithered between green leaf-laden branches, slowing her breath as she melded into the shadows. With the sun set, and no lights illuminating this forgotten corner of the beach, she was invisible among the saplings and brush. Asado waited, breathing shallowly and noiselessly, eyes scanning the sandy trail for a sign of movement.

Her patience was rewarded a minute later as Ypez padded along quietly. She knew he was one of the hunters sent by Brujillo, wearing the same uniform as the others, a dark windbreaker and jeans, the lightweight jacket covering the bulge of a handgun jammed in his waistband. Asado tensed, ready to make her leap when Ypez paused, speaking into his collar.

The conversation was short and terse. Ypez was the only one left of the group that Brujillo had sent out, and he was speaking to one of her lieutenants, a man named Castillo. The trail they were on led up to a concealed entrance to the tunnels that the first lady had settled as her cult's underground temple. This information was a mixed blessing.

On one hand, being right at the enemy's back door, she now had a quick shot at rescuing Diceverde and Gloria, if they were still alive. On the other, any moment now, Ypez would realize that his quarry had gone off the trail, and he'd call in extra help to hunt her down. As soon as the conversation was over, Asado needed to come down on him like a ton of bricks, and find another place to hide.

Her luck had been good so far, but against an underground temple loaded with heroin-dealing gangsters and death cultists, she had no illusions that she could come out on top. She'd need to contact Cooper's people to see if they had a company of Marines on hand to help her out. Even then, a full-blown military assault might only give Castillo and the other Santa Muerte monsters all the incentive they needed to execute their remaining prisoners out of vengeance and spite.

She needed an alternate entrance into the underground temple, which meant that she had to take Ypez alive so he could talk.

The cultist broke contact with Castillo, and Asado leaped like a panther, tackling Ypez to the ground and pinning him with a chicken-wing armlock. Unfortunately, the hunter-turned-prey was large and strong, and he snapped his head backward, the dome of his skull mashing Asado in the face and staggering her, her grip loosening on Ypez's wrist.

The gunner whirled, driving a fist into Asado's ribs, sending a lightning bolt of agony lancing through her as bone cracked. The hulking sentry lifted a ham-size fist, cocking it to spear down at her. Asado had only a second to avoid or deflect the crippling punch.

CHAPTER NINETEEN

Garza's gunmen, strewed about like ragdolls after the concussion of the Executioner's flash-bang grenade, were no resistance as he plowed into the room that lead to the catwalk over the greenhouse. The room was a pantry of sorts, with various supplies for the faux jungle setting, as well as bags of food for the two enormous reptiles. A small stairway led down, presumably to a doorway leading to the chicken-wire cage where Garza stored his prisoners to soften them up emotionally at the sight of a pair of agitated reptiles. There was an emergency gate at the top of the steps, and the little chamber at the bottom was cut off from the rest of the penthouse complex.

Thinking quickly, Bolan rolled another flash-bang grenade through the door connecting the pantry to the rest of Garza's head shed, then sprinted down to the small chamber. He threw open the bolt lock and twisted the door open. On the other side, he caught the thick musk of the artificial jungle and the humid weight of settled air mixed with carrion rot flooding through. A heartbeat later, the flash-bang erupted upstairs, raising more chaos and panic, the crack resounding down the stairs, jolting the emaciated prisoner in the chicken wire to his feet.

"No! No! I'll tell you everything about my mistress!" the bony scarecrow muttered.

"Move," Bolan grunted, shuffling up the steps. He turned back and saw the two Komodo dragons whirl at the sound of his voice. Two pairs of black eyes bored into him, and the Executioner noted with some discomfort that the short burst of rifle fire he'd pumped into the larger black beast had only raised a superficial flesh wound. Both of them lurched forward, fury filling their primitive hearts.

"Yeah, that's right. Come and get it," Bolan taunted softly. He raced up the metal steps as four hundred pounds of saurian muscle tore at the chicken-wire mesh, deforming it with jaws that could produce tons of bone-cracking force.

He pushed the staggered prisoner out onto the catwalk and slammed the door shut to keep him safe and contained. The spindly captive gave no protest, and Bolan turned back to see the first of Garza's stunned protectors struggle to his feet. A swipe of the butt of the M-4 across his jaw sent the dazed guard hurtling down the steps, collapsing at the bottom. An instant later, the chicken wire proved how weak it was in comparison to the prehistoric powerhouses it had been meant to hold at bay, and the savage Komodo dragons rocketed at the Mexican. A howl of horror split the air as Zilla became a flaming-backed bullet, her teeth seizing the first human flesh she could find. Razor-sharp teeth and talons ended the fallen gunman's suffering in a matter of moments as Moda turned the corner and released a long, hissing rumble.

The gunners at the top of the stairs, still too weak for

Bolan to consider them a threat, screamed and clawed over one another, getting caught in the doorway of the pantry as terror squeezed squeals of horror from them. Bolan had long left the pantry behind, moving on to go after Garza. Releasing two live wrecking machines put him at a slightly greater risk, but he doubted that the giant lizards were any good at distinguishing between humans. In their agitated state, they'd sow as much confusion as he would, and Bolan counted on his superior agility and intelligence to keep him out of the path of the monsters.

A pistol-packing gunman lurched into Bolan's path, too late for the warrior to swing the rifle around to shoot. Again, the Executioner utilized the tube-steel stock of the rifle as a weapon, hearing the sickly crunch of bone and tearing of muscle as he snapped it across the *pistolero*'s jaw. Head twisted at an impossible angle, blood flooding out of his mouth and nose, the Mexican bounced off the wall and crashed face-first to the floor, seeping out a quickly growing puddle of crimson.

Two more gunmen barked out a challenge, but Bolan whirled, firing from the hip, the suppressed cough of his M-4 whispering its mute testament to the lethal punch of its quiet bullets. The two Juarez Cartel gunmen jerked and spasmed under the hypervelocity assault before crumpling into heaps of carrion. Bolan took a moment and threw another flash-bang down the hallway. Back at the pantry entrance, the squeals of terror dissolved into a chorus of agonized howls as reptilian talon and fang ripped into yielding flesh.

Like a linebacker breaking through a defensive line to make a touchdown, Moda speared through the wall of mangled men and landed in the open. She thrashed her head around, looking for the creature that had caused her pain. An unholy rattle escaped her throat.

Bolan didn't wait around to be seen by his prehistoric enemy. Ducking down the side hall, he rushed into the sudden void created by the detonation of the flash-bang grenade. He reloaded the M-4 on the run, reaching the end of the hallway as it opened out into a wide sunken room. Garza, standing beside a large piano, saw him and cut loose with his Colt pistol, the handgun belching out shots, spurring his protectors to activity. A half dozen men were with the cartel boss, and they whipped up their weapons, opening fire in a conflagration of semi- and full-automatic thunder. Bolan leaped with panther-like quickness and power, diving behind a fully stocked bar and bowling over another of Garza's men who wore a bartender's apron and packed a sawed-off shotgun.

The Executioner's shoulder chopped into the bartender's gut, carrying him off his feet and providing Bolan with a cushioned landing as bullets hammered into the bar. Thick oak splintered under the hail of lead, but the bar would hold as a shield for now. Bolan rose to his knees and drove the heel of his palm under the bartender's chin, the blow rocketing the guy's head back at neck-breaking velocity. With the stomach-churning snap of vertebrae, the Executioner was the only living person hidden behind the bar. He hauled the dead man up and threw him out into the open.

Distracted by the sudden movement, Garza and his defenders opened fire mercilessly, filling the corpse with bullets. By the time they realized that they'd been had, the Executioner rose over the top of the bar, tromboning the slide of the bartender's stubby shotgun. He swept gunmen with salvos of 12-gauge buckshot. Two of the cartel soldiers folded under multiple impacts, double aught pellets whirling through their chests and churning internal organs into soup. A third howled as his right arm was stripped of a baseball-size chunk of muscle, his Uzi falling to the carpet. The wounded gunner turned tail and ran toward a hallway to escape the carnage. Instead of freedom and survival, he screeched to a halt, his face twisting in panic an instant before four hundred pounds of savage dragon struck him in the chest, bowling him off his feet.

"*¡Cristo!*" Garza exclaimed as Moda lifted her gore-drenched head from the gaping hole in the runner's sternum.

Zilla slithered out of the hall behind her sister, head swiveling as she scanned the area. Bolan brought the shotgun around and triggered it at Zilla, but the sleek, crown-backed reptile darted to the side as she charged at a gunman who fired his pistol at her. The .380 auto that the Mexican used was barely enough to stop a full-grown man in combat, let alone an armored, several-hundred-pound carnivore like a Komodo dragon. The stings of the tiny pistol had saved her from being caught by a charge of buckshot.

Bolan discarded the empty shotgun and, remembering the ineffectiveness of the M-4, pulled the mighty Desert Eagle from his hip holster. Heavyweight lead would succeed where lesser cartridges had failed. He pounded out a single .44 Magnum slug into Zilla's shoulder, but it was too late to spare the life of the gunner who had drawn her wrath. The round hammered into the creature's side, fracturing the shoulder joint and throwing the lizard onto her side. The gunner who'd been mauled by Zilla clutched at his torn throat as sprays of arterial blood jetted into the air. Within seconds, the human had stopped thrashing, but the reptile kicked and pulled herself to three legs, releasing a pained roar. Moda heard her sister's suffering and rushed to her side, standing protectively against the hairless apes who still showed signs of life.

Bolan had to turn his attention to another of Garza's gunners, who ripped his Uzi across the bottles behind the bar. Soaked with alcohol, the Executioner realized that he was now flammable. A spark on steel would be as deadly as an Uzi bullet striking dead center. He turned the Desert Eagle on the gunman and triggered another Magnum round. The .44 slug caught the Mexican at the hairline and flipping the top of his skull open like a gory trapdoor. The last of Garza's defenders turned tail and ran into a hallway facing away from Bolan, who didn't blame the gangster. Who wanted to face a man in black and two dragons?

"Don't snarl at me, you stupid bitch!" Garza growled, catching the Executioner's attention. "He's your enemy! I'm your master, Moda!"

The Juarez Cartel commander was pinned in the corner, hidden enough to be safe from a clear shot by Bolan, but held at bay by the larger, black-skinned lizard. Bolan could hear the sound of Garza's efforts to reload his jammed Colt. All the while, he continued to protest. "Didn't you hear me? I'm your master!"

Almost as if to say that no mammal was Moda's master, she shot forward, lunging at the Juarez crime boss, jaws snapping down, generating two tons of crushing force that cut through Garza's forearm in one bite. The drug boss roared in horror as he saw his hand and his pistol drop to the floor, blood hosing out of severed arteries. He tried to get out from behind the piano, but Moda's slashing talons raked down through the gangster's hip and thigh, disconnecting muscle from bone like meat cleavers.

Zilla, wounded and enraged, coiled before she leaped toward Bolan, powerful tail muscles designed for propelling her through rivers like a torpedo catapulted her forward with blinding speed. The Executioner brought up his M-4, not to shoot, but as a spear, the barrel jamming down the hurtling Komodo dragon's throat. Razor-sharp fangs clamped down, splintering and deforming the aluminum that wrapped the barrel, tearing the flip-up front sight off of its mooring on the Picatinny rail. Two hundred pounds of raging reptile and Bolan crashed into the glass behind the bar.

Zilla bit down again and again, thrashing her head and trying to get off of the rifle's barrel. Her good forearm clawed out, slicing through Bolan's blacksuit and cutting the securing strap for his hip holster. Only the toughness of the blacksuit's Kevlar high-tech weave protected Bolan from a crippling wound. As it was, he couldn't last forever. However, his rifle was jammed down the beast's throat, and he pulled his hand back to the pistol grip. A stroke of the trigger and the M-4 ejected a few casings before jamming. The reptile's thrashing had destroyed the rifle's gas tube.

The malfunction came too late to save the smaller of the dragon queens. Bolan's high velocity rounds literally burned down Zilla's throat and split her heart in two, killing her instantly. The lizard's deadweight wrested the broken rifle out of his hands. Feeling the battering of the last few days aggravated by wrestling with a prehistoric opponent, Bolan dragged himself to a standing position, leaning against the bar.

The Executioner saw Garza, laid out, half of his face missing and his arms reduced to stumps. He looked around for Moda, hand instinctively reaching for the Desert Eagle where he'd dropped it on the countertop.

A furious bellow sounded to Bolan's left and he kicked himself over the top of the bar, barely avoiding the monster that torpedoed into the wreckage behind the bar. In midroll, Bolan opened fire, the flaring muzzle blast of the .44 Magnum round igniting the alcohol-soaked shelves, creating a sudden bonfire. The backwash of flames licked at his flammable blacksuit, lighting his arm on fire.

Blind reflex forced Bolan to hurl the Desert Eagle away as he dropped to the shag carpet, digging the burning limb into the deep pile to smother the flames. The bar suddenly lurched, oak splintering as his ears were assaulted by the rattling shrieks of the burning queen of the dragons. The long whiplike tail wrapped around the end of the bar, cracking the wood as a surge of power toppled the counter.

The Executioner barely rolled out from under the falling bar. Moda clambered over the wreckage, her gleaming black skin dulled by char marks. Her eyes were still bright and clear, glaring hatefully at the human before her. Her tongue licked at the air, steam rising from her nostrils. Bolan knew that between the gunshots and burns, the magnificent monstrosity in front of him didn't have much life left in her, but there was a soul-less resignation in the primitive glare. She knew death was imminent, but she wouldn't go alone. Bolan had no doubt that she would try to drag him to hell with her.

All this flashed through his mind in the space of a second, and in the next, Moda had gathered up her energy to charge into battle again. Bolan rolled, once more feeling the rush of air as the prehistoric demon missed him by only a hairbreadth. Sooner or later, he wouldn't have the speed or reaction to avoid those limb-rending jaws, nor her flesh-shredding talons. As it was, Moda's thick tail whipped the Executioner across the small of his back as he tumbled away from her. Even though he rolled with the blow, Bolan had never felt a single impact like that in all of his life, the armored, muscle-wrapped tail cracking down across his kidneys with a force that would have made a bullwhip feel like a lover's caress.

Moda struggled, her head stuck in the wooden frame of the sofa she'd crashed into. Her muscles surged, and the skeleton of the couch splintered, releasing her. The momentary snarl gave Bolan all the time he needed to recover from her stunning tail lash. He reached for the Beretta under his arm and drew it.

Moda pivoted and bounded toward the Executioner as he opened fire with the machine pistol, 3-round bursts ripping out of the end of the barrel. The suppressed 9 mm bullets chopped into the monitor's jaws, tearing through her tongue and the roof of her mouth, while those that struck her armored skin skidded off, leaving only minor welts. The creature's jaws were torn and bloody from Bolan's machine pistol assault, but she bashed the weapon out of his hands, claws digging into his load-bearing vest. Talons punctured rifle magazines and sliced through heavy ballistic nylon pouches.

The Executioner grabbed Moda by the throat, squeezing tight with his left hand to keep those bloody, fang-filled jaws away from him. He dropped his right hand down to pluck his Bowie knife from its sheath and stabbed upward with the mighty blade's sharp point. The dragon's leathery, armored hide deflected the first strike, and she thrashed, trying to break Bolan's hold on her. He felt the muscles in his left arm protesting the impossible weight put on it, but he had lifted Moda's upper body enough so that her hind claws had to dig into the carpet and not his legs, her fore talons grasping at air millimeters above his torn vest.

The Bowie stabbed again, and this time Bolan found the scarring in Moda's side where he'd injured her with his rifle. The point deflected off bone, but now that he'd found her weak spot, he struck again, this time sinking seven inches of strong steel into the dragon queen's ribs. Agony ripped through the reptile and she twisted, snapping the knife handle off in the Executioner's grasp. The creature toppled to the carpet, rolling around as Bolan scrambled away. The whiplike tail kissed him in the shin, his leather combat boot providing protection against the flailing blow. Still, Bolan lost his footing and flopped to the floor. The Desert Eagle lay just a few inches away. He lunged for it.

Moda scurried to her feet, legs wobbly. She crouched, coiling to strike again, but now the Executioner had his Desert Eagle in hand, safety off, barrel locked on to the monster's head. The .44 Magnum pistol roared, punching heavy-caliber slugs into the reptile's bulletlike head. Somewhere in the bottom of the Eagle's eight-shot magazine was the shot that punched through the saurian's primitive brain, killing her instantly.

Panting, exhausted from the battle with fierce foes he'd underestimated, Bolan struggled to sit up. He stuffed a fresh magazine into his pistol and looked around for his fallen Beretta. He heard movement in the hall. With a push, he surged to his feet, Desert Eagle held upright as an extension of his will when he spotted the man who Anibella had described as Jorge Pueblo, Garza's second in command, waving a white handkerchief.

"Hold it! Hold it!" Pueblo called.

Bolan glared silently at the cartel lieutenant. The

three-pound weight of the Desert Eagle aggravated the minor burns on his arm, but his left hung limply, worn out from holding two hundred pounds of rampaging predator at bay. Inwardly, Bolan felt lucky to be standing, but outwardly, he was a grim, implacable foe standing amid the carnage of slaughtered men and beasts.

"All right, you've made your point," Pueblo said. "You don't have to point that thing at me. We give."

The ice-blue, chilling gaze continued, unblinking, making Pueblo squirm under its spotlight intensity. He cleared his throat, continuing to make his sale. "You've kicked our asses. There's only me and a couple of the boys left."

"That's too many for my taste," Bolan replied. The Desert Eagle didn't waver, despite the searing sting of first-degree burns under his sleeve.

"Yeah. Well, would you gun down an unarmed man who surrendered to you?" Pueblo asked.

Bolan's expression didn't change, despite the fact that the gangster had pegged his code of honor.

"You've been tearing through us. It's a good message. We'll take it back to Ciudad Juarez. No more playing in Acapulco. It belongs to you now," Pueblo sputtered.

"Do you know who sent you this message?" Bolan asked.

"Acapulco belongs to Santa Muerte."

Bolan nodded.

"Maybe Anibella would like to work with us. We make better allies than we do enemies," Pueblo added.

"That's Mrs. Brujillo," Bolan corrected, falling into the role of hired gun. "Speak of her with respect."

"Right. Absolutely," Pueblo answered. "We're sorry for trying to take her out. But she's got hers back."

Bolan nodded again, letting the gangster continue to provide him rope to hang Anibella with. Before entering the greenhouse, he'd taken the time to activate a miniature digital recorder. Now, he had all the proof he needed to take out the first lady.

"So…what say you put that gun away, and I'll pour…" Pueblo trailed off when he saw the flaming bar, two hundred pounds of roasting Komodo dragon sizzling. "I'll get us some beer and we'll discuss a nice, polite withdrawal. Peace with honor, like Nixon said."

"Tell Juarez that he'd better keep a low profile. No more hiring army units to shoot at the U.S. Border Patrol," Bolan growled. "If I hear that one more Border Patrol unit even sees a Mexican army jeep, I'll make the past few days seem like a mother's kiss. Got that?"

Pueblo nodded.

"Get back to Juarez, then," Bolan growled.

The gangster whirled and hurried away, grateful for his life. Bolan reached into his pocket and turned off the digital recorder. He had enough to convince Brognola that putting Anibella in a grave was a legitimate course of action. Brognola could then take it to the President to avoid an international incident. He pulled his cell phone and dialed the first lady on the roof.

"Still holding the fort?" he asked.

"Yes. The gunfire died down. Things are pretty excited outside, and there's a police helicopter orbiting the roof."

"I'll meet you at the service elevator. I'll need my arm looked at," Bolan replied.

"Don't worry, Matt. I'll take good care of you," Anibella cooed seductively.

I'm certain you will, Bolan thought, hanging up. He connected the digital recorder to the cell phone and hit transmit. The audio file shot through space, bouncing off satellites before beaming down to Stony Man Farm. With his evidence secured, he took a deep breath and braced himself.

Burned and bruised, he still had Anibella Brujillo and her men to deal with.

At the first step, his foot felt as if it weighed a ton, but with each subsequent stride, his strength returned. He remembered Diceverde and Gonzales, held captive by Brujillo's death cult. The Santa Muerte high priestess's imminent abduction attempt held no dread for the Executioner.

CHAPTER TWENTY

Ypez's barreling fist brushed Blanca Asado's cheek, grinding across her ear and pinning her thick auburn hair into the sand, ripping out locks at the root. The blow, however, was accompanied by the snicker crack of fracturing metacarpals and Ypez's face distorted with the sudden discomfort. That didn't stop the hulking thug from pulling back his huge, swollen fist again.

Asado flashed her hand up into Ypez's face, her short nails raking across his eyes, tearing the fragile skin of his eyelids. The Mexican gangster cut loose with a bark of pain, and Asado squirmed, pushing him off balance. She continued digging her fingers into his sockets, feeling one of his eyeballs pop under pressure, the firm orb gushing out aqueous humor as her middle finger sank into the socket to the first knuckle. Ypez cuffed her with another punch, but blinded and distracted by the pain in his ruptured eye, it was only a glancing blow. Not that Asado felt lucky to receive even that much. Her head whipped to one side, brains rattling inside her skull. Given the power of the hit, she counted herself lucky that she'd jerked aside on the first punch. The massive fist would have crushed her skull like an egg.

The big man pulled back, staggering to his feet, hauling her up, as well. Gritting her teeth, she pulled down hard, her free hand ramming into Ypez's solar plexus. It felt like she was punching a brick wall, wrist aching with abuse, but the sentry's breath exploded through his lips.

The pain maddened Ypez, so that his flailing fists had no focus, slapping at her back while strangled cries poured from his lips. Asado reached up and took a handful of his ear, hanging on as her larger opponent whirled. Centrifugal force swung her, legs flying. Flesh tore and Asado was thrown by the spinning thug. Unfortunately for Ypez, she never let go of the handfuls of his face that she'd clawed on to. Asado tumbled into a bush, and only when she saw her enemy clutching his head did she realize that she had his crushed ear in her hand. A shudder ripped through her and she hurled the grisly souvenir aside, scrambling to her feet.

His remaining eye was red and swollen where her nails had clawed at it, and his mouth hung open, a ghoulish black hole. A fountain of blood overflowed from his excavated socket, painting his ruined face in crimson. An animalistic growl erupted from his lips and Asado knew that this fight had taken a horrible turn as she was no longer dealing with a rational human. Ypez leaped, and the woman barely sidestepped the hurtling beast who crashed through branches and foliage like a renegade bull. She pulled her pistol, turned and leaped onto his back, arm snaking around his throat as she jammed the muzzle against his kidney. It was like riding an enraged bear as he struggled to throw her from his back. The 9 mm pistol buried in his side wasn't making any noise that she could register, and she wondered if she was even pulling the trigger as the Santa Muerte cultist swung clublike hands over his shoulders, catching her in the face and neck. His lack of leverage softened the swinging blows, robbing them of impact, but still they raised bruises and welts on her.

Finally the big man crashed to his knees and Asado rolled off his back. The muzzle of her pistol was caked in gore, and the barrel was plugged with spongy flesh, the slide locked back. She'd emptied all fifteen shots into her adversary's back and even then, he still had enough fight left in him to batter her. With the barrel obstructed by her opponent's flesh, the gun was useless. She tossed it away. She had the smaller XD pistol with her, as well as the little Ruger Magnum. She could use the larger 9 mm's magazines in the tiny pocket pistol.

Asado knew she had to get to cover before the noise of the conflict attracted more attention. Staggering along, she kept her senses sharp for any sign of further pursuit. So far, there was no sign of anyone. She had gotten lucky, and the gunshots had been muffled by Ypez's body absorbing the muzzle-blast. If that was the case, it would be a while before anyone noticed his corpse on the sandy trail. She paused and knelt, catching her breath, obscured behind a low bush from both the path and the beach.

It took her a while to get her strength back up, and by the time she did so, she heard the soft, muffled voices of a pair of men. Her hand fell to the grip of the tiny XD at the small of her back, but she kept her cool. She'd managed to get out of sight, and maybe they could direct her to whatever secret exit they'd come out of.

"My God!" one of them sputtered in exclamation. "Call Castillo."

"She ripped his face apart," the other whispered.

"I said to call Castillo!" the first man snapped. "She's escaped, and she's closer to the loading dock and the temple."

The other man pulled out his walkie-talkie. Asado tensed as the first man scanned the shrubbery surrounding the path, willing herself to become invisible. He clicked on a flashlight, but she didn't flinch as the light stabbed between leaves. Sudden movement would attract attention and the beam passed over her without reaction from its owner. She wished that she could have gotten her pistol out, but any motion to draw the gun now would only pinpoint her position. Asado felt a numbing, dead calm wash over her.

Nothing. They had no clue that she was no more than a few feet from them.

"We're pulling back in. He wants you on the side entrance. Anibella and Cooper just finished off Garza, and she's going to bring him here," the second sentry told the first.

The man with the flashlight clicked it off. "I don't like this."

"It's one woman. What could she do?" the other asked

The guard turned on his flashlight, showing the horrific mask of Ypez's face.

"Smart-ass," the second rumbled, turning back.

The guard turned off his flashlight and followed his partner back toward the cliff.

Padding softly, Blanca Asado followed.

ANIBELLA BRUJILLO GOT OFF the service elevator on the second floor of Garza's suite. No one was around, but she kept her Uzi clamped firmly to her hip, ready to fill someone's belly full of lead at the slightest provocation.

A skeletal, mostly naked figure stepped into the open, its gaunt face looking on her in awe.

"Mistress?" the former captive asked.

Brujillo whirled and looked him over. "They kept you alive?"

He nodded.

She was about to lift the submachine gun when she heard Bolan clear his throat.

"One of yours?" the Executioner asked, stepping into the open.

"An undercover agent of mine," Anibella said as way of explanation. "Thanks for getting him out."

"Anytime," Bolan replied.

The first lady turned to examine the warrior, and was surprised at the state he was in. "You look like you've been through hell."

"He's been through hell," Bolan noted, pointing to the emaciated prisoner. "I just had another day at the office."

"I've got the first-aid kit," Brujillo said. "Where are your burns?"

Bolan grabbed his collar and tore, freeing his right arm from the blacksuit. The limb was red and splotched. The Kevlar weave had protected his arm from serious injury, but what would have been deep-tissue damaging third-degree burns were still painful first-degree burns. He sat on the floor after shrugging out of the blacksuit top. Anibella opened the kit and spread burn salve over the affected areas.

The Santa Muerte priestess had to admit, he didn't even grunt as she touched the raw, livid flesh. A bandage over the burn would keep the salve in place and protect the arm from infection. Her gaze passed appreciatively over his broad, half-naked chest. "Any other injuries to tend to?"

"He could use your help first," Bolan replied.

Anibella glanced back at her prisoner. "He's a hardy man, and he found some water. We've got nothing here to deal with malnutrition. He's rehydrating, and he has no obvious injuries."

"That's correct," the man said. "I'd like to help you stand."

"An unnecessary kindness," Bolan answered, looking at Anibella. "Unless Huitzilopochtli or Santa Muerte demand it of their sacrifice."

The Executioner couldn't have dropped a bigger bomb in Anibella's lap if he'd somehow stowed away a pocket nuke. She took a step back, hand dropping to the Uzi's grip. "Don't move."

"I won't," Bolan replied. "If you'll make a deal with me."

"What's that?" Anibella asked.

"It should be obvious. Diceverde and Gonzales. They're not combatants in this little game of yours. Let them go, and I'll come quietly," Bolan offered.

Anibella took a deep breath, letting it out in a long, disappointed sigh. "You really are too good to be true, aren't you, Cooper?"

"And yet, here I am," Bolan answered. "Take my offer. Otherwise, I know twenty ways to get that weapon out of your hands before you even pull the trigger."

"It's too late for Diceverde's girlfriend, Cooper," Anibella said. "I'd just finished slicing her throat ear to ear when your people called, lying about Asado's death."

She stepped a little farther back, bringing the submachine gun to her shoulder.

"The offer still stands for Diceverde," Bolan stated solemnly. "Set him free. I'll be yours."

The high priestess's eyes narrowed. "You're in no position to make demands."

The Executioner snapped to his full height in the blink of an eye, slamming his bandaged forearm across the frame of the Uzi, swatting it aside. Suddenly, Anibella felt the cold, thin pressure of a knife edge across her throat. The emaciated prisoner let loose with an angry cry, charging the man threatening his mistress. The pressure on the blade disappeared from Anibella's throat, but Bolan's bandaged arm snarled around hers, trapping the Uzi. His long leg rose and lashed out, cracking the weakened prisoner in the ribs, launching him into a table with splintering results.

The knife returned to Anibella's throat.

"Make the call to release Diceverde," Bolan said. "I won't ask you twice."

The woman sneered. "Swipe the blade. I have no fear of death. I am her voice in your pathetic world. But you silence me, another will rise to take my place."

"They always do. Gives me a hobby putting them in the ground," Bolan growled. He looked deep into her hazel eyes, not seeing a flicker of fear as Bolan's blade rested on her carotid artery. There was a chilling calm deep within her, the cold fire of a fanatic steeling her against the threat of death.

"I notice some hesitation," Anibella said. She loosened her grip on the Uzi and the weapon clattered to the floor. "Having qualms about sawing the head off an unarmed woman?"

Bolan grimaced. It would have been so easy to apply a few more ounces of pressure on the knife, splitting skin and muscle, opening a yawning gap in the manipulative witch's throat. But she was right. Killing an unarmed, helpless foe wasn't something he had in him, despite his title.

"Put the knife down, Matt," Anibella ordered. "If that is your real name."

The spindly cultist rose. He'd found a handgun from somewhere, and was aiming it at the Executioner. Though his legs were trembling, his grip was strong and certain, the muzzle unwavering from Bolan's head.

"He's perfectly willing to die to stop you from harming me."

"And what of christening your new empire with the blood of a warrior?" Bolan asked.

"Martha wants you dead and out of the way. And since you swore to exchange yourself for Diceverde, his death will be just as sweet. I'll gather some of your spilled life to pour at the ceremony," Anibella said with a smile. "And let's not forget that feisty little bitch Asado. She's right in my backyard, and you wouldn't want her dead, either, would you?"

"She knew the risks going into this," Bolan countered. "She'll damage your fledgling empire. I've also transmitted Pueblo's statement that you were in charge of the organization fighting the Juarez Cartel for control of Acapulco. You have nothing."

"Except the lives of two people you've sworn to defend," Anibella replied. "You'd give your life for Diceverde and Gonzales, so why can't you trade yourself for the journalist and Asado?"

Bolan looked at the skeletal gunman. Though he could barely stand, he was unwavering. Anibella had to say only one word, and he'd fire. The Executioner had dozens of options, but most of them involved sacrificing the woman, and his quickest, easiest entrance into her underground temple. A direct assault would take time to arrange, to resupply for, and would come too late to rescue the first lady's victims.

Bolan let the knife fall to the floor as he released the high priestess. She retrieved the knife and held the point toward his heart, scraping the skin on his chest in a circle. "Just so you know exactly where I'll cut in order to take your heart out, to burn for Martha."

Bolan nodded.

"Now, you had a route out of here?" Anibella asked.

"It didn't take into account bringing an emaciated prisoner along," Bolan said.

"That will be no problem, right, Raul?" Anibella said, looking to her cultist.

"Yes, mistress," the skeletal man replied, then put the pistol under his chin. The top of his head popped, hair blowing upward on a geyser of blood. He collapsed.

"You're sick," Bolan growled.

"But I'm beautiful, so it all evens out," Anibella replied. "Move."

The Executioner nodded. He had her just where he wanted her. The only problem was that she had exactly the same advantage. The delicate balance of power continued to teeter, with the lives of his allies at stake.

BARBARA PRICE CHEWED at her lower lip. The hotel where Bolan was going for the knockout on Garza had been surrounded by *federales,* and more cops were at the Spanish fort where Blanca Asado had been sent. She pulled herself away from the main monitor screen to listen to Pueblo's conversation with the Executioner, providing the Farm and Brognola with all the data they needed to cover up for Bolan in case he killed the first lady of Acapulco.

Not "in case" she reminded herself—when Bolan

killed Anibella Brujillo. She couldn't comprehend Bolan failing against the woman when he'd battled countless other criminal organizations across the years. She glanced to one side, looking at the printouts Kurtzman had made of Aztec glyphs, displaying sacrifices to the war god Huitzilopochtli. The lyrics of the *narcocorridos* describing horrible mutilation of flayed skin before the heart was ripped out caromed around in her memory. Right now, she had nothing even remotely on hand that could deal with their opposition. She continued running through her options to get a squad of armed *federales* into the mix as a backup SWAT team for Asado and Bolan, but there was no way of doing it in a manner that could convince the Mexicans without exposing Stony Man's involvement.

Bolan was on his own, and his only ally was an outlaw lady cop bearing a grudge for a murdered sister. Asado's phone wasn't picking up messages, everything was going through to voice mail, which meant that she'd turned it off. Every connection went straight to the electronic storage instead of activating the ringer, even if it were set to vibrate.

Bolan's phone was also out of commission. He'd turned it off, and according to the communication's protocol board, the Executioner had stripped out the encryption key, rendering the cell phone a useless lump of plastic. There was only one reason for that, and it was because Bolan had given himself over to Anibella Brujillo. Stripping out the encryption key sterilized the phone, killing all links to Stony Man Farm. It also disabled the GPS tracker that kept Bolan's position updated.

"Blind and deaf," Price murmured.

"Trouble?" Brognola asked, entering the War Room.

The head Fed was rumpled and tired-looking, an unlit stogie locked in the corner of his mouth.

"Both Bolan and Asado have gone dark," Price answered. "And we're pretty sure Striker's surrendered to Brujillo."

Brognola sighed. "She's definitely the opposition force, then."

Price handed over the transcript of Bolan's transmission. Brognola looked it over.

"Well, neither the U.S. nor Mexican presidents can put the blame on us for eliminating her with this," Brognola stated. "It's nothing that would stick in a courtroom, but the two of them believe in Striker. They won't look for his head."

"If they can find his head after this," Price said. "He's put himself in a tight corner, and we've got bupkes on hand to get him out."

Brognola nodded. "There's Asado."

"I'd rather it were Able Team," Price grumbled.

"Barb, the *federales* are moving into the hotel," Kurtzman announced. "Putting the translation over the speakers, since the roof is shielded from our cameras."

"Shielded?" Brognola asked.

"This used to be the Juarez Cartel's headquarters in Acapulco. They know that the DEA would love nothing more than to have the ability to look down their throats from low orbit," Price responded. "They're elusive, and they've learned from cold war–era consultants about operational security."

"Like the Russian *mafiya?*" Brognola asked.

"Exactly," Price replied. "Luckily, Striker put a dent in the Russians' presence in Mexico when he took out Kuriev."

"And about one hundred of his closest friends," Brognola added. "Mack won't let Anibella's prisoners sit. He's offered to trade himself for them."

"That sounds like a death wish," Price said.

"He's offered," Brognola told her. "He's just putting himself in a better position to act. Anibella's people might be brutal, but they've never tried to hold on to a prisoner like him."

"Here's hoping," Price agreed. "But that's even if the *federales* don't take him down trying to escape the hotel. Sometimes I hate this job. Looking for things to go wrong twenty-four hours a day."

"Striker never goes in without an exit strategy. He'll get out."

Price watched the screen, playing the waiting game as her stomach knotted.

THE SERVICE ELEVATOR went down five floors, and Bolan and Anibella got out. Once more in coveralls, but this time stripped of most of their heavy weapons, with the exception of the first lady's Glocks, they were inconspicuous. The deep pockets of her coverall concealed the pistol in her fist. It was twelve flights down to the main floor, but Bolan knew that standard procedure for a police rescue team was to take the elevators, utilizing override keys.

The walk went quickly, and in fifteen minutes they were at the second floor, turning off because they didn't want to deal with the police controlling the stairwells. They headed back toward the service elevators and found them unwatched at this level.

Bolan dug his fingers between the doors and pried them open. A quick glance showed that the car was at the top of the shaft. He motioned for Anibella to get onto ladder rungs.

She shook her head. "You first."

"I'm not going to run away," Bolan countered.

"Not until you get to the temple." She smirked. "You think I was born yesterday?"

"No, that much is obvious," Bolan answered. She bristled at the implication that she looked old. He stepped onto the ladder and climbed down to the basement. Flipping a latch, he opened the doors and got out. Anibella followed, watching him like a hawk.

"I don't see why you're protecting a man who betrayed you."

Bolan shrugged. "He gave me and Asado up because you were torturing Gonzales, most likely. He was protecting the people he loves."

"Sacrificing one for the other?" Brujillo asked.

"Asado would have a chance out in the open. Gloria didn't have a chance under your claws," Bolan returned.

"You're good at rationalization," Anibella said. "You should have been a politician."

"Unlike you, I haven't sold my soul," Bolan answered.

The woman's eyes narrowed. "Find the tunnel under the parking lot and get us out of here."

The corner of Bolan's mouth turned up in a grim smile. He took off toward an access tunnel. In another ten minutes, they had reached the parking lot, stolen a car and were speeding away from the hotel.

CHAPTER TWENTY-ONE

The entrance was tucked between two shelves of stone, the shade from the lip of rock making it invisible from above. Blanca Asado watched the sentry standing against a tree a few feet from the entrance as he lit up a cigarette. With each inhalation, the tip glowed brightly enough so that his deep-set dark eyes glimmered with malevolent alertness.

She knew there weren't too many ways that she could take him down without making a racket that would alert anyone on the other side of the door, or summon cops from the cliff above. Luck had been with her so far, but she could count on good fortune for only so long. It was nice that she seemed to have her sister as a guardian angel. Asado cursed herself for leaning on everyone else as a crutch. She was a smart, capable cop, and had been surviving against incredible odds by her own skills and talents. There had to be some way to silently take out the guard with what she had on hand.

Her jacket's cuff rubbed against the simple braid of yarn she wore around her wrist. There were a few beads on it, a present from Rosa. Her brow furrowed as she brushed the circlet, tugging it out from under the sleeve. A glance at both of her fabric-wrapped forearms, and how the twine wrapped around her wrist sparked something in her.

"Damn it, Rosa, I'd have figured this out by myself," Asado whispered. She shrugged out of the jacket and began winding it up. She found a rock the size of her fist and dumped it in one sleeve, tying off the cuffed end. The rock would give the sleeve enough weight so that it would have the momentum for what she had in mind. Asado only hoped that the shoulder seams were strong enough. The separation of one of the sleeves during the guard's strangulation would leave her further in the hole than she was.

Padding softly, her jacket formed into an improvised garrote, Asado stalked toward the guard. He pulled his cell phone out and pressed a button. The screen lit, and she froze. The glow of the liquid crystal display was bright enough to be a beacon, and she didn't want a glimmer of reflection to betray her presence. She heard a grunt emanate from the sentry and he stuffed the phone back in his pocket. He had to have been expecting a call, or checking for a text message. Asado held her breath, waiting to see if the guard moved, but he simply stood by the tree, letting out a soft sigh of frustration.

The cultist had been on duty for only a few minutes, but for Asado, as she sneaked up on him, each second felt as if it lasted an hour, each inch seemingly as long as a mile. Her eyes darted, looking for signs of other men spreading out to pen her into a trap. She pulled her lips into a tight, bloodless line, and closed the final two steps. She could hear her tendons creak and groan like the wailing of an orchestra warming up. It was the effect of her adrenaline, sharpening her senses to the point of painful awareness. She could smell the sweat on the cultist, the faint scent of tequila and tobacco rushing to her nostrils with each of his exhalations. The guard's breaths sounded like the wheezing of ancient bellows. She could make out his features, despite the darkness and the fact that he'd long ago extinguished his cigarette.

The guard swallowed, then let out another impatient sigh. With the breath leaving his lungs, he was at his most vulnerable. She launched the weighted sleeve out, then whipped the jacket around. The rock, obeying Newton's laws of physics, flew hard, then twirled across the guard's throat, swinging around and striking Asado in the forearm. She clutched the weighted sleeve and pulled back, jamming both feet into the trunk of the tree, hauling on the guard's throat with all of her strength and weight. Fabric squeaked and popped under the stress, but more importantly, the sentry gurgled and sputtered, grabbing at the slick nylon of the jacket.

"Hold on," Asado whispered to her improvised garrote, her shoulders burning with the strain of strangling a man to death. She could see his feet kicking in the air as he tried to pull himself free from the deadly noose. Asado felt the tendons in her hands snap and crack like gunshots, muscles wrenching as she overloaded them with stress. However, she had the advantage of leverage to improve on her surprise attack. Her opponent couldn't stand up or pull away, and the collar of the jacket was pulled tight across his windpipe.

It felt as if she were wrestling a team of wild mustangs. He struggled, trying to remove the lethal pressure on his throat. Fabric burst apart more, nylon making a sickly zip sound as it came apart under her weight. Asado let go and grabbed a section of the jacket farther up, clutching it, but the slick cloth shifted in her grasp.

Her knuckles were exploding under the strain, and again, the jacket started to come apart.

"Just fucking die," she gritted, pulling with all her might. The handful of fabric she had tore free in one squarish clump, and the improvised noose slithered from around her target's neck. She scooped up the weighted end of the sleeve and charged around the tree, smacking the guard in the forehead. Though he was already dead, the rock caved in a crater, pressure popping one eye from its socket. Nausea swept over Asado and she collapsed to her knees.

All that fighting, and she'd successfully crushed his windpipe and closed off the arteries to his brain with the strong nylon. The extra effort she'd put in, the force that had ultimately destroyed the jacket, had killed the guard long before fabric failed and ripped asunder.

She frisked him, finding the cell phone, a Colt .38 Super and some spare ammunition. She looked at the phone display. A text message came in.

"The mistress is almost back," it read. "Find Asado."

She closed the phone and slipped it into her pocket. So, Brujillo had known that she was alive and perhaps even assisting Cooper. The conniving mastermind wasn't an idiot, so it would have been easy to guess that her two enemies would have hooked up. Asado knew that Cooper hadn't given up the information that Asado had been at the fortress, checking it out.

Diceverde had to have given her up, and remembering the discovery of Gloria's severed foot, Asado knew he'd surrendered the information to save his girlfriend, not himself. But would that betrayal have been enough to protect the two hostages from Brujillo's murderous ways? She couldn't blame the journalist. He knew Blanca was more than capable of handling herself, as the six cultist corpses reminded her.

Asado moved to the entrance and opened it gingerly. The door felt like it was made of molded plaster, and on the other side, she saw a thick metal door. The molding and hinges made the doorway nearly invisible even to anyone looking for it. Only the fact that she'd watched the guard's partner go through the gap had given away its existence. Low-powered bulbs at long intervals lit the tunnel. She closed the door behind her and advanced down the corridor.

The phone vibrated in her pocket and she took it out. A new text message had come in.

"Sending more men to help you look. Have you spotted her?"

Asado typed a quick "No" in response. She was glad that they were resorting to text messaging, because there was no way she could have disguised her voice. The enemy had to have felt that the instant messages were far more secure and quiet than vocal communication, and in every other circumstance, she would have agreed. The only flaw in that security system was the fact that she had the presence of mind to check for the guard's cell phone and had spotted the enemy's instant messages.

Luck was still on Asado's side. But it was a luck that she'd made on her own, using her wits and strength. There was motion in the distance, footsteps echoing up the corridor. She pocketed the phone and ducked into a side chamber. The minicave was an unlit storage room, large enough for her and a couple of shelving units. The reinforcements, sent by Castillo to hunt her down, passed by the doorway in silence.

As soon as they reached the door, they'd know that Asado had taken out the sentry.

After that, her time was up. She waited for the guards to disappear farther down the hallway before exiting and delving deeper into the secret tunnels under the old fort. She wanted to be as hard to find as possible when they started looking for her.

Maybe it would buy Cooper enough time to get here and stage his rescue.

BOLAN HAD TO ADMIT, Anibella Brujillo was good to her word at not taking him lightly. Once inside the car, she leveled the muzzle of the Glock right at his gut, never moving even a fraction of an inch. Just to be sure he didn't jar her into an accidental discharge, Bolan drove smoothly and steadily. She settled back in her seat, a wry grin on her face.

"Shame I have to kill you. I've never had a chauffeur as good as you are," Anibella stated.

Bolan shrugged. "Shame I have to kill you. I never had such an easy time finding the opposition before."

The first lady's eyes narrowed. "I'm the one who has you at gunpoint. And you'll be outnumbered and unarmed when we get to the temple."

"Keep telling yourself that," Bolan replied. "But Death's steering you wrong. Not that renouncing her is going to do any good. You've got too much blood on your hands to flip."

"Quiet."

"Just the latest in a long line of manipulators who got jerked around by an even greater evil. That is if you're not just suffering psychotic episodes when Martha talks to you," Bolan continued.

Anibella got her cell phone out. "Tell me again how I'm hallucinating, Cooper. Try to piss me off some more, because I have Castillo on speed-dial, and I'll have him work Diceverde over good and slow."

"And then I'll just take your gun and snap your neck,"

Bolan said coldly. "We have a perfect balance here. A state of equilibrium that keeps us both alive. It's not going to last long, but why ruin it? And why throw away a prize like me, if I'm wrong?"

Anibella sneered. "Keep driving, Matt."

Bolan nodded. She didn't give advanced directions, just telling him a moment before each turn. It was a further element of insurance that allowed her to hold just a large enough hand to last another moment. It was a fleeting advantage, and she was right. When he got to her temple, he'd be outnumbered, and unarmed.

No, she was only partially right. The Executioner was never unarmed. As long as he had his mind and his body, he was in possession of one of the most reliable weapon sets ever. Sure, he was most comfortable taking on enemy forces with an assault rifle and his two favorite handguns, but when it came down to it, he'd been stuck with less and overcome. It wasn't his favorite place in the world to be, but when given the eight ball, Bolan usually ended up bludgeoning his opposition with it until he came across a loaded firearm. Still, he had a small ace in the hole.

Finally, after a half hour of driving, enduring Anibella's piercing gaze, Bolan could see the ocean to the south, and up ahead, down the road, an old Spanish fortress sat atop a cliff. He glanced over to the high priestess. "Your little getaway?"

The first lady squinted, seeing the flicker of mars lights around the walls of the fort. "Just turn down the left side road."

Bolan steered in the direction she indicated, finding a gravel path that looked untouched. However, considering the fact that Anibella seemed unconcerned about the police noticing them, it was no great effort to imagine that the gravel was raked to minimize the footprint of vehicular traffic up and down the side road. He pulled to a halt in a rounded pool of the gravel. Scanning the area, he spotted half a dozen men, keeping to the shadows, away from the spill from his headlights.

"Kill the engine and turn the lights off," Anibella ordered.

Bolan turned the key, flicking off the switch as she had instructed. He faced her. "Give Diceverde his freedom."

"And then it will be just you, me and Asado."

Bolan nodded to the shadows closing in on the car. "And some of your close friends."

"You have such a way of killing an intimate mood," Anibella quipped. "It's a shame that I never got a taste of that fine, strong body of yours."

Bolan shrugged. "I tend to avoid sex with homicidal drug lords. You never know what you'll catch from them."

She sat there, fuming, hefting the chrome-slided Glock as if she were trying to decide if it was worth the effort to pistol-whip him. Instead of striking him, she nodded. "Get out. Slowly."

He followed her instructions. The men around the car took a step back as he rose to his full 6'3" height. The baggy coveralls he wore made him seem larger than his lean 220-pound frame would have suggested. They circled him, eyeing him carefully. Anibella stood on the other side of the stolen vehicle, looking around.

One of them spoke up. "Mistress, we don't have Asado. She's disappeared."

"Well, not completely. She left Ortega by the side entrance. She crushed his throat and took his gun," another clarified. "She's inside the tunnels."

Anibella chuckled. "Well, the gang's all here. Are the men on full alert?"

"Yes, and the guard on Diceverde has been doubled," the first man explained. "Castillo is on the ball with everything. She's not going to last long."

"What are we going to do with this one?" a third gunner asked.

"He's tonight's main event," Anibella said. "This man has been an enemy of our goddess for too long. I'm going to arrange a face-to-face introduction between them. Treat him nicely."

One of the group, as tall as Bolan, with an extra fifty pounds of muscle bulking out his frame, took a step forward. "He doesn't look like much."

The big man backhanded Bolan across the jaw, throwing him across the roof of the car. A ham-size fist rose and clobbered him in the ribs. "This is usually the nice treatment we reserve for our lady's guests, gringo."

Bolan glanced back at the high priestess. He didn't have to give voice to his question.

"Oh, go ahead. No one interfere," Anibella ordered.

"Interfere with what?" the big cultist asked.

Bolan turned back and snapped his right arm straight. It aggravated the first-degree burns under their bandages as he struck like lightning. The heel of his palm hammered the Mexican under his nose, and kept going until the bridge collapsed and was driven back in between his eyes with an ugly crunch. The tallest cultist wavered for a moment, then dropped to his knees. Blood trickled from his nose and the corners of his eyes, splinters of bone having speared through his brain. The blow had also driven his skull hard against his topmost vertebra, bone scissoring against itself and chopping off his spinal cord.

"Your education," Bolan said.

The big cultist collapsed, streams of his lifeblood trickling into the white gravel. The other five looked at him.

Bolan glanced back at Anibella, whose face was lit with a glee that chilled him to the core. It was a gaze of utter adoration, as if she were warmed by the open flame of a campfire.

"Do you see the gift I have brought you, Saint Martha?" Anibella asked. "The power, just pouring off of this… You are not a mere man, Matt. You have a glow about you, a charge that sizzles off your skin, with each kill."

"Probably why I didn't even notice that I've pissed off a goddess," Bolan retorted. He glared at her. He could feel the madness like an electric charge in the air. Her excitement spread to the other five, overwhelming their reinforced respect for the Executioner.

"Oh, you know your enemies, warrior," Anibella said, her voice taking a deeper, heavier timbre. Her hazel eyes had gone black and shiny, a transfiguration that could have been a trick of the dark night, but that didn't explain the shift in her voice. "And I've known you since you took your first confirmed kill. You've culled my armies around the globe, but tonight, I will cull you."

"Playing mind tricks with me at this point?" Bolan asked, being guided toward the entrance. Anibella's cultists kept their distance, but she slinked up to him, hooking him arm in arm.

"You still think you're speaking to the puppet?" Anibella asked. "After all I've done to forge you into the god that you've become?"

"I'm just a man," Bolan replied, walking into the corridor with her.

"But you represent so much more. The Soviets don't know your real name, but they remember you," she whispered. "She's waiting for you on the other side of this night, you know."

"Who?" Bolan asked.

"Your little flower, the one who died for you. I always get choked up at these reunions."

"You're crazy, Anibella," Bolan told her. He couldn't help but think of April Rose, who had died so many years ago, taking a bullet meant for him. The insane woman in front of him was utilizing a blend of simple mind-reading tricks and rumors to try to throw him off balance. Still, her voice had changed, her demeanor shifting. No. Anibella was a skilled actress, Bolan had seen her talents at work. It was all a game she was playing.

"Martha," she corrected. "But not for much longer. It's such a strain taking her over."

"Multiple personalities do that," Bolan chided.

Anibella shook her head, then ran her fingers over his chest. Her fingertips sparked, striking deep into his heart, when a flood of memories crashed into Bolan's mind, dozens of fallen friends, a nail for each of his friendly dead punched into his ribs. Bolan felt his legs go rubbery, and the woman held him up effortlessly, smiling.

"Right. And hallucinations are contagious, warrior," she said. "I've been there for all of their ends."

"Or it could just be a delayed spasm of pain from the hammering I took from your dead ape," Bolan growled. "Or a last twinge of reaction from my scorpion sting."

"Rationalize all you want."

Bolan regained his strength and the woman at his side looked as if she were recovering from a waking dream. She slithered from his side, stepping away.

"Psychotic episode," Bolan told her.

"No, the goddess, speaking through me," Anibella replied. "I know the feeling."

"You also can put together a pretty story," Bolan

said. "Doesn't take much to link me to the man that the Russians live in terror of."

"It won't be much longer," Anibella promised. They'd traversed the tunnels until they reached a small cavern lined with dungeon doors. Bolan could smell the copper of freshly spilled blood. "Castillo?"

Diceverde was pushed out of the cell first, Castillo following.

"You're free to go, little truth teller," Anibella said.

"You're free to go to hell, witch," Diceverde replied.

"Not tonight. I've got a hot date," she answered.

Castillo cuffed Diceverde in the back of the head, and pushed him along. Diceverde was only about 5'6", while Castillo was only a few inches shorter than Bolan, with a lean, hard face speaking of decades of rough life. This man was a stone killer, and while Anibella seemed to have a large supply of hooligans who'd think nothing of breaking open a skull for a few pesos, Castillo was different. He met Bolan's gaze unflinchingly, only a half nod of acknowledgment, a token of respect from an equal and an opposite.

"This one lives, mistress?" Castillo asked.

"He goes free," she said, her tone lowering.

Bolan looked to Diceverde, realizing that they couldn't allow the journalist to go free. The Executioner lunged, but Castillo whipped around, crashing an elbow with blinding speed into the American's jaw. Bolan bounced off the wall, and the other guards charged in, fists flying with wild abandon, hammering his already battered ribs. Bolan had been so concerned with giving Diceverde a chance to break and run, he drew down the attention of Anibella's thugs.

He grabbed one of them by the throat, crushing his

windpipe with powerful fingers, and his knee cracked the pelvis of a second one.

"Damn it!" Anibella shouted, her Glock booming in the hall. "Get the punk!"

Bolan used the skull of the man whose throat he'd crushed as a hammer. Bone struck bone and a third of the bodyguards collapsed in a heap. Castillo's fists crashed down on the Executioner. Off balance, Bolan was knocked to the floor. The first lady spun and aimed the Glock at him, rage flashing in her eyes.

"You sorry bastard," she snarled. "If he gets away—"

"You'll cut my heart out?" Bolan asked.

Castillo looked at her. "Let me break his arms at least."

Anibella glared at Castillo. "No. He has his destiny. I intend to make it happen."

Castillo turned and shoved Bolan into an open dungeon, slamming the door shut and throwing the bolt. "You two stay here. I'll send more help. If he breaks loose, open fire and keep reloading until you have nothing but a smear."

"Sir!" the survivors said.

"I'll recover Diceverde and Asado," Castillo told Anibella.

"Do that. Turn the tunnels upside down. We won't need to be concerned with using them any more after tonight," the priestess replied.

Bolan rose to his feet, visible to her now through the dungeon cell's door. He wiped blood from a split lip, his torso covered in bruises. The coveralls had been torn at the zipper in the melee, so his chest was naked beneath, only his blacksuit pants providing him with a modicum of privacy. He shrugged out of the tattered jumpsuit, kicking it into the corner.

"No, Anibella. You're not going to be using them any more after tonight," Bolan promised. "But your new home isn't going to be Garza's penthouse suite. Your neighbors will be maggots in a pauper's grave."

The high priestess glared at him.

"It will only take a minute to capture that little prick," Anibella promised. "When he's mine, I'll behead him right in front of you. You'll watch another one of your failures, like that bitch, Gloria."

"You've had a run of luck. Luck ends, and so will you," Bolan said.

Anibella spun and stormed away.

The Executioner took a seat in the center of his cell, reaching for some hidden tools he'd stashed away in anticipation of his imprisonment. It wouldn't take long for him to get out and back into action. Asado and Diceverde still needed his help.

CHAPTER TWENTY-TWO

Armando Diceverde tore around the corner and yelped as a pair of arms wrapped around him, one hand clamping over his mouth. Yanked off his feet, he was dragged into a darkened room in the tunnels, and held in place.

"Armi," a familiar voice whispered. "Quiet and stop fighting."

Diceverde twisted. He cupped a face in the shadows. "Blanca?"

"We keep bumping into each other," Asado whispered. He could feel her cheek rise with a smile.

"Gloria's dead," he said softly.

Her features flattened, a numbed silence washing over her. She put her hand over his mouth again, the clatter of boots in the hall shocking both of them into remembering where they were, deep behind enemy lines and hunted as prey. When the footsteps died away, Blanca's hand brushed from his mouth to the back of his neck, and he felt her forehead press to his. Her shoulders jerked in a suppressed, reflexive sob.

"I'm so sorry," she answered, voice low. "Oh, God…"

"I gave you up to protect her, too," Diceverde added. He tried to pull away from her, but she didn't let him go. His voice rose a few octaves. "Blanca, I betrayed you, and Gloria still died."

Asado put her finger to his lips. "No. You didn't."

Diceverde finally broke from her hold and crawled back against the wall. His shoulder hurt like hell, but at least it took his mind off the throbbing bruises covering his face and chest. Even the ache of his shot-up joint couldn't hide the numbing agony that was at his core. "I told her that you were working with Cooper."

"She'd have figured it out anyway," Asado returned. "She probably already knew."

Diceverde bit back his own sob. "She took Rosa away, she took Gloria—"

"They'll never be gone," Asado cut him off. "But we have to live for them. That means we need to stay quiet."

Diceverde clamped his hand across his eyes, taking deep breaths to hold his sorrow at bay. "I want to kill Anibella Brujillo."

"You'll get your chance," Asado whispered. She crawled over to his side, and he felt her warmth against him. She pressed something hard into his hand. It was a pistol. He inspected it by feel, and it was a Colt .38 Super.

"Blanca—"

"Shh," she admonished.

"She told me she was going to kill you in front of me, too," Diceverde said. "She told me…"

Asado put her arm around his shoulders, and she ran her fingers through his hair, their heads touching in the dark. It was an expression of shared pain and mutual comforting. "We came here to save you. You're still alive."

"They captured Cooper," Diceverde informed her.

Asado nodded. "He told me that was his plan. To get here and be in position to break you out."

"The last I saw, he was being beaten black and blue," Diceverde continued.

"Which word in 'be quiet' did you not understand?" Asado asked.

"I don't want to hide," the reporter said. He thumbed back the hammer on the Colt. "I want to make that woman pay."

"I know," Asado replied. She pressed her lips to his forehead. "I know, Armi. I want her dead, too. We just need to regather our strength."

Diceverde nodded.

The sound of footsteps echoed through the halls. Asado took out her mini-XD pistol. Diceverde kept his finger off the trigger. Asado didn't have to tell him that the minute they opened fire on the men searching through the supposedly abandoned rooms, the rest of Anibella's cult would swoop down on them in over-whelming numbers. Blanca pressed a button on the cell phone, and the tiny screen threw off a weak illumination that gave them a better view of their surroundings. Two large cabinets stood in one corner, and they crawled quickly toward it.

Gently opening the doors, they found them empty, but there was enough room in each to hide. Diceverde stepped into one, Colt at the ready as he closed the doors to a crack. Asado climbed into the next one. The door to the room popped open the minute they were both settled, a flashlight spearing through the darkness. Two men entered, one flicking on a light switch.

"Blood," one of them noted, pointing to a smear where they'd been sitting. Diceverde didn't think he'd been bleeding, but the guards were alert.

Asado exploded from her cabinet, her pistol cracking, punching bullets into the pair. She cut loose with an animalistic howl that exploded from a week of torment building up in her soul. The two cultists jerked violently under multiple impacts, their bodies crashing to the floor. Now, Diceverde knew where the blood had come from.

Asado's hands were gloved in crimson, and blood was trickling from the cheek opposite the one he'd cradled. She looked at him as she stood over the two dead men.

"My God, Blanca," Diceverde gasped. He stepped out of the cabinet, uncertain of the woman in front of him. She came to her senses in a moment, foraging for more weapons and ammunition off the fresh corpses. "Blanca, we can't wait around—"

"We're not. But we have to be able to fight back," Asado explained. She stuffed magazines into her pockets. She held up a full-size Glock and checked its load. "Take it."

She tossed him the pistol. "It's just point and shoot."

"I know," Diceverde answered. Asado stuffed a second Glock in her waistband.

"Come on. Before we're penned in," Asado ordered.

Feeling as if he were caught up in a whirlwind, the journalist took off after his last surviving best friend, ready to fight and die to protect her life.

FOUR STONE WALLS and a heavy door made up this current prison, but the Executioner was rarely without a trick up his sleeve. He sat cross-legged on the straw matting of the dungeon floor and twisted the heels off both of his combat boots. Inside the hollowed cups were a few things he had stashed there, anticipating being taken captive by Anibella Brujillo. He'd had no intention of staying longer than a few minutes in the cult's custody, and he was doubly thankful for the distraction that Dice-verde and Asado provided. Thrown into the dungeon and locked there, rather than being thoroughly searched, had given him the window of opportunity he'd need to escape. He just had to act quickly before Castillo's extra guards showed up.

The left heel was packed with several ounces of plastic explosives, rolled into detonation cord. The right heel held detonators and a small cutting blade. He used the blade to slit the ribs at the heels of his soles, removing two U's of metal. The prongs of the U's were sharp and flat, able to be used as either screwdrivers or hellaciously effective fist loads, the ends sticking out three inches from the ends of his fists. He looped them into his waistband before stuffing the tiny explosive charge against the ancient cross-bolt lock. Sticking in a pencil detonator, he twisted the end and stood back. Bolan put the U-prongs in each fist, his middle and ring fingers pinning them in place, as if he had a pair of steel spikes jutting from his knuckles.

The pencil detonator's time burned down to zero, and the plastic explosive flared for a moment before it exploded. Powerful pressures overloaded the steel of the lock and smashed it open, the bolt deforming as it tore free from the door's surface.

Spanish curses filled the air as the dungeon door swung open. One of the guards filled the doorway, handgun up and ready, but Bolan, standing off to the side, took him by surprise with a punch to the side of the head. The steel tines of the U-fork speared through his temple and ear, bone cracking with the force of Bolan's strength. Brain perforated, neck broken by the Executioner's strike, the gunman's pistol clattered to the floor of the cell.

The second guard howled in terror and opened fire, pumping bullets into the corpse's back. Using the dead man as a shield, Bolan powered into the hall and cut loose with a second punch to the panicked shooter's face. Each flattened steel spike found an eyeball and stabbed deep. Blinded, the gunman's howl turned to an agonized shriek. Bolan turned off the racket with a savage twist of the U-fork, breaking the blinded guard's neck.

Bolan dropped their corpses, taking the shooter's pistol, a Glock 22. He pocketed spare 15-round magazines from both men, then reloaded the pistol that the second guard had emptied, racking a round into the chamber an instant before he heard the sound of rushing footsteps. Bolan threw himself prone as the first of Castillo's reinforcements lurched into view, weapon sweeping, looking for the escaped prisoner. Bolan introduced himself with a .40-caliber round to the guy's heart. Cored, the gunman folded over, a couple of rushing cultists stumbling into his corpse. The impact left both of them caught flat-footed for the Executioner. Though the two unfortunate cultists were helpless as they struggled to recover their balance, Bolan had no qualms about emptying another half dozen rounds into them. A blaze of .40-caliber thunder chopped into their upper chests, 180-grain slugs splintering through rib cages and deforming as they plowed through muscle and organ, killing them both almost instantly.

The Executioner pushed quickly to his feet, reloading the partially spent Glock, listening for further reinforcements as he gathered another handgun, a Colt .38 Super, and more magazines for the Glock and Colt. He stripped a gunbelt off one of the dead men, tying it on to have a place for his second weapon and the extra ammunition he'd taken off of the newcomers.

Bolan noted that their cell phones had a provision not only for text messaging, but also quick walkie-talkie-style communications. Faster and more efficient than using the phone function, it would give him an opportunity to listen in on their conversation. He turned it on, picking up the Spanish communications among the cultists.

The soldier clipped the phone to his belt so that he could hear everything, and have both hands free. He backed to the corner, checking both branches of the intersection. He caught a glimpse of Castillo's powerful frame and snapped up the Glock, but Anibella's lieutenant saw Bolan and dived to the side, barely avoiding a blistering salvo of .40-caliber slugs. Castillo poked around the corner and triggered his Colt, forcing Bolan behind cover.

By the time the Executioner whipped around the corner again, Castillo was long gone.

Bolan reloaded the Glock and took off after Castillo, hoping the cultist would lead him to Anibella Brujillo.

CASTILLO KNEW THINGS had gone out of control when Diceverde made tracks out of the detention area. He switched his cell phone over to its walkie-talkie function and got in touch with more of his men, calling for three of them to reinforce the pair who were currently guarding Cooper's dungeon. He hadn't had a chance to frisk the man, and despite the fact that he was wearing only the skintight lower-half of a blacksuit and boots, there was a possibility that the American warrior had secreted away some form of tools or weaponry to break loose.

"Sir! We've got gunfire in the western section, third level," one of his men said.

"Cordon it off and keep it contained," Castillo ordered. "I want Diceverde sewn up tight."

"Yes, chief," the cultist replied.

Back toward the detention block, he heard the sudden crack of a small explosion. Castillo drew his pistol, sneering in disgust. If he hadn't been distracted by the little journalist, he'd have had the time to strip Cooper and look for explosives. With the chatter of gunfire and screams of fear, Castillo's doubts were confirmed.

The American was escaping. Castillo realized that the soldier wasn't just going to make a beeline for the nearest exit. The moment he was free, his first priority would be to get a weapon and begin killing everyone in the underground temple. He rushed to the hallway, hearing the rip-roar of a Glock in rapid fire. Reaching the end of the corridor, he skidded to a halt and threw himself to the floor, barely avoiding having his head shorn off by a spray of .40-caliber bullets.

Gathering himself up, Brujillo's right-hand man swung his Colt around the corner and opened fire, peppering his adversary's position with a storm of .38 Super rounds. Each shot was a miss, but it was enough to hold the American at bay. Castillo retreated, remembering that the armory had been broken down and loaded into one of their moving vans. With a threat like this warrior on the loose, Castillo realized he needed every ounce of firepower he could bring to bear. He put his walkie-talkie to his lips.

"We need to break out the heavier weapons. Get some AKs and meet me at the mess hall," he ordered. "Anibella, mistress, we've got a situation. Cooper's broken loose!"

"I guessed that much," the high priestess responded.

"Are we going to take this bastard alive?" Castillo asked.

"I can cut the heart out of a corpse with less effort," Anibella told him. "Take no chances with him."

"Now you're talking some sense, boss," Castillo grumbled. "I'll make it up to Saint Martha some other way."

"Make certain you do," Anibella responded. "I'll head over to the western section and take charge of Diceverde and Asado's containment."

"Asado hooked up with Diceverde?" Castillo asked. "At least it saves us the trouble for turning the whole mountain upside down looking for her."

"Cooper's your responsibility, Castillo. Don't let him go."

Castillo smirked. "I've been waiting to get my chance at this overrated gunslinger."

He clipped his phone to his belt and poured on the speed to hook up with his men and get his hands on an AK-47.

THE NEWS OF CASTILLO breaking out the heavier weapons wasn't welcome at first in the Executioner's ears. Still, Bolan was flexible enough to realize that if he was able to survive the first skirmish, he'd get his hands on an assault rifle once more. He stayed tight on Castillo's heels as the big henchman raced through the corridors.

The pocking of a bullet in the wall inches in front of Bolan jerked him into a somersault that saved his life. Gunfire lanced through the air at chest height as the Executioner tucked into a ball. Pistols chattered and Bolan took cover, kneeling at the corner of the intersection where he'd been ambushed. He fired the Glock dry, hammering out rounds at navel height.

One of the cultists took a bullet in his belly and skidded to a halt. The heavy .40-caliber slug churned through his intestines and struck his lumbar spine, cracking it like an egg. Legs suddenly useless, the wounded guard dropped like a rock. A second gunman was in the midst of throwing himself prone when Bolan's second 180-grain round took him at the juncture of his neck and shoulder, drilling down into his rib cage. The bullet deflected across the tough muscle of the heart, but it didn't matter as one of his lungs was whipped into a foamy froth instants before his diaphragm was punctured. Blood vomited from the dying gunman's mouth and he tumbled face-first into the stone floor, features crushed and scraped by cruel momentum and gravity.

The third and fourth of the cult gunners were pounded by another six bullets, hipbones pulverized by shovel-shaped hollow-point bullets that ground into them. Crippled, the pair crashed atop the cushioning shapes of their allies, screaming in pain at the mutilating force of the .40-caliber slugs. Bolan glanced toward the hallway that Castillo had escaped down, and jogged over to the wounded.

"¿Dónde está el cafetería?" Bolan asked after kicking the guns out of their hands.

"Fuck off," one of them snarled, his face twisted in pain and drenched in sweat.

Bolan grimaced. He looked to the other one, muzzle of his captured Glock shoved in the man's face. "Same question."

The wounded cultist coughed, the convulsion sparking a tidal wave of fresh pain through his tortured body. "The hall you were just in. Straight until the third intersection, then take a right."

"Rest easy," Bolan said. He pulled the trigger, a mercy round through the brain ending the wounded guard's pain forever.

"What…what about me?" the other man asked.

"You didn't earn an easy way out. Enjoy prison as a cripple."

The mutilated survivor let out a sob. "No…*por favor,* I want to die a man…."

The Executioner didn't intend to allow either man to suffer, but a moment of frustration with the taciturn guard had strained his sense of mercy. A quick and easy death was preferable to slowly bleeding to death, or being a helpless paraplegic in a Mexican prison full of predatory felons long denied the touch of a lover. Rather than condemn the man to a life of continual rape and abuse, or prolonged agony, he spent a round of ammunition for the sake of kindness.

He turned back and followed the first guard's directions, keeping his eyes peeled for the presence of any more patrolling goons. The fact that they were traveling in knots of three and four meant that both Castillo and Anibella were fully aware of the monster let loose in their midst. There was a quick sputter in Spanish as the quartet that he'd just cut down was discovered. Bolan glanced at his back trail and saw that half circles of dried blood in the shape of his boot toes pointed to him like a row of arrows.

"He's headed toward the mess hall," the team that had found his most recent kills announced to Castillo.

"We're ready for him," Castillo answered. "Did you hear that, Cooper?"

Bolan took the walkie-talkie phone off his belt. "Nothing gets past you, Castillo."

"I'm not stupid, and I know that you aren't, either," the head cultist snapped. "You must be some kind of ex-military, to have shrugged off a beating like that. Probably Special Forces, and those kind always like to listen in on private conversations."

"Color me curious," Bolan said, closing in on the cafeteria. He reloaded the Glock and drew the .38 Super from its belt holster. A pistol in each hand, his accuracy would suffer slightly, but the warrior had trained to use both guns blazing as a legitimate combat strategy. Against multiple opponents with automatic weapons, he'd need the extra firepower.

"Well, curiosity killed the cat, Cooper," Castillo responded. "I've had the same training you've received. Ever hear of the School of the Americas?"

Bolan knew of it. He and the members of Able Team had engaged in countless conflicts against the fanatical forces who had been spawned by an era of anti-Communist paranoia. Instead of tearing into the Soviet puppet states of Nicaragua and Cuba, though, most of the veterans of the School of the Americas had turned their talents toward supporting fascist regimes by engaging in death-squad assaults on indigenous populations. The thugs who didn't find ultimate power supporting Central American dictators found a more profitable position working for drug cartels. Castillo, if he had been educated by the SoA, would be a truly formidable opponent.

"You haven't answered me, Cooper," Castillo taunted.

"I've heard of it. I've been cleaning up their psycho spawn for enough years," Bolan replied. "Between Juarez, the Russians and now you, this has been a one-stop shopping spot for maniacs."

"You're too flattering, Cooper," Castillo answered. "At least of those dime-store dropout Commies and the losers who called them in, I'm the real deal."

"I'm sure you are," Bolan returned. He clipped the walkie-talkie to his belt.

The spill of light through an archway told Bolan that he was close, but as he got within a couple of yards of the door, a familiar egg-shaped object bounced on the stone floor, ricocheting toward his feet.

Bolan looked down at the fragmentation grenade, knowing he had only a few seconds of life left before the minibomb detonated.

BLANCA ASADO PEERED around the corner at the barricade of armed gunmen penning her and Armando Diceverde into the third-floor level of the western part of the underground complex. She ducked back as an assault rifle barked, bullets splattering against the wall. The bodies of two dead lay at the far end of the hall, casualties of the first charge of their position.

The assault weapons had been brought up, which would give the enemy the edge they needed on the second wave of the assault. Asado didn't doubt that grenades would be added to the mix. She looked back, wondering where Diceverde had disappeared to. He showed up with four-gallon bottles in his hands.

"What the hell is that?" Asado asked.

"Cleaning chemicals," Diceverde replied. "We're going to need an ace in the hole."

"So you're going to offer to mop their floors?" Asado pressed.

Diceverde smirked. "Just be ready to run."

He took out a screwdriver he'd found and he started punching holes in the bottles. Asado realized that two of the bottles were bleach, and two were caustic cleanser. Her mind locked on to the purpose of the bottles after a few moments. Diceverde wedged a square plastic bucket over the top of them, then hefted it.

"Cover me," Diceverde requested.

Asado whipped around the corner and cut loose with all fifteen rounds in her Glock's reservoir, driving the enemy to cover. The tough little journalist swung with all his might, hurling the bucket stuffed with cleaning chemicals by its handle. He released it at the apex of its swing, and the jammed-together concoction whirled through the air down the corridor. The bucket struck the ceiling of the tunnel, bottles bursting from its base.

Chopped full of holes by Diceverde's screwdriver, bleach and cleanser gushed everywhere, mixing in the air. The bottles hit the floor hard, bursting and emptying their contents into large mixed puddles that immediately began to smoke. Asado remembered one of Diceverde's first news stories, about an incident where a restaurant worker had mixed bleach and drain opener in the hopes of cleaning out a troublesome stain. The small amount of deadly chlorine gas released killed the worker and rendered a dozen of the eatery's patrons sick. In the gallon amounts that Diceverde improvised to mix up, the choking clouds of chlorine began spilling out quickly.

"Go!" Diceverde called.

The men at the other end of the hallway opened fire with their rifles as the strangling fumes reached out for them. They had to have assumed that the pair was creating a smoke screen to escape, not realizing the toxicity of the fog until their limbs went as limp as string. One of the cultists struggled through the crowd, pulling at the pin in his grenade. He freed the cotter pin, but then the strength left his form. The spoon popped free as he tumbled back toward the barricade. A heartbeat later, the grenade detonated, shredding the guards.

Asado darted after Diceverde, who had towels soaking in a sink. She knew what they were for and immediately wrapped one around her head. Diceverde did the same and they rushed back. The wet terry cloth would filter out the deadly chlorine temporarily, giving them a chance to escape. As it was, they didn't waste time with a casual stroll, running full-out down the corridor, leaping over the larger, slippery puddles that poured out noxious streams of smoke.

Asado stooped and picked up an AK and bandolier off of one of the dead men. It only took a second's pause, but even then, Diceverde shouted, muffled by the wet towel, to hurry. She was back on his heels within a moment. The instant they were away from the poisonous cloud, they ripped the towels free so that they could make full use of their peripheral vision to watch for any other ambushes.

They'd broken free of their trap for now, but there was an entire complex left to escape through. Behind them, they heard the hostile bark of Anibella Brujillo as she came upon the shattered guards. The two of them slowed, looking at each other. Diceverde spoke first. "Kill her now?"

Asado squinted. She couldn't see Anibella down the corridor. "No telling how many men she has on hand. It'd be a suicide mission, and it might not even work."

"Then we thin them out," Diceverde said. He opened fire with his pistol, raising a racket that would bring Anibella running.

CHAPTER TWENTY-THREE

The Exccutioner saw the grenade tumbling toward him, adrenaline kicking his senses into overdrive to the point where the world seemed to pass in slow motion. He swung up his foot with all his might, catching the egg-shaped bomb on the inner curve of his instep, sweeping it into the air like a soccer kick. The grenade launched away from him, seemingly crawling through the air. Bolan twisted, turning so that he leaped away from the grenade. The world whirled around him at a painfully slow crawl. It felt as if he were trying to swim through molasses as he strained his muscles to dive to the floor. Finally his grounded foot rose into the air behind him, arms spearing straight ahead as if he were taking flight.

He sliced down the corridor, time crawling until the rolling roar of the grenade's shock wave caught up with him. Sheets of air pressure slapped at him, but streamlining through the air, he didn't feel their disruption against his feet. The thunderbolt crack of the explosion snapped him back into the here and now, however, and after five yards of flight, he skidded to the floor, his naked chest clawed up by imperfections in the stone.

Only his force of will enabled him to maintain his grasp on the pair of handguns he'd appropriated.

It was a good thing, too, because as he looked up from the ground, a squad of gunmen burst around the corner. The Mexican cultists skidded to a halt, trying to drag their muzzles down to aim at him, but Bolan triggered the Colt and the Glock, spitting high-powered bullets into the knees and shins of the quartet of gunners, slugs smashing through bone and ripping apart muscles. Collapsing, the four of them fell so that their vital organs and heads were in line with the twin muzzles of Bolan's death-dealing pistols. As they hit the floor, their hearts and brains were cored by the continuation of the Executioner's murderous salvo.

Bolan stabbed at the releases on both pistols, dumping spent magazines. He rolled onto his back, shoving their muzzles into his waistband, pulling spare ammunition from the various pockets. With deft twists of his wrists, he slid the clips home, locking them in place, and drew them with lightning precision. The Colt's slide was locked back, so he speared his finger into the slide release, bringing the .38 Super into instant battery.

Castillo and his men came around the corner, but the School of the Americas' graduate saw his quarry was still in fighting condition and whirled toward cover. Bolan's handguns spoke a fraction of a second too late to catch the cult's second in command, but he had plenty of time and room to rip off a dozen bullets into the chests of Castillo's men. Twin lances of fire-riding lead raked across the trio that tried to get the drop on the Executioner. The first man took a 130-grain .38-caliber slug through the nose at a speed of 1400 feet per second, the powerful bullet carrying half of his brain out the back of his head in a blossom of gore.

The second jerked violently as a pair of .40-caliber chest-bursters sizzled through his lungs, slicing his brachial arteries to spongy ribbons. With the blood vessels gushing fluid into his air sacs, the man drowned on his feet. The last of Castillo's gunmen caught a pair of .38s and a .40-caliber round through his heart. With his heart blown apart, he dropped to his knees, then folded backward, staring lifelessly at the ceiling.

Bolan sat up and looked over his shoulder. No one charged up from the rear, and he took a moment to regain his footing. He holstered the Glock, reloaded his Colt and got ready to go after Castillo. He looked around, but none of the men who had burst into the hall had been packing AK-47s, only pistols.

Castillo had been sharp enough to know better than to provide the Executioner with an arsenal that would put him on equal footing. Bolan lifted one of the dead and hurled him out into the open. A short, concise burst slammed into the corpse, the fire of a trained professional.

He wouldn't have much of a chance, and he was counting down the doomsday numbers before Castillo chose to cut loose with more grenades. Bolan retreated to the group who'd tried to rush him from behind, stripping ammunition and handguns off their bodies. He tucked himself in around the corner, taking inventory of the firepower he had on hand.

Two of the guns were 9 mm Berettas, and Bolan had a half dozen magazines for them. Having burned up three of the mags for the Colt, leaving him with only half a load, he discarded the .38 Super. The Berettas were old familiar friends and fit his large hands better. He still had four magazines for the .40 caliber, so he wasn't going to trade that in. None of them had a heavy

Magnum round to augment his 9 mm ammo, so he decided to keep with the larger bore Glock.

"Still alive, Cooper?" Castillo's voice queried from the walkie-talkie.

"You hear me reloading here," Bolan answered. "Though, that was a good surprise. You almost caught me."

"Trained by the best, Cooper. And working for the finest," Castillo replied. "Face it, you're yesterday's news. I'm the new wave. You used to be the fist of retribution. But I'll be taking over that position. Huitzilopochtli has chosen me himself."

"I thought he was just an aspect of a goddess," Bolan chided.

"She only tells Anibella that. Girls work best for girls, but we men and our male gods, we've got to stick together, no?" Castillo asked. "Why not step into the open and we'll settle this like men?"

The clank of bouncing grenades resounded down the hall and Bolan burst to his feet, rushing away from the blast zone. One after the other, the grenades detonated, shock waves rebounding off walls and battering the warrior's skull mercilessly. Bolan ducked into a side room and took inventory of himself, checking for new injuries.

His ears rang, but he'd equalized the pressure inside and outside his head with a yell earlier, otherwise the cacophony of gunfire in the confined tunnels would have racked him with crippling pain. Bolan checked his equilibrium, and it was fine. He looked through the doorway and saw Castillo duck out of sight, rolling another grenade toward him.

The Executioner pulled his Beretta and fired once, the 9 mm bullet striking the fragger and bounced it back toward Castillo's position. He spun away as the grenade ripped apart at the corner, men screaming from their shrapnel-induced wounds. Bolan stepped into the hall, Beretta leading the way. He looked around the corner and saw a large man, his face decimated by a blast of shrapnel. Others twisted and writhed on the ground, suffering from multiple lacerations. A 9 mm pill in each of their heads cured their pain for good. Bolan looked at the corpse he thought could be Castillo. The AK-47s held by the corpses had been chewed mercilessly by the fragmentation grenade. They were rendered useless for his purposes, so Bolan pressed on, ready for anything, especially Castillo, who might have avoided being torn to ribbons by his own grenade.

Bolan paused as he heard Anibella Brujillo calling for reinforcements. Diceverde and Asado had just taken out a large group of her men, and she was in hot pursuit. Castillo's voice answered her.

"I'll be there. Cooper will be on my tail by the time he hears this," Castillo promised. "You missed me, gringo."

Bolan lifted the walkie-talkie. "There's a last time for everything, pal."

He took off toward Anibella's last reported position.

THE MAN SHE KNEW as Special Agent Matt Cooper still lived, and he had somehow gone from being a half-naked prisoner to a man who had blown through well over a dozen armed gunmen. Anibella Brujillo felt a twinge of nervous energy crackle through her body as she finally understood what the goddess had been whispering in her ear.

The warrior she'd drawn into her service was a walking nightmare. Santa Muerte was the patron of drug dealers, killers and thieves, forgiving sins in exchange for a token of worship and servitude, paying a small stipend of belief to pay off past wrongs. As long as she was worshiped in some form or another, she maintained power, an ancient entity who had transcended the taming hand of civilization. Her worship had gone back thousands of years, before even the classical deities such as Zeus and Marduk were adored by humankind. She was Death itself, and in the New World where savagery was as common as a breath of air, she had flourished among the Aztecs and Mayans under other names while Hades and Pluto fell into disrespect.

Saint Martha had only asked one boon—the destruction of this Cooper. He was a thorn in her side, and now, trying to maintain control of her temple, Anibella realized that she'd uncorked a force of nature.

"Martha…please," she prayed. "Give me the strength I need to do your bidding."

She opened her eyes. Somehow Asado and Diceverde had concocted poison gas and broken free of the force containing them. She'd taken a whiff of the stuff, and her skin still crawled, fingers numbed by the toxic chlorine gas.

An AK rattled down the hall, and one of the men she'd sent as a scout screamed, dying under a hail of assault-rifle bullets. Anibella cursed, realizing that they'd captured an automatic weapon. They'd managed to even the odds.

"Do we have any grenades?" she asked.

"The group that had cornered them had them," one of her followers said. "Unfortunately, the man armed with them pulled the pin before he succumbed to the gas."

"So he blew up with any extra grenades he had with him," Brujillo concluded.

"Yes," the cultist confirmed.

"Thank you, Martha. At least they don't have grenades."

The cultist believer nodded. "A small consolation. But they've found a defensible position. It'll take hours and too many lives to root them out."

"I called everyone to the temple for our victory ceremony," Anibella snarled. "Seventy men!"

"Thirty-five have died so far tonight," the cultist answered.

"It's that bad," Castillo said, catching up to her group. "Who the hell mixed bleach and soap?"

"Apparently Diceverde or Asado. They'd managed to make poison gas," Anibella growled. "What about Cooper?"

"He had explosives on him. We found the heels of his boots had been pried off. The guards we left watching him were killed by U-shaped shanks of steel punched into their skulls," Castillo explained. "This man is amazing."

"He's also cut our force by half," Anibella said. "And you're still chatting it up with him on the radio!"

"Trying to get a sense of him," Castillo answered. "And keeping track of him."

Anibella glared at him. "Dead. I want them all dead now! I'm the high priestess of Death herself, and when I want people dead, they're supposed to die! So why aren't they dead?"

"Because I outrank you, Anibella," Bolan's voice said over the walkie-talkie.

Castillo whirled, bringing up his AK, throwing himself against Anibella to knock them both to the floor. Bolan swung around the corner, both Berettas spitting 9 mm devastation. Cultists who'd been caught in the open danced under the spearing impacts of the Executioner's surprise attack. In a heartbeat, Anibella watched five more men scythed down by Bolan's onslaught. The rest of her group spun in reaction, weapons barking. Bullets hosed in streams of flaming lead, but the Executioner had ducked back behind cover.

Castillo struggled to his feet, his face twisted in rage.

From the other end of the corridor, an AK opened up, slicing into her gunmen from behind. Anibella grabbed a fistful of Castillo's shirt, dragging him into the hallway that led to the ceremonial temple front. The space they'd just been in was filled with a cross fire of rifle and handgun fire. One of her cultists spun into the tunnel they'd ducked into, bleeding from multiple gunshot wounds. He looked to her, pleading. He opened his mouth to ask for help, but a waterfall of crimson bubbled out. With a shudder, he sank to the floor, crumpled in a puddle of his own blood.

Anibella did the math as she and Castillo retreated, the SoA graduate's rifle chopping out short bursts to discourage Bolan and his allies. She'd had a dozen soldiers with her when she'd gone after Asado and Diceverde, and in the space of ten seconds, only Castillo remained.

"Meet up at the temple," Anibella ordered. "Fall back to the temple! That's where we'll make our stand!"

There were several cries of confirmation to her demand. Unfortunately, it wasn't the seventy-man force she'd summoned to the temple. Only slightly more than twenty remained out of the throng she had expected to witness her ultimate blessing before the goddess of death.

Now, the worshipers of death were on the run, trying to escape their own demise.

"This is a test," she whispered.

"What?" Castillo asked.

"A test. She's pushing me. The final crucible that I have to make it through. It doesn't matter how many we lose. We will always have more followers. But we have to win this fight. We win, and we'll be gods ourselves."

Castillo looked askance at her. Doubt flashed across his features, but he dispelled it. A moment of weakness in front of an insane woman would likely cost him his life. "Yes, mistress."

Anibella raced off. She had to be fully prepared for the final conflict.

BOLAN ADVANCED AND MET Asado and Diceverde halfway. He thought both of them looked like hell, but then, Bolan figured he wasn't in the best condition of his life.

"Are you two okay?" he asked.

Diceverde's wounded shoulder had opened up. Asado's attempts at wrapping it were good, but blood was soaking through, and his arm hung limply at his side. He was gaunt, face swollen from countless beatings, and there was an empty numbness in his eyes from his accumulated losses. Asado finally spoke up despite Diceverde's emotional condition.

"We'll make it the rest of the way," Asado said.

Bolan shook his head. He stooped and picked up a dead cultist's discarded rifle. He checked the load, then stuffed spare magazines into his belt.

"We're accompanying you." Diceverde's voice cut through the silence.

"You're losing blood," Bolan warned.

Diceverde's eyes locked with his. The dullness had been washed away by a flood of catharsis. "You're going to have to kill me to stop me."

"I don't have time for this, Armi," Bolan told him.

"My friends call me Armi," Diceverde answered. "If you're going to keep me from seeing this through to the end, then you don't get to call me anything!"

"I tried talking sense into him, too," Asado said.

Bolan looked over the scrappy little journalist. He knelt and pulled belts out of pants and went to work on Diceverde, pinning the wounded limb tightly to his side. He also took a moment to fix a three-point sling, which would help the injured reporter control an AK-47. "If you die, you're going to be riding with my soul for a long time. I don't have enough room for the other friendly dead I've accumulated. So I'm giving you a direct order. Don't do anything stupid, and don't die."

Diceverde's eyes narrowed. "Call me Armi."

Bolan looked to Asado. "You good?"

"Ready as I'll ever be," she answered. "Do you have a plan?"

"I'm just working on fire and maneuver," Bolan said. "I'll figure out something when we get a look at the temple itself."

"I've seen it," Diceverde said. There was a long, uncomfortable silence before he continued. "They dragged me there to watch them throw Gloria's corpse down the steps."

He shuddered at the memory. Asado's face twitched with sympathetic pain. Bolan understood too well, having had too many loved ones die in his arms.

"Armi, what's the ceiling like? Is it a natural cavern? Stalagmites?" Bolan asked, resting his hand on Diceverde's good shoulder.

"It's smooth, and reinforced with steel and concrete crossbars. I don't think anything short of a tank shell could bring it down," the journalist said.

"Anything flammable?" Bolan pressed.

"They have torches. Actually these big pottery pieces with what looked like gas spouts sticking out of them. All up and down the steps," Diceverde explained.

"What about at the base of the steps?"

"This is the third level, and it leads out to the ceremonial altar, which is the top. The bottom of the temple looks accessible from walkways down at the first level. They're safer than the steep incline of the ziggurat. The temple face is designed the way it is to simulate the old ways, when Aztecs hurled their used-up sacrifices down, shattering their bones so their spirits wouldn't haunt them."

Bolan nodded. "The first level should be where the fuel tanks for the torches are. If they're portable propane canisters, I might just have our equalizer."

"And if there's nothing down there?" Asado asked.

"It's going to be a long time until dawn," Bolan said. "Because we'll be taking the hard road to morning."

ANIBELLA HAD CHANGED OUT of her commando clothing and walked out to the ceremonial altar, topless save for a classically Aztec necklace that reached from her throat to the center of her cleavage, the full swells of her breasts lifting the bottom, her naked brown nipples perky and erect in the cool cavern. Around her waist was a loincloth, trimmed in golden thread, held in place by a fine gold chain that draped across her curvaceous hips. She wore her ceremonial headdress, and on a leather thong that was slung from one shoulder to her hip, was her ceremonial *athame*. The foot-long blade with the jeweled hilt was razor-sharp and capable of cutting through bone.

The only thing that broke from tradition was a modern, ballistic-nylon gunbelt that housed her Glock 22 and two spare magazines, an ugly black thing that crossed her bronzed, bare midriff.

Castillo looked at her. He wondered if he'd thrown

away his life in the service of a complete psychopath. Here they were, put on the run by only three people, and she took the time to play dress-up. Half-naked, she seemed vulnerable and out of place, despite the modern weapon she wore on her hip. He gazed into her eyes, and his doubts disappeared. She was calm.

Around them were twenty armed men, all of whom had sworn to give their lives for her. A mixture of handguns and AK-47s made up their arsenal, and Castillo knew they were all trained, hardened fighters. Unless Cooper could call down the fires of heaven, three people were going to be overwhelmed by the firepower.

They were behind the cover of stone benches and obelisks atop their ceremonial ziggurat. The ceiling above them, ribbed in steel and reinforced concrete, would require a nuclear explosion to disrupt. Dug in around the altar, Cooper and his allies would need artillery to take them out.

He remembered the fate of Kuriev and his compound. The American had employed mortars to destroy the Russian and his army of hired guns. Fortunately, Castillo and his crew had stripped the vans of every weapon. They had even found the last of the grenades, ready to repel even the most strident of forces.

"The warrior is coming," Anibella announced. She smiled. "How clever."

Castillo raised an eyebrow and looked toward the hallway leading to the altar. Even as he closed with the archway, he heard the rumble and rattle of wheels bouncing on concrete. When he peered around the corner, what he saw turned his blood to ice.

He'd forgotten about the propane tanks that they used to keep the ceremonial torch pots burning for their sacrifices. Six of them were tied to a rolling pallet, and duct-taped to the top were at least ten burning road flares. In the shadows at the far end of the corridor, he saw a kneeling shape, taking careful aim at the rolling six-pack of propane.

"Fall back!" Castillo roared. "Fall back!"

He wondered if he'd be fast enough to escape the fireball when he heard the burp of a distant AK over the clatter of the bouncing pallet. Steel-cored bullets punctured through the metal skins of the half dozen propane tanks, liquid vaporizing on contact with air and spraying from the new vents punched for it to escape. When the aerosolized propane came in contact with the sputtering sparks of the road flares, ignition occurred. All of this happened in the space of a second, even though Castillo felt as though he had a full minute to go over each segment of the chain reaction. He tried to savor that last heartbeat of clarity, drinking it in because he knew there would be nothing worthwhile on the other side.

Liquid propane went up with an earth-shattering fireball, a rolling blossom of orange grinding over Castillo like the press of a steamroller. He didn't even have time to scream as the skin was stripped from his face, his clothes bursting into ash and embedding in the raw sticky mass of melted flesh on his chest and arms. He jerked the trigger on the AK-47 in deadly reflex, and his skull cracked the instant after his eyes burst in their sockets, vaporized by the intense heat. His final sensation were the dying screams of his compatriots, their limbs blackening with the rush of superheated flames peeling flesh off their skeletons.

His charred corpse crashed to the roof of the ziggurat, bones and carbonized flesh bursting in puffs of black smoke.

BOLAN OPENED THE DOOR. The backwash of the propane explosion wasn't something he wanted to experience, but the towels jammed under the door had spared them. Pulling the towels away, he could see blackened crisped strips where they'd been exposed to the intense heat. The door itself almost came apart in his hands, charred to flimsiness.

"Just stay back, about ten feet behind me," Bolan ordered. "Otherwise…"

"All right, Matt," Asado said.

The Executioner stepped out and began the walk down the long, slanted hall. His improvised bomb had been a success. The air was thick and hard to breathe, the walls licked with carbonized ash. When he reached the altar, he could see the first of several incinerated bodies, ribs encased in the blackened husks that used to be skin and muscle tissue. Wreckage from the pallet and shrapnel from the destroyed propane tanks littered the area. He couldn't identify who was who, the corpses all rendered similar mummies of charred skin shrink-wrapped to skeletons.

The stench of cooked human flesh was overwhelming, but it was nothing new to him. He looked back, and could see the queasiness evident on Asado's and Diceverde's faces.

Bolan kept his rifle at the ready. Someone might have been able to escape the conflagration by throwing themselves over the edge. The ziggurat's steps would be a bone-shattering drop, but the smooth slopes on either side of the stairway would have proved an easy way to slide out of the way of danger. He approached the ledge, rifle raised, ready to open fire on anyone still kicking.

He exposed himself just enough to see a figure twenty feet below. A muzzle flashed and a half dozen

.40-caliber bullets flew through the air. The AK-47 took the brunt of the onslaught, steel and wood absorbing five bullets before being driven up into Bolan's jaw. The sixth bullet creased across his forehead, stunning him.

Blanca Asado raced to the Executioner's side as he collapsed, dazed beside the altar. A bullet sliced across her ribs and spun her off the edge of the ziggurat's roof, taking the plunge down the smooth sloped face of the pyramid. Anibella Brujillo ignored the falling woman. She had her eyes on a more important prize, and she scurried up the steep steps like a spider, driven with maniacal rage that gave her uncanny speed. She climbed atop the ziggurat and saw Bolan reaching for the Beretta he had jammed in his belt.

"Oh, no," Anibella grated. She leaped like a panther, the *athame* in her hand, a foot-long gleaming steel fang aimed toward Bolan's exposed heart. Her other hand swatted the Beretta out of the way.

The Executioner, reactions slowed by the hammering of a bullet grazing across his forehead, still had the presence of mind and reflexes to grab Anibella's wrists. The ceremonial knife stopped, an inch above his naked chest, but the madwoman's strength was phenomenal. Adrenaline had supercharged her to the point where even though Bolan could feel her wristbones crunching under the pressure of his grip, she wasn't letting go of the knife. Without the ability to feel pain, nothing limited Anibella's strength. Her empty hand ripped free from Bolan's grasp and hammered down with a punch that left him seeing stars.

"Damn you!" Diceverde shouted. The wounded reporter opened fire, his one-handed control on the AK-47 imperfect. His first two shots punched into Anibella's collarbone, exploding out the back of her shoulder.

Her hazel eyes turned up, gazing at the journalist. "Guns? Against me?"

She wrenched her knife hand free from Bolan's grasp and hurled the blade at Diceverde. It was all that the reporter could do to twist so that he took the point in his arm. A foot of steel carved through muscle and skin.

He screamed in pain and dropped to the roof, the rifle clattering free.

"Oh, dear, I seem to have lost my knife," Anibella said. She swatted Bolan across the jaw again, bouncing his head off the concrete floor of the altar. "I'll just have to kill you the old-fashioned way."

"Lady, shut up," Bolan snarled. With a surge, he tossed her off him. Though her madness gave her strength, she was still under 150 pounds, and recovering his leverage, he shed her like a grizzly tossing aside a fox.

He gathered his feet under him and looked at the insane priestess. Despite the two rifle rounds through her shoulder, her arm was still moving. She charged again, reminding the Executioner of the deadly dragon queens he'd battled only hours before. The lizards and Anibella had the same soulless rage burning in their eyes, and as far as the warrior was concerned, they shared the same level of humanity. Bolan lunged and met her charge, their bodies crashing.

The Executioner had rammed his fist into the woman's sternum, a powerful blow that broke ribs and drove the breath from her lungs, but the madwoman brought her hand down on his chest like an iron claw. Her nails tore through the skin over his pectoral muscle and dug painful furrows into his flesh. Her other hand rammed up into his armpit and she lifted Bolan's 220-pound weight with a primal roar and shoved him brutally into a stone bench.

Bolan rolled off the concrete block, reaching for the Glock in its holster. Anibella let loose an inhuman shriek and pounced once more. In midair, she was a floating target as the .40-caliber pistol cleared leather.

The Executioner milked the trigger, pouring bullets down Anibella's throat as she leaped across the space between them, recoil walking rounds up through the centerline of her face. Madness might have supplied her with the strength to hurl him about, but nothing toughened her flesh and bone against a storm of 180-grain slugs that split her heart in two and crashed through the bones of her face, blowing her brains out the back of her head.

Asado crawled to the top of the ziggurat in time to see the high priestess's corpse collapse atop Bolan. With a grunt, he pushed the dead woman aside and sat up, blood pouring from the claw wounds in his chest.

Diceverde staggered to his feet and walked over to the lifeless first lady, a mirthless smile crossing his face. Blood poured from his ruined arm, but single-minded determination pushed him these final steps.

"I told you I'd see you dead, witch," Diceverde snarled.

Bolan nodded to Diceverde and got to his feet, looking for something to bandage the journalist's cut. Asado handed him her shirt, then looked at Anibella's face, split apart by a merciless rain of bullets. Most of them had gone into her open, howling mouth, but there was a wound in the bridge of her nose, and one in her forehead.

"One for each of them," Asado said. "Rosa and Gloria."

Bolan tied off the pressure dressing. "They're at peace now. Let's get the hell out of here."

The trio limped out of the underground tunnels. Making use of a confiscated cell phone, they arranged for *federales* and paramedics to meet them at the base of the cliff.

The goddess of death had been denied.

* * * * *

ROOM 59

*Welcome to Room 59, a top secret,
international intelligence agency sanctioned
to terminate global threats that governments
can't touch.
Its high-level spymasters operate in a virtual
environment
and are seasoned in the dangerous game
of espionage and counterterrorism.*

*A Room 59 mission puts everything on the line;
emotions run high, and so does the body count.*

Take a sneak preview of
THE POWERS THAT BE
by Cliff Ryder.

*Available January 8,
wherever books are sold.*

"Shot fired aft! Shot fired aft!" Jonas broadcast to all positions. "P-Six, report! P-Five, cover aft deck. Everyone else, remain at your positions."

Pistol in hand, he left the saloon and ran to the sundeck rail. Although the back of the yacht had been designed in a cutaway style, with every higher level set farther ahead than the one below it, the staggered tops effectively cut his vision. But if he couldn't see them, they couldn't see him, either. He scooted down the ladder to the second level, leading with his gun the entire way. Pausing by the right spiral stairway, he tapped his receiver. Just as he was about to speak, he heard the distinctive *chuff* of a silenced weapon, followed by breaking glass. Immediately the loud, twin barks of a Glock answered.

"This is P-Five. Have encountered at least three hostiles on the aft deck, right side. Can't raise P-Six—" Two more shots sounded. "Hostiles may attempt to gain access through starboard side of ship, repeat, hostiles may attempt access through starboard side of ship—" The transmission was cut off again by the sustained burst of a silenced submachine gun stitching holes in the ship wall. "Request backup immediately," P-Five said.

Jonas was impressed by the calm tone of the speaker—it had to be the former Las Vegas cop, Martinson. He was about to see if he could move to assist when he spotted the muzzle of another subgun, perhaps an HK MP-5K, poke up through the open stairwell. It was immediately followed by the hands holding it, then the upper body of a black-clad infiltrator. Jonas ducked behind the solid stairway railing, biding his time. For a moment there was only silence, broken by the soft lap of the waves on the hull, and a faint whiff of gunpowder on the breeze.

Although Jonas hadn't been in a firefight in years, his combat reflexes took over, manipulating time so that every second seemed to slow, allowing him to see and react faster than normal. He heard the impact of the intruder's neoprene boot on the deck, and pushed himself out, falling on his back as he came around the curved railing. His target had been leading with the MP-5K held high, and before he could bring it down, Jonas lined up his low-light sights on the man's abdomen and squeezed the trigger twice. The 9 mm bullets punched in under the bottom edge of his vest, mangling his stomach and intestines, and dropping him with a strangled grunt to the deck. As soon as he hit, Jonas capped the man with a third shot to his face.

"This is Lead One. I have secured the second aft deck. P-Two and P-Three—"

He was cut off again as more shots sounded, this time from the front of the yacht. Jonas looked back. *A second team?*

And then he realized what the plan was, and how they had been suckered. "All positions, all positions, they mean to take the ship! Repeat, hostiles intend to take the ship! Lead Two, secure the bridge. P-Three, remain where you are, and target any hostiles crossing your area. Will clear from this end and meet you in the middle."

A chorus of affirmatives answered him, but Jonas was already moving. He stripped the dead man of his MP-5K and slipped three thirty-round magazines into his pockets. As he stood, a small tube came spinning up the stairway, leaving a small trail of smoke as it bounced onto the deck.

Dropping the submachine gun, Jonas hurled himself around the other side of the stairway railing, clapping his hands over his ears, squeezing his eyes shut and opening his mouth as he landed painfully on his right elbow. The flash-bang grenade went off with a deafening sound and a white burst of light that Jonas sensed even through his closed eyelids. He heard more pistol shots below, followed by the canvas-ripping sounds of the silenced MP-5Ks firing back. That kid is going to get his ass shot off if I don't get down there, he thought.

Jonas shook his head and pushed himself up, grabbing the submachine gun and checking its load. He knew the stairs had to be covered, so that way would be suicide. But there was a narrow space, perhaps a yard wide, between the back of the stairwell and the railing of the ship's main level. If he could get down there that way, he could possibly take them by surprise, and he'd also have the stairway as cover. It might be crazy, but it was the last thing they'd be expecting.

He crawled around the stairway again and grabbed the dead body, now smoking from the grenade. The man had two XM-84 flash-bangs on him.

Jonas grabbed one and set it for the shortest fuse time—one second. It should go off right as it hits the deck, he thought. He still heard the silenced guns firing below him, so somehow the two trainees had kept the second team from advancing. He crawled to the edge of the platform, checked that his drop zone was clear, then pulled the pin and let the grenade go, pulling back and assuming the *fire in the hole* position again.

The flash-bang detonated, letting loose its 120-decibel explosion and one-million-candlepower flash. As soon as the shock died away, Jonas rolled to the side of the boat just as a stream of bullets ripped through the floor where he had been. He jumped over the stairway, using one hand to keep in touch with his cover so he didn't jump too far out and miss the boat entirely. The moment he sailed into the air, he saw a huge problem— one of the assault team had had the same idea of using the stairway for cover, and had moved right under him.

Unable to stop, Jonas stuck his feet straight down and tried to aim for the man's head. The hijacker glanced up, so surprised by what he saw that for a moment he forgot he had a gun in his hand. He had just started to bring it up when Jonas's deck shoes crunched into his face. The force on the man's head pushed him to the deck as Jonas drove his entire body down on him. The mercenary collapsed to the floor, unmoving. Jonas didn't check him, but stepped on his gun hand, snapping his wrist as he steadied his own MP-5K, tracking anything moving on the aft deck.

The second team member rolled on the deck, clutching his bleeding ears, his tearing eyes screwed tightly shut. Jonas cleared the rest of the area, then came out and slapped the frame of his subgun against the man's skull, knocking him unconscious. He then cleared the rest of the area, stepping over Hartung's corpse as he did so. Only when he was sure there were no hostiles lying in wait did he activate his transceiver.

"P-Five, this is Lead. Lock word is tango. Have secured the aft deck. Report."

"This is P-Five, key word is salsa. I took a couple in the vest, maybe cracked a rib, but I'm all right. What should we do?"

"Take P-Six's area and defend it. Hole up in the rear saloon, and keep watch as best you can. As soon as we've secured the ship, someone will come and relieve you."

"Got it. I'll be going forward by the left side, so please don't shoot me."

"If you're not wearing black, you'll be okay."

Jonas heard steps coming and raised the subgun, just in case a hostile was using the ex-cop as a hostage to get to him. When he saw the stocky Native American come around the corner, Glock first, Jonas held up his hand before the other man could draw a bead on him.

Martinson nodded, and Jonas pointed to the motionless man in front of him and the other guy bleeding in the corner of the deck. "Search these two and secure them, then hole up. I'm heading forward. Anyone comes back that doesn't give you the key word, kill them."

"Right. And sir—be careful."

"Always." Jonas left the soon-to-be-full operative to clear the deck and headed topside, figuring he'd take the high ground advantage. Scattered shots came from the bow, and he planned to get the drop on the other team—hell, it had worked once already. "P-One through P-Four, Lock word is tango. Report."

"P-One here, we've got two hostiles pinned at the bow, behind the watercraft. Attempts to dislodge have met with heavy resistance, including flash-bangs. P-Two is down with superficial injuries. We're under cover on the starboard side, trying to keep them in place."

"Affirmative. P-Three?"

"I'm moving up on the port side to cut off their escape route."

"P-Four? Come in, P-Four?" There was no answer. "P-Four, if you can't speak, key your phone." Nothing. *Shit.* "All right. P-One, hold tight, P-Three, advance to the corner and keep them busy. I'll be there in a second. Lead Two, if you are in position, key twice."

There was a pause, then Jonas heard two beeps. *Good.* Jonas climbed onto the roof of the yacht, crept past the radar and radio antennas, then crossed the roof of the bridge, walking lightly. As he came upon the forward observation room, he saw a black shadow crawling up onto the roof below him. Jonas hit the deck and drew a bead on the man. Before he could fire, however, three shots sounded from below him, slamming into the man's side. He jerked as the bullets hit him, then rolled off the observation roof.

That gave Jonas an idea. "P-Two and Three, fire in the hole." He set the timer on his last XM-84 and skittered it across the roof of the observation deck, the flash-bang disappearing from sight and exploding, lighting the night in a brilliant flash.

"Advance now!" Jonas jumped down to the observation roof and ran forward, training his pistol on the two prostrate, moaning men as the two trainees also came from both corners and covered them, kicking their weapons away. Jonas walked to the edge of the roof and let himself down, then checked the prone body lying underneath the shattered windows. He glanced up to see the two men, their wrists and ankles neatly zip-tied, back-to-back in the middle of the bow area.

"Lead Two, this is Lead. Bow is secure. Tally is six hostiles, two dead, four captured. Our side has one KIA, two WIA, one MIA."

"Acknowledged. Bridge is secure."

Jonas got the two trainees' attention. "P-One, make

sure P-Two is stable, then head back and reinforce P-Five, and make sure you give him the key word. P-Three, you're with me."

Leading the way, Jonas and the trainee swept and cleared the entire ship, room by room. Along the way, they found the body of the young woman who had been at position four, taken out with a clean head shot. Jonas checked her vitals anyway, even though he knew it was a lost cause, then covered her face with a towel and kept moving. Only when he was satisfied that no one else was aboard did he contact everyone. "The ship is clear, repeat, the ship is clear. Karen, let's head in, we've got wounded to take care of."

"What happens afterward?" she asked on a separate channel.

"I'm going to visit Mr. Castilo and ask him a few questions."

"Do you want to interrogate any of the captives?"

Jonas considered that for only a moment. "Negative. All of them are either deaf from the flash-bangs or concussed or both, and besides, I doubt they know anything about what's really going down today, anyway. No, I need to go to the source."

"I'll contact Primary and update—"

"I'm the agent in charge, I'll do it," Jonas said. He sent a call to headquarters on a second line. "No doubt Judy will flip over this. Do you still have a fix on that Stinger crate?"

"Yes, it's heading south-southwest, probably to Paradise," Karen replied.

"Naturally. See if you can get this behemoth to go any faster, will you? I just got a really bad feeling that this thing is going down faster than we thought." He gripped the handrail and waited for the connection, will-

ing the yacht to speed them to their destination more
quickly, all the while trying to reconcile the fact that his
son was involved in a plot that could very well tear a
country apart.

* * * * *

*Look for THE POWERS THAT BE
by Cliff Ryder in January 2008
from Room 59™.
Available wherever books are sold.*

CRISIS: A massive armed insurgency—
ninety miles off America's coast.

MISSION: CUBA

A Cuban revolution threatens to force the U.S.
into a dangerous game of global brinksmanship,
thrusting spymaster Jonas Schrader into an
emotional war zone—exacting the highest price
for a mission completed.

Look for

THE powers THAT be

by cliff RYDER

Look for

AleX Archer
SERPENT'S KISS

While working on a dig on the southern coast of India, Annja finds several artifacts that may have originated from a mythical lost city. Then Annja is kidnapped by a modern-day pirate seeking the lost city. But she quickly sides with him and his thieves to ward off an even greater evil—the people deep in the Nilgiris Mountains, who aren't quite human...and they don't like strangers.

Available January wherever you buy books.

GOLD EAGLE ®

GRA10

James Axler
Outlanders

GRAILSTONE GAMBIT

Across mystical Celtic lands a devious enemy has resurfaced, a new messiah of the Druidic religion. Ushering in a new age of magic, terror and human sacrifice, the interloper seeks an ancient relic that will resurrect the dead. To rescue a culture from barbarism, the Cerberus warriors stand with a warrior queen in a final challenge to turn the tide of ancient madness that threatens to engulf the entire world.

Available February wherever you buy books.